PARIAH

THOMAS EMSON

snowbooks

Proudly Published by Snowbooks in 2011

Snowbooks Ltd
email: info@snowbooks.com
www.snowbooks.com

British Library Cataloguing in Publication Data
A catalogue record for this book is available from the British
Library.

Paperback 978-1-906727-34-5
Hardcover 978-1-906727-26-0

PARIAH

THOMAS EMSON

"EVIL IS WOVEN INTO OUR MOST BASIC BIOLOGICAL FABRIC"

Howard Bloom
The Lucifer Principle

"THEREFORE, JUST AS THROUGH ONE MAN SIN ENTERED INTO THE WORLD, AND DEATH THROUGH SIN, AND SO DEATH SPREAD TO ALL MEN, BECAUSE ALL SINNED"

Romans 5:12
The Bible (New American Standard Version)

"A UNIVERSE OF DEATH, WHICH GOD BY CURSE / CREATED EVIL… "

John Milton
Paradise Lost

"GOD SAID TO MOSES, 'I AM WHO I AM'"

Exodus 3:14
The Bible (New American Standard Version)

PART ONE.

THE WOMEN OF MOAB AND MIDIAN.

CHAPTER 1.
THE FIFTH.

IT was going to be bloody, she knew that. The knife-man would cut her throat and disembowel her – he'd have to, if he wanted what was inside.

He loomed over her. His green eyes glittered through the holes in the terrifying, asylum-style hood he wore, and his breathing hissed.

In a whisper he said, "You scared of me?"

She said nothing, just stared at the blade gripped tightly in the killer's hand.

Again he said, "You scared of me like your sister was?"

She struggled but couldn't get loose. They'd tied her on a rusty bed frame. The room was tiny. It was filled with shadows. It smelled old, very old – because it was. She knew that. More than a hundred years old and lost in time.

This room had also seen murder. It had tasted blood in the past. For decades it lay hidden, buried in time. But now it was about to become a slaughterhouse again.

Death would come full circle.

The woman ached all over. She felt doomed. Steeling herself, she prepared to die. It was difficult. Death wasn't so terrifying, but dying was.

"Do it, you bastard," she told him. "If you're going to do it, do it now."

She tried to stop her voice from quivering. Her guts churned with dread.

But she wouldn't show it. Not to him. Not to the other two figures in the room, both lurking in the shadows, waiting for her to die.

The knife-man came closer and kneeled next to her and pressed the knife to her throat.

He said, "You'll show me you're scared."

She cried out, and he laughed.

"See?" he said. "See? I was right."

She spat in his face. He recoiled. The blade went from her throat. She struggled again, and the rope around her wrists and ankles cut into her skin.

She screamed, more in frustration than fear.

The knife-man wheeled to face her again, and fury burned in his eyes.

"Cow," he said. "You cow – you show me some respect. You show me awe."

"Fuck you," she said.

"Bitch."

He raised the knife, ready to plunge it into her.

She screamed for help. But help wouldn't come. Anyone who could have saved her was either dead or disappeared. She'd been abandoned to the fate of her ancestors.

The blade arced down. It sliced through the darkness heading straight for her throat.

She braced herself.

A voice boomed:

"Stop it there!"

The knife-man froze. The blade stopped two inches from her jugular vein.

"Stop it there," said the voice again, quieter this time. It sent a chill through her. The atmosphere grew colder. The shadows thickened.

The knife-man stumbled away. "I was… was going to open her up for you," he said.

The shadows in the room moved, and out of them stepped the knife-man's master. The one who'd controlled him. The one who'd been in his head all these years. The one who had called the knife-man to prepare the way for his return.

The master said, "We've got trespassers."

"What?" said the knife-man.

"A seer and… something else. The seer – it's this one's child again." He gestured at the woman, and she screamed. Her daughter was here. She yelled out the child's name and urged her to run.

The master told the knife-man, "Go get them," and the knife-man went to the door and opened it. Lying on the bed, her mind reeling, the woman thought she heard the sound of wind beating against sails. Or perhaps wings flapping, although they sounded too large for any bird. Maybe it was just her sanity dissolving, and all the noises of the earth were filling her head.

The master said, "You go too, eunuch."

The eunuch shambled out of the shadows.

"You bastard," the woman shouted at the neutered man.

He looked at her and whispered, "I'll look after your girl when you're gone, don't you worry," and he gave her a sneer, spit dribbling down his chin.

The woman stiffened with fear, and a scream locked in her throat.

The eunuch followed the knife-man out into the darkness.

10

The master loomed over the woman.

His chalk-white face was framed with long, black, greasy hair. His blue lips spread out in a smile, revealing rotting teeth, and his black eyes sparkled. A tuft of hair grew from his chin.

He looked dead.

He was dead.

But he'd never really been alive.

"Now, you be quiet," he said, right in her face. "Or I'll have them cut up your kid in front of you, just for show. You saved her the last time, but not again. This time she'll die. But if you behave, I'll have you killed first, so you won't have to watch. You understand?"

She whimpered.

The master laughed. It was a chilling sound.

She thought of the hope she'd found in this horror – the man who'd already saved her and her daughter once. Where was he now? Had he died too? Had everyone she loved now died? Everyone apart from her child, who was also facing death.

She screamed in desperation.

The chalk-faced monster laughed at her, and his breath stank of sewers. She retched.

He said, "You be sick, whore. Puke all over yourself. Choke on it. Make it easier to cut you open and pull it out of you. You're the fifth. Once you're done, I'll be free. Free of this place. Free of these streets. Then London'll be mine. I'll make it a slaughterhouse. Blood will colour her grey concrete towers. Gore will garland her thoroughfares."

A noise erupted outside the room.

The master's eyes suddenly showed concern. He straightened. There was shrieking and that sound of wind on sails again.

The woman felt drowsy, but she tried to focus.

She said, "Death's coming for you."

The master scowled at her.

Then from outside, a voice shouted, "I've got her."

Now the master smiled again, bearing his yellow teeth. "Now we have two seers to kill. Mother and child."

The woman thrashed about, trying to get loose. But there was no hope. No hope for her or her daughter. Her body slackened, and she slumped into the bed frame. She started to cry. The master laughed at her. But through her tears and his hysterics, she could hear that sound again.

And she knew it wasn't wind on sails.

It was wings. Vast wings that were powerful enough to carry something much larger than a bird. Something like a man. Or maybe an angel.

PART TWO.

THE DEATH OF
MARY KELLY.

CHAPTER 2.
SWEET VIOLETS.

"SWEET violets... "
She sang to keep the fear at bay.
"...sweeter than the roses... "
It made her feel better, but only a little.
"...covered all over from head to toe... "
It wasn't going to heal things. It wasn't going to wash away the dread.
"...covered all over with sweet violets."
But it was a nice tune, one her father used to sing to her when she was a kid.

She cried, thinking about her dad. It had been years since she'd seen him. He was working at an iron foundry in North Wales, the last she'd heard. He wasn't happy with what she was doing, being a whore in the East End of London.

But she wasn't either. What kind of life was it? But what choice did she have? She had to eat. She had to survive.

Despite having had terrible experiences with men, Mary still dreamed of the perfect one coming along and rescuing her. A

14

prince to whisk her away. A farmer, maybe, like the one in Sweet Violets. Although he wasn't that nice, taking a girl into a barn. But any man would do. Any decent man.

But Mary was getting on a bit. Most twenty-four year olds she knew were married and had kids. Not her. She was an old maid. But not for long. Soon, her misery would be over. Soon, Mary would be dead.

She sat on her bed, humming and looking around the room. This was the sum of her life, what her twenty-four years amounted to – this grubby hole with a table and two chairs, a bed, and two small windows.

The room cost four shillings a week. It was in a three-storey house off Dorset Street, a narrow, 400-foot-long thoroughfare off Commercial Street. It was a rough part of Whitechapel, and that was saying something. Some said it was the worst street in England.

Common lodging-houses crammed the avenue. Slum landlords ran things and controlled most of the activities, many of them illegal. Whores roamed and thugs prowled. Drunkenness and violence were rife. Illegal prize-fighting left blood and body parts in the dirt. Stolen goods were fenced. Anyone stupid enough to get lost down here was beaten and robbed.

There was grease and there was grime. There was piss and shit. There were rats, there were dogs, and there were humans, all packed together. The air carried a putrid smell. It was the odour of thousands of unfortunates who'd lived and died there over the years.

Mary's skin would layer the ground before morning. Her bones would powder the walls. Her blood would fill the drains.

They would rip her like they'd ripped the others. Tear her open and plough around inside her for the treasure, the thing that gave *him* strength.

Him.

The ghost that stalked Whitechapel. The most terrifying killer in history. The one they called Jack.

And he was hunting her. She shivered. There was not much she could do. Nowhere to hide, nowhere to run. She knew he was coming, because she could see him. She had gifts. She had foresight. She could see the future.

And her future was death.

"Sweet violets, sweeter than the roses ... "

Such a funny song. Jokey and naughty.

Mary tried to smile while thinking about the lyrics. But it was a struggle to make her mouth curve up into a grin. Her lips quivered. Her eyes welled. Tears were easier. Her fear was strong.

Outside, someone screamed. A woman. Mary didn't flinch. It was normal. Silence, not noise, made you alert in Dorset Street.

A man cursed, saying, "Fucking tart."

The woman screamed again, begging to be left alone.

Another man said, "Cut her fucking nose off, Charlie."

Mary shut her eyes and laced her fingers together. Would a prayer do any good? It hadn't helped the others. Not Mary Ann, who'd been butchered in Bucks' Row on August 31. Throat cut, guts opened. A policeman had found her lying in a pool of blood. She'd put up a fight. Her teeth had been knocked out, punched after she'd punched first, probably.

That was Mary Ann – five-foot-two and hard as nails.

But being tough hadn't saved her.

Two days later, the man came from Austria. He came to look for Mary and found her in the Ten Bells, drinking. He said, "You have to come with me," and he gathered them all at an inn – Mary, Annie Chapman, Catherine Eddowes, Elizabeth Stride. They'd never met. But they were all prostitutes in Whitechapel. And according to the man, they all had a special gift.

A gift that would make their lives even more dangerous than they already were. A gift that could kill them.

He told them everything, and not all of them believed. Mary wasn't sure. Hearing what he said made her feel special. She'd always wanted to be special. But not so special that she might die.

Annie had refused to accept what the man had said, and she left in a huff.

But a week after Mary Ann's death, she was dead too, just like the man had warned.

Mary looked out of the small window. It was dark. But it was always dark there. Very little light found its way down Dorset Street. It was as if the day kept its distance. The night owned this part of the East End. The night and the darkness.

And a short walk from where Mary sat now, it had swallowed up Annie.

She had left her common-lodging house at 35 Dorset Street at 2.00am on September 8. She'd been drunk and needed money for a bed. Annie was happy to fuck for it. "Means nothing to me," she'd say. "And means nothing to them, after it's done."

She'd walked up Little Paternoster Row, and was heading towards Christ Church, Spitalfields.

But they got her in the darkness. They got her and cut her throat. They got her and ripped her open, taking her womb and parts of her cunny and bladder. They got her and stole her soul, just like the man had said.

Two down.

"Another three must be ripped."

Ever since Annie's death, that had been the whisper wending its way through the streets.

"Another three must be ripped."

Mary heard it wherever she went. She'd wheel round in a panic, expecting to see his terrible face.

But he was never there. Only his voice.

"Another three must be ripped."

And Mary knew one of those three would be her. She knew it

the moment the man had met her at the Ten Bells and told her who she really was, told her she had a gift – a gift for hunting evil.

There was a fight going on outside. Shouts and curses filled the night. Mary heard a struggle. Men kicked and punched. Flesh and bone being smashed. Mary winced with every blow. But it comforted her. A fight attracting a crowd meant her killers would not be able to skulk to her door unseen.

Glass smashed. A crowd bellowed. Voices said, "Smash him, Bill," and, "Glass him, cut him up."

Women screamed.

"Break his face!"

"Cut his balls off!"

"Fucking Jew!"

"Christ killer!"

Jew, thought Mary. The East End was full of them, Spitalfields especially. But they stayed away from Dorset Street. But plenty of Irish. Plenty of Frenchies and Italians. Scots and Welsh, too. The place was a melting pot.

Outside, the noise grew. Insults were hurled. More Jew abuse.

They didn't usually come round here. They rarely caused trouble. But every race had its thugs. And maybe a few young Jew bulls had swaggered down here to booze at the Ringers pub on the corner of Dorset Street, where Mary sometimes drank.

She listened now. The fight went on. But now there was more than one tussle. She could make out a few. Gangs going at each other. Blades and bottles drawn.

A whistle pierced the cacophony.

Mary jerked, sitting up.

The whistle came again.

"Coppers," someone shouted.

Another whistle speared through the noise.

The fighters and the spectators scarpered. Mary heard their feet pound the pavement, saw their dark shapes shooting past her window.

And then came silence.

Cold, deadly silence.

The silence you should fear on Dorset Street.

She froze, her skin crawling.

A dark shape moved past her door. She saw it in the gap at the bottom – the two-inch space where the cold and the rain and the fog came in, and through which evil could seep.

Dread turned her heart to stone.

And it cracked into a thousand pieces when a pale, white hand slipped under the door, the fingers scuttling like spiders' legs.

CHAPTER 3.
VIENNESE WALTZ.

THE Ten Bells boiled over.

The drinkers poured out. Fists and boots flew. Curses filled the air – mothers insulted, wives slurred, manhoods mocked.

Customers not following the fight outside grabbed drinks left by the departing crowd and downed them. Beer soaked the wooden floor. Dogs lapped it up. A woman's voice rose above the noise, singing Sweet Violets.

Jonas Troy put down his drink.

Mary's song, he thought.

He looked around, searching for the singer. He spotted her through the crowd. An old crone, her face speckled with warts, her mouth empty of teeth, and grey hair sprouting like weeds from beneath her black hat.

Not Mary. Tall, slim, fair-haired, and attractive.

Not Mary. The last of them. Four dead already, and she was the fifth.

Four dead, but only three ripped. They only got to cut Elizabeth Stride's throat. Someone must have disturbed them.

Catherine Eddowes had died earlier that same night. Throat cut, disembowelled, and her face mutilated. The killer posted part of her kidney to the Whitechapel Vigilance Committee as if to say, *Watch all you like, you'll never catch me – I'll keep ripping till I'm done.*

But the bastard wasn't done. He'd not be done till he'd got five.

Five. The perfect number, the pentagram, the five senses, the five fingers, and the five wounds of Christ.

Five, and he was free.

But he never got Long Liz Stride properly, did he. Never got to cut her open and dig it out of her.

Only three ripped. And of the five Jonas Troy had found in Whitechapel, just one remained.

Mary Jane Kelly.

So what would the Ripper do now? He had two more to find before he could be free.

Troy turned back to his drink.

He'll probably come for me, he thought. *Me and Mary left.*

Someone bumped into him, but he ignored them. Stand at the bar of the Ten Bells, you were going to get shoved.

The pub stood on the corner of Commercial Street and Fournier Street. On Fournier, back in the 18th century, London's authorities had built houses for Huguenot weavers and merchants who'd fled Catholic butchery in France.

But it was the same evil that drove the Papist French to ethnically cleanse their protestant countrymen as steered the recent murders in Whitechapel.

The same evil.

Troy drank. In the street, men fought. In the pub, they drank. Somewhere – it might've been just outside the doors of the pub, or inside – a fiddler played a Viennese waltz.

Troy stopped to listen. It had been months since he'd heard

such music. The day he'd left Vienna. The day after Mary Ann Nichols had been ripped. The day Troy knew would come.

Someone grabbed him from behind. He spun, ready to defend himself. But he delayed his punch.

Mick Perry, descendant of a Huguenot weaver who had fled France, said, "Fucking immigrants."

Perry had a bulbous nose and missing teeth. He was short and squat and always had his fists bunched, as if ready for a fight. It looked like he'd just been in one. Blood poured from his mouth, and a welt bulbed under his left eye.

Troy ignored Perry's complaint and his injury and said, "What do you know?"

Perry only turned up when he knew something. That had been the deal. "I don't want to see you, otherwise," Troy had told him. Perry was his bloodhound in Spitalfields. His tracker, his eyes and ears.

"Just been fighting round Dorset Street," said Perry. "And as we cleared out, I saw someone loiter near Mary Kelly's lodgings. Thought you'd want to – "

But Troy was gone, bolting out of the Ten Bells, elbowing himself through the crowd out in the street – hoping he could save Mary from the Ripper.

Then something hit him across the back of the skull, and his vision went blurry.

CHAPTER 4.
ENDLESS NIGHT.

DETECTIVE Inspector Frederick George Abberline, leading the inquiry into the Whitechapel murders, had not properly slept for weeks. He couldn't sleep. It was too dangerous. If he slept, the dreams would come. And you wouldn't want to dream Fred Abberline's dreams. They were terrifying. They could kill you in your sleep. Stop your heart and freeze your blood.

And he didn't want to die in his sleep. He wanted to die with his eyes open, face to face with his tormentor.

And since his tormentor was stalking Whitechapel, that's what Fred planned to do.

Go eye to eye with him – if he could keep his eyes open – and tell him: "No more atrocities."

No more atrocities.

He began to shake. He opened the drawer of his desk and took out a flask. He drank from it, and the liquid – hot down his throat – jerked him awake. But the shakes continued. He always had the shakes. They were caused by fatigue, drink, and a lack of food.

When was the last time he'd eaten a decent meal?

He looked at his pocket watch. Time to go out again and wander the streets. He would do this every night – stroll the alleys and passageways of Whitechapel and Spitalfields till 5.00am.

The time drifted. He was usually in a haze. He hallucinated, for sure, because he saw terrible things that he knew were not real. At least, he hoped they weren't.

When 5.00am came, he would wander home and collapse on his bed, only to be awakened perhaps minutes later by the delivery of a telegraph summoning him to the Whitechapel station to interrogate yet another suspect.

Another maniac. Another lunatic. Another false dawn. At this rate, his bosses at Scotland Yard grumbled, the killer would never be caught.

Abberline rose from his chair, turning to head for the door.

He stopped dead.

The face looking into his was fog-grey, and red rings circled the eyes.

"Evening, Fred," said Inspector Walter Andrews. Andrews had been sent from Scotland Yard to help with the investigation into the Whitechapel murders. *Hinder* was perhaps a better description. Andrews was a short man with red hair. Like Abberline, he appeared to suffer from sleeplessness. His skin and his eyes gave it away.

Abberline greeted his colleague with a nod.

"Off out again?" said Andrews.

Abberline said nothing. He tucked his pipe into his coat pocket. He picked up his briefcase. It was heavy with documents and implements. It jangled as he raised it off the floor. His throat became dry with nerves.

"What've you got in there, Fred?" said Andrews. "The Crown Jewels?"

Abberline said, "I have to leave, Walter. If you'll excuse – "

"We need to sit down and chat, Fred."

24

"Chat?"

"You, me, and Moore."

Henry Moore was the third inspector sent with Abberline and Andrews.

"I'll think about it," said Abberline. He was the eldest of the trio, the most senior – promoted to inspector in 1873, when he was thirty. It would've made Martha proud. Tears welled at the thought. She had died five years before his elevation, only two months after they were married. It was TB that killed her – a hacking, withering death. Although he'd married again – sweet, dear Emma – his heart still ached for Martha.

"Think about it?" said Andrews, frowning. "What's to think? We're no closer to catching this chap. We've got suspects coming out of our arseholes. None of them fits the bill. We've got panic on the streets. We've got the press baying, and even Her Majesty's fretting, they say. What's to think, Fred?"

Abberline's skin goosefleshed, and he shivered. A tingling sensation ran through his fingers. "Come along, Walter," he said, trying to keep his voice calm. "I must go, now."

"Where're you going, Fred? See your whores?"

Anger flared in Abberline's breast. He said nothing, containing the rage behind pursed lips.

Walter Andrews went on. "They say you give 'em money, Fred. Is that true? You pay for it?"

"I give them a few shillings so they can have a bed for the night."

"So you can have a bed, more like."

He leaned into Andrews, going nose to nose with him. "I spent fifteen years in Whitechapel. I know these people. I know these streets. You should count yourself lucky, Walter. It is only by the grace of God that you were born in pleasant Suffolk, you know. You could have been the wretched offspring of some poor unfortunate. And you know what they do with their offspring, Walter? Leave them on street corners or toss them into the Thames. That's what they do."

For a few seconds, they looked each other in the eye, neither giving way.

Then, Andrews laughed and turned away. "There you are, Fred. A right preacher. Ranting on. Off you go, then."

Abberline stayed where he was. He wasn't going to allow Andrews to dismiss him. "We'll speak tomorrow," he told the other inspector. "First thing."

Abberline strode away towards the stairs at the far end of the office.

Behind him Andrews said, "If we don't catch this chap, we might have another body to discuss."

We might, thought Abberline. And he quaked with dread.

CHAPTER 5.
THE SHAPES OF SCREAMS.

"HELLO, Mary," he said. "You've got a fine pair of tits on you. I might have him cut them off, keep 'em as a souvenir."

The door stood open. He lurked on the threshold, a silhouette framed by the darkness. The street behind him was empty. The night was quiet. The fog rolled in. The cold came too. And then him, stepping into the light, bringing with him an odour of decay. The flame of the lamp quivered. Mary stepped back. The door slammed shut. She would have sworn he'd never touched it. She pressed herself up against the wall. He took off his top hat. His hair moved as if it were snakes. His chalk-white face made her bladder sag. It was horror. It was dread. He was a human leech. But he wasn't human. He was something else. He was evil.

Evil itself.

Mary tried to be brave. "If you're here to kill me, kill me."

He laughed. It made her spine watery. He placed a brown, leather briefcase on the floor and sat on the bed. His cape flapped. In its folds, contorted faces appeared, their mouths making the shapes of screams. Dozens of them seemed to be trapped in the material, each one in agony.

But then they were gone.

The light, she thought. *The trembling flame casting shadows, surely.*

Surely...

"Sit," he said.

She slithered down the wall and sat on the floor.

His gaze drifted over her lodgings.

"You live miserably," he said. "The lot of you. Is it worth it?"

"To stop you, yes."

"I could give you thrones. I could give you palaces. I could give you empires."

"You're a liar."

"Well... perhaps. But I could give you more than this."

"You bring fear and death – that's all you can give."

He said nothing. He made a show of checking his nails. But they weren't manicured. They were long and yellow and cracked. Talons that could rip you open.

Mary said, "You think you're strong, but you're not. We can find you. We can always find you. We always have."

"You're a whore."

"You're scared of us."

"A slag, a tart."

"You'll never be free of this place, and tonight... tonight will be the last night of your freedom."

He shook his head. "You could've been the fifth, Mary. Unfortunately, I was hindered when I courted dear Elizabeth. Never mind. There are more of you, and they will come."

"They're hunting you."

"Good – let them hunt. I welcome them. Any pussy among them, Mary? Any cunt I can cut out and keep?"

Mary said nothing.

Then he said, "You know what they're calling me? Jack. A working man's name. A human name. You can call me that, if you

28

like. But I like this name, too." He pointed to a brass nameplate on the briefcase. "Stole it from a fool I killed. Drowned him, I did. Went down with him. Down into the grey, cold depths of the Thames. Shitty old river, she is. Just like the Euphrates."

"You can kill them, but you can't kill *me*. You can't kill *us*."

"*I* can't, Mary… "

Someone knocked on the door.

Mary held her breath.

The man on the bed said, "Come in."

The door opened slowly, and a figure stood there. Terror raced through Mary's veins. Her heart pounded. She began to whine, knowing death was very near.

The newcomer entered. He looked Mary in the eye. Her jaw dropped. "Not you," she said, "please not you."

"I'm sorry, Mary," he said, his voice quaking.

"Rip her," said the man who liked being called Jack.

CHAPTER 6.
ANOTHER NIGHT,
ANOTHER RIOT.

HIS head ached. Blood dripped from his scalp on to the pavement. He crawled along through the moving forest of legs.

He heard someone say, "Come back here, you bastard," and never thought it was directed at him. Not until the agony of a leather boot smashing into his thigh was followed by the same voice saying, "I told you to stop, you fucking Jew."

Jonas Troy rolled on his back and writhed in pain, clutching his leg.

Above him stood a policeman, wielding his truncheon. Around him, men fought. The noise was deafening. The violence was brutal. Not only fists and feet, but knives and broken bottles were being used. And Troy glimpsed one fellow cracking another over the head with a brick. The crowd swarmed. It came close. Too close. Feet stamped near Troy's head. The bobby swung his club to clear space for himself.

He looked down at Troy again and said, "Now get up, you; you're under arrest."

"What for?" said Troy.

The policeman, a big bear with claws and whiskers to match, grabbed Troy's jacket and then lifted him off his feet.

Like being on a swing as a child, Troy wheeled in the air, and his belly tumbled.

The bobby bashed him against the window of the Ten Bells. Troy's head snapped back. Glass smashed. His nape stung, shards piercing his skin. Blood ran warm down his back. He was dizzy, seeing double. His thigh was numb, and he thought he might not be able to put any weight on his leg. And to prove his theory, it buckled when the constable put him down roughly.

Troy staggered away. The bobby followed – cheeks red, huffing and puffing, bashing over the head anyone who came to close.

Troy said, "Tell me why you're arresting me."

"You're a Jew troublemaker."

"I'm not a Jew. I'm not a troublemaker."

"Shut your mouth – and stop trying to get away from me."

"There's a woman… "

"There always is."

"She's in danger."

"It's them that are dangerous round here, mate."

"Constable, you can come with me."

"No, mate, you're coming with me."

He nailed Troy – cracked him on the shoulder with his truncheon. But Troy threw a punch. The right hook caught the policeman on the jaw, making him stagger but not dropping him. Troy's hand hurt now. He shook it, grimacing. He'd broken his knuckles on the constable's face.

The bobby shook off the blow. "Assaulting a police constable is a serious fucking offence, son. You're getting a hell of a thrashing when I get you back to the station." Rage reddened his face, and he snarled at Troy, attacking.

No choice, he thought; *I've got no choice.*

31

He slipped his hand into his pocket and told the constable, "Forget about this. Let me go. I'm warning you – forget it."

"Don't you fucking threaten me, Jew."

The constable charged. He ran straight into the knife and dropped to the street, writhing and clutching his belly.

"Keep your hands there," Troy told him, blood dripping from his knife. He wheeled, ready to sprint down Commercial Street towards Miller's Court, but he stopped in his tracks.

Standing a few yards away was a young girl. But she was not an ordinary girl. She was a vision. She was a ghost. He could see right through her. But she was still staring at him. He looked at her face, and he thought he knew her. He studied her clothes. They were unlike anything a girl would wear – to start with, she wore trousers and a strange, peaked cap with the letters "NY" emblazoned on it.

Troy reached out for the girl, and she reached for him.

He felt a connection. He felt as if she were part of him. As if she were his future.

Then he saw into the girl's heart and knew everything about her. And with that knowledge, he realized that the war he was fighting today would be fought again tomorrow and for many tomorrows to come.

"Go and save her, little seer," he told the girl, and then he ran past her, looking into her face. He saw himself in her features. The girl watched him. He kept looking at her and bumped into someone. He staggered and got ready to defend himself.

"Murdering police constables, now, are we, Mr Troy?" said the man he'd bumped into.

Troy quickly looked back and the girl was gone, and then he spoke to the man. "He's going to kill Mary Kelly, detective inspector."

The policeman raised his eyebrows. "Are you sure?"

CHAPTER 7.
REMAINS.

AS Troy and the detective inspector hurtled down Commercial Street, others of their kind joined them in the race to save Mary Kelly from the Ripper.

But Troy knew they were too late. He could sense it.

Another seer was dead.

Another one ripped.

Another soul lost to the darkness.

Four, now. Four ripped since the evil was freed a few months before. One more, and it would be five.

The perfect number. The pentagram. The five senses. The five fingers. The five wounds of Christ.

As he ran, he was in pain. Covered in blood and aching all over after the policeman attacked him, he was operating on adrenaline.

He looked over his shoulder. Eleven others accompanied him, all running silently. He thought, *It could be any one of us – we could be the fifth*.

"Wait," he said and slowed down.

"Jonas, what are we stopping for?" said the detective inspector, out of breath.

"He's killed her," he said.

"You don't know that," said a black man.

"I know," said Troy. "And you know, too – all of you."

They did. He saw it in their eyes. He saw it in their souls.

CHAPTER 8.
THE WELL.

FROM hell, it said, and it was signed, *Jack*. It was a letter published in a local newspaper. The letter that gave him his name. Like he told Mary before having her killed, he thought it was a good name.

But hell. What did they know? Their squalor. Their suffering. Their poverty. It was nothing – nothing to the *real* hell.

He knew the real hell.

And he wasn't going back there.

So he ran, pelting along the dirty streets.

They followed him.

Bastards.

Never let him be. Always on his tail. Curbing his freedoms.

They reined him in, just like they'd been made to do.

He fumed as he ran through the fog. It swirled around him. It was damp on his skin. It was cold. It reeked of the river.

Shitty old river, she is. Just like the Euphrates.

He thought about the man he'd drowned. The man whose case he now carried. A brown briefcase brimming with blades – blood-covered blades. Knives to cut and knives to gut. Knives to hack and knives to scalp. Knives to saw and knives to slash.

He wouldn't get to use them all. He cursed. He raged. His pursuers were gaining on him. He could hear their feet tramping through the streets. He could hear them call his name, his real name. An unspeakable name. A name so powerful it would burn off a man's skin. A name known only to them.

To them and to *Him*.

He who made them.

He who made Jack.

Shapes moved around him in the fog. Men grunted and women cried. Curses flew. Police whistles pierced the night.

He kept running. They kept coming.

He looked over his shoulder.

Their torches flickered in the fog. The buildings cast shadows.

He quickened his pace. His chest ached. Someone had put a knife in there, driven it deep to where his heart was – or where it should've been.

He had no heart.

Heartless. Soulless. Shameless. No guilt. No conscience. No regret.

Only desire.

They'd smashed their way in just after he'd devoured what had been ripped out of Mary Kelly. The one who had done the ripping stood covered in blood while Jack ate. And it was then that they stormed the lodging house. There were twelve of them, led by Jonas Troy.

Troy, the seer of seers.

The bastard of bastards.

God's own *cunt*.

One of Troy's horde had stabbed Jack. They'd manhandled him, trying to fight him to the floor, Troy ready with his iron. But Jack kicked off. He got loose. He raised hell. He slashed and hacked and flailed, red mist falling, white rage burning.

He barged his way out of the door, out into the street – and started running.

He had no idea what had happened to the one whose mind he had poisoned. The one who'd done the ripping. It didn't matter now.

Get away, that was all that mattered.

Find shelter. Get your strength back. Find a mind to warp. A mind willing to rip for him. A mind willing to murder. Then find a fifth – Jonas Troy or that detective inspector. He was also one of them.

Rip them open. Cut it out. Devour it.

Jack turned down an alley. Pitch black and stinking of piss. Shit-coloured water running in the gutters. Brick buildings covered in mould and damp. The brick gone black with smoke and age. Along the other side of the road ran slum properties. Doss houses for human debris. Inside the buildings, babies cried and women screamed.

He ran down a side street and came into a yard.

Trapped.

He froze.

A well stood in the middle of the yard.

He turned to leave the way he'd come, but shadows flickered in the narrow passageway, and raised voices told him they were here.

The fires of their torches flared as they spilled into the yard.

He backed up.

Twelve of them. They circled him.

"Go quietly," said Troy.

"I've never gone quietly," he said.

They mobbed him. He struggled. He hated this. He feared it. The dread was mounting. They had him. "*Noooooooooooo…* " he screamed.

Why can't I be free?

They forced him to the ground and spread-eagled him.

37

Troy loomed over him, brandishing the iron. He held it up to heaven and shouted a prayer. Lightning sliced the night. It struck the iron. Troy lit up. The iron became red hot. The fire of God. The flames of hell. Jack writhed with dread.

"Hold him still," said Troy.

He fought against them.

Troy brought the iron down and pressed it to Jack's left palm.

Blinding white pain seared through him. He arched his back and screamed. He cursed his maker and cursed him again when Troy burned his right palm.

When he was done, Troy ordered Jack bound.

His skin was melting from his hands and his feet, and from the gash in his side, beneath his ribs, seeped a black, tarry fluid.

They tied him with chains and hoisted him to his feet.

Troy said, "You are bound by the five wounds of Christ. Only blood can unbind you. And five deaths will free you."

"Fucker," said Jack, drooling and sick with pain.

Again. A-fucking-gain.

How many times had he suffered this?

How many times?

The wounds of Christ. The casting down.

"Throw him in the well," said Troy.

They lifted him and took him to the well.

"I will butcher your children's children," he shrieked as they dropped him into the pit.

CHAPTER 9.
NEVER ENDING.

JONAS Troy looked down into the well. Darkness looked back up at him.

A hand on his shoulder made him start.

"It's all right, Troy," said the detective inspector. "It's done. That's him gone."

Troy said, "He's not gone."

"As good as gone."

"The poison he spreads has infected the world. Because of that, he can always call out to it. He can summon it and make it work for him. Just like he did with the fellow who killed Mary."

The detective inspector tutted. "I don't know what to do about that."

"You should lock him away."

"He's a man of high regard."

"He is a murderer," said Jonas.

The detective furrowed his brow.

Troy said, "Many men of high regard have been used by that monster to kill us, inspector. To rip us and… and gouge out… "

He trailed off. He stared down into the abyss. He heard voices. The voices of the dead. The voices of the victims. The voices of the seers.

Those who went before. Those murdered at his command.

They hailed him. Hymns wafted from the deep. Hymns to Jonas. They called him "saint" and "angel".

But the praise was empty. It meant nothing. Words and songs. He knew, ultimately, he would fail. All mortals fail.

We die, he thought. *But evil never does. It goes on and on, never ending.*

"He'll be back one day," he said.

"Get it out of your mind for now," said the detective inspector. "You're hurt, and you need to see a doctor."

"What about the knife-man?"

"We'll deal with him."

"Who, the police?"

The detective inspector nodded.

"What will you do?" asked Jonas.

* * * *

The water sucked him down and he funnelled through the arteries of London, plunging deeper, deeper into the city's guts.

The chains bit into his flesh. The wounds on his hands and feet and side pulsed. His rage bubbled.

Bastards… bastards…

The voice of a child said, "Locked again in the womb of the earth, locked again until blood gives you birth… " and the child's voice laughed.

"Fucking bastard," said the one they'd called Jack. "Let me loose."

"You are bound, my Evening Star," said the child's voice.

He was hauled through the dark water. It plugged his throat. It filled his lungs. It swelled his stomach.

"I am the lord who gapes," he screamed, "let me go."

"You can't make me, you can't make me… " sang the child's voice.

"I am the lantern of the tomb… "

"You can't make me, you can't make me… "

"I am the moth eating at the law… "

"You can't make me, you can't make me… "

"I am your – "

The water whirled. He wheeled, his voice stolen from him. The swirling pool drilled him downwards into the earth, driving him into the chalk and the lime, burying him. He tried to scream, but his voice was gone. Instead, the rage blossomed inside his head, his mind screaming, *I AM YOUR OFFSPRING…*

PART THREE.

HOMECOMING.

CHAPTER 10.
STAMPING GROUND.

IF it had been anyone other than Charlie Faultless walking down this street dressed in the Paul Smith navy blue suit, the Patrick Cox shoes, and the Yves Saint Laurent shirt and silk tie, they probably would have been mugged by now.

But Charlie Faultless wasn't just anyone. He had an air of menace – something about him that made it clear you'd be messing with the wrong fella.

The way he walked made you eye him up but stay well back.

He might *not* be tough. He might just look it. But a mugger had to make a split-second decision. And a swagger, a strut, and scary eyes that were different colours made all the difference when it came to making a choice – to mug or not to mug.

With Charlie Faultless, the right decision was to walk away and choose another victim.

Good call. Because the swagger, the strut, and the scary eyes weren't just show – he could back them up.

44

Faultless wasn't big. Five-nine, a hundred-and-sixty-eight pounds. Lean and sharp-edged, as if he'd been cut from flint.

But he was pit-bull tough. You kick off with him, he'd not let go till one of you wasn't moving much – and it wouldn't be him.

You could put him in an expensive suit, give him the handbook on how to behave in company, forge him into one of the best investigative journalists in the country, but Charlie Faultless still had the cold blood of a street fighter racing through his veins, the black heart of a villain beating in his breast.

And this was the place that had made him. The Barrowmore Estate, E1.

It had been fifteen years. Nothing had changed. Graffiti and burned-out cars. Overgrown grass on a piece of open ground. Rusted swings and a climbing frame. Youths loitering, transmitting menace. The smell of booze and fags on the air. The stench of charred metal from the cindered vehicles and petrol and oil fumes from their gutted engines. The reek of dog shit from the hybrid beasts used as weapons by drug dealers. Satellite dishes festooned the tower blocks. Laundry flapped on the balconies. Snatches of arguments wheeled on the breeze.

He stopped outside a row of shops. Most of them had been boarded up. But there was a Costcutter convenience store, its windows protected by metal grilles. A burglar alarm's red light winked above the door. Bracketed to a tree outside, a CCTV camera gazed down at the pavement. Along from the Costcutter, a takeaway offered fish and chips, pizzas, and kebabs. Further down stood a greasy spoon called Ray's that offered a full English for a fiver and chips with everything.

Faultless looked around. The patch of open ground lay on the opposite side of the road. Litter was strewn in the grass. The smell of dog shit filled the air. It was obviously the place to go when your frothing, mad-eyed weapon needed a crap. Smell or no smell, it didn't put off the trio of louts swigging beer on the acre of ground. Faultless eyed them. He gripped the strap of his Gucci shoulder bag. The three wise men might just fancy it – and the MacBook tucked inside.

You ain't having it, thought Faultless. *No one's having it.*

Not even the Hodder & Stoughton publishing exec Faultless and his agent just had a curry with in Brick Lane. If they wanted the MacBook, or, more specifically, the proposal it contained, they'd have to better the offer made by Macmillan.

Faultless turned away from the three youths and looked up the road.

The sight made him shiver.

You're jumpy tonight, Charlie boy, he told himself. But he knew why.

The four tower blocks glimmered against the dark sky. They were each fifteen-storeys. Fifteen floors of misery. They were built in a quadrangle, the centrepiece of Barrowmore. They were named Swanson House, Monsell House, Bradford House, and Monro House. Surrounding the tower blocks were more flats. Rows and rows of two-storey, red-brick, pre-fab housing, raved about in the 1960s, railed against in the 2010s. Streets of these bland, clinical boxes – hailed as modern and stylish when they replaced the slums – snaked around the estate. The buildings were now damp and filthy. They were as soiled as the tower blocks looming over them, as grim as the warehouses lining the estate's forgotten corners.

Staring up at the towers, Faultless thought about the regeneration projects that had redeveloped much of the East End. Money poured in. The tower blocks were demolished and replaced by low-rise housing. Cool Britannia swooped – artists, musicians, actors. Galleries opened. A busy, lively nightlife evolved.

It was bright, it was buzzing – it was a grand illusion.

Because if you wave a magic wand, your sleight of hand will never hide every secret.

Some places you'll miss. Some secrets will stay hidden. Secrets like the Barrowmore Estate.

Faultless cringed. He nearly turned his back on the tower blocks and walked away – headed up the road that led back to Brick Lane and Commercial Street, back to civilization and sanity.

But he steeled himself. He had to do this. He had to cleanse his soul. He needed closure. He needed answers. He needed to repent.

"Hello, chief," said a voice behind him.

He wheeled, ready to kick off, fizzing with tension. This was his old stamping ground, but he'd not been back since 1996 – not since he'd been forced out. But time wouldn't have healed the wounds he'd opened. It had probably made them fester.

And there was a good chance the Graveneys would still be out for his blood.

"Twitchy, ain't you, chief," said the voice, from behind a veil of smoke.

CHAPTER 11.
THREE WISE MEN.

THE cigar smoke cleared and showed an old man with snow-white hair that reached down over his shoulders. His raven-black eyes sparkled as he smiled at Faultless. He scratched the tuft of beard on his chin and said, "This kind of place makes a fella twitchy, I guess. You agree with me, chief?"

Faultless narrowed his eyes, studying the man. His face was speckled with the signs of age. He wore a leather waistcoat. Tattoos swathed his arms and his torso. Faultless stared at the images and lost himself in them as they appeared to move on the old man's body.

He snapped out of it, feeling himself flush. He furrowed his brow and searched his memory, because the old man's face seemed familiar.

"You all right there, chief?" said the stranger.

"Yeah, top notch. Do I know you?"

"Might do."

Faultless thought about introducing himself, but he hesitated. Bad blood made him think twice.

He asked, "You lived here long?"

"Not round here, no. Elsewhere, though. Very long."

"Moving up in the world, are you? To Barrowmore?"

The old man said, "Up, yeah, that's right. Way up. A long way. You ain't got a couple of quid for a can to go with my cigar, have you, chief?"

"Spent all your pension on the Havana, mate?" said Faultless, still trawling his mind for a match of the old man's face.

"No, I killed a man for it."

"Well, if you need a smoke, you need a smoke…"

The old man chortled. "That's right, chief. Now, have you got a couple of quid for a pensioner to have a night-cap?"

Faultless gave him some cash. The old man winked at him and went into the Costcutter. Charlie shook his head, tutting at his own gullibility and dismissing the feeling that he'd seen the elderly man before.

Mind playing tricks, he thought. *Stress of being back.*

He turned to walk away but stopped in his tracks, the three wise men blocking his path.

Not men really – they looked about sixteen.

The betting was they weren't very wise, either.

"What you got in the satchel, mate?" said one of the boys. He was your generic yob – pasty-faced, hooded-top, a swastika tattooed on the back of his hand.

Faultless glared at the youth, and the boy faltered.

"Here," the lout said, "you got one brown eye, one blue eye. You a freak or something?"

"I'm a freak, son," he said. "You know how much of a freak?"

"You what?" said the youth as one of his mates – maybe wise after all – was saying, "Leave it, Paul. He looks weird."

The third lout was already drifting off. He was tall. Well over six-five, but piss-thin. He reminded Faultless of that old toy, Stretch Armstrong.

Faultless, fixing on the first youth, the troublemaker, said, "You take advice, Paul? Is that your name? Paul? Take your mate's advice and leave it."

But he knew he was wasting his time. Still cocky, the lad called Paul said, "What're you going to do if I don't, fucker with your suit on?"

Faultless gave him a long, hard look that appeared to make the youth's knees buckle. Then he lifted the Gucci bag and said, "You know what I've got in here?"

"No, but I'm having it," Paul answered, not backing down.

"You think so? Tell you what's inside. It's your mother. Your fucking mother. Her fucking head right in this fucking bag." The lad's eyes were widening, his jaw dropping. "And if you don't fuck off," Faultless continued, "I'll rip your fucking skull off too, and stuff it in here so you're mouth to mouth with fucking mummy dearest, her cold, dead lips on yours. See what I'm saying, Paul?"

Paul saw. He looked Faultless up and down. He backed off, still staring, still not entirely sold on the retreat option.

"Come on, Paul. We'll get him later if he's around," said the lad's mate. "Let's go find the fucking cunt who nicked the PS3."

They legged it, Paul giving Faultless the finger before he and his buddies scarpered down an alley next to the wasteground.

"Should bring back the lash. What do you say, chief?" Faultless turned. It was the old man, swigging from a can of Carlsberg. "Time we make 'em pay for their indiscretions, eh?"

"They wouldn't be the only ones paying," Faultless said. He stared at the old man, certain he'd seen him before.

He would've bet his life on it.

CHAPTER 12.
SETTLING IN.

HOME. At least for the next few months. A one-bedroom hovel on the tenth floor of Swanson House. The letting agent had promised great views of London and accessibility to all local amenities. Bollocks. You could see the city sprawling east towards Barking and Dagenham – lovely – and you had Costcutter with its metal grilles and CCTV, the culinary delights of the kebab shop, Ray's café, and a pub with boarded up windows. But you'd have to run the gauntlet of the three wise men – and probably a few of their mates – before you got your shopping done, picked up your supper, or had a quiet pint.

Yes, thought Faultless, studying the flat, *it's going to be perfect.*

A shit-pit. Damp darkened the walls. The paint peeling. The floorboards rotted. A musty smell hung in the air. There was a red couch, sunken and sad-looking. By a window that provided smashing vistas of far-distant estates sat a table with two chairs tucked under it.

Faultless placed his MacBook on the table. This flat would be his base while he wrote the book. He'd spend his days researching and the evenings writing. After all, there wasn't much to do around here. Lucky he had a hobby.

He unpacked the rest of his overnight gear – a change of clothes for the following day and bathroom stuff. He'd left his suitcase at his agent's office in Holborn. He wasn't going to walk into Barrowmore with it at night, telegraph the fact he'd moved in – that'd make his flat a target for yobs. Best to sneak in as quietly as possible and get his agent to send the case over tomorrow.

He ate a ready-meal spaghetti bolognese, heated in the dusty microwave. The floor of the kitchen was covered in mouse droppings. He studied them as he ate standing up, wondering if he should get a cat.

With everything done – unpacking, eating, washing – he sat at the table in front of his computer and thought things through.

The noise of the estate drifted up ten floors. It was muffled, but he could still hear it. Wheels screeching. Girls screaming. Boys laughing. Hip-hop throbbing. Babies wailing. Footsteps pounding. Dads leaving. Mothers crying. A cacophony compressed into a tiny ball of noise that was being constantly tossed at his window and his front door.

Good to be home, he thought. *Good to know nothing's changed.*

He took his notebook out, laid it on the table, and opened it to the first page. Her photo stared out at him, and he saw red. He always did. The fiery rage erupting. In the past, he would've burned someone with it – doled out a hiding, a stare enough to provoke him. Now, most of the time, he could master the fury.

He looked into her eyes and breathed, clenching his jaw, bunching his fists, letting the anger seep out of him.

It was a colour photo, taken when she was sitting at the kitchen table. He remembered taking it. The camera had been nicked. Some tourists had lost their way and decided to photograph the tower blocks, only for a seventeen-year-old Charlie Faultless to swagger over and say, "Take a shot of me, mate," the tourist mumbling, "Heh?" and furrowing his brow – and seeing the camera snatched from his grasp. Faultless swaggered off, the tourist and his wife shouting at him. When he got home, she'd been sitting at the kitchen table, smoking.

"Over here," he'd said, and she'd turned and flashed a smile saying, "No, Charlie, I look a right mess, darlin'."

"You look gorgeous, Mum," he'd said.

She did – long, dark red hair, mahogany eyes, and a face that had once appeared on the front of a teen-mag. That had been when she was a kid – just fifteen. A photographer spotted her at Oxford Circus with her mates. He'd handed her a card, told her to come to his studio. "Get your mum's permission." She said she would but never did. Her mum was a drunk who nicked the money her daughter made working weekends at Ray's greasy spoon.

So she'd gone to this photographer's studio with a mate.

"This is my mum."

"Looks young, your mum."

"Yeah, I was a kid," her mate said, grinning. "You know – modern Britain and all that."

The photos were taken. She got paid. Well, her "mum" got the cheque. A month later her picture was on the cover of the magazine, and the photographer said: "You're going to be a star." Three months later, she was pregnant. The star waned. Her skies darkened. Her future faded. Her boyfriend vanished. The child died.

But another came along. A little miracle. A 7lb 10oz bundle she named Charlie.

His murdered mother smiled at him from the photograph. It was how she would always be to him, and how he wanted to remember her. Smiling and beautiful. But the picture had been corrupted by another image – the police photos of her mutilated body.

As Charlie stared at the photo, both images mingled – the

swishing hair, the glance over the shoulder, the cigarette, the half-smile, the open throat, the cleaved abdomen, the cavernous belly, the pile of intestines…

Faultless cried out, venting his wrath.

Anger's no good, now, he thought. *This is not about vengeance.*

At least that's what he told himself, in his suit and his tie, with his middle-class manners and the cut of his dinner-party jib. That's what he told his agent. "Closure, Mike, not revenge."

Closure…

He turned the page of his notebook. Another photo, Sellotaped there, looked up at him. Rachel. Beautiful Rachel.

His heart felt as if it had shattered.

Fuck closure…

CHAPTER 13.
BLOOD BROTHERS.

THREE of them. Michael and Paul Sharpley and Luke – known as "Lethal" – Ellis. They strutted around the underpass, not letting anyone walk by without giving something up – your phone, your wallet, or if you were a girl, you give them a feel.

The underpass. The gates to hell. ADHD central. Stinking of piss. An obstacle course of thugs, dog shit, and litter. Graffiti splashed over the walls.

Kids gathered here in the day to drink and fuck and mug. They gathered there at night to drink and fuck and mug again. It was twenty-four-hour drinking and fucking and mugging.

The underpass stood on the path that snaked round the estate. The bridge overhead walked you from behind a street of houses, along a public footpath, across the common ground, through some back alleys, and into Commercial Street.

Paul, sixteen and with a swastika tattoo on the back of his hand, kicked the grass verge, taking clumps out of it. A rhymthic kick-kick-kick-kick…

He stared at his Adidas trainer as it thumped into the earth – thump-thump-thump-thump…

"Should've let me shank that cunt," he said.

Michael, a year older and wiser – wiser defined as knowing better how not to get caught – bicep-curled a rusty petrol can loaded with soil and rocks, topped off with water to make it heavy.

He said, "His fucking eyes said fuck off, Paul. Don't mess things up. I'm fucked off with Spencer. He's a fucking twat, and he nicked my PS3. I don't want nothing else getting in the way. We do him, we get our fucking property back."

"I want to" – thump-thump-thump-thump – "do that fucker. Don't care who he was – don't give a shit about his eyes or anything."

Michael swapped arms – curl-curl-curl-curl...

He said, "If he's around, we find him after we do Spencer."

Lethal Ellis, sitting on the arch of the underpass and dangling his long leg over the edge, said, "We going to shank him?"

There was a puppy-dog eagerness in his voice.

Michael said, "Yeah, bleed him."

"It's fucking shit without my PS3, man," said Paul.

"Yeah, we'll get it back, though," said Michael. "That Spencer, man – he is so fucked. He's going to bleed for what he did, bruv. Bleed."

"Yeah, that's excellent," said Lethal. "Bleed, man, bleed."

Laughter up the path made Michael stop curling.

"Stop kicking the fucking ground," he told his brother, and shouting to Lethal, "Who's that?"

"Bloke and a bird."

"We do 'em," said Michael.

56

CHAPTER 14.
NEW DAY, OLD WOUNDS.

7.20AM, FEBRUARY 26, 2011

BREAKFAST at the window. A grey sky spitting drizzle. Those residents with a Saturday job off to it. Driving away in cars and vans, lucky if they hadn't been burned, stolen, or damaged overnight.

I wouldn't keep a car there, thought Faultless.

Too much of a target for kids – a kid like he used to be.

From his window, he looked down into the square of concrete hemmed in by the tower blocks. It was a car park. It was somewhere to have a kickabout. A place to hang out, smoke, and drink. A battleground to settle differences.

It was anything you wanted it to be because here, on Barrowmore, there was no one to tell you what it shouldn't be.

He tuned in to the headlines on the radio. Murder, betrayal, and corruption. War, famine, and plague. Sex, celebrity, and sport.

He yawned and rubbed his eyes. He hadn't slept well. It was cold in the flat. The mattress was hard, his sleeping bag thin. And when someone tapped on the front door at 6.32am, he sat straight up and came completely awake.

It was an assistant from his agent's office. He looked twelve. He might have been fourteen. But he was clearly scared and cold, standing on the threshold with Faultless's suitcase. A youngster on work experience who'd been landed with the a job because a top client needed looking after at the weekend.

"Mr… Mr Faultless?" said the youth.

"You'd better hope so," the top client said.

"Oh… are – "

"Yes, I am."

"Oh yes, I… I recognize you now. From the cover of… of *Graveyard Of Empires*."

"Nice. Is that my case?"

He offered the kid a coffee with a caveat. "I guess Mike will want you back at the office, so I better not hold you up." And then with sincerity he added, "When you're walking out of the estate, try not to look like a potential victim."

The youth gawked.

"You look like the proverbial rabbit, son. Try looking more like a wolf. Swagger, don't slump. Head held high. Shoulders back. You should be okay."

The youth left, still looking frightened despite the advice

Faultless sorted his clothes before sitting down for coffee and toast.

Now dressed in a hooded top, low-slung jeans, and trainers, he carried the dishes to the sink and left them to soak.

Slinging his bag over his shoulder, he left the flat and looked right and left along the walkway. He locked the door, double-locked it, padlocked it, and then gave it a wrench – just to check.

A man in his thirties ushered a child out of the flat next door. He wore a Motorhead t-shirt, and mythical beast tattoos decked his arms. The girl was six or seven, wearing a pink coat and pink ribbons in her hair.

"Put your hood on, darlin'," said the man. Then he looked up and saw Faultless, and he froze. "All right," he said, suspiciously.

"Good, thanks," said Charlie.

The fella was looking Faultless in the eye. Fifteen years ago, the little girl might have been an orphan by now. Her dad's eyes narrowed as he stared, and then he said, "Do I know you?"

"I don't know, do you?"

"The eyes… "

One blue, one brown. Once seen, never forgotten.

The dad said, "You moved next door?"

Faultless nodded.

The child said, "Dad, please… "

The dad said, "Okay, darlin'," then to Faultless, "Lots of families on the tenth floor, mate."

"That's nice."

"We don't want trouble."

"That's nice, too."

"Okay, well… I'm – "

His daughter said, "Come on, Daddy," and tugged him away before he could introduce himself. The dad nodded a farewell. Faultless was glad he didn't have to say who he was. The guy might have recognized him. And who knew who he saw down the dole office or on the building site? Gossip galloped round Barrowmore. And if the Graveneys still had their ear to the ground, it would have quickly been filled with tales of Charlie Faultless.

It took him twenty minutes to make his way to Monsell House, the northeast tower block. On the seventh floor, he stopped outside her door.

Rust caked the number. Red paint peeled. He swallowed, his throat dry. His palms were wet with sweat, and he wiped them on his jeans. He knocked on the door. Her words reached him before she did. "Hurry up, Jasmine, I want you ready."

But when she opened the door, she stopped talking. Her mouth fell open. Her sapphire eyes blinked, and she said, "No way."

CHAPTER 15.
THE WRITER.

"A BOOK?" said Tash Hanbury. "What, with words in it, not just pictures?"

"Real words," said Faultless. "Some of them quite big words."

"Who'd've believed it?"

"Not you."

"No way. Charlie Faultless a writer? Writing books? Do people pay you for doing that?"

"I've got an advance, yes."

"Is that a lot?"

"Not a lot, no. Enough to live on for six months."

"I don't know how much that can be, because I live on dust for six months, honestly."

"Can I help at all?"

She blushed. "I'm not begging."

"I know, but ask if you want."

She nodded. "What books have your written?"

He took a sip of coffee. "I wrote one called *Graveyard Of Empires* about Afghanistan."

"The war?"

"The country. The war. All the other wars that have been fought there."

She raised her eyebrows and sliced her hand over her head. "What else?"

"Couple of years ago I had one called *Scapegoat* published. It was about a British soldier who got drummed out of the Army for murdering a civilian. But it wasn't a civilian. It was a suicide bomber. The soldier was a hero, but the authorities didn't want to know."

She looked at him. Her blonde hair was piled up on top of her head. Her eyes were wide. She had pale, smooth skin and long, delicate fingers. She was beautiful – just like Rachel.

His heart ached.

Tash considered him and said, "I never thought it would be safe for you to come back."

"I don't know if it is."

"Have you seen my… " She trailed off.

He shook his head.

She said, "Hang on a sec," and called out. "Jasmine, you are late. I am not amused, now."

"How old is she?" said Faultless.

"Eleven."

"The dad around?"

"What do you think?"

"Would I know him?"

She blushed.

He said, "That's a 'yes'. Who?"

"Pete Rayner."

"Jesus. Rayner?"

"Don't laugh," she said and then: "Jasmine, this is an amber warning."

"What happens when it gets to red?"

62

"A ruck," she said, smiling. It made her even more gorgeous.

Christ, she looked so much like Rachel. He'd never noticed before.

"So how did Pete Rayner happen? I mean you – you're – you know… " he said.

"What? What am I?" She was fishing.

He smiled. "You and Pete Rayner."

They were sitting at her kitchen table. Everything was clean and white. It smelled of disinfectant and flowers. Nothing was broken inside her flat. It was tidy and aspirational.

She said, "There was no one left. I was nineteen. My friends were mums already. He, you know, the old man – he was behind bars. Rachel was – " She stopped. Her lip trembled. Her eyes became glittery. "But Pete was around. He was kind. I was having a bad day. Must have been a very bad one, because they were all pretty shitty back then. Well, I thought, why not – one night. And… Jasmine."

"Where is he now?"

She laughed. "Where they all are, I hope – the bad dads' graveyard. What about you? Girlfriend? Wife? Both?"

"I was married. It didn't work."

"Why?"

"Because I did."

"You did what?"

"Work. I worked. I worked like a fool. We never saw each other. You know… "

"What's the book about?" she said. "The one you're writing."

He drank more coffee. It was cold. The way he liked it. Half an hour ago, when Tash put it on the kitchen table in front of him, steam had billowed from the mug. He'd baulked and left it.

He was about to answer when she called, "Jasmine," again.

Jasmine trudged into the kitchen. She wore a blue school uniform and a glum expression. She was a pretty girl. Natural selection had opted, wisely, for the Hanbury genes, rejecting her dad's heritable traits.

"She looks like you," said Faultless.

"And Rachel."

He nodded. "Hello, Jasmine, I'm Charlie."

Jasmine nodded.

"Say hello properly," said her mum.

"Hello properly," said Jasmine, giving a fake smile.

"Ha, ha," said Faultless. "Have you got any more jokes?"

"Tons," said Jasmine. "Are you mum's boyfriend?"

"Jas – " Tash started to say.

But Faultless interrupted. "No, why? Doesn't she have one?"

"She ain't had one for ages."

"Hasn't, Jasmine, hasn't. Charlie's a writer, so speak proper."

"What do you write? Stories?" said Jasmine.

"Yeah, stories."

"Harry Potter?"

"No. You like Harry Potter?"

Jasmine shrugged and started making toast, getting butter and a knife.

Tash said, "It's not cool, liking books. Jasmine, hurry up and drink your juice."

Charlie looked at Tash. Twenty-nine and drained of hope. She had been about fourteen or fifteen when Charlie was dating Rachel. Both sisters had wanted to be models. Just like his mum. Neither made it. Just like his mum.

Tash said, "Put the knife down, Jasmine, or I'll ring your grandad."

Jasmine slammed the knife down on the table.

Faultless said, "How is he, then? Grandad. Your dad."

"Godly."

"Godly?"

Someone knocked on the front door. Faultless watched Tash leave the kitchen to answer it. He heard her open door and sigh.

"Morning, Hallam," she said. "What can I do for you?"

"You look lovely today, Tash," said a man. Faultless couldn't see him properly. He looked at Jasmine, who was eating her toast.

"You like school?" he said.

Jasmine curled her lip.

"Neither did I," said Faultless.

"It's boring."

"I thought so, too."

"I don't want to go. I've been having headaches."

"Oh, yeah?"

She scowled at him. "You're doing the 'I don't believe you' voice. Mum does it. But it's true. My head hurts. And I get horrible dreams, too."

"Okay. Sorry."

"Who are you, anyway?" Jasmine asked.

"I'm an old friend of the family. I knew your mum and her – "

Tash returned and interrupted him. "Jasmine, time for you to leave."

"Me too," said Faultless.

Tash said, "You going?"

Jasmine, gathering her things, said, "Yeah, mum would like you to stay. She's in love."

"Jasmine," said Tash, scarlet now. "The light is turning red."

Jasmine grumbled and headed for the door.

As she went her mum said, "And don't forget you've got tae kwon do tonight, so no hanging around with Candice."

"Whatever," said Jasmine, and she was gone.

"She's a lovely girl," said Faultless.

"Most times."

He looked at her and she looked right back.

"Tash, I just thought you'd need to get on – "

"On with what?"

"I don't know – stuff. You work?"

"I do care work three afternoons a week."

"Okay. Just thought you'd be busy, that's all."

"Yeah, my life is so full here. It's all go." She bit her lips. "I'm sorry. You know what it's like. You've got to go, I understand. I'm just… "

"What? Just what?"

She cried. "Fucking lonely and sad and desperate, Charlie."

She fell into him, and he held her as she wept, stroking her hair. It felt like her sister's hair. She smelled like Rachel too. He eased her away, because she was jazzing up his biology, and it was the last thing he needed.

"Where does your old man live?"

"If I tell you," she said, eyes wet and red, a smile on her face, "will you stay for another coffee? I'll make it cold this time."

CHAPTER 16.
DREAMS.

"I DON'T know how you cope," said Tash. "I mean, you lost Rachel *and* your mum."

"How do you know that I do?"

"Don't you?"

"Not always."

"You're not needy though. Like me."

"You're not needy, Tash."

"I begged you to stay and keep me company. I blubbed like a baby." She laughed. "God, I'm so stupid. I'm just jumpy lately."

"Why?"

"I've been having dreams. Weird dreams. Dreams… dreams about… I don't know."

"Jasmine said that, too."

Tash smiled. Pride shone in her eyes. "She takes after me. Tries every trick in the book not to go to school. She knows I've been having headaches, so she says she has them, too."

"How do you know she doesn't?"

"She's my little trickster princess. She's her mother's daughter. It's what I did. My mum used to have headaches, so… so I used to say that I suffered, too." Tash creased her brow. "Thinking back, I did, though. I think I did. The past is so… I don't know… vague and unclear. No… no, it's a scam. A 'get-off-school' scam."

"That's a bit cynical of you."

"You get cynical in a place like this, Charlie. You should've stayed. You'd have been a right laugh."

"I'd've been dead."

She was looking at him, her head canted.

"You think they'd still come after you?"

"Are they still around?"

"I don't know. I just don't. I try not to know what's going on around here anymore. I'd leave and take Jasmine somewhere else, somewhere decent. But… but I can't. Council says there ain't nothing available."

"If you feel threatened, they should move you."

"I don't feel threatened. I feel trapped. Trapped doesn't get you another house in a better area. I want to have a chance, Charlie. I want to leave all this behind. It's like a stain on you, Barrowmore. Poisons you for life."

He said nothing.

She went on. "Doesn't it stay with you? Isn't it still in you, the poison of this place?"

"Maybe," he said, knowing it was. He asked Tash about the old man he'd seen the previous night. "He's got long, white hair and a tuft of hair, here, on his chin – Satyric tuft, they call it. Like a goat's beard. He wears a leather vest, smokes cigars."

Tash furrowed her brow. "Five thousand people on Barrowmore, Charlie."

"I know. I just thought you might have seen him round. It's just… I've seen him before, I'm sure of it. He says he's not been here that long. I don't know… something weird about him."

"Weird like my dreams?"

He looked at her and shrugged. A cold sensation snaked down his spine and he shuddered.

She bit her lip. "Lately, you know, I just feel… unsettled."

"Is it Barrowmore?"

"I'm a Barrowmore girl. No. something else. Like… like something's coming… something… " She trailed off.

"What?"

She didn't answer; she just looked down at her hands and fidgeted with them. Then she spoke. "Just before Rachel was… was killed, she was dreaming, Charlie. Did she tell you?"

He searched his memory. Those days were hazy. He was running wild. He loved Rachel, but his attention tended to be elsewhere. Drugs, thieving, assault. He was climbing the ladder. He was marking his territory. He was making his name. He seemed to remember his mum dreaming, but she drank a lot, so it had probably been the booze.

He told Tash, "Everyone dreams."

"Not like this. Real and vivid."

"She never told me."

"What are you writing about? You didn't say."

He looked her in the eye. He didn't have to say anything – she must have read it in his face.

"Oh my God, you can't be. Charlie, why?"

"Catharsis."

"Are you… are you trying to find out who killed them?"

"I hope to."

She looked away. "Why are you digging this up?"

"I'm trying to bury it, Tash. Four women killed, mutilated – "

"I know how they were killed."

"Okay, sorry – but it was my mum, my girlfriend – "

"My sister – "

"I have to do this. That's the poison in me, Tash. That's the stain Barrowmore left on my soul. I have to purge it."

She stood. "I don't know what Dad will say."

"That's why I want to see him."

"He told you never to come back."

"I know he did."

"Usually, when my dad tells someone not to come back, he means it."

"He did mean it," said Faultless.

"Then why are you here?"

* * * *

"Come on, Jasmine, yeah, or I'm going to miss Tyler, yeah, and I want to see him, see if he's got a hickey, yeah, 'cause he was with that skettel, Italy Slater, last night, and she was saying she was going to do it with him, yeah... "

Candice strode down the road. Jasmine trudged behind her. The rain fell. Kids screamed. Mums shouted. The bus roared by. She'd catch the next one.

"Come on, Jasmine," Candice called out again, wanting to see her ex, Tyler, who was now fancying Italy Slater because she was one year older, at thirteen. Candice was already twelve. Jasmine couldn't wait to turn twelve in two months time. Being eleven was boring. It was like still being in year six, in primary school.

Her head throbbed. Her mum didn't believe her. The dreams scared her. Mum still didn't believe her.

She'd cup Jasmine's face in her hands, smile her beautiful smile, and say, "I know every trick in the book, princess – I wrote the book."

She wondered about the man in her mum's flat. Charlie Faultless. He looked cool. Maybe Mum would go out with him. Maybe he could persuade Mum to believe her about the dreams. Maybe he could be her dad. But that didn't matter so much. Not many of her friends had their dads. The only person she knew who had their dad was her mum.

The bus stop heaved. Boys fought. Girls gossiped. The smell of cigarettes hung in the air. Some of her classmates smoked. One kid – Kain Sharpley – was drinking from a can of Carlsberg. Kain was year eight. He had two older brothers. They were bad news.

Kain caught Jasmine looking. She stared right at him. He told her to fuck off and asked her what she was looking at. She stared him down. Jasmine did tae kwon do at the community centre. Nothing scared her.

Nothing except for the dreams.

Kain Sharpley looked away.

CHAPTER 17.
SITTING IN JUDGMENT.

ROY Hanbury, a python draped over his shoulders and Bible verses inked on arms, said, "You think a judge would let you get away with that, Spencer?"

Spencer Drake, seventeen, with close-cropped ginger hair, said, "I ain't got a clue, Mr Hanbury."

The snake coiled. Hanbury sipped mint tea. His lilac eyes fixed on the youth. The stare was usually enough. But that was twenty years ago. It was different today. The young tended to need more encouragement than a dark glare. Maybe not this one, though. He had the jittery look of a coward about him.

Hanbury told him, "You've stolen something, and you should give it back."

Spencer shuffled in the armchair. He looked around the living room. His eyes fell on an image of the Crucifixion, a dazzling light behind the thorn-crowned head. The picture hung over the mantelpiece, which was lined with family photos and religious icons.

Hanbury said, "It's not my favourite thing, Spencer, being asked by your mum to have a word. She's very kindly, your mum, and you disrespect her."

"I… I don't, Mr Hanbury."

"Thou shalt not steal, son. By stealing, you disrespected her. She's very concerned for you. For your soul. You steal, you go to hell."

"But I'm going anyway, so makes no difference."

"Repent, son, and the Lord will wash away your sins. He washed mine away, and I had a fuck load more than you."

Spencer squirmed. "It was just there, Mr Hanbury. The door was open. It was just sitting there. I couldn't resist."

"A judge wouldn't see it like that. God won't neither. But God's got a get-out clause for you. He sent his only son to die on the cross, bleeding like a pig, to cleanse your sins. See up there? The picture of him dying – *for you*."

"I don't get it. If he's died for my sins, why do I have to repent?"

Hanbury curled his lip. "God demands it. After his sacrifice, it's the least we can do. Repent and choose the path of righteousness. That's how He will judge us, Spencer. Righteousness. There is always a judgment."

He rose. Spencer looked up, scared. Hanbury put the snake back in the vivarium and stroked it. The serpent was six feet long. It slithered away from its owner's hand and coiled itself.

"I hate snakes," said Spencer.

"God's creatures," said Hanbury and faced the youth. "There's always a judgment, Spencer. Someone has to pay. You can't get away with things. I learned that. Spent twelve years in prison learning it."

"Prison's soft. It's easy."

Hanbury's tree-trunk arm shot out and grabbed Spencer by the throat. He lifted him off the seat. The teenager's face reddened. He tried to prise Hanbury's fat hand away from his windpipe. No chance. Hanbury was bull-strong – twelve years lifting weights and pushing floor in jail added muscle to the already bulky frame.

Hanbury said, "Attitude like that'll get you hurt, Spencer."

The youth spluttered. He kicked. His feet sliced thin air. His balls shrivelled. His eyes were going blurry. He was off the floor by a good twelve inches. He was only five-six, while Hanbury was six-four. It was a long way down.

"I'm not going to do anything bad to you, Spencer; I'd hate myself – I'm good with my Lord these days, and pain is not what I do. But I demand respect, lad."

He released his grip on Spencer, and the teenager slumped in the armchair, croaking.

Hanbury offered him a glass of Coke and slapped his back.

"You'll be all right, son. Show a little respect. Prison ain't easy. Not if you do it properly."

Hanbury sat down. His heart raced. Not in good shape like he used to be when he was running Barrowmore or when he was inside. In stir he did 500 press-ups a day, and 1000 squats. It made him strong and fit.

And Spencer was right – prison weren't too bad. But Hanbury wasn't about to share that with the boy.

"Now, Spencer," he said, calming himself down with another sip of mint tea, "when are you going to give this property back?"

Spencer spluttered.

Hanbury switched on a big flat-screen TV bracketed to the wall. He clocked Spencer's eyes lighting up. On screen, thousands of black people in a church were singing hymns. Hanbury's heart lifted. He started humming.

"Here's the Word of God to inspire you," he said. "When are you giving it back?"

"Uh… "

"I'll tell you when. Right after you leave my house. Is that good for you? It's certainly good for me, Spencer."

"Yeah… yeah, that's… good."

"Good lad," said Hanbury. He settled on the couch, relaxed. "Twenty years ago, we wouldn't have got to this stage, Spencer. Twenty years ago, I would've cut your right hand off."

Spencer paled.

Hanbury went on. "But I don't do things like that anymore. It's ungodly. I let God punish. He's crueler than I could ever be. You know he had a man stoned to death for picking up sticks on a Sunday?"

"Really?"

"Oh, yes. Fear the Lord, Spencer. He's a right bastard. He loves you, son, but if you don't love him back, He'll burn you forever. When you return the stolen item to its rightful owner, God will be happy."

"And… and he won't burn me?"

"You'll have to repent for your other sins – the lusting, the lying, the greed, the taking-your-mum's-name-in-vain. All that shit. You have to repent."

"So… did you repent, Mr Hanbury?"

He stared at Spencer. "That's why you've still got your balls, son. Otherwise, they'd be on a silver platter now."

Hanbury cracked his knuckles and stood up. He went to the mantelpiece, where there was a packet of menthol cigarettes. He took one out and lit it.

"Can I have one?" said Spencer.

"Fuck off, son, and go with God."

CHAPTER 18.
RUNNING INTO TROUBLE.

JASON Joseph Thomas, known to himself and his only friend Spencer Drake as Jay-T, said, "You're still alive, Spence."

"Looks like it."

Jay-T, known to everyone else as Slow Joe, said, "Twenty years ago, you wouldn't have made it."

"I would've been alive, Jay. He said he would've cut off my right hand."

"Hand?"

"Yeah. Right hand. As I am a thief, he said."

"Fuck."

"And a sinner."

"Sinner?"

They strode away from Roy Hanbury's front gate. As they walked, Spencer clocked the other houses in the terrace. He couldn't help it. It was so tempting. The properties were red brick and white panelling. They were two-storey with high front walls, which were difficult to scale if you were going to rob the place. But once you were in the garden, they provided cover. *Swings and roundabouts*, he thought.

"Yeah," he said, "sinner."

I'm a sinner.

He looked back over his shoulder towards Hanbury's house. He thought about the TV. If he could sell that –

Sinner!

He turned away, looked at his feet as he walked.

You wouldn't want to rob Hanbury's house. That would be stupid. That would be suicide. He'd probably feed you to that snake. He would've eaten you himself in the 1970s.

He shivered again, glad to be out of the house, away from the old man's presence.

Hanbury was a big bloke. He used to be a gangster who tortured and killed, who organized heists and ran drugs and pimped whores. He owned Barrowmore and nearly owned Whitechapel. He tussled with other gangs. Threats were made. Men were killed. Tit-for-tat. Back and forth. Blood for blood. It went on and on, and it still went on. There was always payback.

There is always a judgment.

And Hanbury finally got caught.

Conspiracy to commit armed robbery got him twelve years.

He went in marked by the beast. He came out washed by Christ.

Spencer and Jay-T walked in silence. Jay-T did footballer dribbles with a Coke can. Spencer ran get-out clauses through his head – how to keep the PS3 without (a) the Sharpleys catching him and/or (b) Hanbury finding out?

He couldn't work it out.

He looked up. The sky was grey. Was there a God up there? He'd never thought about it. He supposed there had to be *something*.

This can't be it.

So maybe he should repent. He didn't know how. Was he supposed to say sorry to God? He tutted, confused. Maybe he should ask his sister. He hadn't spoken to her for a year. But she was into astrology. Was that the same as God?

Hanbury's words haunted him.

There is always a judgment.

No one had said that to him before. His mum had said, "You should always try to be a good boy, Spencer." But that wasn't the same. Not the same as, *There is always a judgment.*

He'd always been taught to get away with as much as you can.

His dad got away with it, and he'd burgled all his life – from when his own mum used him in his pushchair to scam old ladies to the day he dropped dead of a heart attack three years ago.

Spencer furrowed his brow.

Maybe that was judgment?

"You think there's judgment, Jay-T?"

"You what?"

"Judgment. Like a judge."

"Only if you get caught. Mostly magistrates, ain't it."

"Hanbury says everyone's got to pay in the end. There's always a judgment."

"Not if you get away with it."

"My dad said he got away with it. He never got caught."

"See?"

"But he died. He was only thirty or forty or something."

"So?"

"So maybe that was judgment."

"No, I think it was fags. I mean, like, he went through three packs a day, Spence. And he'd go mental if we ever nicked a fag. Even though he had loads."

Spencer felt the itch in his chest.

"You got any now?" he said.

"No."

"Let's go to the Paki shop. I need a fag."

They had to turn round now. The Costcutter was on the road leading out of Barrowmore, and Spencer and Jay-T were traipsing aimlessly along the estate's back streets, inhabited by lock-up garages.

He glanced at one of the lock-ups as he turned to head back.

The metal door was rusted. A huge padlock hung off the handle. The words "Trespassers will be hunted down and shot" had been painted in red across the brickwork.

Spencer gulped.

People told scare stories of gangsters like Hanbury torturing people in the lock-ups. Some said he still owned them. Spencer wondered if there were any bones in there. Skeletons of victims hanging from hooks.

It took the boys twenty minutes to reach Costcutter. An old man stood outside, smoking a cigar. He wore a leather waistcoat. He was well tattooed. Weird stuff – language and lettering Spencer had never seen before.

Maybe we can nick a fag off him, he thought.

"Fuck," said Jay-T.

Spencer said, "What?"

Jay-T pointed.

Pissing against the side of the Costcutter was Lethal Ellis. Tall and gangly, Lethal was psycho. He had a very low attack threshold – it wouldn't take any provocation to make him snap, because he was snapped already.

And he was the Sharpleys' cousin. Where he was, they weren't too far away.

Not far at all.

Both of them swaggered out of Costcutter, Paul carrying a bottle of vodka – nicked, Michael carrying a bottle of gin – nicked.

The Sharpleys stopped dead. Spencer froze. Jay-T wheezed. Lethal Ellis said, "I needed that."

"You cunt," Paul said and bolted towards Spencer.

Jay-T legged it. Spencer followed. He bumped into a bloke eating a Twix.

The brothers pursued. Lethal tailed while shouting, "You're going to bleed, Drake. You're going to fucking bleed."

CHAPTER 19.
PASSING ON THE GIFT.

HACKNEY, LONDON – 9.22PM, JANUARY 12, 1903

THE crowd booed. Jonas Troy concentrated. Nothing happened. The crowd booed louder.

But the dead were silent. And that was the problem. No dead, no show.

"You're a fraud," someone shouted from the audience.

It had been a rotten evening. It had been a terrible fifteen years.

And Troy knew why – The Ripper.

The one they called Jack.

The audience bayed. They had come to talk to their dearly departed. But their dearly departed weren't in the mood.

This was his first performance at the Hackney Empire.

"We're getting big crowds," Mr Tolland, the manager, had told him. "I've never had a medium here before. You'd better bring a show."

He promised he would.

But waiting in the wings while a fourteen-year-old singer and dancer named Charlie Chaplin dazzled the crowd, Troy started to feel queasy. Voices echoed in his head – the screams of the

Ripper's victims, the hollering of the crowds that followed the trail of bodies, the trilling of police whistles, always too late, and the cold, cruel laugh of the one who made this madness.

Jack.

In the theatre, the crowd had cheered Chaplin. The kid skipped off the stage. As he entered the wings, he winked at Troy and said, "If you're half as good as me, mate, you'll be all right."

That was asking too much.

He quaked now as the audience crowed. He'd done performances in smaller venues, front rooms. They had been successful. But the money on offer at the Empire was much better. It would put food on Hannah's plate for months and pay for their lodgings for weeks.

After the Ripper plunged into the well, bringing the murders to an end, Troy had stayed in London. It was a grim, dirty city crammed with grim, dirty people. The East End, in particular, was a cesspit of immortality and disease. But he remained. He found lodging and soon he began to advertise his gifts so he could pay the rent.

Your future foretold. Your dearly departed contacted. Medium and fortune teller Jonas Troy will bring the spirits alive for you. Let him guide you to your fate.

The ad appeared in the newspaper. Soon he had customers knocking at his door.

He would only charge what people could pay. Sometimes that was nothing. Sometimes it was: "I'll sew on those buttons for you, sir," "I've got some apples here, guvnor," "I could keep you company this afternoon, love."

The third offer, he'd refuse. He was courting by then. Magda, the daughter of a Polish butcher. She was golden-haired and green-eyed. At eighteen, she was thirteen years younger than Troy. He'd met her when he read for her mother. The woman had been grief-stricken after losing her brother the year before.

Troy made contact. The woman cried. She thanked him in Polish. Magda translated. Troy said, "And can you ask your mother if I might be able to take her daughter out to tea?"

Magda said, "You should ask the daughter yourself."

He did. They went.

On April 7, 1891, six months after they met, Troy and Magda were married.

Ten months later, Hannah was born. Two months later while she was walking home late, after visiting her ailing father, Magda was murdered.

Throat cut. Face mutilated. Gut opened.

Her intestines were spooled on the ground beside her. Her liver and kidney had been removed. The words "A gift from him" had been written in blood on the wall.

Troy wailed. He raged. He cut himself. He tore out his hair. He smashed up the room where he now lived with his motherless daughter.

And then a voice in his head stilled him.

"I will never die."

Troy had frozen in the act of throwing a chair out of the window.

And the voice came again.

"You'll never be rid of me."

Troy had put the chair down and gawped around the room.

Hannah screamed in her cot.

He ignored his child and listened to the voice, which said, "Your lovely, lustful whore of a wife wasn't one of you, Jonas, but I chose to have her ripped, anyway, because I can – even when I'm trapped. Even when I'm buried. My poison seeps through this city's veins, Jonas. It can still stain a heart. It can still twist a mind. Every day I call out to someone for blood, and one day I shall have blood. And when I do, I will live again. Long after you are dead. But I'll hunt your kind, Jonas. I'll rip and I'll rip. I'll eat and I'll eat. Till there's five. Till I'm free."

82

"No!" Troy screamed and hurled the chair through the window.

It snapped him back to the present – Hackney Empire, nearly eleven years later.

The audience howling.

"You're a fraud," shouted a man with golden whiskers.

"You promised my husband would tell me where he left the silver," wailed a fat woman.

Another woman cried out, "My little boy is lost on the other side, and he wants his ma."

Troy raised his hands to quieten them. It made them angrier.

Mr Tolland shuffled on stage in his red velvet jacket and top hat.

Smiling at the audience, he hissed at Troy. "Fuck off, mate, before they kill you." Then he addressed the mob. "Ladies and gents, ladies and gents, please… sometimes, the spirits don't feel like visiting us … "

"Sometimes we don't feel like paying," a man shouted.

Troy plodded off stage and made his way down into the belly of the building, running the gauntlet of smirking entertainers.

In the dressing room, Hannah faced the mirror. She ate an apple and stared at her reflection. Her eyes were brown like chestnuts, her hair gold like her mother's. Troy's red suitcase sat on the floor next to her.

Hannah's gaze skipped across to him as he stood in the doorway.

Without turning she said, "I heard them shout at you, Daddy."

"I… I couldn't get through tonight."

"Perhaps there was no one there."

"There wasn't. Not tonight."

"Perhaps there's no one there, ever."

He came to stand beside her and began removing his stage clothes – the Fez, the brightly-coloured smoking jacket, and the scarlet necktie.

"You shouldn't speak like that, Hannah," he said.

83

"Why not, Daddy?"

"Because I say so."

"Don't be mean."

"I'm... I'm not mean." He lifted the suitcase and laid it flat on the counter where Hannah sat. " But... but the spirits, they can hear you. If we doubt them, they will never come. You have to keep believing, Hannah. If... if you stop, there isn't anyone else to – "

He stopped talking. He was about to say, "There isn't anyone else to watch for *him*."

For the Ripper. For Jack.

No one to see his coming. No one to find him. No one to hunt him. No one to cage him.

But he didn't say those things. He never had. Hannah didn't know she had a gift. Maybe it was time she did.

Jonas opened the suitcase. His newspaper cuttings were laid inside, clipped together neatly. His scribbled notes covered sheets of paper, and a leather journal was tucked into a pocket on the inside cover of the suitcase. He started to pack his stage clothes in the case. When he was done, he said, "You are a special girl, Hannah."

"Thank you, Daddy."

"You have gifts."

She turned to face the mirror.

"Daddy, I'm too old for fairytales – "

"No you are not. And you are not too young for the truth. Listen to me, Hannah."

"Daddy – "

"We are seers. We see the dead. We see the future. We see... we see evil."

"Evil?"

He took a breath and sat next to her. He stared at their reflections in the mirror.

He said, "Before you were born, I fought a monster. An evil thing. They called him Jack back then. But he's had many names."

"Why did you fight him?"

"Because we are the only ones who can."

She said nothing.

"There are a few of us," he told his daughter. "We are watchmen. We must be vigilant. If… if the evil is freed, it is our duty to hunt him down."

"Why?"

"Or he will kill us. He will kill us and…" He paused, wondering if he should tell her everything and then deciding he should. "And he will rip us open and…"

"Daddy, no!" She leapt to her feet, the chair flying across the room. She reeled away, hands clasped over her ears. "Don't tell me, don't tell me!"

He went to follow her, calling her name.

The muffled sound of music came from the stage above.

"Don't tell me, Daddy," said Hannah, cowering.

"I must," he said. "You must know."

She shook her head violently.

He said, "You must know, because he is not truly dead, Hannah. You must know, and your children must know. Promise me. Promise me. Or if he is resurrected and there is no one to know, no one to see, the people of the world will suffer terrible things. Promise me, Hannah. Do you promise?"

CHAPTER 20.
THE VOICE IN THE
DARKNESS.

WHITECHAPEL – 8.47AM, FEBRUARY 26, 2011

HOW had they ended up here?

Spencer had no idea.

They'd been running hard, the brothers tailing them.

Lethal brought up the rear and was shouting, "I got my shank out, Drake. You're gonna bleed, cunt."

Spencer ran. Blinded by fear. Blinded by rain. The sky like lead. The terror heavy in his limbs. His heart nearly bursting. Jay-T behind him, wheezing.

They ran along the roads. Down the alleys. Over parked vehicles. In front of *moving* vehicles – brakes shrieking and drivers cursing. Ploughing through pedestrians. Weaving past cyclists. Flipping over a pram – the mum screeching and threatening death.

Running till Spencer saw hope.

One of the garages – the padlock unlatched, the door slightly ajar.

As they entered the building, they looked back. No sign of Lethal and the Sharpleys.

Spencer could hear them, though – pounding the pavements a few dozen yards around the corner.

"What is this place?" Jay-T asked.

"Just get inside," Spencer told him.

Into darkness. Into cold. Into stink.

"Jeeee-sus," said Jay-T. "It goes way back down there, way back. Can you see?"

Just, but it was pretty dark. Light seeped in through gaps in the ceiling. But very little. Barely enough to show them the way.

But the way where?

"Where are we going?" Jay-T said.

"I don't fucking know."

At the back of the warehouse, they found an office. The door hung off its hinges. Cobwebs curtained the entrance, but the boys waded through.

Rats scuttled. The place smelled old. Yellowing papers curled on a table. Spiders crawled over a typewriter. A coffee mug was half full of something green and thick.

A wooden door at the rear of the office, marked *Do Not Enter*, looked tempting.

"Let's go," said Spencer. "They'll never find us."

They nearly tumbled down stone stairs that led into pitch black.

"Not sure about this, Spencer," Jay-T said.

"Lethal's going to cut you," Spencer replied.

They went down into the dark.

Their eyes adjusted to the gloom, and a little light also filtered from a crack where the wall and the ceiling met. It helped them see enough of their surroundings.

Wooden crates, rotting and stinking, were piled around the walls. The floor was littered with debris – pieces of wood, bricks, chunks of cement.

Damp soaked into everything. It smelled fusty and old. It smelled dead.

How did we end up here? Spencer thought.

How? By having itchy fingers and failing to walk past an opportunity, that's how.

Like he told Mr Hanbury, he had never meant to nick the PS3.

But when he'd swaggered past the Sharpleys' flat in Bradford House the previous afternoon, he couldn't resist poking his head through the open door.

Paul was fighting with his dad, reeling around the living room. They swore and shouted. Both sounded drunk.

The PS3 sat by the door. It was still in its box. It had a price tag on it. One of the Sharpleys had probably nicked it from somewhere. A house or maybe even somewhere in town.

With his brain telling him not to do it, Spencer had reached out and grabbed the box.

He thought he'd got away with it. But just before he legged it, he'd looked up and Paul caught his eye. He hadn't said anything, only carried on laying into his dad.

And when Spencer finally bolted, he was pretty sure he'd got away with it.

But something had slowly uncoiled in his belly during the rest of the day.

It was fear.

And it became fully unfurled when news rifled through the tenements that the Sharpleys were looking for the bastard who nabbed their PS3.

Spencer had been up all night on the games console. If the Sharpleys were coming to get it back, he was going to make the most of it.

Jay-T had also been up all night – smoking dope with his sister.

The mates had met at 8.00am.

"Come over to the squat; I got a PS3," Spencer had said.

"Yeah, and the Sharpleys want it back," Jay-T had said.

"Better hurry up and play it to fuck, then."

They'd nicked some cereal from Costcutter and ate it from the box, heading back towards Spencer's squat.

Then, as they strolled past Roy Hanbury's house, a voice had called out, "Spencer Drake, you heathen bastard, get in here, child of God."

Spencer had frozen. His balls had shrivelled. That happened when Roy Hanbury spoke to you. He was a legend. Not the fearsome figure he used to be when Spencer's dad was a dealer round the estate. But he still had that reputation. You respected Roy Hanbury. He'd earned it.

Now in the cellar beneath the garage, Spencer regretted ever setting eyes on the PS3.

"Look at this," said Jay-T.

"What the fuck is it?" said Spencer.

It was an area of concrete floor that had been bricked off. Ten feet wide and six feet deep, the red of the bricks stood out against the dark stone of the cellar floor.

"Can you smell something?" said Jay-T.

Spencer felt dizzy. There was a drain set in the middle of the brickwork. He stared at the hole, narrowing his eyes.

"It's coming from the drain," said Jay-T. "And… and can you hear that noise?"

Spencer listened. He sniffed. He heard rushing water and smelled dirty river.

He listened to a cold voice whisper, *Blood… blood… blood…*

It chilled him. Froze his bones and made his brain hurt.

"What… what was that, Jay-T?"

Jay-T crouched at the drain and said, "Sounds like a river down there."

Pick up a brick… crack his skull… make him bleed…

Spencer trembled. He felt dizzy, a bit sick.

Jay-T was saying something about a smell and a river and maybe something about treasure, but Spencer wasn't sure. By then he'd bent down to pick up a brick and was lifting it above his head.

Do it, came the voice again, like acid in Spencer's veins. Like a hammer in his skull. *Do it and be my witness – be the instrument of my savagery. Do it...*

Spencer saw white light.

With all his strength, he brought the brick down on the back of Jay-T's head.

CHAPTER 21.
REBORN.

SPENCER panted and stood over Jay-T's dead body. Blood seeped from the mangled skull and drizzled down the drain.

The ground trembled.

Spencer came to. He gasped and staggered back.

"J... Jay, man, get up," he said.

But Jay-T stayed still.

The only thing moving was the ground.

It shuddered, making it difficult for Spencer to keep his feet.

"Oh fuck, what have I done?" he said, his voice high pitched.

He felt something in his hand and looked – a brick stained with blood and matted with hair.

He yelped and flung it aside.

He checked his hand. Blood. He screamed and wiped it on his tracksuit bottoms.

The ground shook.

Spencer swayed.

The sound of water rushing grew louder – a torrent, now.

And then the cold voice from Spencer's head said, "Freedom tastes so good... "

But it wasn't in Spencer's head, any more. It was right there in the cellar.

A plume of black smoke drifted up from the drain. Spencer's insides turned watery. His legs buckled, and he fell to his knees.

The smoke swirled and became a shadow, which grew solid and took the form of a man.

Spencer was frozen with fear.

The figure loomed. It wore black – hat, cape, trousers, boots. But the clothes were damp and covered in dirt and blood. The stranger carried a tattered brown leather briefcase. He grinned, showing rotting teeth. His eyes shone like black pearls. They fixed Spencer like a hawk's would fix on a mouse.

"You're mine, little man," said the figure. "Slave or eunuch, you can choose."

Spencer said nothing. His voice had abandoned him. His sanity seemed to have made a run for it, too.

I am mad, he was thinking, *I am mad.*

The figure cocked its head and kept looking at Spencer.

I am mad...

The pale, white face shimmered in the gloom.

I am mad...

CHAPTER 22.
YOU HAVE AN EDGE.

FAULTESS had been leaving for the last hour. But cold coffee kept him seated. Cold coffee and warm eyes. The way she looked at him made him think of her sister.

"Does Jasmine know about Rachel?" he asked.

"She knows she died – that she was murdered. You can't protect kids these days. Rumours spread like the plague here. They riffle through the streets, and you can't stop them. Might as well tell the truth at the out. It saves a lot of hassle."

"How did she deal with it?"

"She's okay. But it's so far away for her. Before she was born." She looked into her tea and rubbed her eyes. "Jesus, who would do such a thing to her? To all of them." She stared up into Faultless's eyes. "To your mum."

"How's your dad taken it?"

"You know what it was like at the beginning. He was going to smash down every door on Barrowmore, find the bastard and hang him on the common. But just a year later he was under arrest, and after that he went inside. Twelve years. I honestly thought he'd tear that prison down to get out. He was going to find this guy and kill him – kill him slowly and painfully."

"What happened?"

"Dad found God."

Faultless remembered that Tash had described her father as godly earlier.

"Fire and damnation," she said. "The real deal. So when he comes out of jail a couple of years ago on licence, he's got no intention of finding out who killed Rachel. He'd forgiven him, he said. And Rachel, she was – she was with Jesus."

"Is he still God squad?"

"Dad's practically the pope of Barrowmore. People are still scared of him, but he just doesn't do what he used to do."

They were quiet for a few seconds.

"Are you still on the warpath?" said Tash.

He thought carefully before saying, "I want to find who killed them."

"You're not a detective."

"I'd do a better job than the bunch of layabouts who ran the investigation. I could've killed that Don Wilks. I had a few run-ins with him."

"He was out to get you."

"Everyone was out to get me."

"Oh, poor Charlie Faultless." She smiled and everything lit up. He smiled back, unused to the sensation.

She said, "You think the killer's still around?"

"Maybe he died. Maybe he went away. Maybe" – he furrowed his brow and looked her in the eye – "he went to jail."

Her face hardened. "You came here with a suspect in mind, Charlie? Is that it? My dad wouldn't do that. To his own daughter?"

"He was a suspect."

She leapt to her feet. "So were you. I can't believe this. And we were getting on so sweetly, weren't we. Just like you to bring an edge to things. Rachel always said that about you."

Faultless bristled.

Tash went on. "She said you were cold, that you were sometimes like the blade of a knife." She turned her back and folded her arms. "Christ. You come here, drink my coffee. Then blame my – "

"I'm not blaming anyone."

"Especially not yourself."

"I better go," he said, rising.

"You better had."

He touched her shoulder. She didn't flinch. He kissed her cheek. She smelled of roses. Her skin was silk. He stayed near her face for a second too long. Wisps of her golden hair brushed his mouth. She gasped.

He said, "Seeing you was great, Tash."

"Go find out what seeing my father's like."

"Maybe not so nice."

CHAPTER 23.
RIP THE FIFTH.

THE dark man hovered. His cape flapped. Writhing figures and agonised faces appeared in the folds of the cloak. It might have been his eyes playing tricks on him, but it looked real to Spencer, and his bowels trembled.

He gazed up, terrified.

The man came down, and his feet settled on the ground.

"You fear me," he said.

The voice went through Spencer like wire.

He was going to piss himself.

"Do you know who I am?" said the stranger.

"Jesus, no… I never saw a thing, mate."

The dark man laughed. "You never saw a thing?"

"Nothing. Honest. I'm not a grass."

"You've no steel in you. You're a coward, I think."

"I won't tell. Please let me go."

The stranger clicked his tongue. "I don't care who you tell. Tell the world. My name will be known, soon. My legend will again ripple through the streets. How are the streets, by the way? Still bloody? Still grim and desolate? I miss the grim and the desolate."

Spencer screwed up his face in horror.

The stranger cocked his head and studied him. "You're not the one, are you?"

Spencer gasped, shaking his head. The one? Whatever it was, he didn't want to be it. His balls had shrivelled to marbles. He was cold and scared and wanted to be safe in his bed.

"The one who's been doing my work for me," said the stranger. "The one who came to me years ago. The one who has been preparing the way for this homecoming. You're not the one, are you?" He scratched his chin, pondering Spencer.

"I'll... I'd do anything," said the youth.

"You're squeaking."

"Anything, mate."

"I'm not your mate, chap."

"Are... are you the devil or something?"

"Or something, I think's better."

Spencer was looking for a way out, his eyes flitting around the gloomy cellar, when he clocked Jay-T. "He's... he's dead, ain't he."

"You killed him for me. His blood freed me. The sacrifice. You know, like goats are sacrificed. Like sheep. Sometimes humans have to be sacrificed. Now what to do with you."

Killed him? thought Spencer. *Killed Jay-T?*

The stranger said, "Do you want to die, or do you want me to torment you for the rest of your life?"

"None of them... please... I can help you. Who are you?"

"Would you kill for me?"

"Kill?"

"One must be ripped."

"Ripped?"

"One more, and I'll be free."

"F-free?"

"Stop repeating what I just said, or I'll cut your tongue out and eat it."

Spencer clamped his mouth shut.

The dark man said, "I am a bringer of death. A spreader of dread. A spiller of blood."

"O… o… okay… "

"Are you with me?"

Spencer nodded.

The stranger said, "Slave or eunuch, then?"

"S-s-slave?"

"Good. I need to be free of this place. Somewhere, there are things waiting for me – things I need to devour. And a man, too. He's waiting for me. A killer. The one who has prepared the way. A killer of four. You must bring him to me. And then we find the fifth. Bring ripper and victim together. Rip the fifth. Rip the fifth, and I'm free of these streets. Are you still with me?"

Spencer nodded again. He was scared. The weird man was obviously nuts.

"Have you heard of someone called Troy?" said the stranger.

Spencer shook his head.

"Do you know what seers are?"

Spencer shook his head once more.

"You don't know much. Seers have very bright souls. They shine brighter than anyone else. Because they shine so brightly, they can shed light on secret things. Things other people can't see. Things like evil. Things like me. You understand?"

Spencer shrugged.

"You don't even know who I am," said the dark man.

"O… okay… who… who are you?"

"I'm Jack. And I'm back."

The door at the top of the stairs flew open. Spencer wheeled. The Sharpley brothers and Lethal Ellis raced down, shouting, swearing, and threatening to shank him.

Spencer turned, but the stranger had disappeared.

His briefcase remained. It was open. Something glinted inside. Something steel and sharp.

CHAPTER 24.
TEA AND BISCUITS.

ROY Hanbury sneered and looked him up and down before holding Faultless's gaze.

"What do you call that thing with the eyes again, Charlie? The one brown, one blue?"

"Heterochromia iridum."

"Sin."

"Sin?"

"Adam sinned, sin is passed down through the genes, and we are all sinners. It causes disease, corruption, earthquakes, it makes land barren."

"And it makes one eye blue, the other one brown?"

"That's right – sin. You know sin, Charlie."

They looked at each other for a few seconds. Hard seconds. The moment filled with rage.

Hanbury cooled things by saying, "You made it big, then. Done well for yourself."

"I done all right."

"When I urged you to leave – "

"Told me to fuck off, or you'd kill me yourself – "

"When I fucking asked you to leave – I thought you were fucked. Dead fucked. Or banged up, for sure."

"Thanks for the vote of confidence."

"Where did it all go right, Charlie?"

Faultless looked up at the portrait of the crucified Christ over Hanbury's mantelpiece and thought, *He got a shit deal from his dad.*

He looked at Hanbury again. "When you exiled me, Roy, I didn't know where to go. I was a kid, eighteen. I'd hardly been out of East London. Barrowmore was my patch. I thought I'd stay away for a few weeks and then come back."

"That wasn't going to happen." Hanbury lit a menthol cigarette.

The minty smell made made Faultless screw up his nose. He sniffed and then said, "You made that pretty clear. If I came back, they'd kill me."

"If you'd come back, *I'd* kill you, Charlie."

"I thought about doing myself in. I had no clue about anything except running these streets."

"You were a first-rate thug, I'll give you that."

"I wasn't that mean."

"You were as mean as a fucking honey badger. You seen those things? They fight lions and leopards. Take on anything. They rip your balls off. Fucking vicious. That's you, Faultless – a fucking honey badger."

"Ain't they fluffy?"

"One of the nastiest of God's creatures."

They were quiet for a while.

Faultless had arrived twenty minutes ago, hoping to surprise Hanbury. No such luck. When Charlie was invited in, a coffee pot sat on the low table. Two cups, china, flower patterned, waited to be filled. Hanbury had even made sandwiches and cut the crusts off. And digestives were piled on another plate.

Tea and biscuits with the beast of Barrowmore.

"Haven't spoken to your daughter in the past few minutes, have you, Roy?" Faultless had asked.

"I still don't grass, son," Hanbury answered, inviting Charlie to sit down.

Faultless stared at Hanbury. A big bear of a man with a snake draped over his shoulder. His arms were muscled and tattooed. His head was shaven. A scar, white on his bronze skin, raced across his throat.

Hanbury had been twenty-one. Thug brothers named Bobby and Benny Malone kidnapped him. They were old school. They owned Barrowmore. They ran the drugs and the pimps, and they decided who lived and who died. Hanbury barged into their territory. He was a bulldog. He didn't go around – he went through. Right through the Malones' defences.

They got the rage. They killed his mates. They told him, *You're in the deep end – get out.*

But Hanbury kept coming. That bulldog in him.

Finally, they got him – five brutes breaking down his door and dragging him out at three in the morning.

They trussed him with wire and tossed him in the back of a van.

He kicked and he bit and dished out some pain. But there were too many of them, and they were too strong.

The wire cut into him. Blood turned him red all over, glistening and wet.

From the back of the van, he heard his wife, pregnant with twins she'd lose because of the stress, scream in the street.

"I promised I'd see her again," he'd say when he told the story.

And he did.

An hour later.

He staggered home with his throat cut from ear to ear, Ripper style.

Doctors said he would die. Man cannot live without blood, and Roy Hanbury barely had a thimbleful left in his veins. But he survived. That bulldog in him – barge through doors, barge through borders, and barge through death.

Old Bill came and asked what happened, but he said nothing.

"Was it the Malones?" asked a detective.

Hanbury stared at the carnations his mates had sent round.

"Where are they, Roy?" the detective had asked.

Hanbury switched his gaze to the piles of fruit a market trader had delivered as a get-well-soon gift.

"Where will we find them?" the detective had said.

Hanbury looked him in the eye.

He said, "You won't."

And they never did. Neither Bobby nor Benny Malone, nor their five attack dogs, were ever seen again.

Now Hanbury asked, "Tell me about your transformation from yob to yuppie."

"I ain't a yuppie, Roy." He shrugged. "You dumped me at Waterloo Station, told me never to show my face again."

"Or I'd cut it off for you."

"Yeah. That kind of thing. Well, I slipped into WH Smith, planning to nick something to eat. For some reason I found myself in the books section, browsing the travel guides. I saw this – "

He reached into his bag and fished out a travel guide to the United States. It was scribbled on, creased, and well thumbed.

He continued. "I got a train to Heathrow, and with the £500 you gave me, booked a ticket to Miami. I'd never been on a plane before. I had no passport. But I blagged myself on to the flight. Gave them some sob story about my mum being in Florida. She was dying, blah, blah, blah. Customs gave me the third degree. Immigration grilled me in the States. But that was nothing. I'd been fronting up to filth and teachers, social workers, anyone, since I was toddling. I didn't give a shit. I made it through. They were taking me to some immigration centre when I gave them the slip. They never saw me again."

"Weren't they looking for you? You some kind of illegal alien in the US?"

"No, I gave them a false name when I got there."

"Yeah? What'd you call yourself? Donny Osmond or something?" Hanbury smiled at his own remark.

"No," said Faultless. "I called myself Roy Hanbury."

Hanbury stopped smiling.

CHAPTER 25.
BLOODBATH.

PAUL Sharpley straddled Spencer and slapped him across the face.

"Where's my fucking console?" he said.

Michael Sharpley stood over them, sneering. Lethal prowled the cellar, punching his palm over and over, spitting and mumbling.

Spencer looked directly into Paul's eyes.

He got another slap across the face. It stung, but he didn't care. Not anymore. He felt different.

It had happened when he'd fished the butcher's knife from the briefcase. It was as if a surge of electricity had powered through him when he gripped the weapon.

Acid pulsed through his veins. Darkness filled his heart. The devil had his back.

"Where's my PS3?" growled Paul.

"Weren't yours in the first place," said Spencer.

Paul gawped.

"Smack him again," said Michael.

"Let me stamp on his head," said Lethal. "When can I shank him?"

Two years before, Lethal had killed a boy of fourteen. The kid had been walking home from the Barrowmore youth centre with his ten-year-old brother. Lethal was walking the other way.

"What d'you say to me?" he asked the boy.

The boy had said nothing, according to his little brother.

Lethal attacked him. He punched him. The boy keeled over and hit the ground. Lethal stamped on his head till it popped like a balloon.

Lethal bolted. The brother named him. But Lethal was somewhere else. The Sharpleys said so. His mother said so. A girl he was screwing at the time said so.

There is always a judgment.

Paul said to Spencer, "That was mine. I nicked it. It was above board. Fucking grabbed it off the shelf and legged it. It was me who took the risk, you wallad."

"I took the same risk coming into your flat."

They laughed. Paul said, "Too right, man. Big risk. Risk that's costing you your balls." He smacked Spencer again and then stood up. "Where's your mate, Slow Joe?"

"Back there in the shadows," said Spencer. "He's dead. I killed him. Go see. In the shadows."

There was a moment of silence, and Spencer sensed the trio's fear. They were looking around in the dark, their eyes skating the gloom. They were tense, ready to leg it at any sign of danger.

Then Lethal said, "You couldn't kill the light."

"Go see, Lethal. Go see his body. Back there in the dark. I sacrificed him."

"You what?" said Paul.

"Fuck, it's gone cold in here," said Michael Sharpley. "What is this fucking place? How'd you find it, Spencer?"

"I think it found me," he said.

In one movement, he sprang to his feet and plunged the knife into Paul's belly.

The Sharpley boy folded. His mouth dropped open, astonishment in his eyes, his shirt soaked with blood.

He gurgled and staggered, and his brother shouted, "You fucking bastard, Drake," and lunged at Spencer.

A shriek halted him.

Spencer followed the noise.

Lethal screamed again. But his cry was cut short. A darkness enveloped him.

Michael said, "What the fuck is that?" Panic laced his voice. He staggered about. "Where's Lethal? Paul? Paul, where's Lethal?"

Paul groaned, the knife in his guts. He fell to his knees. He made a noise that sounded like *pleeeeeease* to Spencer, but it may have just been the air wheezing out of his body.

The darkness moved away from Lethal, as if a magician had whipped a cloak away to reveal his trick – a red raw grin widening across Lethal's throat. His head tilted backwards. Blood poured from the ear-to-ear smile. The weight of his skull made him topple over, and his body hit the ground, hard.

"Help me," said Paul, squealing. "Bruv, help me, I'm dying. I want our mum. Get our mum."

But Michael backed away. Unlike Spencer, he hadn't seen what was behind him. It was that darkness again.

He retreated into it, disappearing. From within it came his screams.

And then he stumbled out of the pitch-black, screaming still. He wheeled, and Spencer saw that his back, from nape to arse, had been sliced open. The skin had been pulled apart like a coat.

Spencer gasped at the sight of the throbbing organs caged inside Michael's ribs.

Blood gushed from his cleaved body.

He shrieked and twitched.

Paul moaned. He called for his mother again. His brother died, his body arcing and spewing blood.

Spencer stared at Paul. He wondered if he should help him. The Sharpley lad was groaning. He was obviously in agony. He clutched his belly. Blood soaked his shirt. His face was pale. He was crying and asking for his mum.

"What part of him would you like as a memento of this occasion, Spencer?" said a voice.

He looked up.

It was Jack.

The dark man bent down and plucked the knife out of Paul's belly. He licked the blade.

"Good knife, this," he said. "Butcher's knife."

Paul unleashed a scream that almost peeled the skin off Spencer's face.

Jack knelt.

"Let me help you, bright eyes," he told Paul.

Jack eased Paul's hands away from the wound.

Black blood pulsed from his belly.

"Help me," wailed Paul.

Jack plunged his hand into the wound.

Paul shrieked, his body stiffening.

Jack laughed and held him round the neck with his free hand. He dug around in Paul's belly, the Sharpley boy twitching. His eyes were like an antelope's in the jaws of a lion.

Jack pulled the intestines out of Paul's belly. They coiled from his body, a blue-grey snake. The youth howled. He twitched. His face stretched. Yards of innards came out, and Jack piled them next to the boy, who screamed and screamed and took a very long while to die.

Spencer smelled death and shit before he fainted.

CHAPTER 26.
TIME TO REPENT.

"I MADE peace with my enemies on your behalf," Hanbury said.

"I know," Faultless said.

Hanbury's cold, lilac eyes measured him. "And you mocked me like that? Using my name."

"I owe you, Roy."

Hanbury stubbed out his cigarette. "Not me, Charlie. You owe the Lord."

Thank Christ, thought Faultless.

Hanbury went on. "Everyone pays in the end. We have to. Our sins are too great. They stain creation. There's no getting away with it."

"Many have."

"No they ain't, son. What d'you think happens when you die?"

Faultless said nothing.

"I'll tell you. You face the Lord your God, maker of heaven and earth, and you submit to his judgment."

"I thought he loved us. That's what the Bible says. Why should we face his judgment?"

108

"He does love you, Charlie. But he wants you to love him back."

"Or he'll torture me forever."

"That's right, son."

"So I've got a payment overdue."

"Not overdue. But when you die, the Lord will demand repentance on the last day. Repent or suffer burning hell. That's why you need to do it now. Let Christ into your life. He saved me. Fuck knows what would've happened had the Lord not entered my cell all those years ago."

"You would've been hunting Rachel's killer."

Hanbury looked him in the eye. When Hanbury looked you in the eye, you felt your brain boil. His cold eyes fired lasers into your soul.

Faultless dropped his gaze and then looked at Jesus over the fireplace. His wounds flared red. The artist had mixed up a good shade.

He said, "You on the straight and narrow these days, Roy?"

"God's path, son. None straighter."

"What do you do with yourself?"

"I got my pension, you know. Enjoy my granddaughter. Little Jasmine. She's a handful, but what kid isn't. I was. You were. She's a gem."

"I met her."

Hanbury nodded and went on. "And I try to keep the kids here out of trouble. You know how it is. Unemployment. Gangs. Drugs. The devil marches through Barrowmore. His works are increasing. The bad days are coming, Charlie."

"I thought they'd always been bad."

"You wait. You think what man can do is bad? You wait. Armageddon is around the corner. God's wrath. You wait."

"I will."

Hanbury placed the python back in its vivarium.

109

He said, "So you're here to dig up the past?"

"I'm here to bury it."

"Forgiveness is the key, Charlie."

"You telling me you've forgiven whoever murdered Rachel? Who opened her up and – "

"Enough." Hanbury's face had turned crimson.

Faultless said, "I want to know who did that to her, Roy. To her and my mum. I want to know."

"You thought you did know, son."

"I was wrong."

"You were wrong, and it cost a man's life. You were wrong, and it gave me a serious headache."

Faultless shrugged. "It brought peace between you and the Graveneys."

"Don't try to be funny with me, Charlie. Humour was never your strong point. Being a little shit was your strong point."

The past reared up in Faultless's mind – him running wild, feeling rage, and being a pain in everyone's arse. But then he shut off the memories. He didn't want to see what he'd been. He stowed the recollections away.

1996 was 1996.

You couldn't change it.

You could only…

Repent?

Hanbury said, "Had you stayed, Charlie, they would've killed you. And they're still on the maps, the Graveneys. They won't have forgotten."

"I thought you made peace."

"I did. But part of the peace was that you would never be seen again. Charlie Faultless is gone, I said. He ain't coming back. Christ, you were trouble, son. You were like a son to me. Especially when you were with Rachel. When you saved…"

He trailed off and crunched his knuckles. Veins swelled on his bulldog neck.

110

He found his voice again. "But – Jesus forgive me – I sometimes thought of killing you myself."

"Once this is done, I'm gone."

"This book?"

Faultless nodded. "Interviews. Photos. Can you help me? Be my point man?"

"No, I can't. I helped you once before."

"You know you were a suspect."

Hanbury narrowed his eyes. "I don't mind being accused of the things I've done – and I've done bucket loads – but telling me I did things I would never do, that's injustice. I hate that, son. You put that in your book, I may have to forget I'm a Christian for an hour or two."

"God wouldn't be happy."

"I'm saved. The Lord keeps me from harm, Charlie. And he keeps me from harming others. Remember that."

Hanbury rose. His knees clicked. He went to the mantelpiece, kissed his finger and touched it to the stigmata on Christ's foot.

"I don't want old wounds re-opened," he said. "Rachel's or yours. I don't want revenge. I don't want nothing, Charlie. Only peace on earth and goodwill to all fucking men. Even the Graveneys. I love seeing you again, son, it makes my heart sing, it does. But it's not a good thing. And it makes me look like a liar."

"Fair enough. But I ain't going."

"You're a bastard, Charlie. If things were as they were, I'd have to kill you."

"My mum deserves justice. Your Rachel deserves justice. Their killers deserve judgment."

"All killers do. Don't they, Charlie."

"I know. Maybe my day will come."

"It will. Count on it."

Hanbury sat down again and poured more coffee into his cup.

Faultless said, "Is Wilks still around?"

"Don Wilks." The name came out of Hanbury like a growl. "Cunt," he cursed. "The Lord forgive my foul language. But cunt. Wilks. The bastard. He's a detective chief superintendent, now. Heads up some serious crime squad. Bollocks, he was. You'd have thought he was on the side of the killer back then."

"He liked you for Rachel's killing."

"The bastard. I've known some useless filth in my day, but he took the fucking digestives when it came to being a crap copper. He should've been a villain. He is a fucking villain. Bent as Larry Grayson. Bent and twisted. I thought I was a mean bastard. But Wilks. You ain't seen nothing."

"I did see." He rolled up his sleeve. A scar, four inches long, sliced across his forearm. The skin was withered – a burn mark.

"Hot poker," said Faultless. "I was thirteen. He caught me with some of your dope, Roy."

Hanbury grimaced.

"I kept my mouth shut, and this is what he does," said Faultless.

"You were a good boy, Charlie. I should've killed Wilks for that. I don't know why I didn't. Maybe 'cause he gave me back the dope. I still wanted to do him, though. That's why I need God, see. If I didn't have the Lord, there'd be blood, Charlie. Blood and vengeance."

CHAPTER 27.
AN ITCH TO SCRATCH.

"I SPEAK to the evil in men's minds," said Jack. "I spoke to yours, Spencer. I reached out to you. See what you did?"

Spencer surveyed the bloody carnage. Mutilated bodies everywhere. The Sharpleys and Lethal Ellis dismembered. Jay-T brained. He said, "I never did nothing to them."

"You battered your friend with a brick. And you stabbed that fella in the gut."

Spencer's head ached. He felt dizzy. When he had come round after fainting, Jack was in his face. It scared him even more. He'd scrabbled away, right into Michael Sharpley's remains. Now he was covered in gore.

"You have a lodging house?" said Jack.

"A lodging what?"

"A place to stay. A doss-house."

"It is a doss-house."

"Take me there."

"Are… are you staying at mine?"

"I am sheltering there, Spencer. I have work to do. One more must be ripped. The walls around this place, they cage me. I must be free of them. One more must be ripped. London will be mine."

113

"You're off your head."

"So would you be, trapped where I've been trapped for more than a hundred and twenty years. I had one hell of an itch, Spencer. And now" – he gestured to the bodies – "I've scratched it."

Spencer looked at Michael Sharpley, whose body had been opened up like a box. He bit his lip. He thought of something.

"Can I keep the PS3 now?" he asked.

Jack smiled. Yellow teeth showed. He said, "You help me put my art on display, and you can keep anything you find forever more."

"On display? What're you talking about?"

CHAPTER 28.
NEED TO KNOW.

HALLAM Buck, dragging thirty-seven bitter, lonely years behind him and looking at decades behind bars if they ever caught him, always poked his nose where it didn't belong.

It was about wanting to know. It was a fear of being left out.

That had been Hallam's life – isolation.

Skirting the playground while other kids clustered and gossiped about him. Trudging through Barrowmore, trying to attach himself to various groups, all of them telling him to fuck off, if he was lucky, or kicking his head in.

So knowing what was going on kept him in the loop. He could loiter near tittle-tattle and toss in his two-penneth. He could be part of the conversation; he could be part of life.

As usual, Hallam had woken up at 5.00am. He dressed and made breakfast. He put on his yellow bib with "Tower Hamlets London Borough Council" written on the back. On the breast it sported the council's logo, and the motto, FROM GREAT THINGS TO GREATER.

When he was ready, he'd gone out and traipsed the walkways of Monsell House, picking up glass and wiping up piss, cleaning up vomit and scooping up needles, sweeping up litter and sprucing up stairwells.

It wasn't hard work. He did it at his own pace. After all, he wasn't getting paid. The bib he'd nicked off a street cleaner a couple of years ago. The equipment was his own – bin bags, brushes, disinfectant. He mostly focused on the eighth floor, where he lived, and the seventh – where she lived.

Tash. Lovely Tash. Delicious Tash. *His* Tash.

Should've been. Would've been had it not been for –

Approaching her door that morning, he went through it all again – hot flushes, racing heartbeat, stiff cock, dry throat, and buckling knees.

He knocked. He wore his smile. He pushed his hips out, his erection pressing against the nylon of his boiler suit with nothing underneath it. Just thin material between todger and Tash.

She opened the door and said, "Hi, Hallam," and looked him in the face.

Look at my cock, he was thinking. *Look at my cock.*

But she didn't flinch. A straight-ahead stare.

She had beautiful eyes. So blue. Like two sapphires.

"I… I've been busy this morning," he said.

"Oh, good for you," she said. "Actually, Hallam, I'm busy… "

Rage flared in his chest. He trembled with shame. He mumbled something and turned, plodding off down the walkway.

Back in his flat, he'd fumed.

He stripped naked and masturbated. And when he came, he screamed her name in anger and imagined himself ramming into her while she could do nothing but beg and cry.

One day, he thought. *One day…*

Sweating, exhausted, he slumped on the floor. The dust and the debris stuck to his sticky body.

He thought about Tash. Had she got a boyfriend, or was it a one-night stand that made her "busy"?

His guts churned.

Slag. Tart. Whore.

He got on all fours. He stared at the floor. She was right beneath him in the flat below.

If he put his ear down, he could sometimes hear her when she sang along to the radio and when she called Jasmine.

Get out of the bath, Jasmine.

Jesus. Too much. The thought of them made fire in Hallam's belly.

He had considered drilling a hole through the floor so he could watch her – watch them both.

But it was risky. His life was risky. It had always been risky.

So easy to get caught. Especially these days with DNA and forensic evidence being so good.

After catching his breath, he got to his feet. His blubber itched. Sweat and dust coated his body. His sperm stained the dusty wooden floor.

He showered and then dressed in his dad's old shirt, trousers, and shoes before going out.

Scudding clouds spat rain. The gloom weighed heavily. His heart was a lump of lead. His life, worthless.

At the shop he bought *The Sun*, two cans of beans, and a Twix.

He munched the chocolate as he trudged back towards the high rises.

Behind him, shouts erupted. Hate in the air. Threats on the breeze.

He'd wheeled and faced them – two charging towards him, fear on their faces.

He knew one by name. Spencer Drake. He knew the other youth's face.

They barged past him. Hallam reeled. The Twix fell out of his hands. He yelled out and squatted to pick it up.

"You're going to bleed, Drake. You're going to fucking bleed."

Hallam looked up. He froze. The Sharpleys, Paul and Michael, raced past him, and after them – *You're going to bleed, Drake. You're going to fucking bleed* – came Lethal Ellis.

As he raced by, Lethal's twisted, angry face turned to Hallam and said in a shriek, "What are you fucking looking at, flid?"

Hallam watched as the chase hurtled down the road that swerved around the tower blocks.

Goosepimples raced up his back.

He followed the hunt. He couldn't help himself. He had to know. He had to be part of life.

CHAPTER 29.
THE RED ON THE DOOR.

HALLAM'S dad would've told him, "Don't get involved."

But then, Hallam's dad kept himself to himself. He needed to – being gay on Barrowmore wasn't something you advertised. Apart from in the beaten-up telephone kiosks where you pinned a scrap of paper with your number on it. Apart from the piss-smelling elevators where you graffitied an image of your cock with your contact details on the shaft. Apart from the shit-coated public toilet where you lurked in the cubicles, staring through the round hole at groin level in the wall… waiting.

His dad had come out fifteen years ago. His mum walked out.

Hallam was twenty-two, Mummy's boy and Daddy's punchbag.

And it didn't change. His father started drinking heavily. He beat Hallam. He sneaked men back to the flat. Tough guys who'd say, "I'm not fucking queer, right, but… "

Hallam listened to their sex and pined for his mother. He'd weep while his father fucked truckers and doormen. And after he was done, Dad would come into Hallam's room and say, "Stop your fucking crying, you little queer – she's gone. Women are no fucking good. You hear me? You hear me? You hear me, you little – "

Mummy's boy and Daddy's punchbag.

His dad died three years ago. He left Hallam with nothing.

The council let him stay in the flat. They'd never chuck him out. He was on benefits and couldn't work because of his mental state. He'd be homeless and more doomed than he already was.

He still cried for his mum. Photos of her plastered the corkboard in the kitchen, covered the door of the fridge, and crammed the mantelpiece.

But she wasn't coming back.

What would she have said?

Don't get involved.

Too late. He followed the road around the tower blocks. It led him along streets of low-rise housing. It took him to an area dominated by lock-ups.

The silence was heavy.

In the distance, you could hear Barrowmore's voice – the traffic, the music, and the shouting.

But the sound was muffled, as if an invisible wall separated life on the estate from this other dimension.

He sneaked down the road, staying close to the red brick wall on his right. On the left lay the garages, lined up like coffins.

They were black with age, rotted and battered. They creaked in the wind.

Where had the lads gone?

He looked to his right. They might have scaled the wall. But it was twelve feet high. It would take some climbing. And security wire curled along the top of it. That would slice up your hands.

He dismissed that option and moved on.

Noises came from a lock-up. He flinched. It sounded like scuttling.

Rats, probably. He shuddered. They were everywhere. The flats were plagued by them. He'd had a Jack-Russell-sized one in his kitchen a few months ago.

He hurried past the garage, hearing a squealing behind him as he went.

He groaned.

What the hell was that? Maybe a cat caught a rat?

He stopped dead. Up ahead, a garage door sagged off its hinges. Red paint covered the corrugated steel. Hallam narrowed his eyes, trying to make out what the paint said.

He swallowed and moved nearer.

The door swayed. The hinges creaked. Hallam held his breath.

THIS IS HELL was daubed there.

The words glistened. The letters ran. It was freshly written. He smelled the paint. It wasn't paint. It smelled different. He approached. The red was dark. The red smelled coppery. The red was blood.

THIS IS HELL.

The hinges creaked. Hallam screamed. His balls went up into his belly. The door swung open. Paul Sharpley hung crucified on the back of it.

PART FOUR.

MY KNIFE'S SO NICE AND SHARP.

CHAPTER 30.
AN HEIR TO ATROCITIES.

AT the time, the papers named him the New Ripper because, like the old one, he ripped women.

He cut their throats, mutilated their flesh, and opened their bellies.

He removed organs, scooping them out as if he were searching for something inside the body.

He *was* searching.

And he always found what he was searching for.

The papers knew nothing about the missing portion. Neither did the police, nor the pathologists who post-mortemed the victims.

Why should they?

What he took was not a normal part of the human anatomy. Not a kidney. Not a liver. Not a heart.

In fact, it was highly unusual.

But when he extracted it from the blood and the gore, he would take it home. He'd wrap it in newspaper and stow it in a mini-freezer hidden away in his attic.

From April to July 1996, he collected four of these treasures.

They had come from his four victims. Rachel Hanbury, Patricia

Faultless, Susan Murray, and Nancy Sherwood.

The women lived in the Whitechapel and Spitalfields districts of East London. Two of them – Hanbury and Faultless – were from the Barrowmore Estate.

Nothing had changed. In 1996 it was blood and fear, and in 2011 it was blood and fear again.

Nothing had changed. In 1996 four women were butchered by an unknown killer, and in 2011 four youths are butchered by –

He narrowed his eyes and surveyed the area.

It had been fifteen years. Nothing had changed. Graffiti and burned-out cars. Overgrown grass on a piece of open ground. Rusted swings and a climbing frame. Youths loitering, transmitting menace. The smell of booze and fags on the air. The stench of charred metal from the cindered vehicles, and petrol and oil fumes from their gutted engines. The reek of dog shit from the hybrid beasts used as weapons by drug dealers...

Four youths are butchered by –

Not me, he thought. *Not this time.*

He shuddered. He remembered the voice.

I am the lord who gapes... I am the lantern of the tomb... I am the moth eating at the law...

"Jesus Christ," he said.

Four youths are butchered by –

It had been carnage. One had his brains bashed in. One had been decapitated. One had been opened up like a book. One had his entrails removed. Two of them had been crucified. Someone had written *THIS IS HELL* on the building where they'd been found.

"Jesus Christ," he said again.

I am the lord who gapes... I am the lantern of the tomb... I am the moth eating at the law...

He was only a kid when the voice came to him – eight or nine years old. He knew who it was in his head straight away.

Him.

He owned books about him. He watched TV shows about him. He walked the same streets as him.

He regaled guests by raving about the killings, "… and he sent part of a kidney he took from one woman to Mr Lusk of the Whitechapel Vigilance Committee, and he said he'd eaten – "

And his mother would scold him. "Your auntie doesn't want to hear about those things, darlin'. Little boys shouldn't be thinking about those things, either."

But he couldn't stop thinking. The voice was in his head. The voice was calling him. The voice wanted him to serve.

I am the lord who gapes… I am the lantern of the tomb… I am the moth eating at the law…

As he got older, he studied the brutal murders more forensically.

Like many before him, he tried to identify the killer. But he just could not make the evidence against any of the suspects stack up. Circumstantially, perhaps, but not forensically.

It was as if the killer were truly a ghost.

And maybe he was.

Maybe Jack the Ripper only existed in his head, and that's why he took on the mantle in 1996.

That's why he became the New Ripper, an heir to past atrocities.

He strolled along the passageway separating two of the tower blocks. It smelled of piss. Beer cans and pizza boxes littered the path. He stomped on them and kicked them.

The passage led into the quad that was hemmed in by all four high rises. He studied the space. It was a car park. It was somewhere to have a kickabout. A place to hang out, smoke and drink. A battleground to settle differences.

It was anything you wanted it to be, because here, on Barrowmore, there was no one to tell you what it shouldn't be.

An odour of petrol clung to the air. A large, once-white wall stood by a grass verge. It was a canvas for the local graffiti artists. Or yobs, as he preferred to call them. He bristled. Another useless, politically-correct gesture by the lefty-liberals running the council.

As he could have predicted, the wall hadn't spawned the new Banksy. It had only bred a new hatred.

Instead of art, the wall was decked in abuse towards Old Bill, parents, teachers, boyfriends, girlfriends, football teams, other estates, foreigners.

It had become a place to vent fury, not creativity.

The hate had no meaning.

Does what I do have meaning? he wondered.

I am the lord who gapes… I am the lantern of the tomb… I am the moth eating at the law…

It had to have meaning. The voice in his head gave it meaning. The voice told him what to do. It urged him, encouraged him. It said, *Prepare the way for my homecoming.* It said, *Spill blood and gather gifts.* It said, *Kill one, kill two, kill three, kill four… prepare for the fifth… the fifth we share… our reign shall begin with her blood… the blood of the fifth…*

And on it went. The voice was always in his head. It would come to him as he stood over an eviscerated victim, drenched in her blood. *Dig, boy, dig,* it would say. *Find the treasure. Find it for when I return…*

And he dug, and he gouged, and he scoured – and he found.

He stared at the hate on the graffiti wall.

He thought, *The death of these youths means something.*

The bloodbath had a point.

The carnage had a reason.

It wasn't some madman – it was an artist.

An artist like him.

Meaning, he thought, and walked back down the passageway. *And the meaning is Jack the Ripper.*

And he was here.

Prepare for my homecoming.

Jack was back.

CHAPTER 31.
FALLING MAN.

"YOU'RE up early," said Tash.

"I went for a walk," said Faultless.

"Is it him?"

He said nothing, just looked at her standing on the threshold.

"Can I come in, Tash?" It was 7.00am, it was cold, and he wanted a drink.

In the kitchen, she stood with her arms folded, her back against the fridge. She chewed her nails now and again. She put strands of her hair in her mouth.

Faultless drank cold coffee.

"How's Jasmine?" he asked. "Is she okay?"

"She's okay. Sleeping."

They were quiet, Tash fretting and Faultless watching. "It'll be all right," he said.

"Is it him?"

He lifted his shoulders. "I don't know."

She reached for a packet of cigarettes, took one out and lit it.

"It's definitely him – the… the one who killed Rachel…"

"We can't say that – "

"Funny that you're back, too."

He raised his eyebrow. "I don't know what to say to that."

"Something's wrong, Charlie. I feel it. Something... something *evil* is here."

"Your dreams again?"

"Don't make fun of me."

"Christ, Tash, I'm not making fun of you."

"I wake up screaming. Jasmine too. Christ, how could I have doubted her? I... I thought she was making it up. You think people can have the same dream?"

He shook his head.

"They named the dead ones yet?" she said.

"Not yet. The news headlines said four dead. Teenagers."

"Jasmine probably knew them. They say how they died?"

"Badly."

"You know who found them?"

"Some guy named Hallam Buck," said Faultless.

Tash gaped. "Hallam?"

"You know him?"

"He lives next floor up. He's a bit weird. He comes round every morning to tell me he's cleaned up, swept away the litter."

"That his job?"

"No, he's on the dole, but he just does it."

"Sweet," said Faultless.

"Don't say it if you don't mean it."

"Fine."

"He fancies me."

Faultless nearly said, *Why shouldn't he?* but instead said, "Does he hassle you?"

"No. He's okay. Weird, like I say. I think he's probably lonely. He invites me round, sometimes." She shuddered. "He likes horror films, I think. He says, 'Do you want to come and watch

Texas Chainsaw Massacre IV,' or whatever, and he's saying it in all innocence – like it's a great date movie."

"It might be. If you like that kind of thing."

"I don't."

"So what d'you say to him?"

"That I'm washing my hair. He must think I spend a fortune on shampoo."

"Does he take rejection well, this Hallam?"

"He smiles, nods, says, 'Okay, Tash, just wondering.' He's fine. Harmless. Worst he probably does is have a wank thinking about me. Ugh. Anyway. Feel sick, now. Bet this is going to help your book."

"Just makes it more complicated."

She looked at him hard, as if she were trying to read his mind. He kept it blank – just in case.

She took her eyes away from him and said, "I need to talk to some of the other mums, see what's up with school tomorrow. I can't see them opening."

She picked up her phone off the worktop and dialled.

Someone rapped on the door.

Tash said, "Can you get that, Charlie? D'you mind – Oh, hi, it's Tash Hanbury, Jasmine's mum…"

Faultless got up and went through the living room to the front door and opened it.

A short, round man in his mid-thirties stared back at Faultless. The man wore a yellow bib with a logo on the right breast pocket. His thin, ginger hair lay flat and wet on his scalp. He had an inch-long scar just under his left eye.

Something flashed into Faultless's mind but was quickly gone.

He looked at the man and said, "Yeah?"

The man made goldfish movements with his mouth. He looked as if he'd seen a ghost – or perhaps something worse.

Faultless said, "You Hallam Buck?"

The man continued to open and close his mouth, making no sound.

"Tash is on the phone," said Faultless, and then added, "I'm Charlie Faultless."

It was as if the man had just been shot in the chest.

He reared back, stumbling towards the safety barrier. It was four-and-a-half feet high, but he crashed into it as such pace, he started to topple over.

Faultless lunged out of the doorway to grab the falling man.

CHAPTER 32.
MURDER IN MIND.

DETECTIVE Chief Superintendent Donald Christopher Wilks, aged fifty-two, with one eye on the yacht moored in Ramsgate harbour and the other on nailing someone, anyone, for the murder of the four Barrowmore scumbags.

Born in the East End, hated in the East End, Wilks was despised by his own people.

And he despised them right back.

But Don Wilks despised pretty much everyone.

His heart was black with hate, his soul tarnished by bitterness, and his blood hot with rage.

Tough shit, he thought, watching the residents of Barrowmore crawl out of their lairs.

He saw a girl wearing the uniform of a high street computer retailer trudge along the road. Off to do her Sunday shift. Unemployment stood at more than 40 percent on Barrowmore, so she should have counted herself lucky she had a job, in Wilks's opinion.

The estate crawled with cops. Wilks nodded to a couple of uniforms just arrived at the tower blocks. They were on door-to-door duty.

Yeah, good luck with that, thought Wilks.

Up in the high rises, youths who, according to Wilks, should either be in internment camps or doing national service, were shouting obscenities at the police as they gathered for the first full day's investigation.

Wilks walked on, heading along the road running to the left of the tower blocks. It was lined with low-rise housing. Red brick boxes. White panelled frontages. High walls festooned with graffiti or hanging baskets.

Dogs barked. Children screamed. Sirens wailed. Horns blared.

Fucking Barrowmore.

Wilks gritted his teeth. Being here brought murder to his mind.

Nuke the bloody lot of them, he was thinking.

But wait till we leave.

Wilks and his team were based in Barrowmore for the duration of the murder investigation. The major incident room, set up at the scene of any serious crime, was at the local community hall. Offices in the rear of the building had been commandeered by detectives. The hall itself was a jungle of computer stations, fax machines, telephones, and television screens, operated by the civilian workforce. Here, they sifted through the evidence as it came in. However, it was only a trickle at the moment. Barrowmore wasn't too keen on helping the cops.

Wilks walked along the row of houses. A swaggering youth came towards him, dragged along by a panting, black-and-white Staffordshire bull terrier on a chain.

Wilks hated dogs. Dirty animals. It was one thing the Muslims had right. That and chopping people's hands off.

The youth strutted. The dog strained. Wilks glared. When he was ten yards away, he said to the youth, "Get that fucking dog off my pavement before I have you taken down the nick for being armed and dangerous."

The youth squared his shoulders. "What'd you fucking say, mate? You want to fucking go?"

Wilks whipped out his badge and flashed it at the youth. The dog panted. Spit oozed from its jaws. It was built like a beer barrel.

Wilks said, "Let's fucking go, son, let's fucking go."

The youth baulked. He mumbled something. He stepped off the pavement, dragging his dog with him. The Staffie wagged his tail at Wilks.

Wilks grumbled as he strode on. But after a few yards, he stopped. He blinked. His vision blurred. A headache pulsed in his temples. He grunted and bared his teeth against the pain. Images flashed in his mind. He shut his eyes and tried to relax, breathing deeply.

I'm all right, he said to himself, and opened his eyes again. *I'm all right. The price I have to pay for my burdens.*

He walked. Two minutes later he found the house and pushed open the gate, smiling at the sign that said, "Beware Of The Snake."

CHAPTER 33.
DOES HE KNOW?

HALLAM'S skin crawled. He was hot and sweaty, and his nerves were wire-tight. Trying to make conversation, he said, "Are you Tash's boyfriend now?"

"No, Hallam," said Charlie Faultless. "Are you?"

Hallam blushed. "Yes" nearly came out of his mouth without him thinking, but he managed to disguise the word by mumbling.

"You fancy her, mate?" said Faultless.

Hallam felt really uncomfortable. He squirmed. He flushed. He stalled. Faultless was obviously making fun of him.

Does he know? thought Hallam. *Does he know?*

He considered running away, but if he did that, maybe Faultless would guess.

"I don't blame you, Hallam," the other man said. "She is attractive. I used to go out with her sister. You remember her sister?"

Hallam looked into his coffee. Faultless had brought him to Ray's greasy spoon café. Earlier, when they were coming down in the lift, Hallam thought he would piss himself. Faultless stared at him all the way down. Stared and said nothing.

He knows… he knows… Hallam was thinking.

But Faultless didn't do anything if he did know. He brought him here, smiled, bought him a coffee.

They sat at a red Formica table. The place was packed and teeming with gossip. Steam rose. Bacon sizzled. You could hear the Sunday crowd talking about the murders and slagging off the Old Bill.

Hallam wanted to stand up and say, "It was me who found them," but he resisted.

Now he answered Faultless. "Yes… yes, I remember."

"You remember me?"

Fear turned his spine into an icy rope. He looked Faultless in the eyes – one brown, one blue, both cold. He tried to say something, but no words came out. His heart thundered.

"Don't worry," said Faultless. "I've changed, mate. I know I was a bit of a bad lad in my youth, but I'm all right, now. Honest."

"Oh… oh, yes, 'course," said Hallam, pouncing on Faultless's misunderstanding. He obviously thought Hallam was scared of his reputation, which he was. But he was also scared of something else.

He was scared of vengeance.

He doesn't know, thought Hallam. *It's okay, he doesn't know.*

He blew air out of his cheeks and took a sip of his coffee. It was hot and comforting. Faultless hadn't touched his drink yet.

"You remember the New Ripper?" said Faultless.

Hallam held his breath.

Faultless went on. "He killed my mum fifteen years ago."

Hallam nodded.

"I've come back to write a book about it."

Hallam opened his mouth but said nothing.

"And yesterday's killings, they looked pretty violent, not so different to back then."

Hallam blinked.

136

"You found the bodies, Hallam; you're the famous one… "

Hallam blushed.

"… so I thought maybe you could tell me what you saw?"

Hallam swelled with pride.

"You want to tell me, mate?"

Hallam told.

And when he'd finished half-an-hour later, Faultless said, "Good stuff."

Hallam said, "Will you tell Tash I helped you?"

Faultless, rising from his seat, smiled. "You want me to?"

Hallam looked away.

Faultless said, "I'll say you were really helpful."

Hallam licked his lips.

CHAPTER 34.
TWO OLD BULLS.

ROY Hanbury folded his big arms and leaned against the doorframe. "It's always me first, ain't it, Wilks."

"You're a good place to start, Roy."

"Why's that?"

"You're the main bastard round these parts."

"Ain't no bastard no more, Wilks."

"Once a bastard, always a bastard – and I should know."

Wilks had Dick Van Dyke silver hair, John Sergeant jowls, Dolph Lundgren height, and Nick Griffin hate.

Like Hanbury once had, but not any more. "My heart's pure, now," he said. "Filled with the holy spirit."

"Don't think you can be forgiven for your ways, Roy."

"Everyone can be forgiven – even you."

"No one's in a position to forgive me – I am my own judge."

"God's your judge, Wilks."

"Fuck God."

"You better start believing in him."

"I do, Roy."

"Good – then you better start worshipping him."

"I only worship me."

"You'll be no good in the end times."

"I'll survive. I'm like a cockroach. Get through anything – disciplinary panels, nuclear war, and Day of Judgment."

Hanbury clenched his jaw.

Wilks clocked it. "Am I pissing you off, Roy?"

"You always pissed me off, Wilks."

"Where's that pure heart of yours?"

Hanbury grunted.

Wilks said, "How about showing me some Christian charity and making me a cup of tea, warm the cockles of my cold, black heart on this grim old day?"

"Fuck off."

"I can have you hauled in for obstruction."

"For not making you a cup of tea?"

"Come on, Roy." His face darkened, the fake mateyness rapidly fading. "Bygones and all that."

"You come back when you've nailed my daughter's killer."

Wilks narrowed his eyes.

Hanbury said, "You royally fucked up, Wilks. There are people round here who ain't had closure. We're still suffering."

Wilks looked away for a moment. His jowls shook. Then his cruel, green eyes were back on Hanbury.

He said, "Don't fuck about with me, Roy. You ain't got the balls anymore, son."

Hanbury leaned forward, and Wilks reared back.

Hanbury said, "You'd be surprised at the balls I carry round with me, DCS Wilks."

Wilks smiled. "All right. All right. That's good. Two old bulls going head to head here. No harm done, eh? We didn't see eye to eye back then, Roy, that's true. Many reasons. But you're on the straight and narrow, now. Me, I'm a couple of years away from my yacht, cruising around the Med, tanned tarts spread-eagled on deck, in – or out of – their bikinis. Let's not ruck when there's no need to ruck. Let's try to be civil, eh?"

Hanbury said nothing.

Wilks's smile went. "All I'm asking, Roy, is have you heard anything?"

"I heard nothing, Wilks."

"That lad Jason Joseph Thomas. Called him Slow Joe round here. The kid who got his head bashed in. I know something about him."

"Bet it's made up, Wilks."

"I don't know. Made up or not, he was seen hanging around here, just outside your place, early yesterday morning. What do you say to that?"

"I say you see a lot."

"I do, Roy. I am the all-seeing eye."

Hanbury shrugged. "I never saw him. If he was out here, so what? They hang about all over the estate.

Wilks looked him in the eye. "Kids have been killed, you know."

"I fucking know that. Don't give me that bollocks. You ain't got a heart of gold. You ain't on a crusade for justice. Fifteen years ago you wasn't, and you ain't had an epiphany in the meantime."

"Why not? You have. Or is it just show? You still the bastard you once were, Roy? Not planning to sort this out yourself are you?"

"Vengeance is mine, sayeth the Lord."

"I bet he does, the bloodthirsty cunt."

"Take my name in vain, Wilks, but not the Lord's."

Wilks sneered. "Another thing the rumour mill churned out," he said, "is that a bloke was hanging around your Tash's place this morning."

Hanbury said nothing.

"She got a boyfriend? New fella? No one seemed to know his name."

Hanbury stayed silent.

"Thing is," said Wilks, "we just need to eliminate him from our inquiries, see. Every 'i', every 't', that kind of thing."

"Can't help you," said Hanbury. "Now, I need to feed my snake."

He shut the door in Wilks's face.

CHAPTER 35.
HE'S HERE.

"THE roof, the roof," said Jack, stumbling out of the lift on the fifteenth floor of Bradford House. "I need to get to the roof."

He panted. He reeled. His cape flapped, and Spencer saw faces in its folds – faces twisting into the shapes of screams.

He stepped back, his throat dry.

Behind him, the elevator clanked and went down. Jack leaned against the lift.

Spencer watched him, scared.

It had been more than a day since the murders. During that time, Spencer had been in a daze. He'd given Jack a tour of the estate. But it was Jack who knew his way around. And he'd shown Spencer hiding places, alleyways, and dark corners he never knew existed. Places history had forgotten.

"You have to look hard," Jack had told him, "but if you do, you will always find a way through from your world to these lost places, these hidden locations."

In all of these places, Spencer had seen terrible things, and he tried his best not to remember them…

A fucking goat. Fucking bones. Fucking corpses on hooks. Fucking ghosts. Fucking... Hell.

But they had stained his memory. They had corrupted him. They were foul, and they were in his heart.

Night and day, Spencer and his new friend had trawled this alternative Barrowmore, Jack saying he was reacquainting himself with his territory.

And now, he wanted to survey his domain.

"What's the matter?" said Spencer.

"The roof, I need the roof," said Jack.

"I don't think I can – "

Jack moved like lightning. A black flash. He scooped Spencer up and dangled him over the edge of the fifteenth floor .

The world wheeled. A scream clogged in his throat. Wind whipped his hair.

He swung like a pendulum, a hundred-and-fifty feet above the earth.

Jack held him by his ankle.

As he stopped swaying, Spencer found his voice. He used it to shriek.

Jack leaned over the side. Spit oozed from his jaws.

It spattered over Spencer, and he said, "I'm going to be sick."

"Puke then," Jack said.

"Please, let me up."

"Do as I say, Spencer."

"Please... "

Jack hoisted him up. Spencer fell on his arse on the walkway. He felt dizzy.

"You're crazy," he whined.

"I'm psycho, Spencer."

"Are you dead?"

"I never die."

"Are you an angel?"

143

Jack shrugged.

"Where'd you come from, man?"

"From hell. Now hurry. Show me how to get to the roof."

Spencer showed him a metal door at the far end of the walkway.

"It's how the council blokes get up there. It's locked – "

Jack grabbed the padlock with his hand and crushed it. It twisted and snapped.

"Now it isn't," he said.

Spencer gawped.

The narrow stairwell was dark. It led up to another door. Jack kicked through it, and the wind nearly shoved him back into Spencer.

Out on the roof, it was gusting. It sliced into Spencer, right down into his bones. His thin, fraying Adidas hoodie and matching tracksuit bottoms were no match for the elements up here.

He stayed where he was, near the broken door.

Jack rushed towards the edge, and Spencer hoped he would leap off.

He didn't. He jumped on the high wall skirting the roof and looked down. His cape flapped. He looked like a giant bat.

"He's here," he called out, the wind trying its best to steal his voice.

"W… who's here?" said Spencer, desperate to get off the roof, desperate to roll back time.

The Sharpleys' flat. The door open. The PS3 sitting in the hallway. The price tag still on it. Paul and his dad fighting…

He cursed himself for not walking by.

"The law are everywhere," said Jack.

Spencer said nothing.

He could end this now.

He stared at Jack up on the wall.

Nothing between him and the streets and pavements of Barrowmore.

Spencer stepped forward.

He could run to him in less than five seconds, shove him.

Do it. End it. Do it...

Spencer took two steps, ready to build up his speed.

Jack turned slowly and stared, and the look stopped Spencer in his tracks.

Jack hopped off the wall. He strode towards Spencer, who felt the fear rise up from his belly like lava.

"He's here, Spencer. He's here. There's a psychic storm blowing through this place. He's here, and there are seers, too. Seers on Barrowmore."

He was in Spencer's face. His breath smelled of rotting meat. He grabbed Spencer's arms and lifted him off his feet. He blustered, words spilling out: "One more to rip... one more and I'm free... I need to kill again, Spencer... I'm itching for it... one more to rip... one more... and *him*, we have to find *him*... *him*... he's here... *and he has them for me... for me to devour...* "

145

CHAPTER 36.
A DARKNESS IN THE
CORNER OF HER EYE.

TASH woke up from her nap screaming, her body drenched in sweat.

The dreams again.

She dreamt a lot. They were vivid. But they'd not been as scary as this for a long time – for nearly fifteen years.

Not since Rachel and those other women had been murdered had she visualized such terrors.

Christ, she thought, crossing to the table where her handbag sat, digging out her cigarettes but then remembering that Jasmine was in the flat.

She put the fags away, the itch for one clawing at her chest, the panic rising.

Sit down, she told herself. *Have a sit down*, and she returned to the couch where she'd been dozing.

She wiped sleep from her eyes. The dream stained her mind. Most of the time they faded, and she had to grab at them as they floated off.

But this one was staying put.

She shut her eyes, trying to blind herself to the images reeling through her mind. But that didn't help. The dream replayed itself behind her eyelids. It drove her mad. It made her shake.

In her dream, she was walking through the estate.

It was a bright day, brighter than any she could remember. Everything was blindingly white.

Almost everything.

Just outside her eyeline, a shadow lurked.

Every time she turned towards it, thinking it would come into view, it stayed where it was – a notch in the side of her vision.

It panicked her. In her dream, she tried to escape it. But it was always there.

A darkness in the corner of her eye.

Trying to flee the wraith, or whatever it was, she raced along the streets, the light still blindingly white.

Somehow, she came to a spiral staircase that sunk down into the earth, into a well.

She stared down into the abyss.

Screams came up from the darkness.

The cries of agony.

She could even smell something in her dream, and she recognized the odour. It was sulphur.

Deep in the depth of the well, a fire glowed orange.

Her conscious self told her, "No, no… " Tash's unconscious form descended the staircase. The darkness was still in her eye. She wanted it to go away. It was claustrophobic.

She raced down the staircase. She noticed the stairs were glistening under her feet. At first she ignored the strange sheen. But then she stopped and squatted and touched the stair, and frantically tried to wipe the blood from her fingers.

She screamed in her dream, and maybe in her flat, and began to descend again until she came to the shore of a lake.

A lake of fire.

Bubbling lava splashing at the shore.

She looked around. She was in a cellar. It was dirty and smelly. Damp on the walls. Rats scurrying behind crates. Cobwebs draped everywhere – and this burning lagoon.

A small raft the size of a tea towel bobbed on the blistering waves. Something sat on the raft. In her dream, she stared at it, focusing. Also in the distance, a voice whispered. It said a word that she couldn't make out. Although it sounded like "yellow" or "pillow", Tash knew it wasn't either of those. It was something much worse. A terrible word. A terrible name.

Ignoring the voice, she reached out for the raft. It was too far. She stretched. The heat seared her face. But she had to get to it. She leaned forward.

Something dark and terrifying reared up out of the lake of fire and engulfed Tash, and that was when she screamed herself awake and sat bolt upright.

Now, sitting on the sofa, her mind spinning, Tash felt a dread slowly washing over her – and over Barrowmore.

Something terrible was here; she could feel it. The killing of the boys was more than just savagery – it had a meaning. Just like Rachel's killing all those years ago. It indicated a coming of something – it foretold an arrival.

She shook. Her dad spoke of Armageddon. The "end times". The Day of Judgment.

Maybe Rachel's death had something to do with that. Maybe the youths' murders were also linked.

"Mum, I'm sick."

Tash started. She looked up. Jasmine stood in the door of her bedroom. Her daughter was pale. Her brow was furrowed, and tears wetted her cheeks.

"Come here, sweetheart," said Tash, and she embraced her daughter.

The girl said, "I'm not lying about the dreams, Mum, honest."

"I know, it's okay.

"I'm really feeling weird. I had a horrible nightmare."

Tash eased her away. "It's all right to tell me."

"It was about a fiery lake and… and something in my eye. And someone whispering 'pillow' or something."

CHAPTER 37.
BLOOD AND BLUE LIGHTS.

THE road leading down to the lock-ups had been closed. A police car blocked the route. Yellow tape marked with the words POLICE: DO NOT CROSS ribboned across the street.

Three coppers loitered near the vehicle, ignoring the insults and the jibes streaming from the kids gathered nearby.

Quite a crowd swanned about. The noisy kids insulting the cops. Mums with prams, fearing for their children. Thugs claiming immigrants were to blame. Old men telling stories of 1996 and four dead women. Old women tutting about the state of the world. Journalists digging the dirt on the slaughtered youths.

Faultless looked beyond the roadblock.

In the distance, figures in white coveralls shuffled in and out of a large tent. The bivouac had been erected to protect the crime scene. It covered the entrance of the lock-up where the bodies had been found. Police vehicles were parked across the road. Their spinning lights sprayed blue into the gloomy sky. Faultless clocked uniformed officers and plain-clothed CID striding around the murder site.

Memories streamed through his mind. He'd stood in a similar spot fifteen years ago, watching as an ambulance ferried his mother's butchered body to the morgue.

Back then there were police loitering, kids jibing, mums dreading, louts accusing, old men boasting, old women scorning, and hacks sniffing.

Back then it was blood and blue lights.

Back then a fire burned in his breast.

Just like now.

Was the New Ripper back? If so, how come he'd returned at the same time as Faultless? Was that a coincidence?

Something cold and multi-legged crawled down his spine.

Did the killer know who he was?

Had Faultless's return triggered his re-emergence?

Hallam Buck had named the youths. They were Jason Joseph Thomas, Paul and Michael Sharpley, and Luke Ellis.

Hallam had described their injuries – ripped apart, gutted, disembowelled, brains bashed in, and blood everywhere.

Hallam had offered a piece of evidence: "I'll bring it round to Tash's flat."

Faultless wondered what it could be. *Nothing of value,* he thought. *Hallam's just using whatever he's found to get into Tash's place. You sicko, Buck.*

He remembered the scar under Hallam's eye. He creased his brow, focusing on the blemish. Something he knew but had forgotten lurked in the shadowy corners of his mind. He reached for it, but couldn't grab hold. He focused. The gloom started to lift. He started to see what was there, his memory slowly revealing the dusty, old recollection.

The light was about to shine on the lost knowledge when someone shoved Faultless in the back.

He staggered forward a couple of steps.

He stared ahead, letting the anger build.

He very slowly turned to face whoever pushed him.

Someone had it coming.

But when he saw the grinning, jowly face, he just curled his lip and said, "Bad smells never go away, do they."

CHAPTER 38.
OFFICIAL THREATS.

DON Wilks lit a cigarette and said, "Do you have permission?"

Faultless said, "For what?"

"To write this fucking book, son."

Faultless looked straight at him. "I ain't your son. Donny."

"Don't call me fucking Donny. Or Don. I remember you when you were a little cunt, running around here causing trouble. Now you're just a big cunt, back to cause more. Not on my patch, son."

"Your patch."

"Yeah, my fucking patch."

Faultless slipped a hand into the pocket of his hooded jacket and switched on the mini-disc recorder tucked inside.

If Wilks was going beyond the call of duty, Faultless thought it would be better to have a record of it.

He knew from experience that your word against a cop's counted for nothing.

Especially if you were from Barrowmore.

"Funny how these scum die just when you turn up like a bad fucking penny, Faultless," the DCS said.

He tossed the fag aside, making sure it landed close to Faultless's feet. Charlie glanced down at the stub, smoke pluming from it.

"Not very convenient for me, Don," he said.

Wilks grimaced. They were standing next to his silver Mondeo. He leaned on the vehicle. Faultless leaned on a wall.

The copper looked over at the kids and the mums and the jobless and the old and the reporters.

"Fuckers," he said.

"They think the world of you, too," said Faultless.

"Here, Charlie, why don't we put aside our differences and go to Ray's for a cuppa and a catch-up?"

"What a fucking tempting offer. But I'm having my fingernails removed with pliers. It's a more pleasant experience than spending time in your company, Wilks."

The detective's grin drooped, becoming a frown. "You misunderstand. We need to catch up. You need to talk to me. You can do it freely, or I drag you down the nick."

"What is it you're so keen to chat about, Wilks? Your love life? Still fancy young Asian boys?" Faultless chuckled.

Wilks went purple.

He spluttered. "You... it's fucking you... you like fucking Paki queers, you fuck... don't you fucking ever call me a fucking homo... don't you – "

"You're the ideal modern cop, ain't you, Wilks. I bet they love you down at New Scotland Yard. You're a star in diversity training, is my guess."

Faultless leaned back. He'd hit a nerve. It was easy. Wilks was homophobic and racist. Winding him up was a doddle. The knife was in, so Charlie kept twisting. "Case still closed on my mum and Rachel and the other two women, is it?"

"Case ain't closed, son." Wilks was cooling down. "No evidence. No suspects. Apart from the one who legged it, of course. Eh, Charlie? Ran off like you had something to hide."

"I remember you dragged me in after my mum died. You were very sympathetic. Oh no, that was someone else."

"I don't do sympathy, son. I do detective work."

"You didn't do much of it back then, Donny."

Wilks reddened again. He leaned into Faultless. "Don't fucking push your luck with me, toe rag. I know what you're like – street scum. You ain't rehabilitated. You're the same. Bad genes, son. You get it off your mum –"

Charlie's blood boiled. "Don't you dare, Wilks."

Wilks grinned. "Or what?"

"I'll write about you. I'll fucking name and shame you. I'll dig up all the shit about you, Wilks. Every fucking disciplinary you've wriggled out of, every fucking suspect you've abused, every innocent you've framed. Papers love a dodgy copper tale."

"I'll fucking sue your balls off if you publish a word about me, Faultless."

"You can't sue if it's true."

"All right, so you won't mind me writing a report about your involvement in Tony Graveney's unsolved murder, then?"

Faultless said nothing.

"You want to tell me where you were on the night of the twenty-sixth of July 1996?" said Wilks.

"Shagging your mother."

Wilks shook with anger, but he didn't snap. He said, "You wouldn't have been smashing Tony Graveney's head in, would you?"

"I don't think so."

"And two days later, when we were hoping to have a word, you know, help us with inquiries – you disappeared like a magician's rabbit. Where d'you go?"

"Got fed up. Went looking for work."

"You work? Don't make me laugh, Faultless."

"I'm working now."

155

Wilks looked him up and down. "Writing books. That ain't work. That's poncing about."

"I get paid for poncing about."

"This book, what's it going to say?"

"Don't know yet."

"I'd like a look."

"I don't think I'll require your insights, thanks, Don."

Wilks narrowed his eyes. "Don't say anything about me, son." It wasn't an appeal.

"Anything I do say, you'll have a right of reply."

"I'll fucking reply with my fist up your arse if you write anything shit about me."

"Is that an official threat?"

"I'll fucking write it down if you like."

Faultless said, "That'd be great," and he walked off.

Wilks called out his name.

"What?" said Faultless, turning.

Wilks looked him in the eye. "I'm having you for Graveney's murder, son. And any other cold case that needs a tick next to it. You and me, we're going to talk soon. Down the nick. Now, off you fucking pop." Wilks reached into his pocket and took out his phone. He started dialling. Without looking at Faultless he said, "I got a very interesting call to make. Passing on some fascinating news to an old mate."

Faultless turned and walked away.

He had a good idea who Wilks was ringing. And it wasn't fascinating news. It was very bad news.

He put his hand in his pocket and switched off the recorder.

CHAPTER 39.
THE SPECIAL ONE.

HER mother had always told Tash she was special girl.

"You're a gift from God, darlin'," she'd say. "Just like those who have passed."

"Passed what, Mum?" the nine-year-old Tash would say.

Mum would smile and her white teeth were like pearls. "To the other side, darlin'. With the angels."

But then Dad would say, "Don't fill her head with that ghost rubbish."

"It ain't rubbish, Roy," Mum would say. "It's a gift, and Tash has it."

She was Dad's third wife and the only one to produce children. They married in 1975. She was eighteen, and he was thirty-five. Three years later, Rachel was born. Tash came along in 1981. Ten years later, her mum died in a hit-and-run. Dad went mental. He traced the driver's address. But the police got to him first. He was arrested for causing death by dangerous driving. He was in protective custody during his trial, and after he'd spent six years inside, he was given a new identity. But Dad kept hunting him.

He didn't speak about it now, but Tash sometimes wondered if her dad had ever found the driver.

She thought about her mother and why that particular conversation had come to mind.

You're a gift from God, darlin'.

Had it been the dream?

Had it been the same dream Jasmine experienced?

Her daughter was curled up in Tash's arms. They were lying together on the couch. The girl had gone to sleep. Now and again, she jerked, and Tash wondered if the dream was returning to haunt the child again.

Tash kissed Jasmine's hair and breathed her in. The scent of her offspring sparked something in Tash's heart – an ache that she could only name as love.

It's what it feels like, she thought.

She felt it when Jasmine was born. It sliced through the hate and anger that filled Tash's veins at the time – hate and anger towards her newborn's feckless father.

Pete Rayner.

She shuddered at the thought of him.

How had that happened?

Through her teens, she had been barely aware of the lanky clown.

The girls, thinking they were cool, would roll their eyes or tut at him as he clambered on top of a car or a wall and shouted, "Look at this," and he'd dive off, hit the ground, and hurt himself. And Tash and her mates would strut past, ignoring him.

Pete always fancied her, but there were better options around, and Tash blanked him.

By her late teens, with her mates pregnant or already mums and all the better options either in jail or warned off by her dad, Pete wangled his way into her life.

158

She'd been dumped by Neil Uxford, one of Charlie Faultless's former lieutenants. Charlie had left a couple of years before, soon after Rachel had died. Soon after his own mum had died. Neil tried to take over Charlie's business, but he didn't have the brains, he didn't have the brawn, and he didn't have the brutality.

He dumped her for a forty-year-old ex-prostitute living in Monro House.

"Her ex, he runs some business up north," Neil had said, "and she says, if I… you know… if I shack up with her, she'll get me in with him. It's business, darlin'."

"Was I business?" she'd asked.

He'd shrugged.

Her tears had brought Pete Rayner to her door. He could sniff out Tash's sadness like a bloodhound could hit a trail.

She was fragile. She was young. She was lost. Her heart had been broken. Her hopes shattered. Her future obliterated.

It happened on the couch at her dad's house. Lucky for Pete, Roy Hanbury was on remand, awaiting trial.

Tash could barely remember the event. She was blind with grief. But nine months later, the result of the episode came along.

And so did that ache in her heart.

She stroked Jasmine's hair. The child continued to sleep. She flinched, still dreaming her awful dreams. Tash wanted to keep her safe from those terrible things going through her head. But that was impossible. It was impossible, even, to keep her safe from the outside world, let alone what was inside her mind. Tash was furious with herself for ever doubting Jasmine, for accusing her of lying about her headaches and her nightmares.

She looked through the window. A grey sky loomed. Rain spattered the pane. There was a chill in the air. Tash shivered. Her anxiety grew. Something was here on the Barrowmore estate. Something that was poison. Something that was dark. Something that was evil.

And it was speaking to her and Jasmine through their dreams. *Pillow*... Was that what she'd heard? *Pillow*...

There was a knock on the door. It made Tash start. She eased herself away from Jasmine and went to answer it.

It was Hallam Buck. He was carrying something. A brown leather briefcase. Her flesh crawled with dread. She'd seen it before.

* * * *

Jack froze. He stayed very still. The wind ruffled his long hair, but nothing else moved. It was as if he'd turned into a statue. He didn't blink, and his chest didn't rise and fall as he breathed.

"You okay?" said Spencer.

They were still on the roof. Spencer was freezing. He was covered in goosepimples and had been shivering for ages.

"What's the matter?" he said.

"There is a woman and a child," said Jack.

"You what?"

"There are others, but they're weak... but the woman and the child... "

"What about them?"

"My bones are trembling."

"Your bones?"

"My blood runs cold."

"That's 'cause it's freezing up here."

"They are dreaming me."

"They're... "

"I need a ripper."

"You need a... "

"I must find him."

"Who – "

"I need a ripper... "

160

"I don't understand," said Spencer.

"The woman and child."

"What about them?"

"They must be ripped."

"Jesus… "

"But there's something else."

Spencer quaked. It was so cold he was burning. His skin was turning red. He couldn't feel his hands. He couldn't feel his legs.

"W…what else?" he said.

Jack gazed out across the estate. Police cars trawled the streets. Blue flashing lights lit up the grey sky. Sirens wailed over hip-hop beats.

Jack said, "There's a darkness."

"A… a… a what?"

"A darkness in the corner of my eye."

CHAPTER 40.
MONTAGUE JOHN
DRUITT.

FAULTLESS asked her, "Are you all right?"

Tash nodded and said it was okay.

He narrowed his eyes, fixing on her.

"You don't look it."

"It's fine. I'll tell you later."

"You look pale."

"I'm all right."

The briefcase sat on her kitchen table. Time had blemished the brown leather. Time and blood. It was still wet in places. Faultless had wiped it with his hand, and his skin went red. Slime was also draped over the briefcase. The clasps were rusty. There was a brass name tag. It was covered in mud.

"I'm sorry about this," Faultless had told Tash ten minutes earlier when she'd let him and Hallam into her flat. "He said he had something to show me, something he found where those boys were killed. He wanted to bring it here. I thought it would be… "

"Yeah, fine," she'd said, her voice filled with panic. She gaped at the briefcase. To Faultless, it looked as if she were staring at an animal that could kill her. She was carefully watching it as it sneaked by. She was hoping it wouldn't see her and attack.

When they had walked into the living room, Jasmine was sitting up of the sofa, rubbing her eyes.

"Hello, Jasmine," Hallam had said, and the way he'd said it made Faultless squirm. He thought about something. It reawakened a memory. He tried to dig it up, but it was buried deep.

Tash had suggested Jasmine go to her room, and the girl had tottered off, looking tired.

Now in the kitchen, Charlie kept a close eye on Tash. She looked twitchy. He clocked her problem, or thought he did, and said, "Hallam, you've been really helpful, but me and Tash, we need to talk, now."

Buck stared, his mouth open. The scar under his left eye wiggled.

"I think it's time you went," Faultless said.

"But… but what about my… my case?"

Faultless stared at him. Buck cowered. He reared back.

Faultless said, "You've been a great help, Hallam, see you around."

Buck mumbled.

"You say something?" said Faultless.

"It's mine."

"You want me to call the cops, Hallam? You want to say it's yours to them?"

Buck mumbled again.

"Go on, off you fuck," said Faultless.

Hallam slipped out of the kitchen. Faultless looked at Tash. She stared at the case, chewing her nails.

"What's the matter?" he asked.

"I… I've seen it before, Charlie."

163

"This?" he said, pointing at the case.

She nodded and then asked, "What does the name tag say?"

He wiped the dirt away and read. "Montague John Druitt."

They looked at each other and shrugged – but fifteen minutes later, they were staring at Faultless's MacBook, both speechless.

"He was a Ripper suspect," said Faultless, reading from the Web page. "Druitt was one of many suspected of the Whitechapel murders in 1888."

"What... what's his briefcase doing here?"

Faultless shook his head.

"Did he do it?" she asked.

"No one knows. No one knows who the Ripper was."

"What happened to him?"

Faultless studied the page. After reading he said, "In November 1888, days before the body of Mary Kelly, the Ripper's last victim, was found, Druitt apparently lost his job as a teacher. He was said to have drowned in the Thames. Committed suicide, it says here."

He stared at the briefcase. Bloody history on Tash's kitchen table. An artefact worth a fortune to Ripper buffs.

He looked at the page again for a while and then he continued. "Three years later, an MP called Richard Farquharson claimed Jack the Ripper had been 'the son of a surgeon' who topped himself the same night as Druitt did. Says here Farquharson lived ten miles from Druitt's family and knew them. A journalist called George R. Sims wrote a few years later that the Ripper's body had been found in the Thames."

"So it was him?"

"According to this stuff, most of those who are into this Ripper stuff don't think there's any evidence against Druitt."

Faultless sat back, knitting his fingers behind his head. He gazed at the photo of Druitt on the internet page, a young man resting his head on his hand. Then he said to Tash, "You said you'd seen his case before. How come?"

Her eyes were wide with fear. "I… I saw it on a fiery raft."

"A what?"

She told him, and while she did, he completely rejected her explanation in his head and tried to see reason and logic in this slowly evolving pandemonium.

There was none.

CHAPTER 41.
THE CURSE.

SOMEONE grabbed him by the back of the neck, shook him violently, and tossed him against a tree.

He blacked out for a moment, then came to with a pain in his skull.

He blinked, staring into the light. He tried to look at it, but his eyes strained, and finally he had to turn away. It made him feel as if his body were melting.

"What have I done?" he said.

"Spoiler. Tempter," said a voice coming from the light, a deep voice that squeezed the air out of a person.

"I haven't done anything."

"You've destroyed everything."

"It's not my fault, it's yours."

"Look at what you've done."

He scanned the garden. Already things were dying. Leaves browned and fell from the trees. Branches withered. The grass yellowed. A dog's corpse lay near a rock. Its belly had been sliced

166

open. Flies buzzed around the carcass. Further away, lions feasted on an antelope. Off to the right, the entrance to a cave was coated in blood.

"Can you smell it?" said the voice.

He could.

"It's death," said the voice, "and you brought it – you brought death."

"It's your fault," he said, whining. "You didn't make them strong enough. You made them weak. They broke. They broke too easily. It's your fault."

"Spoiler. Curse you. Curse you, tempter, killer, coward. Serpent. I'll make you suffer so you wish you'd never been born."

"I wish that already."

* * * *

WHITECHAPEL – 11.12AM, FEBRUARY 27, 2011

Jack entered Spencer's flat and tossed what they'd found on the doorstep into the living room, and it slammed against the wall, slumping in a heap.

"You have a lovely home, Spencer," Jack said.

Spencer looked around. Holes in the ceiling. Plaster peeling off the walls. Damp blackening the corners. Rotten floorboards. Pizza boxes and empty beer cans littered the flat. Beneath a huge TV on the wall was the PS3 console Spencer had nicked from the Sharpleys' flat.

"It smells of dead flesh," Jack continued.

"Dead flesh?"

"You know, everywhere smells of dead flesh."

"Does it?"

"Of course, lad. It must do. Every city is built on the dead. Bones lie below. For miles and miles. Rotting corpses. Wormriddled skeletons. Piles of them. London would sink into the earth, were it not for its foundation of bones. I close my eyes, I can see them – a white tangle of them, a scaffold of them, holding everything upright. And gluing them together, like concrete, the flesh and the blood. Death is everything, Spencer. Without it, you wouldn't be alive. Without death, you'd be dead. And d'you know who brings you death so you can live?"

Spencer gaped and shook his head.

"I do. I am the bringer of death, and I drape fear over the world. I am the plagues that kill the sick. I am the wars that make refugees of the innocent. I am the famines that make the poor hungry. I am the fires that burn your cities. I am the curse."

He paused, smiling. His eyes glittered. Saliva dribbled from his grinning mouth.

After a second he said, "You've got to find this woman and child for me, Spencer. The child would be easier."

"Yeah?"

"And the ripper, I must find the ripper."

Spencer shook. What had he got himself into? "Christ," he said.

"The work he did while I was captive makes things so much easier this time. Just one left to kill. One left to rip." Jack was ranting again, his eyes glittering with madness. "It will be the child, and... and I shall devour what she has inside her, and will be free. The city will be my playground. This nation will tremble at my name. My real name. Now, help me pin this to the wall."

He went over to the thing that had been outside Spencer's door when they arrived. Spencer stared, not wanting to move. This was going too far.

But I've gone further than far already, he thought.

"Get some nails, Spencer," said Jack, lifting the thing up against the wall.

"We shouldn't do this," said Spencer.

"Why ever not?"

"Because… because he's Old Bill."

"Get me nails, Spencer."

Jack spread the policeman's arms out.

CHAPTER 42.
REACH FOR THE SKY.

TERRI Slater felt safe with the cops here. She didn't want to admit that, but it was the truth.

She hated the cops. They'd put Wayne in jail.

Bastard pigs.

Always picking on him, knocking on her door at all hours asking, "Is Wayne in, Terri?" just because he went out robbing.

Bastard pigs.

Then the social came round and discovered she and Wayne were living as a couple.

Terri had told them she was a single mum, living alone with her kids.

How else was she supposed to get all the benefits she needed?

How else could she buy Italy and Rome the Ted Baker, Nike, and Ralph Lauren gear they had to have?

How else do you get Domino's delivered every night and Sky Movies on tap?

The girls were thirteen and nine and wanted to dress up nice. They wanted the best food and the latest music.

Dole money was the only way.

But when they found Wayne was living there, they cut it.

Terri fumed. She'd had to get a job. Her clients wouldn't cover the costs. So she ended up doing the early morning shift at Costcutter four days a week, including Sundays.

And then the cops picked Wayne up again. It was three weeks ago. He'd mugged a pensioner near the post office.

He'd barely touched her, but she put up a fight when he tried to snatch her purse. Why hadn't she just let go? Stupid bitch. She tugged and wrenched and screamed, but you can't fight Wayne off when he wants something. He kicked her in the belly, and she fell, hitting her head on the pavement.

A week later, the old cow died.

Wayne faced murder.

I hate the cops.

But thank God they were crawling all over Barrowmore today.

She knew the Sharpleys. She thought she might've sucked off the eldest one, Michael, a couple of years ago.

Wasn't he the one who refused to pay after she swallowed the lot?

She threatened to call Wayne in unless the kid paid.

She hurried along the tenth-floor walkway of Bradford House.

Home to Terri since she'd been born.

Home to her parents before her and home to their parents.

In fact, her mother's mum and dad were among Barrowmore's first residents.

They'd lived in the slums that scarred the East End. They'd crammed ten kids into their hovel. They'd lived on bread and potatoes. Four of the kids had died.

The authorities razed the tenements. They built swanky new tower blocks. They said, "Look at what we've made for you, and be grateful for it."

Reach for the sky.

Terri's gran and grandad moved in. Thousands more came with them. They crawled from their fleapits and scaled their high rises.

Reach for the sky.

Work dried up. Crime leached in. The benefits culture became the way of life. It was cool Britannia. The immigrants kept coming – Bangladeshis at first, before the East Europeans swarmed in.

"No white Englishman left," Wayne would say.

It was nearly midday. With her shift at Costcutter over, she was planning to snooze for the rest of the afternoon. Italy and Rome were probably out somewhere. Terri should've stayed home as well. But Mr Khan was a bastard when it came to sickies. You had to come in even if you had a cold.

"Fucking Paki," Wayne would say. "Thinks he owns the place. They never gave a white person a chance – just gave it to a Paki."

Terri had thought about it and said, "Yeah, but it was shut for years, Wayne, 'cause no one local wanted to open it."

He said, "Shut up, slag. I wasn't asking your opinion," and he slapped her. "Fucking Paki lover."

Mr Khan and his wife were actually Bangladeshi – but they were all Pakis, Terri supposed. The store had been closed for three or four years before the couple took it over and re-opened it as a Costcutter. Some people – like Wayne – moaned. But most people were happy to have a mini-supermarket on the estate.

And at least it gave Terri and some of the other girls a job.

Better than being slobbered over by a fat, violent drunk for twenty quid.

Thirty yards to her door. The walkway was empty. The wind whistled along the passage. A Pepsi can rolled back and forth on the ground. Litter fluttered on the breeze. Screams and shouts filtered from down below in the streets. Sirens blared. A police helicopter hovered in the west.

Terri bricked it. Her legs felt weak as she strode. Her chest was tight. The walkway suddenly became gloomy. She hurried along.

Her door looked so far away. She wanted to be inside, drunk – all her troubles drowned in a sea of cider.

More sirens screeched.

Maybe the cops were on to the killer. They had him in their sights.

She felt sick.

Her heart pounded.

She remembered her mother speaking about the New Ripper. It was fifteen years ago. Four women butchered.

Terri had been thirteen.

No worries back then. Only where the next bottle of Thunderbird was coming from.

Even that wasn't a heavy concern. A blowie for a few boys would get her some dosh, and then it was down to the offie.

But now it was different. She felt threatened. Now she knew what life was about, and death was very near.

She reached for her key. The bunch jangled in her sweaty fingers. They slipped. She gasped, flailed at them. They clattered to the concrete.

She bit her lip and whined.

She squatted to pick them up.

The shadow passed over Terri and made everything dark.

She became very cold, and a creepy voice said, "I can *see* you."

She looked up slowly, catching her breath.

She tried to scream, but he was quick.

And then her world turned upside down, and she wheeled, and the clouds became earth and the earth, clouds, and she flapped and flailed and fell and found her screaming voice as she hurtled ten floors down, thinking, *Reach for the sky, reach for the –*

CHAPTER 43.
TIE-DOWNS.

DON Wilks eyed every one of them in turn, fixing each with a cold, hard, three-second stare to make sure they all experienced a balls-shrivelling moment – including the women.

Then he unleashed his anger. "How the fuck did this happen right under our noses? You're fucking useless. You should all be fucking demoted. I'd have you helping fucking old ladies across the street, if I had my way."

They were in Wilks's office in the major incident room. It was glass-fronted, so he could see into the room across the corridor where Faith Drummond, the office manager, was based.

She made his balls ache.

She'd look good in a bikini, sunning herself on his yacht. She'd look good out of a bikini, splaying herself on his bed.

He watched her while the detectives digested his tirade.

He might ask her to join him when he retired and sailed off. She was married, but that didn't matter. Maybe he'd warn the husband off. Spread some shit about Faith fucking the dog section during her lunch hour.

He thought about that for a few seconds before switching his attention back to the senior detectives shitting themselves in his office.

He said, "The fucking press is going to piss all over this – all over us. Who the fucking hell was on duty here this morning?"

A female detective inspector gave two names.

"Have 'em flogged, for fuck's sake," said Wilks. "What was the bird's name again?"

The female DI spoke again: "Teresa Jane Slater, twenty-eight. Her boyfriend, Wayne Dalton, is being held on remand. A pensioner he mugged three weeks ago died."

"Anything else?" said Wilks.

Another detective gave details about Slater's place of work.

"Drag the Paki in," said Wilks, when told the store was managed by a Mr Khan.

"He's Bangladeshi, sir," said the detective, a do-gooder with red-rimmed glasses who was probably queer, Wilks guessed, despite the wedding ring.

Mind you, he thought, *poofs can get married these days.*

"Whatever," he said. "Pull him in. Grill him. Tandoori him. Kebab him. Or do you want me to do it?"

"Okay, sir," said red-specs, "we'll have a chat, sure."

They ran through a few other details, including Slater's children.

"We're not sure where they are yet, but there's two girls called Italy and Rome," said the female detective.

"You what?" said Wilks.

"Apparently," said the woman DI, "Miss Slater named them after her two favourite countries."

"But Rome ain't – " Wilks started to say before trailing off. "These scum," he added under his breath. "Brain-dead scum. Okay." He sighed. "We're focusing on TIEs," he said.

TIE – trace, interview, and eliminate. The process of identifying suspects and incidents, and making sure they were not connected to the crime.

Wilks said, "We've got two fucking separate crimes, five murders. Anyone find this Spencer character yet?"

"We've checked his mum's address," one of the detectives said, "and he's not been there for months. Apparently crashes at an empty flat. We checked, but it's locked. We did have someone outside his door, but they've gone AWOL, sir."

"You're fucking joking."

The detectives said nothing.

Another officer said, "We got enough to smash Spencer's door down?"

Wilks, without thinking, said, "I don't think so." He reddened, unsure why he'd said that. He cringed, thinking about this Drake character's doss-house. Gut instinct seemed to be telling Wilks to stay away. There was nothing there. Or if there were, it was not meant to be found – just yet.

Wilks snapped out of his daydream and turned on the charm. "Fucking find out where he is, you fuckers. That's what you're paid to do. I want him in a cell by *Songs Of Praise*. And what about Charlie Faultless? That shite should be in the nick by now."

"Nothing on him yet, sir," said red-specs. "His alibi's sound."

"Bollocks," said Wilks.

"You want him watched, sir?" said red-specs.

Wilks thought about the phone call he'd made earlier that morning. No one had picked up, but he'd left a message. And once the person he rang got his voicemail, he'd be on the blower to Wilks in a flash.

"No, he probably won't be around for long."

"Are we re-opening the Graveney case?" red-specs asked.

"It never closed, inspector. Okay. That's enough. Fuck off. I'm going to have a wank."

The detectives shuffled out, mumbling.

Wilks stood and went to the glass partition. He stared at Faith Drummond. She was on the phone, the handset buried in her blonde hair. Wilks groaned. He thought of slashing her tyres and offering her a lift home, driving her down some quiet street somewhere off the Whitechapel Road.

I bet you smell nice, he thought.

She looked up and caught him staring. He didn't budge. He smiled at her. Her eyes stayed on him for a second, then dropped away.

He chuckled. He didn't care. Nothing fazed Don Wilks. He was the boss. He owned Faith Drummond. He owned the lot of them, detectives and uniforms.

He also owned these streets, only the residents didn't know it yet. They would. Soon enough.

He'd always been the boss. He'd always been the bastard. A bully from birth. It was the only way to be, or you'd never survive. And what better vocation for a tormentor like Wilks than the police force.

After working with his old man in a bottling factory for a couple of years, he'd joined the Met at eighteen.

Best job ever. Suited him down to the bone.

It was the hate. It was the blood. It was the hunt.

That's what gave him hard-ons, what got him going.

His blood was up. This was a big one. Bigger than fifteen years back. Much bigger. And after this one, he'd be like a king.

CHAPTER 44.
THE SOUND OF WAR.

WITH the policeman still pinned to his wall, Spencer wondered how much further Jack would take things.

He'd already butchered Paul and Michael Sharpley and Lethal Ellis. He'd made Spencer murder Jay-T, nailed the copper up in the flat, and then thrown a woman off the tenth-floor balcony for a laugh.

It wasn't going well.

Spencer looked at the filth. Jack had driven nails through the cop's wrists. Blood ran down his arms and stained the wall. His head hung on his chest, but he wasn't dead yet. He lifted his head now and again and groaned. Sweat seeped from his black hair, down his face. He was only a few years older than Spencer. Twenty, maybe.

Spencer opened a can of beer and took a gulp. He stared at the copper again. He thought about things and decided there wasn't much he could do.

He turned on the TV and the games console, and the flat filled with the sound of war as he played Medal Of Honour. The gloomy flat came alive with flashing images. Spencer stared at the screen, hardly blinking. His brain filled with carnage.

Animated guns barked. Animated bombs exploded. Animated men died.

Spencer stalked the streets of Kabul, killing, killing, killing.

Time went. It could have been a minute, an hour, a year. Spencer in his bubble and the world outside moving on. But the flat had suddenly grown colder, and the drop in temperature brought Spencer back to reality.

He paused the game and turned, and Jack stood there, dark and vast in the half-light.

"Where did you go?" asked Spencer.

"He's here, Spencer. The one who prepared the way. My willing servant."

"I thought I was your servant."

"You're my dog."

"Nice."

"I sense the evil in his heart. It's like a lighthouse, pulsing. He has gifts for me. He has what he took from the seers. Gifts that will set me free."

CHAPTER 45.
JUST LIKE RACHEL.

CHARLIE Faultless stared up at the Jesus over Roy Hanbury's mantelpiece and delved into what he'd found out by searching the internet.

1888, Druitt, a Jack-the-Ripper suspect, dies.

1996, four women murdered in Ripper fashion.

2011, five dead in two days, three of them mutilated the Jack way.

2011, Tash and Jasmine Hanbury dream about a lake of fire and floating on it was the Ripper suspect's briefcase.

2011, the Ripper suspect's briefcase is found where the four boys were killed the previous morning.

He turned away from the crucifixion and faced Roy Hanbury, Tash, and Jasmine. They'd been talking. He'd been aware of their voices, but he hadn't really caught what they were saying. He was delving too deeply.

He said, "We have to find Spencer. He was mates with this Jay-T fella. Roy, you say he'd nicked a games console off the Sharpleys."

"What about our dreams?" said Tash.

Faultless looked at her and then at Jasmine.

The mum looked back at him. The girl watched a DVD.

He didn't know what to say. Dreams didn't count to him. They weren't concrete. He wanted to say what Tash had experienced meant nothing. But seeing the fire in her eyes, it was clear it meant something to her.

He said, "I don't know."

"Me and Jasmine dreamt this briefcase."

It sat on a towel on Hanbury's floor.

"And then," she said, "Hallam finds it where those boys got killed. You don't think that means something?"

Faultless said nothing.

Tash reddened. "You think what we dreamt is crap, don't you? You think it's just... just stupid."

"Tash, I'm – "

"You think we're mad."

"No, I don't, I – "

"What are you saying?"

She was fiery. *Just like Rachel,* he thought, not for the first time.

He remembered something. Rachel and him in a dodgy pub down in Stepney. Late in the evening, last orders called. The clientele drifting away.

Faultless, eighteen and a distress beacon for trouble, determined to finish the dregs in his pint.

Rachel saying, "Let's go."

Faultless saying, "I've got booze left."

A voice behind him saying, "Listen to your mummy, son."

Faultless turning.

Seven hard-cases – scars, tattoos, noses out of joint, number-one scalps, teeth missing, and muscles ballooned on steroids.

Faultless picking up his pint.

Faultless drinking it dry.

Faultless smashing the glass on the bar.

Faultless wielding it, a jagged weapon.

Face twisted, saying, "Come on, then… all of you… all of you… you cunts… "

The hard-cases cracking knuckles and flexing muscles, moving in on him.

Rachel blocking their way, saying, "You come on then, but first one to take a step loses his eyes." She clawed her hands, showing her long, red fingernails. "And I don't give a shit what the rest of you do. But who's first? Who's going to need a guide dog?"

For ten seconds, a stand-off.

Then a hard-case laughs and says, "Lucky she's here to look after you, son; we would've cut your balls off. Now kindly fuck off back to Barrowmore, Faultless."

The men had known him. He was Hanbury's acolyte. He was Hanbury's pit-bull pup. And they were going to neuter him before he got too dangerous.

Just like Rachel, he thought again, looking at Tash.

She said, "I dreamt this, Charlie. Jasmine dreamt it." She looked scared, this knowledge terrifying her. "It's real. Just because it's beyond your understanding doesn't mean you can dismiss it. Dad, tell him."

Hanbury was feeding dead mice to his snake.

Tash said, "Dad… "

Hanbury turned. He had worry-lines all over his face.

"Don't worry about it, darlin'," he told his daughter.

"Don't 'darlin'' me, Dad."

She looked at her father and her eyes narrowed. "You know something."

"Tash, I'm telling you – "

"Dad, you know something. Something about our dreams."

Now Jasmine was looking up from her movie.

Faultless caught her eye.

The girl said, "I'm scared, Grandad."

Hanbury went to her and hugged her, Jasmine tiny in his huge embrace. "Don't you fret, little angel, I won't let anyone hurt you."

She wriggled out of his grasp. "I'm scared of my dreams."

"It's just a dream," said Faultless.

Tash said, "Not to Jasmine, not to me."

Faultless said, "There's a lot of tension around the place, and that can contribute to – "

"Tash is right," said Hanbury.

Faultless gawped. Hanbury starting to believe crazy things was the last thing he needed.

He tried to think of a rational explanation. Coincidence was the only one he could come up with, but he'd offered that before.

"Dad," said Tash, desperation in her voice. "Dad, tell me what's going on."

Hanbury sighed. "You've got to go see old Bet, Tash. You've got to talk to her. Or try to. She's the one who knows. She'll know about all this… this dream stuff."

"I don't want to go see that old cow," said Jasmine. "Last time I went, she spat at me."

CHAPTER 46.
A GIFT IN THE GUTTER.

WHITECHAPEL – 1945

"YOU got to tell her when she gets to an age, love," said Mother.

"Christ, Mum, don't go on about it," said Bet.

She took another drag and blew out the smoke in a cloud that hid her mother for a moment.

Wish I could make you disappear in a puff of smoke, she thought.

"Don't blaspheme, Bet," said Mother.

Jesus, thought Bet.

Mother had been here all week, berating her.

There was always something.

You ain't doing the potatoes right, Bet.

You ain't cleaning the dishes right.

You ain't changing the kid's nappy properly.

Now she sat in the armchair and stared at Bet with those blue eyes that seemed to drill straight into your soul.

Get out of my life, Bet thought. *Leave me alone.*

Bet was twenty. The youngest daughter and fifth child of seven.

Born when her mother was thirty-three.

She looked at her daughter. She was eighteen months old. She cried in her crib. Bet felt cold towards the child. But maybe that's because she felt cold towards the kid's father.

Everybody said Derek Cooper was bad news. The police kept arresting him. They beat him up sometimes and threatened to jail him.

But Derek hadn't done anything. Or at least he hadn't been caught.

"Did he give you that?" asked Mother now and reached out to touch Bet's black eye.

She slapped her mum's hand away. "I fell. Tripped over the kid."

"Child's got a name, you know."

"Yeah, I know."

"You should use it, or she won't know it." Her mother leaned in. "And then she won't know where she's from."

"She's from the gutter, Ma. Just like the rest of us."

Bet and the baby lived in a cold, damp, dark room on the top floor of a tenement building. Beneath her, the neighbours rowed. Above her, the rats scuttled. She had to piss and shit in a pot, which stank the place out, because she rarely bothered to clean it. The kitchen reeked of rotting vegetables and sour milk. And now there was the baby – screaming and puking and shitting all night and all day. Life was hell. She'd been left in the abyss. No Derek, no hope. He promised mansions in Kensington. She was desperate enough to believe him. Nothing came of his pledge. She was left in the gutter.

They should've carried on from where Hitler left off and flattened the whole of the East End.

Bet hadn't seen much of Derek during the war. He was away a lot.

"Busy, darlin'," he'd said.

He argued that he was too sick to fight and duly failed a medical. But he kept himself occupied, although rarely in Bet's company.

He turned up when he wanted something – money, food, sex.

It was a visit for the latter that got her lumbered with the kid.

She dragged on the cigarette.

"You ain't showing any motherly inclinations, Bet," said Mother. "I don't know what's wrong with you."

"I don't feel none."

"Shame on you. It ain't natural. You behave like this, who knows how the little one will turn out."

"We don't know anyway, Ma."

"You know that's not true, Bet."

"Oh, Mother. We can't see the future. We can't see anything. If we could, we wouldn't live in shit."

The baby cried.

Mother rose from the armchair, tutting.

Bet said, "Leave her," and got up as well. "I'll sort it."

She went to the infant and scooped her out of the crib. The kid stank. She needed changing. The idea sickened Bet. She never saw herself like this. She'd pictured herself on stage, in movies – she'd pictured herself glamorous.

Another Derek promise. "Stick with me, sweetheart," he'd said, "and you'll be quaffing champagne and dressed in silk in no time."

No champagne, no silk. Only dirty water and threadbare cloth.

Cringing, she set about changing the baby's dirty napkin. While doing it, she thought about her grandad, who'd been on the stage. Not an actor. He'd go mad if you called him that. And so would Mother.

"My dad, he weren't no actor," she'd say. "He was for real."

Grandad Jonas was a medium. He spoke to the dead. He looked into the future.

Never looked into mine, thought Bet, safety pinning a clean cotton cloth around her daughter's waist.

Mother said, "That little girl deserves to know where she's come from, Bet."

"I told you, she's come from the gutter like the rest of us. And that's where she'll end up."

"She's got the gift."

"Shut up, Ma. No one can speak to the dead. The dead are dead. They're gone. We'll all be gone in the end. What's the point?"

Mother's face darkened. "Don't you speak ill, my girl."

"I ain't speaking ill."

The baby cried. Bet laid her in the crib again and went back to smoke her fag. She stared out of the window. The rain fell. Her chest felt heavy. The baby wailed. Mother cooed over it.

Bet listened to her mother's words.

"Don't you worry, little darlin', Granny will tell you how special you are. Granny will tell you everything. You're a special little girl, Gracie."

Tears filled Bet's eyes.

CHAPTER 47
OLD TIMES' SAKE.

"WHY the fuck are you calling me?" said Allan Graveney.

"Old times' sake," said Don Wilks. He switched the wipers on. The rain fell heavily now. He was parked outside the community centre. He'd eaten a sandwich and drunk some tea. He wanted to be on his own, away from the commotion of the incident room.

Graveney said, "That's not a good reason. So what's this about?"

"You think it's about anything, Allan?"

"It's always about something."

"We've got a mess here."

"These murders?"

"These murders."

Graveney grunted. "You think it's anything to do with me, you're wrong."

"I don't think that, pal. You heard anything?"

"I don't hear anything about Barrowmore these days, Wilks. I'm well away from that shit-hole. Bad memories."

Wilks paused before saying, "I never offered you my condolences for the loss of your brother."

"I never expected you to."

"I should've sent flowers or something. He was my snitch. He was my boy."

Wilks could sense Graveney bristling on the other end of the line. To describe someone like Tony Graveney as "my boy" was disrespectful. And disrespectful got you killed in Graveney country. It got you killed if you weren't Don Wilks.

Before his death on July 26, 1996, Tony Graveney and his brother were in a cold war with Roy Hanbury for possession of the streets.

Tony was found bludgeoned to death on waste ground. His face was pulped. His skull shattered. No arrests were made, mainly because the prime suspect did a runner a few hours after the body was found.

But that prime suspect was back.

Sounding tired of their brief conversation, Allan Graveney said, "If you're only ringing up for a chat, I could do without it. I'm legit these days, you know. I got a few arcades going and run a cab firm."

"That's what you were doing thirty years ago, Allan."

Graveney sighed. "Yeah, but I'm as white as a virgin's knickers these days, I'm telling you. I don't need Old Bill phoning me or coming round – it's bad for business."

"You won't hear from me again, Allan. Ever. Whether you're straight or bent, whatever you do, you'll never hear from me or any other filth. You hear me?"

"Yeah… yeah, I heard you. What's going on?"

"I just got some news for you, that's all. Just thought you'd be interested."

Wilks told him.

* * * *

Job done, thought Wilks, putting his phone away. He poured another coffee laced with scotch from his flask.

He watched uniformed officers talking to residents. Door-to-door continued. It would continue till every flat, every house had been ticked off the list. They were already having to make a third or fourth visit to some properties because no one had been home earlier.

They probably were at home, thought Wilks, *and just couldn't be bothered answering the door to cops.*

It was true they were getting a mixed response. But that wasn't surprising. Everyone wanted the killer caught, but they weren't sure if they wanted the cops to do the catching.

And talking to the Old Bill was a no-no in places like this.

Wilks's eyes scanned the parking ground.

Scum everywhere, he thought.

It was time he took control.

It was time *real* fear came back to haunt Barrowmore.

It was time the law grabbed this place by the balls and crushed the life out of it.

CHAPTER 48.
FEAR AND INTIMIDATION.

HALLAM was furious. He trudged the tower blocks, plotting revenge and planning murder.

Charlie Faultless's murder.

Faultless had stolen the briefcase.

Faultless had embarrassed him in front of Tash.

He'd kicked Hallam out of her flat.

I found the case, he thought. *It's mine… it's mine, and so is she.*

If he'd had the chance, he would have had her. He would have talked to her and persuaded her. And if she hadn't listened, he would have *made* her listen. But only if Charlie Faultless weren't there. But he was.

"Bastard," mumbled Hallam as he moped through Bradford House. The Sharpleys had lived here. Spencer Drake had lived here. Jason Joseph Thomas had lived here. Hallam would find secrets here. He would find things to show Tash, things to tell her. Stuff that would make her worship him. Stuff that would make her go on her knees for him. And if she didn't…

That bastard Charlie Faultless, he thought. *He spoiled everything.*

Hallam wished he were hard, tough, and fearless.

He wasn't. He was a coward and a softy, scared of his own shadow and terrified of other people's.

He walked up to the tenth floor of Bradford House. The lift was out. It always was in this tower block – it was the worst of the four high rises.

Good people lived here. They lived everywhere. But the bad overwhelmed them.

Fear and intimidation ruled the streets.

You only needed a few, and the many would cower.

They're cowards, too, thought Hallam. *The good are always cowards.*

He plodded up the stairwell. It stank of piss. The Bradford House Crew moniker had been sprayed on the wall – BHC. They were a local crew. One of many. Mobs ruled the four tower blocks. Sometimes they fought each other, but mostly they were aligned under the Barrowmore banner to battle gangs from other estates. The majority were just kids with nothing better to do. Truants with no prospect of a job. Children whose parents had abandoned them to the streets. The gangs gave them a family. Gave them security.

Fear and intimidation, thought Hallam. They were everywhere – even among those who spread them.

Some senior members of the crews worked for local gangsters. Tash's dad used to control the mobs on the estate before he went to prison and found God. He had dozens of thugs on his books.

Charlie Faultless among them.

Hallam's hate for Faultless grew as he reached the tenth floor. He peeked around the corner to make sure the police weren't loitering. They were everywhere now. You couldn't stop and look over at a bunch of girls without some PC poking his nose in and saying, "Can I help you, mate?"

Hallam edged along the walkway. He felt shivery. His nerves jangled. Fear made him feel sick.

No one had seen Spencer Drake since the murders. The police had been round to his flat a few times. They'd hammered on the door and shouted through the letter box.

"You sure he lives here?" Hallam had heard one cop say to another after he followed them up the previous day.

The second cop said, "They say he squats here, that's all."

The police would probably knock once or twice more. Then they'd smash the door down. They were already priming their battering ram. They liked smashing down doors. It happened quite often on Barrowmore. Hallam's next door neighbour suffered an early-morning raid a few months before. The 6.00am wake-up call had been very effective. It got the whole eighth floor out of bed. They battered their way in, shouting and trampling over everything. They dragged the bloke out. They tossed him on the ground. They let an Alsatian growl and slobber six inches from his face. The fellow was a drug dealer. But they could have knocked.

Hallam knew he had to be quick, or they'd ram their way into Spencer's hovel.

He knew if he could get into his flat, have a poke around, he would be able to go back to Faultless and Tash and claim some knowledge.

The door was padlocked and caged. A strange smell came from inside the flat. Something wet drizzled from beneath the door. It looked like black water.

Hallam cringed. He wanted to go home and hide. But his desire to prove himself was overwhelming. He wanted to impress Tash, to make her want him.

Every morning he was round at her flat, saying hello and asking if she wanted anything.

Every morning she wanted nothing.

One day, he thought, *one day.*

He was thinking about the hole he wanted drill in his floor so he could watch Tash and Jasmine. His mind whirled. Images cascaded through his brain. He stared at the caged door and thought of caged women and children – a caged woman and a caged child.

Tash and Jasmine.

His slaves.

He groaned.

Something hissed. He thought it was the serpent in his soul, the evil that lived in him. The evil that made him do what he did and think what he thought.

But the noise didn't come from inside him. It came from the flat. And from beneath the door, a fog billowed out. It was thin and wispy and swirled around Hallam's legs. He stared at it and listened to its hiss. And behind the hiss, a word lurked.

A word he knew.

A name. His name.

And as the fog crept up his thighs and spooled around his groin, it called to him.

He answered.

CHAPTER 49.
ATTACKED.

FAULTLESS thought about Druitt's briefcase while he walked.

Hallam Buck claimed he'd found it at the murder scene. He'd hidden it before ringing the police.

Why had he done that?

According to what Tash said, Buck was besotted with her and might have taken the briefcase to impress her.

The opportunity to do that arose when Faultless approached him earlier that morning.

But was the briefcase authentic?

Faultless found that difficult to believe – a Jack the Ripper suspect's briefcase turns up at the scene of 21st century murder.

He thought, *Perhaps the case has been there since the 1880s.*

No, that was impossible. The lock-ups were only built in the 1950s. Before then, warehouses crowded the area. Warehouses and terraces fit for nothing but rats and cockroaches. Those old building had been flattened along with the rest of the slums. New homes had been built. And the lock-ups to go with them. Most of the garages were empty.

As a youth, Faultless had seen them used to stow class-A drugs, hide pinched motors, hoard stolen cash, and interrogate kidnapped grasses.

It was impossible that the briefcase had just been sitting there for more than a 120 years.

Faultless walked along a street of red-brick houses. Toys littered front gardens. Dogs barked. Music blared from an open window. Two men sat talking in a silver BMW up a side road. A wheelless red Toyota, with its engine on the pavement next to it, perched on piles of bricks.

The lock-ups lay up ahead. Trees draped over them, as if protecting the garages from prying eyes.

He stopped walking and looked around. The streets were pretty empty. A group of boys rode their bikes on a grassy slope. Two teenaged girls waited at a bus stop. The silver BMW appeared at the end of the junction and stopped. There was no traffic, so the driver could have pulled out. For some reason, he stayed where he was, the engine still running.

Faultless clocked the guy behind the wheel. Then he turned away and kept walking.

The driver's face stayed in his mind. He tried to place him. But then the scar under Hallam Buck's eye suddenly flashed up in his thoughts, and then the bearded old man came to his head.

I've seen these people before, he thought.

He heard the car scream up the road, and he turned to see it skid to a halt next to him.

Faultless cocked his head. He wasn't scared. He'd never been scared.

The passenger leapt out – a big black guy wielding a baseball bat.

Before he could defend himself, something hit Faultless on the back of the head.

Dazed, he staggered towards the black man who struck him across the face with his club.

196

CHAPTER 50.
GREAT-GRANDMOTHER
COOPER.

BET Cooper, eighty-six years old, her bones marrowed with hate and vitriol, said, "Did you bring that bastard with you?"

Tash's hackles rose.

Bet laughed, seeing Tash's discomfort. "She is a bastard, ain't she – born out of wedlock."

"Shut up, Bet," said Tash's dad. "We came here to talk nicely."

"Fuck you and nicely," said the old woman. "You put me in this home, Roy Hanbury. You ain't even family."

"Rose was my wife."

"Shut up," said the old woman. "Locked me up in here. I never put my mother in a home."

"No," said Tash, "you locked her in the bedroom and let her starve to death."

Bet's blue eyes flashed coldly. Tash stared into the old woman's hate-filled eyes.

Why was she so bitter, so twisted?

When Tash had brought Jasmine to meet her – "Say hello to your great-great-gran, Jasmine" – Bet Cooper had spat in the child's face.

"She's a cow, that's all," said Tash's dad at the time. "She's a hateful old woman. Has to have something to hate or she doesn't feel alive. When you and Jasmine visited, she hated single mums and their kids – bastards, as she calls them."

Tash glared at the old woman now and remembered her dad's words. "She stores up every hate she hates," he'd said, "and plucks them out now and again."

Just like now, calling Jasmine a bastard.

Tash bristled but controlled her fury.

"Let's all sit down and take it easy," said Roy, dressed in a blue shirt and a red tie.

Tash never saw him dressed up. He was always in his vest with his tattoos and his muscles on show. His hair was nicely brushed too, and his brown, leather shoes polished. Tash thought he looked like a grandfather, and she felt love for him in her heart.

She scanned the room where Bet Cooper vented her fury and spat out her hate.

It was decorated in floral wallpaper. Red carnations sat in a vase on a chest of drawers. The room smelled of soap and flowers.

There was a television set and a stereo, with CDs of Andrea Bocelli and Russell Watson piled on a table. A large window looked out on to a garden. Winter had stripped the trees of their leaves.

The residential home was in Bromley, Kent. Tash's father had been paying Bet's keep at the institution for fifteen years. In the past, he could afford it. Crime paid. But when he left prison, he gave most of his money to charity. He stored a pile of cash in a trust fund for Jasmine. And now Tash wondered how he funded Bet's stay in a floral-wallpapered room with a garden view.

"What do you want?" said the old woman. "I ain't got no money. And I don't know where the treasure's buried, neither."

"Treasure?" said Tash.

"She's joking," said dad.

"I don't joke," the old woman said. "I take the piss, but I don't joke."

Someone knocked on the door and entered without being invited. It was a care assistant. She said, "Good morning, good morning. How are we today, Mrs Cooper?"

Bet looked away and mumbled something that Tash couldn't hear.

The care assistant was a heavy girl with black hair and an emerald stud in her nose. She wore a blue, nylon tunic and black trousers that were too tight around her hips. On the coffee table, she placed a tray containing three cups, a silver pot, and a plate of biscuits.

"I'm Simone," said the girl, "and if you want anything, just ring the bell, there." She pointed to a switch near the door marked BELL in biro.

After Simone left, Tash's dad went on. "Bet, you got to tell us about your grandad."

The old woman's eyes narrowed. "Why?"

"Because," said Tash, "me and Jasmine, we've started dreaming things."

Bet blinked.

"It's all nonsense," she said.

"You saw things," said Tash's dad. "Rose told me. She saw things too. And her mum."

Bet grimaced.

Tash's dad said, "This is important, Bet. You're a grumpy old cow; you've always been one. But something's up on Barrowmore."

"There's always something up on Barrowmore," said Bet.

"You can see," said Tash. "I can see, and my daughter can see. What are we?"

199

Bet said nothing.

"You know what I dreamed?" said Tash.

The old women stayed quiet.

After a moment Tash said, "I dreamed something to do with Jack the Ripper."

Bet looked her in the eye.

"What do you know about Jack the Ripper?" asked Tash.

"You want to know what I know?" said the old woman. "I know too much, darlin'. We all do. We're cursed – me, you, your kid, my mum. My girl, too. My Grace. You know what it's like to know your child's going to die? You know what it's like to see it's going to happen and you can't do nothing about it?"

CHAPTER 51.
DEADLY VISIONS.

"WHAT you seen, girl, what you seen?" said Bet, shaking her daughter by her shoulders. "Tell me what you seen."

Grace yanked herself free and said, "Nothing, Mum, leave me alone."

The girl, nearly fourteen now, threw herself on the bed.

Bet said, "What did you see?"

"I saw nothing."

"You dreamed something… or you had a vision."

"Mum, don't… " Grace curled up on the bed. She sucked her thumb and shut her eyes.

Bet watched her daughter with horror. She knew what the girl had seen. She'd seen it herself.

"You dreamt Derek, didn't you darlin'?"

"Mum… "

"You dreamt your dad."

"Oh God, Mum… "

Bet seethed. She cursed her gift. She damned her family. For so long she had rejected her visions. But they kept coming, flooding her brain and sending waves of panic surging through her. She only saw the bad, only saw death.

The death of her daughter.

Her heart raced. Cold sweat soaked her back. She grabbed her daughter and shook her again. Anger pulsed through Bet, and she couldn't contain herself. She slapped Grace across the face.

"It's your own fault, you little tart, your own fault."

The girl screamed. Bet threw her back on the bed and wheeled away. She put her fist in her mouth and bit down to stop the tears. But they came. Her body trembled with grief, with jealousy, with shame.

Behind her on the bed, Grace whimpered.

When Derek came back in '53 and said, "This time it's for keeps, darlin'," Bet thought everything would finally be all right. He'd been back and forth over the years, showering her with those promises he made, promises that were never fulfilled.

"This time, darlin'," he'd said, standing on the doorstep, the rain pelting down. "This time it's for keeps. I'm done with running around. I'm on the straight and narrow from now on, and I'll make an honest woman of you. Country's got a queen, now I want mine. And I'll be a dad to that sprog of ours."

Remembering his words made the tears come harder, made her shake even more.

I'll be a dad to that sprog of ours.

But he'd done more than that.

During that time, Grace had grown. From ten to thirteen, she changed, showing the first glimpses of what she would look like as a woman. Men stared and saw that too. Some wanted to taste it early. And Derek Cooper was one of them.

"I don't feel much like her dad," he'd told Bet one morning. At the time, Bet thought little of it. But a few months later she realized how significant his words had been.

Nearing her fourteenth birthday, Grace became pregnant. And when Bet found out, Derek once again vanished.

Then, the visions started to seep into her brain. They disturbed her when she was asleep and when she was awake. They came in nightly dreams and daily hallucinations. The made her faint in the street, the blinding white pain in her head overwhelming. They drenched her in sweat and gave her stomach cramps. They made her sick with fear. They were terrifying. They showed a terrible future – they showed Grace's death in childbirth.

And now, the girl was having them too.

Grace dreamt her own destruction. And the worst thing was, she knew her dreams were real. She knew she had a gift, because her grandmother had told her. If Grace had thought they were merely dreams, it would've been bearable. It would have been horrible to think of her daughter suffering nightmares. But that was all they would have been – nightmares. But Grace's visions were more than that. They were real. Just like Bet's. Just like Bet's mother. And just like her grandfather, Jonas.

Now Grace said, "I'm not going to die, am I, Mum?"

Bet bit her lips. She said nothing.

"Mum, please say I'm not going to die. Please promise me I'll be all right. Please say my baby will be all right."

Bet stayed quiet. Hot tears ran down her cheeks. Cold sweat ran down her neck.

Grace sat up and her face twisted with dread, and she screamed, "Tell me I'm not going to die, Mum, tell me."

CHAPTER 52.
THE SUITCASE.

BROMLEY, KENT – 3.41PM, FEBRUARY 27, 2011

"AND I never did tell her," said Bet. "It would've been a lie."

"A lie that would have given her some comfort," said Tash. She was crying and looked at her father. "Did you know this?"

He shook his head, his face pale.

"You let her die," said Tash.

"I never let her die, stupid girl," said Bet. "And lots of women died in childbirth back then. She was young, remember. Her body not ready for it. And it was destiny. It was written."

"Written where?"

"Wherever our futures are written, I don't know," cried the old woman. "You don't believe this stuff. I can tell."

Tash glared at her, her mouth open.

Bet went on. "Well I didn't, neither. I hated it. It was all crap. My grandad, he made a few bob out of it. Seances. Psychic readings. But by the time the war came along, no one was interested. Everyone busy surviving. I tell you, if I thought it would've made me rich, I'd have been on that stage or in some posh cow's sitting room, spouting bullshit about those who'd passed over."

They lapsed into silence.

Then Tash asked, "Could my mother see?"

"'Course she could," said Bet. "We all bloody can. It's a curse."

Tash thought about her mum, her birth so deadly. Rose coming into the world had caused her own mother to die. Her conception came about because Grace was raped by her own father.

Tash shuddered. Her skin crawled.

My great-grandfather's my grandfather, she thought.

"Where did he go?" she said.

"Who?" said Bet.

"Him. Derek."

Bet shook her head. "Never saw him again. Happy not to."

"He should pay for what he did." Tash looked at her dad. "Don't you think?"

He said, "There's always judgment. Maybe not here. Maybe in the afterlife. But there's always a judgment. He'll pay, darlin'. He'll pay."

Tash's eyes dropped to the coffee table. The biscuits were untouched. Seeing the food made her tummy rumble. But she would bear the hunger. It was nothing compared to Grace's agony.

"We have to go," she said. "I have to pick up Jasmine." She rose and looked at Bet, sitting in her armchair. For the first time since they'd arrived, the old woman looked her age. She looked fragile. She looked near death. Maybe she was ready for it. Maybe she'd wanted to reveal this terrible secret, a confession before her passing. Tash told her, "Thank you," but there was very little warmth in the gratitude.

Tash's dad matter-of-factly kissed Bet on the cheek.

He came to Tash, waiting by the door. Bet stared out of the window.

Her dad told Tash, "Come on, let's leave her to it."

They turned to leave.

"Hang on a minute," said Bet.

Facing her again, Tash saw the old woman lift herself out of the chair and toddle over to a large, white wardrobe. She opened its door said, "Come over here and help me, for Christ's sake."

When Tash went over, Bet pointed to the bottom of the wardrobe.

"In there, underneath those shoeboxes," she said.

"What am I looking for?" Tash squatted and reached into the wardrobe. It smelled musty. The odour of mothballs.

"Shift a few of those boxes; you'll see it."

Tash obeyed, piling the shoeboxes to the side. She saw something and took it out, laying it on the carpet. It was a red suitcase. It looked ancient. Rust covered the hinges. The casing was split and torn. One of the clasps was missing.

"It was my grandad's," said Bet. "I got no need for it. Nor the terrible old things inside it, neither."

CHAPTER 53.
BIRTHDAY PRESENT.

ALLAN Graveney had reason to celebrate. Not only was it his forty-third birthday, and to mark the event he was getting his forty-third tattoo, it would also be the occasion of Charlie Faultless's death.

"The spineless, gutless, attack-from-behind, murdering bastard," he'd said an hour earlier when his son, Ryan, called him to say they had Faultless.

Graveney was sitting in the tattoo parlour. His skin burned with fresh ink, which had been drawn in the shape of Death. The cowled, sickle-wielding figure reached from Graveney's belly button to his solar plexus.

He had planned to have an angel done. He already had one – a golden-haired figure with a halo, its wings spread as if ready to fly. Graveney was also adorned in scarier images. On his back, a samurai warrior brandished an uchigatana sword. Across his upper chest, a dragon breathed fire over his shoulder. Down his thigh, a snake coiled, its tail wrapped tightly around Graveney's knee.

The snake had been his first. He was fifteen. During that same year, he was tattooed another fourteen times. His elder brother, Tony, rest his soul, had said, "Now you got one for every year you been on this earth, kid."

And that triggered the idea – he'd get one every birthday from then on.

When Tony was murdered, he had a portrait of him inked right over where his heart beat with fury. Beneath Tony's image, the words *RIP, My Big Brother, Tony, 24.4.66-26.7.96* were written.

Finally, he would be avenged.

I'm going to slit you open and send you to hell where you belong, Faultless, he thought.

At the time of Tony's murder, a war had threatened to break out on Barrowmore. Faultless was one of Hanbury's pit bulls. He was a name in the gangster's organization. Despite being a teenager, Faultless was highly regarded by the big guns. He planned heists. He dealt drugs. He ordered beatings.

And he dished them out. Plenty. Charlie Faultless was a hard case.

But Hanbury and the Graveneys had a pact. Trouble always simmered, but Allan and Tony's dad, Arthur Graveney, had made peace with Roy Hanbury in the 1970s. And that peace held – until Faultless murdered Tony.

Charlie blamed Graveney for his mother's murder. Pat Faultless had been butchered by the killer the newspapers called the New Ripper. At the time, she was seeing Tony off and on. Faultless hated that, but there was nothing he could do. The pact was in place. No cross-border raids. No hit-and-runs against Graveney's men. Sleeping with the enemy was approved from on high.

"Old Roy's told him there ain't nothing he can do," Tony once told his brother. "I'm screwing the little bastard's mother, and that's all there is to it."

Hours before she died, Patricia rowed with Tony. It was a public spat. They swore and fought in the pub. She smashed a bottle over his head. He smacked her, slicing open her lip. She stormed out of the pub. Later that evening, she died. Her killer cut her throat, ear to ear. Then he sliced her open and scooped out her guts. He cut her breasts off and took her kidney as a souvenir.

Faultless went ballistic. He nailed Tony. The cold war became hot.

Arthur Graveney told Roy Hanbury, "I want the little fucker's balls on my breakfast table."

Roy Hanbury said, "His balls, your arse, Artie."

"He's broken the code," Graveney's father had said.

"And he'll pay for that."

"Blood for blood, Roy."

"You've got to give the kid a break. He's lost his mother, and Tony smacked her, Artie."

"Yeah, but he didn't kill her."

Allan had been there, watching the two bulls going head to head. You never messed with Hanbury, but that day Dad was close to going bare-knuckle with him. He wanted blood. Charlie Faultless's blood.

"I'll give you something else," Roy Hanbury had said.

In business terms, it was a good deal. Hanbury handed over his cannabis trade. It was big money, and it came with Dutch contacts and street dealers. It came with Charlie Faultless's exile.

At the time, Allan urged his father to reject the deal. His blood was up. He wanted revenge for his brother.

But Arthur Graveney saw the commercial value in accepting Hanbury's terms.

Faultless disappeared. The Graveneys made money. Hanbury went to prison. But still, the rage burned in Allan's heart. And when his old man died in 2004, he pledged to break the pact made with Hanbury if he ever got the chance. He pledged to kill Charlie Faultless.

He was about to fulfil that pledge.

On his phone, he dialled Ryan.

His son answered.

Allan said, "What state's he in?"

"A fucking state, Dad," said Ryan.

"Good, I'll be there in ten."

CHAPTER 54.
EVIL PLACES.

HALLAM sat on the mattress in Spencer's squat. He looked around. The place was worse than his flat. At least he had furniture. And dishes and cutlery. Spencer seemed to eat mostly out of pizza boxes. They were scattered around, bits of food going green in some of them. One thing Spencer had that Hallam coveted was the TV. It was huge. Hallam's was an old-fashioned one with a tube. It was a big, lumpy thing. Not lean and cool like these flat screens everyone had these days.

His eyes went round the flat, and they rested again on the one thing Hallam was glad he'd never had in his flat.

A policeman crucified on the wall. That was definitely something to avoid.

Hallam stared at the officer. He wondered if he were dead. But then the man spluttered, and blood dribbled from his mouth. He groaned and trembled.

Seeing him nailed to the wall reminded Hallam of Paul Sharpley hanging on the door of the garage as it swung open.

The difference was that Paul Sharpley was dead.

Lucky him, thought Hallam. *I'd rather be dead than alive if someone nailed my hands and feet to a wall.*

Looking at the dying policeman made Hallam excited. He should've been scared. He should've run away the moment the door opened and the fog surrounded him and the voice called him inside. He should've known that the evil in Spencer's flat would possess him.

But it was what Hallam wanted.

He wanted to serve. He wanted to belong. He wanted to see things like the crucified cop. He wanted to be part of the culture that fashioned such horrors.

He'd been nothing all his life. An outsider. A joke. Someone to laugh at. But he knew deep in his sick, dark soul that he surely belonged somewhere. Others must have felt what he felt. He wasn't alone in the grim and cruel world. And when the fog slithered all over him, crawling inside his clothes and chilling his flesh, he knew that finally he was close to home.

Spencer, his face white with fear, his whole body shaking, had said, "If it was anything to do with me, there's no way you'd be here, Hallam. You're a pervert, and everybody knows it. But it ain't got nothing to do with me, so you're here, and that's that."

"W-where is he?" Hallam had said, knowing there was another presence here – something cold and sickly and dangerous, something like decay.

Spencer had shaken his head. "He comes and he goes. I got no clue. All I know is I'm shitting myself most of the time, and that's the truth. I don't know nothing else 'cept I'm scared."

Hallam had asked what happened in the lockup. "Was it him?"

Spencer had explained. He'd told Hallam about the places Jack had taken him. "I thought I knew every inch of Barrowmore, but there's places I'm glad I didn't know. Places I can never go again, man. Actually, I don't think no human can go there. Not unless they're cursed or something."

"What kind of places?"

"Places full of bones. You can hear people – or maybe they're not people – but you can hear screaming. Far off. Way away. Places that smell like death. Makes you sick and weak. Makes you feel like you're dirty all over and you'll never wash it off. These places are near here, Hallam. Like, round corners I recognize. Down passageways I've pissed in. Behind walls where I've smoked dope. They're there. They're here. All around us. Dark, dark places. Evil places. Fucking lost places."

Hallam had said, "You know the police are looking for you?"

Spencer nodded.

Hallam said, "And they'll be smashing down your door very soon."

Spencer nodded again.

"What will you do?" Hallam had asked.

"I don't decide anymore – Jack does. I got to go lie down, Hallam. You wait here. He wants you."

"He wants me?"

"He wants you."

And Spencer had gone through a door, shutting it, leaving Hallam in the living room with his heart leaping.

He wants you.

I'm wanted, thought Hallam. *I'm wanted.*

Now, sitting on the mattress, waiting, he wondered why this Jack wanted him.

Suddenly the room darkened. It grew colder. The sheet draped over the window flapped.

Hallam's mouth and throat dried out, as if all the moisture had been sucked from his body.

A dark shape swept across the room – a shadow or a cloud.

Hallam curled up into a ball. His bones clattered. His nerves frayed. His excitement grew.

As if out of thin air, the figure stepped forward and stood in front of him.

The man's cape flapped. Hallam was sure he could see anguished faces in the material, but it was probably his eyes playing tricks. He looked into the man's face. The skin was deathly pale. The eyes were coal-black. A tuft of hair sprouted from his chin. It looked like a goat's beard. The man smiled, and his thin, red lips parted.

He spoke, and his voice was like something very cold being injected directly into Hallam's veins.

"You want to be of service, don't you?"

Hallam trembled.

"I can tell. There's something in you, Hallam. Something foul. Something putrid."

For a second, Hallam thought he was being insulted.

But then the strange man said, "I mean that as a compliment. There are many bad men. Most men are bad in some way. Some are malicious. Wicked. Cruel. But not many have that beautiful, pure evil in them that I sense in you. It's very sad that you've not had the chance to properly share it with the world."

Hallam tried to speak. Tried to say "thank you" to his saviour. But no words came. Only a bubble of spit filling his mouth.

"But don't fret, Hallam. I'm here, now. Jack's here. And Jack will help you fulfil your potential. Stick with me, Hallam, and all your dreams will come true."

Hallam swooned.

"I'll do anything," he said.

"Yes, you will," said Jack.

"Anything at all."

"That's right."

"What do you want me to do?"

"I want you do what what you've always wanted to do."

Hallam gawped.

"I want you to kill a child."

CHAPTER 55.
SHOWREEL.

CANDICE said, "It's really evil that Italy's mum, like, died."

Jasmine hurried down the road. She wanted to be home. Her mum was back. She'd called and said, "Jasmine, where are you?" and Jasmine had lied and said, "I'm at Candice's" when she was actually hanging around with some friends, some of them smoking.

Mum had said, "Come home, wherever you are."

"I'm at Candice's."

"I don't care. Come home."

Mum knew she was lying. Mum always knew. But Jasmine knew things too. She knew that fear had laced her mother's voice when she'd spoken to her on the phone. And it was the same fear that had stalked Barrowmore since the murders.

Candice, walking alongside Jasmine, went on. "I mean I wished, like, she was dead, like. Not Italy's mum, like, but Italy, 'cause she's been getting off with Tyler, like, and I've been sick, Jasmine, really sick with it."

"You can't wish people dead, Candice."

"Why not, babe?"

"You can't."

"I'm cold. Can I get your top, babe? Till tomorrow."

Jasmine took off her hoodie. She had a thick jumper underneath that kept the cold at bay. As she handed over her hoodie, Candice, taking it, said, "You think it's Jack the Ripper?"

Jasmine furrowed her brow. "What?"

"Like, someone said they found his knife or something. Found Jack the Ripper's knife. They said, like, he was reincarnated or something. He's come back from the dead. I mean, he killed... I mean, he killed your auntie, yeah? He killed her ages ago."

Jasmine shivered. She felt cold all over. She quickened her pace. Her head filled with pictures, and she tried to shut them out, but they had stained her mind. They made her sick. They made her scared. They made her cry but now she kept the tears at bay, biting her lip.

"Why are you walking so fast, man?" said Candice.

Jasmine nearly said, *Because I'm trying to get away from the pictures in my head of someone cutting my aunt open and pulling out her guts.*

But she said nothing. She held her breath. The images reeled, like a film. It was worse than *Saw* and worse than *Hostel*. Jasmine had seen both those films at Candice's place. Candice's big brother had them on DVD. They were horrible films, but the showreel in her head right now made those movies seem like Disney.

"Are you coming to tae kwon do tonight?" said Candice. "'Cause I don't think Tyler's going, like, as he's distressed about Italy's mum, so I don't think I'll go neither, and maybe I'll go round to Tyler's, see if he's okay. You think I should do that?"

"I've got to go, Candice," said Jasmine, wanting to run.

The pictures in her head were clearer than they'd ever been. She'd always seen them, mostly as if through gauze. But in the past few days, it was like normal TV suddenly becoming HDTV. And even 3D TV. Everything became clearer. The blood was redder. The guts were wetter. The knife was sharper. The screams were louder. And Aunt Rachel was screaming Jasmine's name, begging her niece, who was unborn when she was murdered, to save her from the Ripper.

She left Candice gawping near the stairwell on Monsell House and raced up the high rise. She was in a panic, the pictures in her head just not fading. And as she ran along the walkway towards her front door, she failed to see the man blocking her path until the very last moment.

And by then it was too late.

CHAPTER 56.
THE TASTE OF POWER.

HALF an hour after she'd been snatched, she was dead. Assaulted first, then strangled.

After doing what he did, Hallam left her body on the stairwell of the seventh storey, the floor where she'd lived. Before leaving her, he'd poured a can of red emulsion paint over the body in an attempt to destroy any forensic evidence. It looked bizarre, twisted and dead, soaked in paint that drizzled down the stairs. Hallam's instinct would have been to hide the corpse. But Jack said, "Leave it somewhere for the world to find. Killing's no good if no one knows about it. It's the fear that spreads after a murder that's the real gift, not the murder itself."

Hallam would probably disagree. The murder had been a great relief to him. And the assault before it. The desires he unleashed on the girl had been simmering in him since adolescence. Now, scuttling away from the scene, he was coated in sweat and shuddering with excitement.

So this was what killing was like. This was what power tasted of. He liked it. He liked it a lot. He felt fulfilled at last. After an age of being nothing, nobody, now he was something, someone.

He hurried back to his flat, clutching to his chest what he'd taken from the girl.

"Bring a gift," Jack had told him. "Something warm."

Reaching his door, his heart thumping, he began to understand what Jack had meant when he said the dread caused by a killing was the true prize.

The girl's murder would send shockwaves through Barrowmore. In many ways it was worse than the slaughter in the lock-up and the throwing to her death of Terri Slater. It was worse because the victim was a child. Eleven or twelve. The tragedy would result in more outrage and horror. It would send parents into a frenzy.

He entered his flat, but before shutting the door, he peeked out at Barrowmore.

Hallam could already sense the alarm leaching through the streets.

Fifteen minutes later, he lay in the bath. The radio was on, but his focus was elsewhere. He was replaying the attack while lathering soap on his fat belly.

It had been the first time Hallam had attacked a child since he attempted to kidnap Tash Hanbury nearly twenty years before.

That attempt failed.

He had her all lined up. He had his hood up over his head. Dark glasses hid his eyes. His fingers flexed inside his leather gloves. He was ready.

She was walking home from the youth club. It was 9.00pm. She was ten and alone. But Tash was Roy Hanbury's daughter. No one would dare touch her. No one except for a desperate, dangerous pervert whose desires outweighed his personal safety.

She was so pretty. He'd rough her during the assault, and then he'd strangle her.

He'd grabbed her from behind, lifting her off her feet, one hand clamped over her mouth. The plan was to drag her into the alley and punch her lights out and then do what he needed to do.

But as he was dragging her into the darkness, someone attacked him. Threw punches at him and cursed him, calling him a "fucking pervert" and saying, "I'm going to cut off your balls and make you eat them."

Hallam had to let Tash go, and he reeled, trying to get away from the assault. He remembered being scared. He hated being hurt. So many bullies at school had wounded him, and pain was terrifying.

He whimpered and begged as his attacker pummelled him. A fist caught him under the eye. He felt a sharp pain. He'd been cut. Blood ran down his cheeks. He cried out, and an adrenaline surge gave him a bit of extra strength. He got loose and spun away from the pasting, and his assailant lost his balance because he was so angry.

As he ran away, Hallam looked over his shoulder.

He saw a youth bend over Tash and help her to her feet. The boy was about fourteen or fifteen. When he looked up, Hallam had a good look at his face, which made him turn away and quicken his pace. The youth's face imprinted itself on Hallam's mind. And in the next few months and years he saw it many more times. During those times he witnessed what the youth was capable of doing. It made him glad that he ran away. It made him glad that Charlie Faultless never laid into him properly.

Now, twenty years on, full circle from the attempted attack on Tash Hanbury, Hallam blew air out his cheeks.

The bathwater cooled. The next door neighbour played hip-hop loudly. The radio reported financial collapse.

Hallam shut his eyes. For the first time in his life, he felt strong.

CHAPTER 57.
FIFTEEN YEARS OF HATE.

THE first thing he remembered was the glare of a powerful light forcing him to squint.

The second thing he remembered was the pain – from the pulsing ache in his skull to the searing fire in his chest, shoulders, and arms.

His eyes were shut, and the light made him shut them tighter.

He thought, *I'm dead and I'm going towards the light.*

He kept his eyes closed. Opening them and seeing where he was headed scared him. And scared was something he rarely felt.

But he wanted to look. He opened his eyes. They were sticky, and he had to blink away the sleep. He squinted, the big white light right in his face.

Am I here? he thought. *Is this it?*

"Here he is, the bastard," said a voice. "Waking up, more's the pity. You should've stayed sleeping, Faultless."

Faultless? He wondered. *Who's –*

And then he came fully awake, shaking his head. It was like birth – a violent, rapid, agonizing casting out. He jerked, his body stiffening. He gasped, the pain levels increasing.

"Take that away for now, Ryan," said another voice, deeper, made craggy by cigarettes.

The light angled away from his eyes, and he saw where he was. A low-ceilinged room. No windows. Damp drizzling down the walls. A single light bulb meshed in wire. The floor was wooden. It creaked as people trod on it.

His sense of smell reactivated, and his nose filled with the musty odour of somewhere old, somewhere without light and air. The reek of tobacco also saturated the atmosphere.

Then he became aware of his condition. He looked up. Two chains hung from two rusty rings pinned into the ceiling. Faultless's wrists were cuffed to the chains. He'd been stripped to his boxer shorts. Sweat and blood soaked his torso. The pain in his shoulders was volcanic. He gritted his teeth and groaned.

And then he clocked his captors.

Three of them. Two he recognized from the car. A young bloke, early twenties. Short in stature, but built hard and mean. He moved a video camera and tripod across the room. The light from the camera, which had moments ago blinded Faultless, now showed him more of his prison.

Four wooden steps led up to up a door. It was barred and padlocked. No way out.

The second guy was the black. The one who'd smashed him across the head with the baseball bat. He brandished it now, letting it swing menacingly next to his leg.

The third man came into view, moving into Faultless's eye line.

It took a few seconds, but the years peeled away from the man's face.

"Graveney," said Faultless.

"You fucking, murdering bastard," said Graveney. "You've made a big mistake coming back. You should've stayed exiled, son."

"I was missing your friendly face, Allan. Just had to come home."

222

Graveney smiled, but only his mouth moved. His eyes remained cold and steady.

"That's nice," he said. "Since you missed it so much, it can be the last face you see."

Graveney clutched Faultless's jaws and squeezed. Rage twisted his face. Spit came from between his gritted teeth. He went dark red.

He said, "My hate for you has been brewing fifteen years, Faultless. You made a bad mistake killing my brother. You know there was a truce. But you made an even worse mistake killing him, because he was innocent."

He snapped his hand away.

Faultless flexed his jaw. It hurt, but he just added the pain to the already-mounting agony he was feeling.

He said, "I never put Tony down as an innocent, myself."

Graveney shuddered with wrath. He punched Faultless in the ribs. The air was knocked out of him. Pins and needles surged up his flank. He felt his left side go dead, all the nerves in there locked up. Then the feeling in his body returned and revealed yet another new pain.

He coughed, every breath he took hurting his ribs.

"Before this is done, you'll beg for mercy," said Graveney. "And you'll say sorry a thousand times for killing my brother. You'll say sorry till you can't speak no more, Faultless. And you know what, son?"

"What, mate?"

"It'll make no difference, because you're going to die, and it's going to be long and very painful." Eyes fixed on Faultless, he gestured with his hand as if he were beckoning a dog.

The younger thug appeared again, carrying the camera and tripod.

Graveney said, "This is my youngest, Ryan."

"Lovely to meet you, junior," said Faultless.

"Shut up, bitch," said Ryan, drenching Faultless in spit.

"Set it up," Graveney told his son, and while the younger man fixed the tripod and adjusted the camera, his dad went on. "It's going to be recorded for posterity, your death, Faultless."

"Nice, make sure you send the royalties cheque to Roy Hanbury. He'll want to know what you've done."

"You think Hanbury scares me? Hanbury's gone good, Faultless. He's gone all decent, now. He ain't got evil in him no more."

"You'd be surprised."

"Shut it," said Graveney and then to Ryan, "Is it ready?"

The camera's light shone into Faultless's eyes again. He squinted and turned his head away.

Graveney said, "Buckley, fire it up."

Faultless looked at the big black guy as he crouched over a sports bag. He stood and turned, goggles resting on his forehead. He carried a handheld butane blowlamp.

Faultless grimaced. Fear wrenched his stomach.

Buckley grinned, and his white teeth stood out against his black face.

Graveney flicked a Zippo lighter and held it to the lamp, and a tongue of blue fire jutted from the torch.

Every muscle in Faultless's body tightened as Buckley moved towards him.

CHAPTER 58.
SINNER AND SAVED.

STANDING in the middle of Tash's living room, Don Wilks frowned. He held his shoulders back and his chest out, and his arms were folded.

Arrogant bastard, thought Hanbury.

Roy and his daughter were sitting. Tash was terrified. The last thing you need is a visit from the cops, especially one with a bad-news face on.

Tash clutched her chest. Hanbury put an arm around her shoulder. A big dad's arm that should have been a comfort to his daughter more often over the years.

The two decades since Rose died had been tough. After her death, Roy got more vicious; he got more violent.

Maybe if he'd caught the hit-and-run driver, the valve on his hate would have opened and extinguished the bad feelings.

But that never happened. He was left with hate in his heart and two young daughters to bring up. To Hanbury, rearing children was woman's work. Especially if they were girls. If he'd had a son, it would have been different. The boy would have been out with him. Learning the business. But girls had to be protected.

Although he neglected to spend a lot of time with them, they were given the best care. He showered them with gifts. He paid nannies and chaperones. He cushioned them from the evil he wreaked and the evil he faced. Or he tried to. All his power, all his influence, had failed to protect Rachel.

Grief and fury turned him psychotic.

But a year later he was arrested over a botched armed robbery. Two of his troops made a hash of a Post Office raid in Stepney. They traced the pair's getaway motorbike to Hanbury. The morons were supposed to have dumped the vehicle after a previous job.

You can't trust no one, he thought.

One of the robbers folded under Old Bill pressure. He spilled his guts. He'd have lost them if Hanbury had ever got hold of him. The guy's testimony put Roy behind bars for twelve years. Conspiracy charges. Not the first time he'd been inside, but it was the longest stretch. And it started badly. His anger grew daily. Fury towards the men who'd killed Rose and Rachel. He would take it out on his cell, punching the wall. He would take it out on fellow prisoners, time in the hole.

It would have continued, had it not been for Ernie Page.

Aged sixty-three, Page was a lifer. He'd been inside thirty years and was looking at another five before he was out.

"Not much point in them letting me go, to be honest with you," he once told Hanbury.

Page went down for murdering three people. Piled on top of those charges were indictments for armed robbery (two counts), assault (four counts), and handling stolen goods.

But something had happened to Ernie Page inside. He got saved. He found Jesus.

"It's a blanket, brother," he told Roy. "A shield. To be honest with you, I can't say if it's the truth or not. But some of it sounds good. And a fear of God, or whatever's up there in heaven, keeps us in check."

Over three weeks of talking, praying, and reading the Bible, Roy moved from sinner to saved.

He grasped what Ernie had told him – believing a higher power could stop you doing bad things. Just like he'd used fear to hold people to account, God did the same. He was the ultimate scare-story. There was nothing like the threat of hell to keep you on the straight and narrow.

A probabtion officer had once asked him, "Are you telling me, Roy, that if you didn't believe in God, you'd go back to being a criminal?"

"That's about right, I'm afraid," Hanbury said. "It's in my DNA. It's in my genes. It's who I am. Like the scorpion, you know?"

The probation officer shook his head.

Hanbury said, "The frog offers to take the scorpion across the river. 'Just don't sting me,' he says. 'No problem,' says the scorpion. But halfway across, the scorpion stings the frog. As they're both drowning, the frog goes, "'Why d'you do that?' The scorpion says, 'It's what I am, and I can't help it.' See? I can't help it neither."

"But you can now."

"Because I've got someone watching over me."

Now, with his arm around his daughter's shoulder, he looked another bad man in the eye. Another bad man who could have done with a dose of fear in his heart to have stopped him doing the things he had done.

Wilks, still standing there full of himself, finally said, "We believe that Charlie Faultless has been assaulted."

Tash leapt to her feet: "No!"

Wilks said, "We found his top. It was covered in blood. We wanted to speak to him in connection with the killings, but unfortunately, unless he turns up, we have to assume the worst. Or, of course" – Wilks grinned – "he's done a runner. Same as he did fifteen years ago."

"Charlie's not done a runner," said Tash.

Wilks said, "Has he not? You know where he is, Miss Hanbury?"

"Fuck off, Wilks," said Hanbury.

"Don't tell me to fuck off, old fella."

"I'll tell you whatever I please. Fuck off."

Wilks was about to say something else when his phone rang. He answered it by saying, "What?" loudly. But then his face paled. His mouth dropped open. He listened for twenty seconds. He put the phone down.

"Someone died?" said Hanbury.

"Yes, a kid," said Wilks.

Roy's blood froze.

CHAPTER 59.
BURNING FLESH.

THEY blowtorched him from his collar bone to the middle of his chest.

He smelled his flesh cooking.

The pain was appalling.

It felt as if his head was going to explode.

He was trembling, every muscle corded, every nerve wire-tight.

He clenched his teeth.

He thought his jaw would crack.

Sweat poured down his face.

His blood sizzled. His skin melted.

He screamed.

His heart seemed about to burst.

Buckley stepped away.

The pain stayed. He looked down at his wound. A strip of black-red flesh, smoke coming off it. The skin still frying, still hissing away in the heat.

"You ain't going to faint, are you?" said Graveney. "It ain't going to be fun if you pass out – like a girl."

"He ain't begged yet, Dad," said Ryan Graveney, loosening his grip on the rope tied around Faultless's legs to stop him from kicking.

"He will, son. When we do his face, maybe."

Faultless growled. Spit flew from his mouth. He was still shaking, his body in shock. His teeth chattered. But he managed to get words out. "… kill you," he snarled, "… 'ckin kill you… "

Graveney chuckled. His son smiled. Buckley stared. The big man was ready to go again – chomping at the bit to cook up some Charlie meat.

Graveney said, "Check the camera, Ryan. I don't want to miss any of this." The son went over to the tripod. The dad looked Faultless straight in the eye. "I never bothered to waste this amount of time on an enemy before. Bullet to the back of the head or a blade across the throat – it was enough. But the hate I have for you, I just got to unleash it, Faultless. You understand. You'd do the same thing."

Faultless snarled again. He was sick with pain. He wanted to vomit. He wished he would pass out. He took in Graveney's words and thought, *I'd do it to you, you bastard…*

His legs sagged beneath him now. His arms and shoulders took the weight of his body. They struggled with his 168 pounds.

His muscles were tearing. His ligaments were ripping. His nerves were fraying.

He was coming apart.

He was going to die without a fight – and that just wasn't the Charlie Faultless way.

"Come on, you fuck," he said, his voice a growl, "finish me off."

Graveney said, "Your finish is a long way off, Charlie."

He gestured with his head to Buckley and shifted out of the way.

The black man and his blowtorch moved in on Faultless. The blue flame lit up Buckley's eyes. They were bronze in colour. The pupils were large. They reflected the flaring tongue of the lamp.

Faultless's gaze skimmed quickly to Ryan. He was fidgeting with the camera. He'd forgotten his role – stop Faultless from thrashing about or kicking out while Buckley burned him.

Adrenalin coursed through Faultless, ramming his heart.

Buckley stepped forward.

Ryan played with the video camera, eye glued to the viewfinder.

Graveney rolled a cigarette.

Faultless brought both knees up sharply.

They smashed into Buckley's elbow. His arm jerked. The blowtorch snapped up into his face. The flame melted his eye and the flesh around it in a second. He screeched and spun away, dropping the lamp.

Graveney gawped at the writhing Buckley as he shrieked and cupped his dissolving flesh.

Ryan said, "Fucking hell."

Graveney lunged at Faultless, face knotted with rage.

Finding another dose of strength from somewhere, Charlie again lifted his legs and kicked out with both. They smashed into Graveney's chest and sent him sailing across the room. He tripped over Buckley and smashed into the stairs.

Ryan Graveney rushed forward and bent to pick up the blowtorch. Faultless hooked Ryan's neck inbetween his knees, and started to squeeze. He jerk his legs into his backside. Ryan's neck was trapped in a slowly tightening vice. The man tried to ease the pressure around his throat. Faultless strained. He shook with stress. His shoulders felt as if they would snap out of their sockets. His legs were filling with lactic acid, weakening.

But still he tightened his grip around Ryan's neck, and the man's face creased with pain. He was turning red, the red deepening with every second.

Faultless's knees viced around his throat.

Tighter and tighter.

Cutting off the air supply. Stemming the flow of blood to his brain.

Faultless quickly scoped the other two men. Buckley was on all fours, moaning and crying, his eye pulped. Graveney lay on his back, starting to move after being knocked out for a few seconds.

Ryan's tongue popped out of his mouth. His eyes snapped open. His face had gone purple. He sagged. Faultless gave him another squeeze, then loosened his grip. The man hit the ground, dead. Faultless gasped, his energy gone. He slumped, all his weight again on his shoulders and arms.

Graveney started to get his bearings.

Faultless had no plan now.

He looked down. The blowtorch's flame still burned. He kicked it, and it skidded along the floor. It struck Graveney flame-first in the arm. He shrieked, scrabbling away as the heat melted his skin. He leapt to his feet, crying out in agony, clutching his arm.

Buckley was screaming. He was calling for help. He was saying he couldn't see and that his face was on fire.

Graveney looked at Faultless. His hate had gone up a notch again.

"You're a fucking dead man," he said.

"Tell me something I don't know," growled Faultless.

Graveney staggered about and picked up the blowtorch. He came towards Faultless, who braced himself.

At least I've done some damage, he thought. *I've killed one of them, maimed the other two.*

He was ready to suffer. He was ready to die.

Bring it on, he told himself and then shouted, "Bring it on!"

With Graveney three steps away, Faultless noticed from the corner of his eye that the door at the top of the stairs was opening.

As Graveney yelled out and drove the blowtorch directly towards his face, Faultless saw a pale-faced figure clothed in fire rise up behind his attacker.

And everything became suddenly very hot, and the smell of sulphur laced the air.

PART FIVE.
LOST SOUL.

CHAPTER 60.
A GIFT, A CURSE.

HE came down among the people and brought something for them. A child wrapped in the wings of murdered angels. Their blood still stained the feathers. But he had no other swaddling for the child. And the baby cared nothing for flesh and blood. It was sleeping in the softness and the warmth of white feathers.

He came to a place where he could leave the child. Cradling the baby in his arms, he gazed around. He listened. Music boomed. Car horns blared. People shouted.

The middle of the night, he thought, *and this place is still alive.*

But behind the noises, he heard other sounds. Past voices calling out. Forgotten stories begging to be told. Old wounds opening up. Ancient hatreds rising again.

This place had a memory, and it was screaming to be heard.

He smelled the air, and all the earth's odours came to him – death, decay, blood, pain…

They filled him, and he loved them all, including the great evil that lay buried under the concrete, the steel, the asphalt, and the glass.

In fact, he adored that evil more than anything.

Thinking of it warmed him. It made him feel love.

But even love dies.

A father must sacrifice his son.

There has to be a judgment, in the end.

And that end was getting closer.

There had been too much savagery. The game was tedious by now. The rules had to be changed.

He looked at the baby and touched its lips. The infant snorted. It slept deeply, swathed in blood-soaked, heavenly feathers.

He walked towards the door of the flat and crouched. As he eased the baby on to the concrete, he said, "One day I'll be back for you, and then you'll be ready. I will come for you in your darkest place. I will salvage you and give you a chance to save yourself for I am the redeemer and the judge."

Gently, he removed the angel-skin wrapping from the child and left it naked on the doorstep. The cold made the baby writhe. It started to come awake. Already, its pink flesh took on a blue tint. The infant whimpered.

The one who had brought the child bundled up the angels' wings and tucked them under his arm.

He gazed at the wriggling baby and smiled.

The baby opened its eyes and started to cry, suffering in the low temperatures.

By then his deliverer was leaving and going further and further away. But however great the distance between them, he could still see into the baby's newly opened eyes, one brown, one blue, both staring up towards his departing father.

* * * *

Charlie Faultless came awake quickly. His eyes snapped open, and he sat up. He looked around, his gaze skimming the surroundings. He was lying on someone's doorstep, on cold, hard concrete. He was naked and shivering. He tried to remember how he'd gotten there, and at first thought he'd been out and got drunk. But then it all came back to him. And it made him want to scream.

CHAPTER 61.
HEARING THINGS, SEEING THINGS.

HER dreams were of fire. More fire. Just like before. Oceans of it. And a rainbow of colours. Flames of every hue. Among them, a blue tongue of fire brushed flesh. Human flesh. And the flesh melted, pink and red, running like wax. Bone showing and then bone charring. The blue flame liquefied the body and turned everything to ash.

Her eyes snapped open and she sat up in bed, panting.

Charlie, she thought. *Charlie Faultless, burned.*

Tears ran down her face. She whimpered and climbed out of bed. It was cold, and she shivered. Outside it was still dark, although light was just starting to seep into the night sky. She peeked through the curtain. Down in the quad, blue lights flared.

A blue tongue of it…

She flinched and moved away from the window. But she could still see the lights showing in the sky. Police cars filled the parking area. The whole place was lit up. Detectives and forensic officers had been trawling all night, looking for evidence. Two murders yesterday added to the terror leaching through Barrowmore and to the pressure mounting on the police.

She went back to bed and huddled under the covers. She was very scared and very confused.

She remembered her dream again.

Charlie Faultless, burned.

That's what it was telling her.

And it was true.

Someone knocked on her bedroom door, and it made her jump. Her mother's voice said, "Can I come in, darlin'?"

She said nothing.

"Darlin', please let me come in."

"Okay," she said.

She cried when her mum entered the room.

"It's all right, sweetheart," said Mum, hugging her.

She loved that feeling. Her mother's warmth, her softness. She felt safe in her mum's arms. At least she used to. Not so much any more. The world had become more dangerous in the past couple of days. And not even love could keep the peril at bay.

Mum stroked her hair and said, "Do you want to talk about what happened to Candice?"

Jasmine shook her head.

Mum said, "You can ask me whenever you feel like talking."

Jasmine nodded.

It had been a scary few hours. When Jasmine ran home after leaving Candice, she'd bumped into a man standing right outside her door. He was tall and large, and he had a mean face. He said he was Mr Wilks, a policeman, and he was here to see Jasmine's mum and grandad. Inside the house, Mum had told Jasmine to go to her room, but she listened through her door and heard Mr Wilks talk about Charlie Faultless. Hearing what he was saying made

240

Jasmine's nerves jangle. And when he said someone else had been murdered – "a kid" – she wanted to be sick.

She asked her mum now, "Why did... why did Candice get killed?"

"Darlin', there's a lot of bad men in the world. But there are more good people, you know. Sometimes bad things, horrible things, happen, but they don't happen a lot. I don't know why Candice got killed."

"Do you believe in God, mum?"

Her mum's eyes narrowed. She was thinking. Then she said, "I don't know, Jasmine."

"If God was real, why would he let Candice die? And Italy's mum, too."

"I don't know, darlin'. Sometimes things just happen."

"Mum... "

"Yes."

"I... I saw horrible things happen to Charlie."

She felt her mum shudder.

"Do you like him, Mum?"

"Of course. He was your Auntie Rachel's boyfriend. So he's almost like family."

"I saw him being burned."

"W-where did you see this, Jasmine?"

"In my head, Mum... you know."

"In your head."

"Yes, like the other dreams. Like... like the things I see that come true."

Her mum nodded.

"What did old Bet say?" said Jasmine. "Does she still want to spit at me?"

"No, no she doesn't. She's had a very difficult life. It makes her sad. It makes her do horrible things like she did to you when you saw her. She... she doesn't mean it."

"She shouldn't do it, then."

"No, she shouldn't."

"Does she dream too, Mum?"

"Yes, she dreams too."

"And she can see things that haven't happened?"

Mum nodded.

"Did… did your mum do it too?"

"I think she did."

Jasmine buried her face in her mum's chest. "Why are we different?" she said. "I don't want to be different."

CHAPTER 62.
LIKE THE FLAMES WERE HIS WINGS.

"I FOUND you in the early hours of this morning," said Roy Hanbury. "You were lying outside the front door without a stitch on – naked as the day you were born. You had your eyes wide open, looking up towards the sky – but you didn't seem to be seeing anything. You just had this blank look on your face."

Charlie Faultless stared at Christ above Hanbury's mantelpiece. The figure seemed serene in its suffering. But Faultless knew there was no tranquility in anguish. Only dread and terror. Only loneliness and hopelessness.

He looked at his shoulder and ran a finger from his collar bone down to the middle of his chest. He felt a burning pain as his finger traced a line down to his solar plexus.

But his skin was unmarked. No seared flesh. No charred bone. It was as if he'd been healed.

"I remember where I saw the old man," he said.

"You what?"

He told Hanbury what he was talking about.

"That fellow. Must've been a stranger. Told you, Charlie. He didn't ring no bells with me, and I know pretty much every – "

"I saw him in my dream," Faultless interrupted.

"Your dream? Not you as well. Does everyone have dreams and visions except for me? Do you believe all of this?"

Faultless stared at Christ.

"There's not a shred of evidence to back up claims made by psychics and mediums, and dream interpretation is bollocks," he said. "But I saw this guy when I arrived, and I've seen him before, Roy – in my past."

Hanbury shook his head. "I'm getting my snake." He went to the vivarium and opened the lid. He reached inside and gently lifted out the python, draping the serpent over his shoulders. The moment the animal rested on him, Hanbury appeared to relax.

"Did you see anyone?" asked Charlie.

"Told you – I opened the door, and there you were."

Faultless touched his chest again, where Buckley had blowtorched him.

Hanbury said, "Are you sure you're not high on something, and you dreamt – "

Faultless glared at Hanbury. "I didn't dream the pain, Roy. They picked me up, two of them in a black BMW. I woke up in a fucking cellar. Graveney was there. His son. And this Buckley arsehole with his blowtorch. I remember the pain."

"Well, if they scarred you, it cleared up pretty well. Perhaps God healed you, son. Though I don't know why. You ain't repented yet. Tell me again what you saw."

Faultless blew air out of his cheeks. "Graveney was coming towards me, and all of a sudden, this shape just appears behind the bastard. And it was him, Roy. The old fella. The one with the tuft on his chin. Leather waistcoat. Weird tattoos. He was there, and he was surrounded by fire. Like the flames were his wings. I felt the heat. The fire just swallowed Graveney up, and when it cleared, he weren't there no more. I just passed out, I guess. But I got this recollection of being wrapped up warm. It was all soft. Like feathers, you know? But real silky feathers. And there was blood on them, and the smell of meat too."

Hanbury shook his head and stroked his python.

"You don't believe me?" said Faultless.

"I don't know what to believe any more."

"You believe in God, mate."

"He's sound 'cause he's the Lord Jesus Christ, while you're an untrustworthy little shite."

"Cheers, Roy."

"Well, you're better than you were. Get on with your jackanory."

"I was being carried, like I say. Wrapped in these... feathers. Carried around by this old fella. His little beard. His eyes... black and cold, but they felt safe, you know. I shut my eyes, then I went to sleep. Next thing, I'm getting cold. I wake up, and the old fella's putting me down on cold, hard concrete. He's taking my feathers away, mate. And he's gone. Gone into the darkness. And I'm left there, hazy. I must've lost consciousness again. Next thing I remember is just now, waking up in there."

Faultless thought about things.

Then he asked, "Do you know who my dad was?"

Hanbury stared at him. "How the fuck should I know? I'm not Jeremy fucking Kyle with my DNA test, you know."

"You knew everything."

"Bollocks."

"Was it Tony Graveney?"

"What makes you think that?"

"He was messing about with my mum."

"Don't mean nothing. That was years after you was born, son."

"He wasn't coming back for more, then?"

Hanbury shook his head.

"Was it you, Roy?"

Hanbury's face darkened.

"I'm only asking."

"Don't ask fuckwit questions like that, Charlie."

"I want to know."

"Some things we're not meant to know, son."

"Not meant to know? Why aren't we meant to know them?"

"'Cause maybe they can kill us."

"What d'you mean?"

"I mean I'm not your bloody dad, and maybe you'll never find who it is, that's what I mean."

Faultless was quiet for a few seconds, thinking. Then he said, "Was Pat Faultless my mum?"

"You what?"

"You heard."

"Jesus, I don't know."

"I dreamt I was being laid at someone's door."

"You were – at mine, last night."

"But it's happened before. I know it has."

"How can you know, Charlie?"

Faultless gestured at Christ over the mantelpiece. "You know he's your saviour. And that's irrational."

"It fucking ain't."

"It fucking is. You can't prove it. You ain't got evidence."

"I got personal experience."

"Yeah, and every nut in the world's got personal experience of something Roy. Fucking alien abduction. UFOs. Ghosts. Everything's a personal experience."

"So what?"

"If yours is valid, why ain't theirs? Why ain't mine?"

The snake slithered down Hanbury's leg.

CHAPTER 63.
HOW WE HAVE ALL BEEN CURSED.

THEY would learn the truth together. Maybe then it would be easier to bear. Two are stronger than one. Mother and daughter are stronger than everything. That's what Tash told herself.

She laid the red suitcase given to her by Bet on the carpet. She sat on the floor and looked at Jasmine. "It's okay," she said.

"What's that?"

"Bet gave it to me."

"Is it hers?"

"It was her grandfather's first. And maybe his grandfather's, too."

Jasmine came closer.

Tash said, "It's all right."

Her daughter knelt.

Tash touched Jasmine's hair. It was warm and soft, and love came through it and rinsed into Tash's veins, flooding her heart. She nearly cried. It made her grieve that she might fail her child. That this place, this world, might take Jasmine away like it had taken Candice away from her mother, and Terri Slater from her children, and so many others from those who loved them. But love meant nothing. It was only a gesture. A scream drowned out by the storm of violence and hate engulfing them all.

"Okay," said Tash and opened the suitcase.

"It stinks," said Jasmine, crinkling her nose.

"That's just age."

What memories smell of, she thought.

"And look at those clothes," said Jasmine.

There was a Fez, a smoking jacket, and a scarlet necktie. They had holes in them. Moth-eaten.

A voice drifted through Tash's head like a ghost passing a window.

I am the moth eating at the law, it said, but she barely noticed it. Her head was full of voices, crammed with memories she had no idea she'd experienced. She took them for granted. Ignored them and let them flap around in her brain like litter on the breeze. They weren't doing any harm. They were just scraps. They meant nothing.

From the suitcase, she removed the items of clothing. They were dusty on her hands. She laid them gently on the carpet.

"Whose are they?" said Jasmine.

"I think they were your great-great-great-great grandfather's. His name was Jonas Troy. He was… I think he was like a magician. He could… "

"He could see things."

Tash looked at her daughter.

Jasmine gazed at the clothes and went on. "He dreamt things, like we do. He could tell the future." Her eyes lifted to Tash. "That's true, ain't it, Mum?"

Tash had no reason to ask her daughter how she knew. It was obvious. She nodded and said, "That's true." Everything was true. Every fear, every doubt, every uncertainty, every strange feeling

248

Tash had ever experienced was down to this. She felt weirdly calm with this new knowledge. As if it made her complete. The last piece of the jigsaw dropping into place, the picture it made now clear.

Beneath the clothing were piled newspaper cuttings, photographs, notes, and a journal. They were yellowed with age. Time had crumpled the paper.

Tash lifted the journal out of the case. It was fragile, and she thought the pages might disintegrate if she were not careful. She gingerly opened the diary to the first page. The lined paper was grey. The writing slanted to the right and was tiny, the ink smudges making it difficult to read. But the date at the top was written in capital letters.

AUGUST 31, 1888

And she could make out the first paragraph.

"As I feared, he has returned," it said. "Very early this morning, at around 4.00am near Bethnal Green, a cart driver discovered dear Mary Ann Nichols. The devil had nearly decapitated her. She had been cut open from beneath the ribs on the right side of her body, down under her pelvis and to the right of her stomach. How we have been cursed that we must be mutilated in this way. How he has been cursed that he must rip to seek out his sustenance. How we have all been cursed."

And then on one line, written in capital letters:

"DAMN HIM!"

She turned the pages and in the back of the journal discovered old, black-and-white photographs. She clutched her chest. They showed mutilated bodies. Jack the Ripper's victims. They showed where the women had died and what they looked like after death.

A chill ran down Tash's spine. Did she want to be seeing and reading these terrible things? She looked up. Jasmine was studying a letter. Panic gripped her, and she snatched the piece of paper from her daughter's hand.

"Mum, what are you doing?"

"You… you shouldn't be reading this. I'm sorry. I didn't know, I – "

"Mum. Mum. You know what we are?" Her voice was shaking. "It says in the letter. You know what me and you are, Mum?"

CHAPTER 64.
LOOKING FOR AN EXIT.

BY now Spencer was very scared. He was so scared he had to puke every few minutes. His nerves were shot, and his head was messed up.

Hallam Buck had killed a kid.

Jack just told him to, and he did it.

Killed a kid.

Just like he told Spencer to kill Jay-T.

But worse. Candice Daley was a twelve-year-old child. And Hallam had assaulted her and then strangled her.

I'm in over my head, thought Spencer. *Way over my head.*

He wanted a way out. But he guessed there wasn't one. Unless he topped himself or Jack finished him off. He swallowed. That option might not be pleasant. Dying, full-stop, would be unpleasant.

Hallam had only just come back. After killing the girl, he'd holed up in his flat. "I had to spend time getting used to what I did," he'd said, his eyes glittering.

Dirty, sick bastard, thought Spencer. Hallam Buck, child-killer and kiddie-fiddler, had been re-living what he'd done to Candice. *Dirty, sick bastard.*

Spencer sat against the wall of his flat. The place had gotten worse. The policeman had died overnight, and flies buzzed around his body. The squat had started to smell of shit and blood. It had grown darker there, too.

He knew they'd have to leave soon. There was no way the cops were going to hold off from smashing down his door. No way. It was hard to believe they hadn't done it already. He was certainly a suspect in the first four killings, including Jay-T's murder.

And he was missing.

First place they'd look would be where you lived. That made sense. Or it did to Spencer. Maybe the filth thought differently these days. Maybe they'd gone to the wrong address. To his mum's. To his auntie's place. His cousins or his mates.

This place wasn't really home. It was one of the places he crashed.

They stuck a lone copper outside the door, hoping he'd turn up, and he had – with something from hell behind him.

But they'd be round again, for sure. They'd smash the door down and ransack the place. Confiscate the TV and the PS3. All his games.

He looked over at Jack and Hallam.

Hallam had handed Jack a hoodie. Something he took off the girl. A gift.

At first, Jack was angry.

"I meant something from inside her, you insect," he raged. "Her heart. A lung. A kidney. Not this piece of – "

He had smelled the hoodie. And he still smelled it, rubbing it all over his face.

Finally he said, "Seer." He pressed it to his face again. "Seer. I can smell her. I can smell it on her. Did you kill a seer?"

Hallam gawped.

"If you did, you've got to find the body," said Jack. "Where have they taken it? Find it and… and cut it out of her."

"Cut… cut what?" asked Hallam.

Cut what, for Christ's sake? thought Spencer, retching again. *No more cutting. No more stabbing and killing.* He groaned.

Jack looked at him. "Do you know if she was a seer?"

"I… I don't know what you're talking about."

"Do you want me to kill you, Spencer? Have you had enough?"

Despite earlier thinking of death as an option, having it offered up made him decide against it.

"N… no, Jack."

Jack tossed the hoodie at Spencer. It hit him in the face.

"Find out if she was a seer," said Jack.

"How do I do that?"

Jack glared at him. Even in the gloom, the terrible glow emanating from him blinded Spencer.

"Do it, Spencer. Do it or I will dismember you."

Spencer wanted to cry. He felt weak. He bundled the hoodie up into a ball. He started to pull it inside out, his panic growing.

Jack said, "We have to relocate. Hallam, we'll join you."

"Me?" said the dirty, sick bastard.

"You think I want to move from hovel to hovel, living with low-life such as yourselves?" said Jack. "I need to find my ripper. I need to find the seers. A woman and child. The ones who dreamed me."

Spencer had turned the hoodie inside out. It had a name tag in the hood. He said, "This wasn't Candice's."

They turned to face him.

"It says here it was Jasmine Hanbury's. You know her, Hallam. Don't you fancy her mum?"

A silence fell. It grew even colder. Spencer shivered. He thought ice was forming now in the flat. He could see his breath.

Then, cold and cruel, Jack's voice came hissing out of the gloom. "She's the fifth. This Jasmine. The fifth. Hallam, you'll rip her if you have to. You shall stand in my ripper's place. You shall be a ripper, too. She's the fifth, and then London will be bathed in blood."

CHAPTER 65.
ABOUT THE FALLEN ONE.

IT was good to see Tash again. Better than he ever thought it would be. He felt he never wanted to leave her presence now. Always be here with her. Just sitting on her bed, talking. It was enough. More than enough. It was the world.

He and Roy had come over half-an-hour earlier. At the door, Tash nearly threw her arms around his neck. He could tell she wanted to. Roy was happy to look after his granddaughter in the living room while Faultless and Tash had some privacy.

She had wanted to tell him what she'd discovered. But first there were things she had to know.

"What did they do to you?" she asked.

"They tried to barbecue me."

She flinched. Her sapphire eyes welled up.

"What happened?"

He told her.

She said, "You think it was the old geezer you saw when you arrived? The one outside the shop?"

"That's right."

"And he brought you to my dad's place?"

"That's what I think."

"And… and he killed Graveney?"

"He had fire."

"Fire," she said and touched his face.

"Yes. Fire. He came with fire. From fire. I don't know. I was fucked. Radio Rental. Probably hallucinating. But that's what I saw."

She nodded. He held her hand and kissed her wrist.

"Maybe you shouldn't do that," she said but made no effort to pull her hand away.

"Tash, I'd seen him before. The old man."

"Yeah, outside the shop." She shuffled closer, so her knee was touching his thigh.

"No," he said. "Years ago."

"How many years ago?"

"Nearly thirty five."

She furrowed her brow. "What?"

"I… I dreamt him bringing me here as a baby."

"A dream. Are you like me? Like Jasmine?"

He shook his head. "What did the letter say?"

"It said, 'To my children's children and those who follow,' and it was written by someone called Richard Troy. He wrote it in 1666. I guess he was one of my ancestors. One of Jasmine's. He said we are seers."

"Seers?"

"We can see. Dream. Have visions. Psychics, I suppose. Do you believe someone can be psychic?"

"I've heard loads of people claim they were."

"What about them that help the cops?"

"They don't help the cops. They say they do. When there's a murder, they ring up and say stuff like, 'I think the body's here or there,' and 'I saw so-and-so.' Police have just got to follow up on those leads. No choice. A lead is a lead, no matter how shit. When they do, the psychic can say they helped the police – which isn't a lie, despite being bollocks."

"You think if I see something I should tell the cops?"

He thought about it.

"You should, I guess."

"So you think I am psychic?"

He said nothing.

She looked away. "This Richard Troy, he says we go right back to the beginning of time. We… my ancestors… we were chosen to… to hunt this evil. Hunt it wherever it appeared."

He listened. He looked at her. He thought how beautiful she was. For the first time while gazing at her, Rachel stayed out of his mind. Instead, there was only Tash.

"He says, this Troy, he says London had just burned down. A great fire, he called it."

"The Great Fire of London. Started by accident in a baker's in Pudding Lane. Not far from London Bridge."

Tash shook her head. "Not according to Richard. He says they were chasing this… this thing, this dark angel, he calls it. The fallen one. He'd got free. He wrote that, 'Three had been ripped, and the evil sought out two more of my kind.' It was this fallen one who started the fire. But they trapped it. This Troy fella says they burned the wounds of Christ into its body and locked it up in a coffin weighed down with lead. Tossed it into the Thames. Watched it sink."

"What's that got to do with all of this?"

"Charlie, don't you see? It's Jack the Ripper, ain't it."

"You think Jack the Ripper's come back to life?"

"You found that briefcase."

"Montague Druitt's come back to life?"

"Neither, Charlie. It's the fallen one. The dark angel. 'Three had been ripped, and the evil sought out two more of my kind.'

That's what Troy said. And in Jonas Troy's notebooks, he says that the Ripper victims in 1888 in Whitechapel were seers, too."

Faultless narrowed his eyes. He was trying to link everything. Jack the Ripper. The fallen one. Dark angels. Seers. And the old man with the little tuft of hair on his chin. They were all pieces of information flying about, refusing to join up and make sense.

Tash said, "Jonas Troy says that Jack – that's what the newspapers started to call him – failed to rip Elizabeth Stride properly. She wasn't the fifth. There were only four. He was looking for a fifth victim, so he could be freed from a curse. It says in the notebooks that… the five wounds of Christ bound this evil figure. Only blood can unbind him, it says. And five deaths will free him."

Faultless stared into space.

Tash carried on talking. "Jonas says this is how it's always been – this evil thing hunted by… by the seers, and the seers themselves hunted by him in return. They're caught in a vicious circle. He can't be killed, though; he can only be contained, it says."

"Everything can be killed."

"It… it says he can't."

Faultless looked her in the eye. She was terrified. Her confusion and dread was obvious in her face.

"So what's the point if he can't be killed?"

Tash swallowed. She was pale. She said, "Jonas writes that if this evil he hunts kills five seers and takes… takes what he calls 'the gift' from them, he will rule the whole world, and it would be hell on earth."

After a while, Faultless said, "How does he get free in the first place? If this Richard Troy flung him in the river in the 17th century, how did he get out of the coffin to kill in 1888?"

Studying the notes, Tash said, "Blood can unbind him… that's what it says." She flicked through the pages of one of Troy's notebooks. "Here… here, it says that a woman called Martha

Tabram was killed on August 7, 1888 – about three weeks before the first Ripper victim, Mary Ann Nichols, was killed. Jonas says here that… " She tailed off and licked her lips, then coughed.

"You okay?" he asked.

"Yeah, just scared."

He stroked her arm. She held his gaze for a few seconds. Then he said, "Tell me about Martha Tabram."

She looked at the notes again. "J-Jonas says she was found at somewhere called George-yard-buildings in Whitechapel by a labourer. She'd… she'd been stabbed – oh my God, Charlie – she'd been stabbed thirty-nine times. Jonas says she was killed to free this evil from the curse. He says this thing, this spirit, can… can call to the evil in men's hearts. He is always calling out to it, says Jonas here. Even while he's trapped in the curse. He reaches out to anyone who approaches his place of burial, tempting them, urging them to spill blood for him. Blood can unbind him. And then, when he's free, he comes after the seers." She looked up at Faultless. "You… you think those lads in the lock-up freed this… this thing from its curse?"

He shook his head. It was difficult to accept Jonas Troy's ramblings. Faultless liked evidence. Just because there wasn't any, you shouldn't immediately leap to a supernatural conclusion.

"Charlie… Charlie, if this is true, and he's looking for seers to kill, he's looking for me and Jasmine. He's going to kill us."

CHAPTER 66.
JACK'S LETTERS.

ROY Hanbury was purple with rage.

Times like these, Jesus turned a blind eye. Or maybe Hanbury's cold heart became too hot for the Almighty to handle. Because if anyone tried to lay a hand on his daughter or his granddaughter, he would murder them. Just like he should have murdered the one who killed Rachel. He had wanted to. He was going to hunt him down and torture him to death.

But then the Old Bill nabbed Hanbury over the Stepney raid.

Maybe it was fate. Maybe it was heavenly intervention. Maybe it was two pillocks who failed to follow orders.

Whatever it was, he'd ended up doing time and Ernie Page came along with his Bible and Hanbury's hate dwindled.

But now it was back. And it was volcanic.

The eruption occurred when Jasmine told him the killer stalking Barrowmore intended to kill her and her mum.

At first he had tried to comfort her. They were sitting on the sofa together, and he put a big arm around her small body. "You been watching too many scary movies, babe."

Tash had taken a batch of old letters and notebooks with her into the bedroom, but some remained in the living room, scattered about. And Jasmine had showed them to Hanbury.

"He wants to kill us, Grandad," said Jasmine. "Mum and me, we're seers. Just like Bet Cooper. Just like Jonas Troy. And Jack the Ripper, he's going to kill us like he killed all those women in 1888."

Hanbury felt the hate bubble up, and it nearly made his head explode. He read a copy of a letter supposedly sent by Jack the Ripper to Central News Limited, a news agency, on September 25, 1888. The sheet on which it was written was turning yellow. The letter had been typed. The ink smudged. The words said, *"The next job I do I shall clip the ladys ears off and send to the police officers just for jolly… "*

Hanbury trembled with fury.

An image stained his mind, and it was there to stay – this fucker slicing little Jasmine's ears off, her shrieking, and him too far away to save her.

Hanbury read on.

"My knife's so nice and sharp I want to get to work right away if I get a chance."

He put the letter back on the coffee table. A pile of them were stacked there, along with a notebook and clippings from old newspapers

"You're very red, Grandad," said Jasmine.

"I'm angry, darlin'."

"With me?"

He stroked her hair. "No, sweetheart, never. With… with this fella. This man who… I tell you, if he tried to hurt you or your mum, he's going to feel my wrath. No more Mr Nice Roy. No more."

"We'll be okay, won't we?"

"You will, darlin' girl, you will."

He reached for another letter. This one had been sent once more to the news agency and was dated October 5, 1888. His eyes skimmed the words.

"... for the women of Moab and Midian shall die, and their blood shall mingle with the dust... "

Hanbury cursed.

He could feel his trust in God, his faith in Jesus ebb away.

Ernie Page's words came back to him.

"It's a blanket, brother. A shield. To be honest with you, I can't say if it's the truth or not. But some of it sounds good. And a fear of God, or whatever's up there in heaven, keeps us in check."

He could feel Christ in his heart. He was convinced Jesus was there, making him good. Saving his soul. Believing in God made it easy for him to accept what these letters suggested – that there was a supernatural element to what was happening. Accepting the true God made it easier to accept other gods, and also ghosts, UFOs... and psychics.

Seers.

He'd always known his wife had a gift. She could see things coming. Often she'd warn him, "Don't go to the meet tonight, Roy; there's going to be trouble."

He'd ignore her concerns, her tears, and keep the appointment. It would usually be with another villain. Settling debts. Buying drugs or weapons. Exchanging prisoners. Things would normally go without a hitch. But when Rose warned him there would be trouble, she was right. She had foresight. She had a gift. And because he was a bastard back then, he'd disregarded her and her knack for prediction.

He should have got her to forecast some winners for him, because he always lost on the horses.

But then she was gone. The fury came again, rising up from somewhere deep inside him. The place where sin still lurked. He quelled the rage by thinking about Jesus. He tried to feel his saviour's warmth. He'd known it before. It had healed him. It had cleansed him of malice. Or so he thought.

He'd been right when he told the probation officer that evil was in his genes.

It only needed a trigger to reactivate it.

And here was that trigger.

A threat to his family. And a determination not to back down like he did when Rachel had been killed.

Forgive me, Lord, he thought, *but you and me are finished for the time being. Get me through this, I might come back. Fuck it up and let my babies die, I'll fucking hunt you down to heaven and crucify you again.*

He got up and strode over to the bedroom door to get Faultless.

CHAPTER 67.
THE CREATURE FROM THE GARDEN.

"SO according to Jonas Troy's notes, this fallen angel had to be… " said Tash, tailing off to check the notebook, flicking through the pages. "Had to be bound by the five wounds of Christ. And then he says only blood can get him out of the curse. And five deaths will free him. What does that mean?"

Her dad, his face red with rage, said, "Didn't Jack the Ripper kill five women? Ain't that five?"

Faultless stepped forward. He looked down at all the stuff piled on Tash's coffee table. He skimmed the material quickly and then picked up an old newspaper clipping. It was covered in words. *Not like today's newspapers,* he thought. *Big tits, big headlines.* But one thing that a red top in 2011 and an 1888 rag had in common was sensationalism. Sketches portraying some kind of evil figure stalking Whitechapel replaced the paparazzi-snapped photos of the present day. Images of the terrified poor were on every page. Words like "terror", "horror", and "fear" were peppered all over the pages.

He said, "Elizabeth Stride, who was found on September 30, hadn't been ripped open. She'd been killed. Her throat cut. But not… "

He trailed off, glancing at Jasmine. The girl was curled up on the sofa, reading one of Troy's journals.

Tash looked at him and nodded.

He went on. "Thing is, these women were all seers."

Tash paled. Her gaze settled on her daughter. Hanbury must have read her expression. "It's all right, darlin'," he said. "He won't get to you, Tash. Neither of you. Not while Charlie and me are around."

Faultless said, "And when he killed them, he got something from them. That's why they were all cut open. There was something he needed."

"Organs were missing," said Tash, shivering.

"You think… " started Hanbury, before losing his words somewhere.

"What?" said Faultless.

"You think he was a cannibal or something?" said Hanbury.

Faultless shrugged.

Hanbury continued. "Was he killing them for food? Christ almighty."

Faultless started to think about something. This was enough to make you mad. How could it be true? Everything he trusted – rationality, evidence, skepticism – were being tossed out and replaced by an unquestioning acceptance of supernatural things. But the transition felt normal. It was painless. It became perfectly natural to believe that an evil being stalked the Barrowmore Estate and that certain people had a gift enabling them to see this presence.

And those people included some he loved, some he'd lost.

After a while, he said, "Rachel was a seer. Just like you, Tash. Like the rest of your family."

264

This was a declaration of acceptance from Faultless – and acceptance of the bizarre. A statement revealing that he acknowledged everything and rejected nothing. All explanations, however irrational, were valid from now on.

He went on. "Rachel... Rachel was... " He couldn't finish the sentence. She had been ripped open. Her kidney removed. He felt cold, and he saw the fear in Tash and Hanbury. "Were you related to Susan Murray and Nancy Sherwood?" he asked.

Tash shook her head.

"Were you related to my mum?"

"You saying," said Hanbury, "that this Ripper was around fifteen years back?"

Faultless shook his head firmly. "I just don't accept that. It's got to be a copycat killer."

"Are we all related, then?" asked Tash. "Your mum, too?"

Faultless stayed quiet for a few moments before he said, "She weren't my mum."

"It was only a dream," said Hanbury.

"I don't think it was. He brought me to your door yesterday, Roy. I didn't get there by myself, not in my condition. And he laid me at my mother's door when I was a nipper. I'm not her son. I'm a waif and stray, mate. An orphan. But who's he? Who's the old fella?"

"Maybe he's the killer?" said Hanbury.

"No he ain't," said Jasmine.

They all turned to look at her.

"He ain't the killer," she said. "And neither's this Jack fella."

"What do you mean, babe?" said Tash.

"It says it here in Jonas's book," said her daughter. "It says this fallen angel – 'the creature from the Garden,' Jonas calls him – this thing, he can't kill the seers. He ain't allowed to."

"Go on, Jasmine," said Faultless.

265

The girl looked at the old notebook. "It says there's evil in everyone, right. Deep inside. Sometimes it hides itself. It's… " She narrowed her eyes, studying a page. "Dor… dormant, it says."

"What else does he say, sweetheart?" said Hanbury.

"He says, right, that this creature speaks to the evil in men. It's only their evil part that can hear him to begin with, then he infects every bit of them. He loves to kill, to cause carnage and mayhem, but he needs to persuade someone else to kill the seers. Jonas calls him 'the lord who gapes', 'the lantern of the tomb', 'the moth eating at the law'."

She looked up at the adults. Faultless was thinking about what she had said.

What were they dealing with here?

Was it human?

Not from what he was hearing. This killer, the one who'd called himself Jack, was some kind of angel, according to Jonas and Richard Troy. He'd been around for centuries.

The creature from the Garden.

What did that mean?

The Garden…

No way, thought Faultless. It couldn't be true. He wouldn't accept that. There had to be a rational explanation.

"So," said Tash, "he wasn't actually Jack the Ripper."

"Jonas says he took on the name," said Jasmine, "but he didn't actually do the killings. He… " She was studying another word, her brow creasing. "Or… orch… orchest… "

"Orchestrated," said Faultless.

"Then who was the Ripper?" said Tash.

CHAPTER 68.
THE HOLE.

DETECTIVE Inspector Walter Andrews dragged on the cigarette, drawing the smoke deep into his lungs.

He breathed out. Smoke filled the dark little cell. The smell of tobacco mingled with the smells of damp and piss that saturated the air. He studied his surroundings.

This was the hole, one of five punishment cells that lay deep in the bowels of the building in Whitechapel Place, home to Great Scotland Yard.

As you headed down towards the punishment cells, it grew hotter and hotter. The men joked it was because you got nearer to hell. It was a bad joke. It was bad because some of them thought it was true.

The iron door had no window. There was a gap between the bottom of the door and the stony floor. They slipped your food through the gap. Stale bread and a cup of water. Once a day.

Men went into the hole fat and proud. They came out thin and broken.

If you were confined in the cell, you shat and pissed on the floor. And you lived with the stink till they let you out. That could be three days, it could be thirty. It could be till you died. After they removed a body, or hauled out a hardly-living prisoner, they washed the cell. But it was only a cursory wipe. It didn't get rid of the odour.

Andrews felt gloomy being here. He'd brought a chair down and was sitting on it. He looked at the other man, who was huddled in the corner, shivering.

Blood covered virtually every inch of the fellow's body. His clothes were drenched. His hair was matted. His eyes were set white and wide in his blood-dark face.

Andrews dropped his cigarette and crushed it with his shoe.

He asked the question he'd wanted to ask for hours.

"Why?"

The wide, white eyes flickered over to him. But the man in the corner said nothing. Just stared at Andrews.

"Tell me," he asked.

The man trembled.

"You were a clocksmith before you joined up, weren't you?" said Andrews.

Again the man failed to respond.

"That's a delicate trade. Requires dexterity. Skill. Care and attention. Did cutting open those women require dexterity?"

The man stayed quiet.

Andrews said, "We chased him. Mr Troy and myself. Ten others. We cornered him and bound him, cast him down. He failed, my friend. He failed, and so did you."

Andrews considered the man. Jonas Troy's words came to mind.

"We all have evil in us, Andrews. The great challenge is to contain it, keep it leashed. Especially if we are called by darkness."

This man had been unsuccessful. He'd succumbed. He'd weakened. The voice from the pit had whispered in his ear, and he'd been seduced.

But there had been no promises, Andrews knew that. No gifts handed over. No money. No women. No drink. Nothing. There was no need of bribery.

As Troy would say, "Evil is within us. It is part of our nature. All that is required is a trigger. And he, the evil one, knows what that trigger is. He awakens the need in us to be cruel and violent. He unearths it from our deepest, darkest places. He uses it for his own gain. He calls out to the evil, Andrews. He calls out for a Ripper. And a Ripper comes."

And a Ripper comes.

But who would have guessed it would be this man.

When Andrews and a colleague had brought him in nearly four hours earlier, they'd had to provide a false name and also lied about why they had arrested him. His true identity had to be kept hidden for now. The blood covering him made it difficult for the desk sergeant and other police officers who were milling around to recognize the man. But soon they would know. Before they did, Andrews had to deal with the situation.

"You are a seer," Troy had told him. "You keep this secret, and you guard it with your life. This is what we do. We hunt this evil, and we deal with its aftermath."

Andrews had always had visions. When he was a child growing up in Suffolk, his mother would hide things, and he would find them. If he concentrated, the hiding places would appear in his head.

His mother would tell him, "We are special, Walter. We have a gift from God, and we must use it to protect people."

He joined the Metropolitan Police Force in 1869 and was soon using his gift to solve crimes. Nine years after he joined, he was promoted to Inspector. Two months ago, he'd been sent to Whitechapel to investigate the Ripper killings.

When he arrived, he knew immediately who was truly responsible for the murders.

His visions grew more vivid, more violent. He met Jonas Troy and the others. He learned more about his past, about his calling. He learned that the victims of the Ripper crimes were seers like him.

"They are your family," Troy told him. "We are blood. We are made by God to do this work."

Now he thought, *What am I going to do with this man?*

In reality, he was a murderer. He should hang. It was that simple.

It's that simple if you don't know the truth, thought Andrews. And the truth made things more complicated.

"Why didn't you fight it?" he asked the man, exasperation in his voice.

It was easy for Andrews to say that. Easy for him to fight the evil. He was chosen. He had a gift. He had something inside him that kept evil at bay. Something the evil one claimed from all the victims. Something this blood-soaked man had ripped out of them.

But he still thought, *Why don't they reject the darkness?*

Then the man spoke. "I am only human, Andrews."

"You are a murderer."

"He made me do it. You know this is true. He told me about you, Andrews. He said I should kill you because you were a seer. You could hunt him. You had… you had within something he wanted, something he craved."

Andrews nodded.

"So you see," said the man. "You can ward off the evil he speaks, the evil he is. You can parry it away. I cannot. I am merely human."

"So am I."

"No, you are more than human. He told me this. You are more."

They lapsed into silence. Andrews thought about things. After a while he asked, "What shall I do with you?"

"You know I shan't kill again. Not now that you have contained him. He is no longer in my head."

"He can get into your head again, my friend. He can reach you from his confines. He can and does. This is how he releases himself. He calls out to the evil in men, and they kill for him. They spill blood. Then he is released, and so begins another hunt, another quest to kill five seers."

"I am sorry, Andrews," said the man.

"I know you are. Do you see what would have happened if he had succeeded?"

"I realize now, but… but you will never understand what it is like to feel evil within you, feel it corrupting your… your soul."

"The world will die if he is freed from the curse."

"I know… I know."

"He will destroy everything."

"Yes, I realize… "

"His influence is already strong in the world. Evil is everywhere. It always has been. But it will be nothing to what will be unleashed if he ever kills five, and this game is concluded. The damned game."

The man shook his head and wept.

Andrews said, "I don't know what to do with you."

The man shuddered and cried.

Andrews spoke again. "Tell me, my friend, what do you say? If you were standing where I am standing, and *you* had Jack the Ripper in this cell, what would you do?"

Detective Inspector Frederick George Abberline lifted his head and looked Andrews in the eye.

CHAPTER 69.
WHO AM I?

CHARLIE Faultless was reeling. His head swam.

Who am I? he thought.

It was terrifying, not knowing.

His past was now a big, empty hole. There was nothing there. Just a void. A pit. A grave. And he teetered on the edge of the abyss, looking down, hoping to see something he could grab on to when he fell.

But there was nothing. No mother. No father. Nothing.

Hands buried in the pocket of his top, the hood pulled down over his face, he stomped through the streets.

It was still rainy. Dark clouds filled the sky. They were bruise-black. Heavy and foreboding.

Who am I? he thought again.

He kept walking. He was going nowhere. Just thinking, trying to work things out.

He had come here to write a book, to dig into four unsolved murders. But now he was going to have to dig even deeper. Mine another seam of history. A forgotten seam. An undiscovered stratum that would hopefully contain the answers to his heritage.

But where to start?

He knew where. With the old man. The one he'd seen outside Costcutter on that first day. The one he'd seen cloaked in fire when Graveney was trying to kill him. The one he'd seen lay him down on the cold, hard concrete outside Patricia Faultless's house in 1977.

Was he Faultless's dad? It made sense if you were looking for the most logical answer, the simplest explanation. But nothing had been logical or simple over the past few days. He touched his shoulder, where Graveney's thug had blowtorched him. He had been healed. No mark. No scar. How had that happened? Nothing made sense. Nothing at all.

He stopped in front of the pub. Two blokes loitered outside, smoking cigarettes. They were soaked through.

"What're you looking at?" said one of the smokers.

Faultless tensed. He was ready to go, but he stopped himself. Ten years ago, the man's question would've been an invitation to fight. Two days ago, it might have triggered a verbal assault from Faultless. But now, it made him cower. He turned his back and walked on, the smokers laughing behind him.

Who am I?

Everything had been taken away. His strength. His courage. His balls.

He wasn't Charlie Faultless anymore, and that name meant so much. It had caused tremors in the community. It had made men tremble. His name was wrath in years gone by. His name was vengeance and fear. You told a fella that Charlie Faultless was on his way over, you already had him on the back foot. You might even see him leg it, wanting to be as far away as possible from the man with that name.

But now even his name had gone. He wasn't Charlie Faultless

273

anymore. Your parents gave you your name. But if they weren't your parents, what did that mean? The name meant nothing, that's what. It was just two words.

He walked on, shaking with nerves.

He thought about his father. He'd never known him. "He was a lazy cunt," his mother had said. "You're better off without him. He'd get on your tits. You'd want to kill him, darlin'."

Now he knew that was a lie. His mother was a lie. His life was a lie.

He had never believed there was a point to anything.

The only meaning to him was Charlie Faultless.

And the only purpose was also Charlie Faultless.

Nothing else. Everything was down to chance – and you had to take yours while you could.

But now that "Charlie Faultless" had been stripped away, it left him feeling lost and scared.

He had no identity. He was nothing. He was no one. He belonged nowhere.

Not even here, where he thought he was made.

Not even the Barrowmore Estate.

The Barrowmore Estate. Crawling with cops. Stained in blood. Haunted by a monster.

Two options confronted him. He could run, or he could find the old man. He was trying to make a decision when the car skidded to a halt next to him and a voice said, "Faultless, what the fuck…"

CHAPTER 70.
THE GOSPEL OF DEATH.

IT was better to be living here in the house of Hallam Buck.

Menace corrupted the air. Evil lingered in the atmosphere. Jack felt more at home than at Spencer's hovel.

He had certainly savoured the decay over at the youth's squat. But it lacked the malevolence of Buck's apartment, which was the result of the resident's true dark nature.

It was also very near to the child and its mother.

The seers.

Jack tingled with anticipation. One of them would be the fifth. Four had been conveniently killed fifteen years before. The man who killed them was now on the estate. Jack sensed his evil. It shone brightly. That man had prepared the way for Jack's homecoming. Four dead, only one to go. It would be far easier than chasing down all five as he had done in the past. Finding rippers was always straightforward. Man had a dark heart. He was tarnished by sin from the beggining. Tapping into that brutish nature was usually simple. But you had to find the right killer. Some men, although desperate to shed blood, couldn't go through with murder. Some turned away from evil. But Jack had found a powerful ally in the ripper now roaming Barrowmore. He had mercilessly killed those four seers fifteen years before. Killed them for Jack. Killed them and ripped out from each the gift. It didn't matter if that ripper killed the fifth seer or not. Hallam would act as the butcher if need be. But he had to be reached so he could bring Jack the gifts he had taken from the women, and stowed. He had to be beckoned.

After he arrived at Buck's place, Jack set about turning it into hell. He was a whirlwind. He tore down the walls, tossing plaster and hardboard everywhere. Dust and dirt covered everything. Doors were ripped off their hinges. Appliances were yanked out of their sockets. The lights were smashed.

He laid waste to the apartment.

After he had finished, Buck asked, "Why did you do that?"

"I'm frustrated," said Jack. "Would you prefer it if I tore you apart?"

Buck blanched and shook his head.

Jack said, "I need my freedom. Have you found me my ripper?"

Buck shook his head again.

"And what about Spencer, has he?"

Buck shrugged.

"Will you be my ripper, Hallam?"

"Me?"

"Yes. You'll follow in the footsteps of great men. Men who have worshipped me. Men who have washed my feet. Do you worship me? Would you wash my feet?"

Hallam nodded.

"Then you'll be my ripper?"

"I… I don't know."

"I handed you your first victim, Hallam. Did I not give you the strength to kill it? To kill the child? To do with it what you dreamt of doing?"

Hallam nodded.

"Then you should do something for me. Be my ripper."

"What… what is that?"

"The child below," said Jack. "She's a seer. She has something in her that I must have. It gives me power over them. It gives me the strength to break free of my curse. Are you listening? Do you understand?"

Buck nodded.

"I must have the girl. Or her mother. Either one. And they must be ripped."

"Why… why can't you do it?"

Jack shuddered. "They are seers. I can't kill a seer. It's a curse that I can't, but I can't. Those are the laws."

"Laws?"

"The laws that were carved in the fabric of creation."

"Creation?"

"Stop repeating what I say, Hallam, or I'll cut your tongue out. You won't need it to be my ripper."

Buck's mouth dropped open.

Jack shut his eyes and listened. He could hear them breathe in the flat below. He could hear their heartbeats. The child and its mother.

A fifth, at last. He would have the child killed. Hallam would do it.

And then all he had to do then was find the previous ripper and retrieve the tokens he surely took from the four seers he butchered.

He seethed for a moment.

Why was he forced to start all over again after being resurrected? All the work he'd done in previous centuries meant nothing once he was bound. He always had to wangle his way out of the curse, reaching out to the sin embedded in every human. And once he'd done that, he had to seek another ripper and find the seers – or wait for them to find him.

He let out a breath. This time it was different. This time he'd found a strong collaborator. Years ago, he'd reached out from his lonely confinement and found that beautiful sample of evil in the deeply corrupted heart. And when the time came, he had unleashed it.

Four dead, he thought. *One more. Just one more. It will be so easy.*

He opened his eyes, and Buck was still standing there, a loyal servant.

"Do you know what will happen when I'm freed of this curse, Hallam?"

Buck shrugged.

Jack said, "I will be like a sword. I will set son against father and father against son. Mothers will kill daughters. Children will murder parents. A man's enemies will be his friends, his family. Bloodshed shall reign, Hallam. All will hate. All will kill. All will spread my gospel. And my gospel is death."

CHAPTER 71.
GOBBY LITTLE SHITE.

STAYING cool, despite his heart thundering and his balls shrivelling, Don Wilks said, "Where are you off to, Faultless?"

Faultless stopped and stared at him.

Wilks stared right back, although he was a bundle of nerves.

Why the fuck was Faultless still alive? Had Graveney fucked up? Or perhaps the moron had decided to delay the hit.

Then Faultless looked away and started walking again.

Wilks crawled alongside him, leaning out of the driver's side window.

"I'm just asking, Charlie. Where are you off to?"

"A stroll," said Faultless.

Pulling himself together, Wilks said, "Don't stroll too far, son."

"I wouldn't want to be too far away from you. You're electric."

Wilks laughed. It was all right. If Faultless had got away from Graveney, at least he had no idea that Wilks had set him up. Or he gave nothing away if he did know.

Cool little bastard, thought Wilks and said, "Still got that mouth on you."

"Yeah, still got that."

"Big time writer, gobby little shite."

"That's me."

He was dying to ask Faultless if he'd had a run in with Graveney. But that was out of order. He'd give himself away. This bastard would smell a rat and suspect Wilks of being up to no good. Instead, he carried on winding Faultless up.

"Do all those poncy writer people you mix with know you were a lousy little yob, Faultless?"

"They know, Don."

"They like it, do they? Having a bad lad around. You get to shag all those posh birds, do you?"

"Yeah, that's right. I shag 'em all."

"Bet you're mum would be proud, eh?"

Faultless stopped dead and glared at Wilks, who braked.

Faultless said, "You done with me?"

"For now, son. For now." He thought for a few seconds and then added, "We'd like a word about Tony Graveney, though. You've not seen his brother, have you?"

"Should I have, Wilks?"

Wilks felt himself redden. He tried to stem the blood flowing into his cheeks, but preventing it was impossible. He just smiled a big, red-faced smile instead.

"I just like having you around, Charlie boy. It reminds me of the good old days, that's all. Stay close, son."

Wilks sped off. The smile turned into a scowl and the beginnings of a headache pulsed in his temples.

And when he got back to the incident room, his indignation scaled new heights.

CHAPTER 72.
DARK OF HEART AND
COLD OF BLOOD.

AT least he'd pissed off Don Wilks. It made Faultless feel better. He was ready to run. But then the detective had stopped and tried to wind him up. And it was the DCS who ended up being taunted.

Faultless saw something in Wilks's eyes when he'd stopped. It looked for a moment like fear. Or shock.

Why did he ask me if I'd seen Graveney? thought Faultless.

He stopped. He was near to where Ryan Graveney and Buckley had ambushed him.

How did they know I was back? he wondered.

He looked in the direction Wilks had driven, and he knew the answer.

Fuck you, Wilks, he thought. *I'll deal with you later.* For now, he was going to find the old man. He was going to find out who he was. He was going to get answers.

As he walked, he thought of his mother's death. He thought about how he'd killed Tony Graveney. He remembered the fury. He could still taste it.

"You got evil in you, son," Roy Hanbury had told him at the time.

Roy wondered long and hard what to do with him after he'd battered Tony to death.

He said to Faultless, "We are both in mourning, Charlie, and for that reason, I am going to spare you. You were blinded by hate. So am I. The death of my daughter has opened a fucking volcano in me, and hate and rage is just spilling out, hot and deadly. In a way, son, you've done me a favour. My enemy is dead. But there will be a war now. You have to go, if you want to live."

"I ain't going," the young Faultless had said. "I'll fight them. They won't kill me."

"I didn't mean them," Hanbury had said. "If you don't go, I'll have to kill you. There was an impasse, son. There was a peace. Deadlock, you follow? Means no killing. Sadly, you killed. The way round here is revenge, you know that. But you are like a son to me. You've been hurt bad. So I'm offering you deliverance. Here it is." Hanbury had tossed a padded envelope on the table. "Now fuck off, and don't ever let me see you round here again."

Now he walked for a good while, strolling past low-rise blocks. They were four-storey flats. Red-brick boxes built in the early 1990s to accommodate the growing population. St George crosses flapped on the breeze. Two youths watched a rottweiler and an English bull terrier go at each other. The dogs snarled and salivated. The lads laughed and pointed. Across the road, next to a boarded up shop, a police car was parked. The Old Bill had been a heavy presence on Barrowmore these past few days. But the two cops in the vehicle ignored the dog fight.

Faultless walked on. More boarded up shops. Buildings unused for years. A community centre decorated in graffiti – legit graffiti.

It was a blast of colour in the grey grimness of Barrowmore. Faultless admired some of the art. It was excellent. He imagined the smiling, laughing youth at work on the display. There were good kids on the estate. Good people. Not like him.

Not dark of heart and cold of blood.

Shame rose up in him. In his youth, he'd been destroying

creativity like this. He'd be mocking the teens responsible. The kids who tried to make it better. Not like him.

Scum, he thought. *You were scum, Charlie Faultless.*

As he walked, the shadow of the four tower blocks fell across the road. He glanced up at them as he passed. Monsell House loomed above him. He thought about Tash. His heart flipped. But then thoughts of her brought Rachel to his mind. And the pain uncoiled in his chest.

What would've become of them, had she lived? Would they still be together? Married maybe, with little Charlies and Rachels running around.

Perish the fucking thought, he told himself. *One of you is enough.*

And anyway, they would probably have split up. Time kills everything in the end. Nothing lasts. It all dies. Especially love.

Only hate thrives, he thought.

Hate and darkness.

And its profusion in Faultless's life fifteen years ago would have killed him in the end.

Someone would have shot him or stabbed him. A deal gone wrong. Revenge. Bad blood. Something…

If he had been lucky, he would have been banged up.

And then God might have saved him like He saved Hanbury.

He closed his eyes and shrivelled into himself when he realized what had actually saved him.

Rachel's death. Patricia's death. Tony's death.

They got him out of here. They got him exiled. They got him saved.

He came to the lock-ups where the first murders had occurred. It seemed like an age ago now. But the police tape still crisscrossed the entrance. Bollards blocked off the road. A police car was parked on the pavement, two cops inside.

He sensed that he would find the answers in that old lock-up where Montague Druitt's briefcase had been found.

CHAPTER 73.
ZOMBIE MEMORIES.

THE assistant commissioner of the Metropolitan Police said, "This estate is in meltdown, Don."

Wilks said nothing. He nodded like he was supposed to nod – with reverence. But he felt contempt.

The AC was a high-flying female in her forties who was scaling the heights at the Met. In Wilks's opinion, she was doing a job a man could do better – all in the name of political correctness and the feminization of what he regarded as a man's world.

Women weren't meant to be coppers. They could do the civvie stuff. They could file. They could type. They could make tea. But in Wilks's view, the dirty work should be left to men – and men like him.

Some would say his days were numbered. But Wilks knew his time was coming. Inside, he knew he only had to wait and be patient. He'd always known that. He sensed it. A voice within telling him, *Everything you do has a reason; your actions have meaning.*

It was hard sometimes to believe that voice, especially when you saw a dead man walking.

How the fuck was Faultless alive? He'd given him to Graveney on a plate. Not only was Wilks getting rid of Faultless, he was also making Graveney his bitch.

Graveney knew nothing about that. He had the brains of a gnat. But if he stepped out of line or decided not to contribute to Wilks's pension fund, he might find himself facing a murder and kidnapping charge.

Sitting in his office in the incident room, Wilks now rested his elbows on the desk. The AC sat opposite him. Short, blonde, and stern, she reminded him of an old teacher of his. Miss Reilly. A real cow. She always picked on Wilks, making him look foolish in front of the class.

He fumed now, thinking about her, and transferred his hate of the old bitch onto the AC.

She said, "We are being made a mockery, Don. The murder of this child. It really is the final straw for people. Are you making any progress at all?"

"We're following a number of lines of inquiry."

"Don't give me soundbites, Don. It just doesn't suit you. Why haven't you raided the squat where this Spencer Drake is said to live?"

He felt himself grow hotter. "There's no evidence – "

"I thought breaking down doors was your style, Don. Break his down. You've got no excuse."

He trembled with rage. He pictured himself laying her across the desk and showing her who was really in charge.

His anger had given him an erection. It happened a lot. He bunched his fists, trying to control the urge to spring at the AC, trying to ignore the voice in his brain.

"Seven murders in two days," she said. "And two of them happen right under our noses. The community leaders are on my back – "

Wilks shuddered.

" – and now we've got the MP knocking on the Commissioner's door with petitions and demands for his resignation. The press is having a field day."

"Bollocks to the press," he said.

Her brown eyes widened into a stare. "Our relationship with the press is important, Detective Chief Superintendent. It is our route to the public."

Fuck them too, thought Wilks.

Fuck them all.

His mind whirled. His skin crawled. In his mind, memories that had been buried away were rising up like zombies.

Zombie memories.

Chewing him up from the inside.

Turning him into a zombie, too.

"In my experience, ma'am, it don't matter much what you say to the newspapers. They always take the negative line."

"It's why we should manage our relationship with them, Don. Do you speak to our press office at all?"

"I don't have time."

"They are valuable members of the team, and they can advise you – "

"I don't need to liaise with them, ma'am."

"I think you do. I know you have a junior PR here as part of the investigation. Well, I've asked our senior press officer to come down. He'll be here first thing tomorrow. Be nice to him, Don. He has a rank equivalent to yours, remember."

"I don't respect his rank. He hasn't earned it."

"You're such an old school dinosaur."

"Yes, I am."

"That's all very well, Don. I don't mind. But if you intend to be a racist, misogynist artefact, could you please do so while actually solving these crimes?" She stood up. "And by the way, this afternoon, there's a public meeting at the Andrew Mayhew Community Centre. Do you know where it is?"

"I know where it is." Andrew Mayhew had been a fourteen year old kid who died of stab wounds ten years previously. They said the kid never joined a gang and was a bright, popular pupil. They could say what they wanted; Wilks reckoned he was a little thug who deserved what he got.

The AC said, "Be there."

"Excuse me?"

"I want you to be there with me. Answer some questions. Face these people."

"I'm far too busy – "

"No you're not. Good morning, DCS Wilks."

She strutted out of the office.

He fumed. He hurled the desk aside. He punched the whiteboard. It split. He grabbed a chair. He swung it around. He smashed it against the wall. It splintered. He raged. He snarled. He sweated. His blood boiled. He was hot. As hot as he'd ever been.

He thought about Spencer Drake's flat and the AC's criticism. Although Drake officially lived with his mum, it was known he spent most of his time at an empty flat. His mother was a Christian and disapproved of his lifestyle. She'd kicked him out.

Very Christian, thought Wilks.

He slumped in the corner and put his head in his hands.

Something had prevented him from raiding Drake's squat. That voice in his head. He called it instinct. But maybe it was something different. Maybe it was not really part of him and came from somewhere else. Maybe he was merely a host, accommodating the presence he felt deep in his brain.

He groaned.

Fucking AC, he thought. *Fucking Spencer Drake. Fucking Charlie Faultless and Allan Graveney.*

He had to do something. He had to take control. He had to be Don Wilks the monster again.

Right, he thought, getting to his feet. *Right…*

CHAPTER 74.
TAKEN.

IT came through the ceiling. Tash was napping on the sofa at the time. Jasmine was in her bedroom. They were unprepared for it. There was no chance to escape.

Her eyes snapped open.

She gasped, holding her breath.

Her skin crawled.

She kicked up her legs and threw out her arms.

All of this happened in less than a second.

And it all happened as the ceiling collapsed.

Debris rained down. Plaster fell in chunks. Dust showered, filling Tash's eyes and mouth.

Something dark fell from the hole in the ceiling. A black flash. It coiled on the floor and sprang up, becoming a shadow that blocked out the light. The darkness flapped, as if it were a cloak. Faces writhed in the folds of the blackness. They stretched as if in agony. And Tash was convinced she could hear them scream.

The dark shape then narrowed and took on a form – the form of a man.

All this happened in just two seconds.

By then, Tash had let out her breath. Her eyes burned with dust. She spat it out of her mouth and sneezed it from her nose.

An arm reached from the dark shape and grabbed Tash around the throat, and the grip was cold and clammy. It lifted her. It tossed her. She sailed across the room. Everything wheeled. She smashed into the wall. Stars erupted before her eyes. Her head throbbed with pain. She fell and hit the floor, dizzy and disorientated.

And then a voice said, "Seer bitch. I'd kill you if I could. I'd kill you both."

Her vision swam. A chalk-white face blurred before her eyes. It became three, four, five faces. It flickered. It was hazy.

The voice echoed in her head. "But I'm killing your offspring first. Then I'll be back to see you suffer. Taste your grief, you whore. Say 'bye to your baby girl."

The darkness swept away, letting the light return and leaving her flat fuzzy and unclear.

Knowledge suddenly overwhelmed her. It was as if masses of information had been downloaded into her brain. For some reason, she knew the voice. She knew its dangers. She knew the threat it made was real. She knew Jasmine was in danger.

She reached out and cried her daughter's name, but only a moan came from her. It was a mother's desperate lament.

And when a spiteful, cruel laugh drowned out Jasmine's scream, the horror of it was too much for Tash, and she passed out.

* * * *

Faultless had walked back the way he'd come and found a narrow path, crammed with weeds and waist-high grass.

He followed it. Stinging nettles pricked his skin. Rats scuttled over his feet. Thorns tugged at his clothes. But he made it through and found himself at the rear of the lock-ups.

A footpath ran behind the garages, hemmed in by a high wall. He smelled beer and tobacco. Cans of booze peppered the tall grass. He saw syringes and used condoms.

He started walking, making his way along the footpath. He tried to count the lock-ups as he went. He'd walked back ten garages before finding the alley that led to the path. Ten garages from the one where Jason Thomas, the Sharpleys, and Luke Ellis had been murdered. Ten garages from the police car.

He kicked his way through the undergrowth. Thorns and nettles filled the path. He crushed beer cans beneath his feet. There were cigarette ends everywhere. He saw aerosol cans. He saw plastic bags filled with glue. He saw knives and empty bullet casings.

He walked and he counted – eight, seven, six, five…

Ten garages.

… three, two –

"Hey you," said a voice.

He turned.

He cursed.

The two cops sitting in their car outside the garage had decided to make a nuisance of themselves. They must have spotted him and followed.

"What can I do for you, gents?" he said.

The two cops came to a halt five yards away from Faultless. They looked at him and then looked at something one of them was holding in his hand.

They were checking him out.

"What you got there, fellas?" he said.

One of the coppers held up an iPhone. At five yards away, Faultless could make out the image on the screen.

It was him. A photo from the dust jacket of *Graveyard Of Empires*.

"You know who this is?" said the iPhone copper.

"Is it your very handsome boyfriend?" said Faultless.

"You wish, poof," said the second copper.

The iPhone officer gave him a look before staring at Faultless again.

The cop said, "Incident room just sent this over. You're either Charlie Faultless or a very good match. Which one is it?"

"Very good match," said Faultless.

"I think you're him. And Detective Chief Superintendent Don Wilks wants to talk to you," said the copper, still holding up his iPhone.

"I'm not sure I want to talk to him."

"Whatever, mate. You're under arrest for the murder of Anthony David Graveney in 1996."

The coppers stomped through the tall grass towards Faultless.

He bunched his fists, ready.

CHAPTER 75.
DARK PLACES.

THE elevator clanked. It went down, hurtling through the shaft. Spencer had never known it to travel so quickly. He stood in the corner, leaning back in an effort to stay on his feet. He was shaking. His skin felt as if it were peeling away from his bones. It was like one of those films you saw of pilots exposed to G-force.

What the fuck is happening? he thought.

Hallam held on to the girl. She looked terrified. He looked calm. He'd gone really weird in the past few hours. He'd always been a victim. Bullies picked on him. Everyone picked on him. But since he'd broken into Spencer's flat and got involved with Jack, he seemed to have an aura around him.

It made you shiver, being near him. The atmosphere around the bloke was dank. He'd killed Candice, Danny Daley's little sister. After that, the Barrowmore Estate had gone mental. Protesters took to the streets. The Old Bill got slagged off. Some old fella got beaten up because he was a little bit too close to the kids' playground, and the mums clocked him as a paedo.

Fucking nuts, thought Spencer.

And now it was getting even nuttier.

"What the fuck are we doing with fucking Roy Hanbury's granddaughter?" he asked.

"She's a seer," said Hallam, arm snaked around the girl's throat.

She whimpered. She cried. She had tried to kick and bite, but Hallam just stared ahead as if nothing was happening. He never blinked. He never grimaced.

Weird, thought Spencer. *Way too weird.*

"Where the fuck are we going, man?" said Spencer.

"We might be going to hell."

"You what?"

"Hell. Ain't that exciting, Spencer? Hell."

"Hell ain't exciting."

The elevator kept descending. The numbers on the display were just strange symbols by now. They flickered like mad, but they made no sense to Spencer. They'd gone way past GROUND, and he never realized there was anything below that level.

"Didn't he show you?" said Hallam. "Didn't he show you all the secret places? All the arteries of Barrowmore? Where its blood flows? Where you find its life force?"

Jack had dragged him to all kinds of dark, grotty hovels in the hours after he'd killed the Sharpleys and Lethal Ellis. He vaguely remembered them. But it had been like being high. Everything was hazy. He'd been sick and groggy.

They had been places Spencer had never seen. Some of them appeared to be on the same floor as his flat. Dingy coves holed out of the bricks. Alleyways so narrow you had to squeeze through sideways. Pits filled with bodies, some of them alive and in agony. Altar-rooms displaying skulls and crucifixes. Desecrated churches attended by ghosts. Abandoned slaughterhouses exhibiting corpses that hung on hooks.

They had even visited an attic above his mum's flat. Only there was no attic above his mum's flat – just another apartment. But Spencer had been inside the non-existent loft and watched his

293

mother through a pinhole in her ceiling while she had sex with a horned man whose lower body was that of a goat.

A fucking goat.

He had been sick then. He had moaned, puke dribbling down his chin. The next thing he knew, Jack had dragged him to another terrible place, another gut-wrenching scene.

It was a nightmare. Or a drug trip. It had to have been. No way was it real. No way would his mother do that. She was God squad. Big time God squad.

A fucking goat. Fucking bones. Fucking corpses on hooks. Fucking ghosts. Fucking... hell.

"My mum'd never do that with a fucking goat," he remembered groaning.

But Jack, he was sure, had whispered in his ear, saying, "She would, Spencer – and she'd do worse."

The elevator was now screeching as it sped down the shaft. It started to shudder, knocking from side to side.

Spencer stretched out his arms to steady himself. His gaze skimmed around the narrow container. Claustrophobia panicked him. His chest tightened. His gaze fell on Hallam. The man looked calm. His eyes glittered. Jasmine Hanbury sagged in his clutches.

The elevator clunked. It stopped dead. Spencer jerked. His neck whiplashed.

"Where are we, for fuck's sake?" he said.

"The world was made with dark places in it," said Hallam. "Places we can't see. Places we don't know about, but we feel them sometimes. We feel them cold on our skin, we feel them in our bellies. Places were evil hides. That's where we're going, Spencer – one of those places."

The girl whimpered.

"Ain't she lovely," said Hallam.

"You're sick."

"What are you going to do about it?"

Hallam Buck would never have said that in the past. He would scuttle by, scared and nervous. The kids would pester him. They would harass him. They would throw stones at him.

Not anymore.

Hallam had found his place in the world.

"Christ, look at that," said Spencer.

Fog slithered under the elevator door, which then slid open. The mist curled inside. It felt really cold. The smell turned Spencer's stomach.

With the doors open now, he narrowed his eyes and stared into the darkness.

What is this place? Underground parking lot? Cellar or something?

The fog filled the elevator. Jasmine cried. Hallam gasped. Spencer whined. A dark shape came out of the blackness and stood on the elevator's threshold. A white face slowly appeared. It smiled. It showed yellow teeth.

Jack.

His long, white fingers beckoned them out of the lift, and then, seeing Jasmine, he said, "A little seer, ready for ripping."

CHAPTER 76.
JUST SKIN.

"YOU'RE a special girl," said Jack to Jasmine.

Jasmine spat in his face.

He wiped the spit with his fingers and licked them.

"You let me go," she said, struggling in Hallam's grasp.

Spencer watched in horror. This had gone too far. It had to stop. But who was he to stop it? He was nothing. He was no one. He would go down too – for killing Jay-T, for stabbing Paul.

He looked around. It was a large area. It appeared to be an underground car park. But it contained no cars. Pillars reached up to the ceiling, which was too far up and too dark for Spencer to see when he craned his neck. It was very cold in here.

"Where are we?" he said without thinking. His voice echoed.

Jack stared at him. The only sound was Jasmine's cries.

Jack said, "Didn't I show you places you'd never seen, Spencer? Things you'd never seen?"

Fucking goat...

He shuddered, trying to get the image out of his head.

"You think your world is the only world there is?" said Jack.

"I… I don't know." He *had* thought that. Nothing lay beyond Barrowmore. In any direction. The estate was everything to him. It was hell and it was heaven. It was the place he hated and the place he loved. Leave and he'd die; he was sure of that. So were many other kids. On the streets, they felt strong. They owned their territory. Or they thought they did.

"Your world was built on other worlds," Jack said. "Your cities on other cities. Your history cloaks other histories. This is just skin, Spencer. Barrowmore. Whitechapel. London. Just skin. This place" – he gestured to the vast cavern they were in – "is not part of your world."

"I… I thought you couldn't leave."

"I can't. I'm still trapped. A great circle surrounds Whitechapel. It goes to heaven; it stretches to hell. I can't move past it, no matter how deep I go. This is why we have to deal with this seer."

Spencer felt sick.

Jack walked over to the kid and the pervert.

"Don't kill me," said Jasmine.

Her voice cut into Spencer's heart.

"I ain't going to kill you, child," Jack told her.

"What are you going to do to me, then?"

Jack smiled. "I'm going to get someone else to kill you for me."

She cried for her mother.

Jack said, "It's what I have to do. It's the rules. It's how we were made, you and me. You are poison, little girl. You are the only ones who can hunt me down. The only ones who can find me. And when you do, I have you killed, because your deaths will secure my freedom."

"You're crazy." She struggled, but Hallam held her tightly.

"They say so," said Jack, "and it may be true."

"My grandad'll kill you."

He laughed, and it echoed around the underground lot, bouncing off the pillars. Spencer's eyes followed the sound and then came

297

back to Jack. By then he had taken a butcher's knife from inside his cape. It had a wooden handle. It was the one he'd used to gut the Sharpleys and Lethal Ellis. The one he'd taken from the briefcase he left in the lock-up.

"Do it, Hallam," said Jack.

Spencer froze.

Hallam said nothing.

Jack's face darkened. "Hallam, did you hear me?"

Jasmine said, "Please don't, Hallam."

Spencer thought, *Please don't, Hallam.*

"Hallam," said Jack, his voice low and chilling. "Now, Hallam. Now."

"Why can't you do it?" said Hallam.

Jack growled. "Hallam. She is God's own. I can't harm her. I wish I could. I need her dead. Make her dead, Hallam. Now."

CHAPTER 77
THE NEW CHARLIE
FAULTLESS.

IT felt like the first time in days Faultless had been back in the flat he'd rented to write his book. The place was cold and dark. He switched on the light and took off his coat, flinching at the pain in his ribs. One of the filth had smashed him with his truncheon. But not before Faultless had decked his pal. Despite the pain in his side, he'd then turned on the copper who'd attacked him and laid him out with a right and a left. Then he'd legged it. It had felt good, standing up for himself. But it was going to cause problems. The Old Bill would come for him. And not just two of them this time.

He walked into the living room.

Writing felt like the last thing Faultless wanted to do. Things had changed. The book he'd intended to write would be very different if he started it now.

On July 24, 1996, my mother, Patricia Faultless, was murdered. Her killer has never been caught.

That had been his opening. Not anymore. Patricia Faultless wasn't his mother.

He sat at the table near the window. He switched on the radio. The headlines reported more financial gloom, the death of a Mafia godfather, and a Premiership footballer jailed for rape. Faultless half-listened to the bulletin as he stared down into the quad. A large group of people milled around the area. He leaned towards the window. He saw camera crews. He saw placards and heard chanting.

The residents were protesting.

Faultless ignored it. He stared into space.

What would he do?

He'd come here to nail his mother's killer. But not in the old Charlie Faultless way. Not with fists and feet. Not with a shank or a baseball bat.

He'd come here to nail him with words.

This was the new Charlie Faultless.

In the past few years he'd discovered that power lay in the pen. He could cause a lot of damage with a few sentences.

And the injuries caused by an article published widely would be slower to heal.

Sticks and stones might break bones, but they healed. It was being named that could really wound the prey Faultless hunted. Named and shamed. Hunted and humiliated.

He recalled some of his successes as a journalist. His book *Scapegoat,* about a British soldier wrongly accused of killing an Iraqi civilian, had ruffled feathers. And it left a few politicians red-faced.

It had been 2004. The war was going badly. The press and the politicians were looking for someone to blame. You'd had Abu Ghraib. The Yanks abusing Iraqi prisoners. You'd had the insurgency turning the country into a charnel house.

They wanted a fall guy. They got one. The soldier killed a would-be suicide bomber, but footage shot on a mobile phone made it appear he'd murdered an innocent local.

The soldier was drummed out of the Army.

Faultless's book sold okay, but best of all it had government ministers squirming on Question Time and Newsnight.

Faultless remembered another hunt.

Psychic detectives.

He fizzed now thinking about that investigation.

He was working for a news channel in Chicago.

He and a female colleague he was dating at the time had gone undercover, pretending to be the parents of a missing child.

There wasn't a missing child, but that didn't stop three "psychic detectives" from claiming to have pinpointed the made-up kid's body.

A fourth said the fake daughter was still alive but had been taken into slavery in the Far East.

One of the psychics led Faultless and his fellow reporter to a quarry and started having a fit and speaking in tongues.

Another led them to an apartment building in the city and said their bogus baby had been brought there. "But I am truly sorry to say, she was killed here and thrown into the river – but her soul is now at rest and with Jesus in heaven."

Faultless and the investigation team then set up a TV show where the psychics appeared – and were outed as scammers.

The psychics and their supporters were furious. They claimed to have read Faultless and the other reporter's minds. They said they felt there was a child. Their spirit guides or auras, or whatever, had led them to those places.

So how had they all come to different conclusions?

The psychics refused to accept they were making it up. They were either convinced they had a gift, or they were liars.

"Liars," Faultless had said on the TV show.

The psychics fumed. They threatened him with a lawsuit. They told him to "go back to England, where you are all godless".

Faultless then reminded them that God frowned on mediums, quoting the First Book of Samuel in the Bible, which states they should be put to death.

The psychics stormed off the TV show.

Faultless had gloated. And he gloated now. It made him feel better. But he still had no idea what he was going to do. He considered leaving Barrowmore. He looked at the flat. It would be easy to leave some of his stuff here and get out, today. He was thinking seriously about it now, seeing himself taking a train to Heathrow and getting a flight back to New York.

Get away from this hell. Escape the cops. Avoid the judgment.

He blew air out of his cheeks and made his decision.

His phone rang. He checked the caller ID.

Tash.

He thought about not answering.

Easier to go without saying a word, he thought.

But an ache in his chest led him to answer.

"Tash," he said.

And she cried and wailed down the phone.

CHAPTER 78.
LEW.

MOST of Tash's ceiling was on her floor and all over her furniture. It looked as if a bomb had hit her flat. There was dust and debris everywhere. She was crying and shaking on the settee. Her father comforted her. He was saying, "We'll get her back, darlin', we'll find her," and tears had also made his eyes red.

Faultless looked up at the ceiling. Whatever came through had left a large hole. The edges of the hole looked charred, and Faultless could smell a burnt odour.

Hanbury said, "I'm going to find her, Tash, and when I do, I'll – " His face darkened. Faultless thought God might have left Hanbury's heart by now. The devil had moved back in. But Hanbury was resisting. He was trying to hold on to his faith, because if he didn't there would be trouble.

Tash said, "It's him, ain't it? It's that Jack." She looked at Faultless, and her eyes were on fire. "Where were you? You weren't here to… " She trailed off and cried again.

Hanbury said, "Where have you been?"

"I had a spot of bother," said Faultless. He told them. Not about his identity crisis or about his plans to leave. Just about looking for the old man and fighting off the cops.

Hanbury said, "So they'll be on to you, now, son."

"Fuck that. We got to find Jasmine. You told the Old Bill?"

Hanbury nodded.

Tash said, "They thought I was crazy."

Hanbury said, "They got a plateful of shit at the moment. They don't know their arses from their elbows."

Tash leapt to her feet. "We can't just sit here. We've got to find her. He's going to murder her, Dad. He's going to cut her open and – " She slumped back on the couch. "Why didn't he take me? We can exchange. I'll go in her place… I'll – "

"No you won't," said Faultless. "We'll sort this."

"How?" she said.

Faultless had no idea.

Then a voice said, "You got someone to look at this?"

They all looked up at once.

When he saw the speaker, his skin crawled.

It was the old man, peering out of the hole in the ceiling, the stump of a cigar between his lips.

Hanbury said, "Jesus… "

The old man said, "Can I join you?"

They had to help him, Faultless taking his weight on his shoulders as he eased himself down into Tash's flat.

Now he sat on the sofa, smiling and chewing on his unlit cigar. Faultless, Tash, and Hanbury stood and stared at the fella as if he were an alien.

The old man's face triggered memories in Faultless. He remembered being carried and laid at Hanbury's door after the assault by Graveney and his thugs. He remembered being laid at Patricia Faultless's door more than thirty years ago. And it was this old man with the tuft of hair on his chin and his long, snow-white hair who had left him at both thresholds.

As he stared at the man, Faultless started to feel hazy. The tattoos on the stranger's body seemed to move. Faces smiled and grimaced. Figures danced, skipping up and down his arms. Words appeared across his chest, writing themselves on his skin. They were strange words to Faultless, but they looked like they were from an ancient language.

"Do I know you?" said Hanbury.

"You might do, Roy."

"You fucking know me, obviously."

"I have my ear to the ground."

Faultless came to and said, "Who are you?"

"You can call me… Lew," he said, as if he'd just come up with that name.

Faultless narrowed his eyes. "You're not Lew, are you."

"I am Lew. That's what I'm called. Just like you're called Charlie Faultless. You might not be Charlie Faultless, but that's what you're called."

Faultless felt something uncoil in his belly. A feeling of panic rose up into his chest. He wanted to ask this old man, *Who am I?* He wanted to know if he'd saved him from Graveney's men. He wanted to know if he'd killed Graveney. And as if he could read Faultless's mind, Lew said, "I'll answer your questions later, but first – tea."

Tash erupted. "My daughter's missing, my little girl. We have to find her. I am not making fucking tea."

Lew said, "Find her yourself, Tash Marie Hanbury."

Tash gawped. Faultless bristled. Hanbury reddened.

Tash found her voice. "Fuck off out of my home."

"Why?" asked Lew. "For giving you some good advice?"

"Now look, mate," said Hanbury.

"She's a seer," said Lew, and his voice was sharp and loud, and its power made Faultless tremble. "She's a seer and she can find *him*. Where he is, her daughter will be."

Faultless said, "Who the fuck are you? You came with fire. You killed Graveney. I saw you. You carried me home yesterday and… and you brought me here thirty-four years ago. I dreamed you."

305

The man's coal-black eyes glittered. He stared at Faultless but spoke to Tash. "Have you found her yet, Tash Marie Hanbury?"

Tash stared into space, her mouth open. Hanbury went to her, concerned. She held out a hand to keep him at bay.

"What's wrong with her?" said Hanbury.

"Nothing's wrong with her," said Lew. "She's a seer, ain't she. She finds him. She hunts him. She's a seer, and – "

Tash said, "I know where she is."

CHAPTER 79.
SALVATION.

HALLAM looked at the knife.

"Lick the blade," said Jack. "It's got blood on it – old blood. A lot of blood. See how sweet it tastes. You ever tasted blood, Hallam?"

Jack brought the knife up to Hallam's face. He saw his reflection in the blade. He saw his eyes were wide with fear – or maybe it was excitement.

"Taste," said Jack.

Hallam licked. He gasped. It was like honey. It sent shockwaves through him.

Jack laughed and drew the knife away. "The fresher it is, the better it tastes, Hallam."

He looked over to where Spencer had been ordered to take the girl. She lay on the floor with her arms out to her sides. Her wrists and ankles were in manacles, which had been attached to spikes in the floor. She was screaming for her mother.

"Do you see her?" said Jack. "She's waiting for you and the knife. She's waiting to die." He handed Hallam the knife. "Take it. I won't tell you again. Take it."

Hallam took it.

"Can you find me the treasure in her, Hallam?"

"I… I don't know… I… I'll try."

"You don't try. You do. She's the fifth, Hallam. The fifth. You remember the other four, don't you?"

Hallam remembered them. He was obsessed with them.

Rachel Hanbury, Patricia Faultess, Susan Murray, Nancy Sherwood. Four women, mutilated. Their throats cut. Their organs removed. And something else. Something ultimately more precious than a kidney or even a heart. It was a rumour rifling through Barrowmore at the time. Whispers heard on street corners. Murmurs in alleyways. Gossip spread by old women with nothing better to do.

But when they fail to catch a killer, speculation will thrive. Myths will blossom. Tales will grow.

Just like they'd grown around Jack the Ripper in the 19th century.

And just like they'd grown around the New Ripper fifteen years ago.

Never caught. Never understood. Still a mystery.

The "why" had never been answered. Why had these men killed? Why had these women died?

And while that riddle remained, people would make up answers.

But Hallam knew why. He looked into Jack's cold, black eyes and saw the answers to all the questions.

"What if I can't find the… the… what I'm looking for?"

"You'll find it, Hallam. Then you'll find the first four."

"F… first four? F… find them?"

"The killer has their treasures still. I need them. I need all five. And once I have all five, I have my key to the door of the world."

Hallam looked over to where Jasmine had been chained. Spencer squatted nearby, chewing his nail.

Beyond them lay darkness – a deep, cold, eternal darkness. Hallam felt it call out to him. Heard it sing his name. He knew his world had changed, from the moment he'd found the briefcase. He'd wanted to keep it so he could impress Tash, impress anyone who'd listen.

But now he had so much more.

He had salvation.

He'd been salvaged from the wreckage of his life.

The darkness called him again, and then Jack, who came from the darkness, said, "You know you can do this, and when you do you will be a king."

Hallam looked at the knife. He went towards Jasmine and the darkness.

CHAPTER 80.
PEACE AMID THE
CARNAGE.

ANGER laced every word, every statement. You could hear it in their voices. They slagged off the police, and they slagged off the government. They slagged off everyone they could, because they had to have someone to blame.

Blame yourselves, thought Don Wilks. *You're making your own monsters.*

He hated the public.

He folded his arms and leaned back in the chair. He stared out at the crowd packed into the community hall. Sharing the stage with Wilks was the assistant commissioner, a couple of local councillors, the member of Parliament, and two community workers.

Fucking do-gooders who know nothing about what life's really like, thought Wilks.

He glanced at the AC. The bitch had forced him to take part in this circus when he could be out on the streets, doing his job.

The MP raised his hand to quiet the audience. He was Asian, a 29-year-old lawyer. Wilks sneered at the man. He'd only got voted in because most of the population around this part of Whitechapel was Paki – or Bangladeshi, as the politically correct cops these days insisted on calling them.

All the fucking same, thought Wilks. *All fucking foreign.*

Apparently the flashy, young MP had recently been critical of extremist elements of Islam. He'd slagged off nutty imams for leading impressionable young Muslims on the path to terrorism. He'd encouraged integration and co-operation.

Bollocks, Wilks said to himself. *Probably a cover for being a suicide bomber.*

The MP said, "These murders have horrified the world. It's all very well having press and broadcasters from across the globe descending on Barrowmore for their soundbites, but what happens when the story is of no further interest? There will still be anguish here. There will still be fear. And unless the police pull their socks up, there will still be a killer on the loose."

The crowd cheered and clapped.

More fucking votes for you, thought Wilks.

He hated politicians.

He leaned forward now and scanned the faces. He was looking for Faultless. The bastard might have been stupid enough to turn up. If he were here, he'd be pinned to the floor and handcuffed.

After his bollocking from the AC earlier, Wilks had issued an order for Faultless to be arrested.

Two grunts spotted him near the scene of the murders – *very handy*, Wilks had thought, *a bit of circumstantial there* – and approached him.

Unfortunately, Faultless trounced the pair.

Never mind, thought Wilks. *Another good reason to hunt down the bastard – assaulting police officers.* Faultless would go down for that, even if Wilks failed to make any of the other accusations

311

stick. He was going to try to pin the murders on him, although he knew Faultless was clean. What he wasn't clean of was Tony Graveney's death. But too little evidence, too few witnesses, and too much time gone by since the killing meant they'd probably never get a conviction.

Shame Allan Graveney was still missing. That was a Faultless job too; Wilks knew it. Graveney was supposed to finish him off. Wilks had handed the bastard to him on a plate. But somehow prey became predator. And Wilks was sure Graveney's ugly old body lay hidden somewhere on Barrowmore. If they could find the corpse, they might get a charge out of that.

The MP yammered on. The crowd applauded. Wilks sweated.

He hated this world.

He hated everything about it and everyone in it.

He just didn't belong.

He shut his eyes to block it out. The sounds of the meeting grew distant. His mind wandered. It went to a dark place. A place hiding terrible secrets. A place where he kept atrocities like other people kept antiques. He stayed there, and he found peace – peace amid the carnage.

And in that bleak, bloody darkness, he heard a voice.

It was calling to him, now. It was looking for him. He listened. He felt completely relaxed. He waited. The owner of the voice would find soon him. He'd found him before. And when he did, it had been like finding love for Don Wilks.

CHAPTER 81.
THE DESCENT.

"DEEP," said Tash. "Deep somewhere. Underground. Under… under the world. She's deep, deep down."

They were standing outside the lift on the ground floor of Monsell House. A sign saying OUT OF ORDER was pinned to the elevator. Litter was strewn all around the reception area. Someone had tried to burn through a door marked CARETAKER. Its frame was black with soot. The door had been padlocked. At the bottom of the stairwell lay a Costcutter bag full of beer cans. Someone had dropped their booze. Maybe they'd been attacked. Maybe they were being chased and dumped the alcohol while they were running away.

Faultless's gaze returned to the elevator door. It was steel. The word HELL and an arrow pointing down had been painted on the door.

It was maybe more accurate a description than the vandal responsible had imagined.

Tash was staring at the lift door.

Faultless said, "You saying she's in there?"

Tash said nothing.

Faultless looked over his shoulder. Hanbury nodded at him. Charlie shrugged. He looked at Tash. She was fixated on the door, focusing on something.

He was trusting in her psychic abilities. He was trusting something he'd been convinced was bollocks.

He thought about Lew. His weird tattoos. The black eyes. The face that came up from the depths of Faultless's memories. The old man had left them soon after Tash announced she knew Jasmine's whereabouts. Outside the flat, Faultless had watched him stroll down the passageway, smoke wafting from the old fella's cigar. Soon the smoke was a thick mist around Lew, and in a few seconds he'd disappeared completely.

Tash laid her hand on the door. "He's down there somewhere. Him. The… the evil thing. Down there. And Jasmine, he's got – "

Faultless eased her out of the way and started kicking the door. Hanbury appeared next to him and was driving his heavy boot into the door. It buckled. After a while, Faultless was able to pry it open. He stood in the narrow gap and stared down. His legs turned to liquid. The abyss stared up at him. A burning breeze wafted up from the pit and boiled his blood.

"I can see way down," he said. "But that doesn't make sense. This is the fucking ground floor. There's nothing down there, is there?"

Using all his strength, he pushed the doors apart. They groaned and eventually jammed, providing a twenty-four-inch space for Tash and Hanbury to join Faultless in looking down.

"That's not supposed to be there," said Hanbury. "What is it? It's impossible."

"There's nothing there," said Faultless again.

"There's something," said Tash. "There's Jasmine."

He looked up. It was wires and cables and scaffolding. They looked like veins and ligaments and bones to Faultless.

He looked down again. There were none of the mechanisms of modern elevator systems down there. It was as if the 21st century ended there on the ground floor, and beyond it was a place lost in time. The shaft was mud and clay. In places, bones jutted out of the walls. They looked human. Faultless took a deep breath and shook his fear away. An old, wooden ladder, some of its rungs decaying, was bracketed to the side of the chute. Weeds coiled around it, and moss covered some of the steps, making them look slippery.

Faultless said, "We go down."

As they descended, it became hotter and hotter.

Hell, he thought. *The sign was right.*

Faultless led the way, followed by Tash, with Hanbury taking up the rear.

"Are you sure this is right?" he asked Tash above him.

"No, I'm not, but it's what I'm… "

"What you're what?"

"What I'm seeing, Charlie. That's all I can tell you."

It was dark. It was hot. Sweat poured down his face. The shaft stank of rotting meat. On occasion he was convinced he could hear voices – wailing voices. He was also sure that he could smell something.

Ammonia, maybe. Or sulphur. Or death.

"Can you see the bottom?" asked Hanbury. He sounded out of breath.

Faultless looked down. The darkness stretched. He saw no end. He said, "Not far now, mate."

Above them, something grinded – like metal grating against metal.

In the heat of the shaft, a cold fear ran through Faultless. He looked up. The sound came again, followed by a loud clank and then a hum.

"What the fuck is that?" said Hanbury.

315

The humming grew louder.
Faultless recognized it.
It was an elevator – coming down.

CHAPTER 82.
CHARNEL HOUSE.

FAULTLESS swung sideways, holding on to the ladder with one hand. "Hurry up, Tash, get past me," he called up, and she descended quickly.

When she got level with him, she stopped. She looked into his eyes. He stared right back. He wanted to leap at her, kiss her. She wanted the same, he could tell. But instead he said, "Get moving."

She did, heading down.

He looked up and hurried Hanbury along.

He could hear the lift. He craned his neck as Hanbury went past. Up in the shaft, he could make out the elevator's shape coming down. Its hum grew louder. He glanced below him and started to descend again.

He was sweating. His heart raced. There was an ache in his ribs where the copper had truncheoned him. He was exhausted, his vision swimming.

But he had to go on. He had to survive. He had to find out.

"Move," he told them below him. "Move."

"Where are we going?" said Hanbury.

"Ask your daughter, mate. She's the psychic."

"You've called me mate twice in the last few minutes. You'd have done that fifteen years ago, I'd have cut your tongue out."

"You did worse than that, Roy. You threatened to kill me."

"You what?" said Tash. "Dad, you did what?"

"Didn't you know?" said Faultless. "Thought you were psychic."

"Shut up, Charlie," she said. "Dad, were you going to kill him?"

"Save your breath, darlin'," said her father. "Save your breath and keep going. It's all in the past now."

Fucking past, thought Faultless. You can say "it's all in the past" and try to forget it, but not when the past made you. Not when it left you lost. Not when it had stolen everything you thought you were.

He looked up. His legs grew weak. The elevator was coming closer. He could see it now.

"The ladder's out," said Tash.

"Jump, then," said Faultless. "You're nearly there."

"Nearly where?"

He said, "Leap, Tash."

"She ain't leaping into the dark like that," said Hanbury.

"She's here somewhere," said Tash. "I... I can see him... his eyes, his face – he's here."

"Jump," said Faultless.

"No," said Hanbury.

Faultless leapt off the ladder. He plunged, sweeping past Hanbury, past Tash. He fell and was thinking, *Please let there be –*

He hit the ground and rolled into what felt like branches. They cracked and crunched as he flailed around in them.

"It's okay," he said. Before he could get up and check out his surroundings, Tash landed on him. Then Hanbury fell in a heap to the side.

"You okay?" he said to Tash. He was holding her. Everything

was calm for a second. Everything was right. She nodded. He was looking into her sapphire eyes. They glittered, even in the gloom. He nearly kissed her.

"Jesus Christ, save us," said Hanbury.

"W… what?" said Faultless, the moment between him and Tash gone. He got up, scrabbling through the stuff that covered the ground.

Branches, he thought. *Trees. White –*

Tash gasped.

"They're bones," said Hanbury.

The elevator screeched. Faultless looked up. He held his breath, thinking they were going to get crushed. But it stopped about ten feet above them, sparks flying. And the light they made lit up the room. The few seconds of illumination showed Faultless what Hanbury had seen.

Bones. Human bones.

Hanbury said, "It's a fucking charnel house."

CHAPTER 83.
KING, NOT PRINCE.

JACK salivated. He was shaking, and his teeth were chattering.

"Do it, fucking do it," he was hissing at Hallam Buck, the useless, cowardly *cunt* of a human.

He had waited an eternity for this. During the long ages of his existence, many men had bowed before him. They had cowered and obeyed. He had spoken to the evil in them. He had called them to their duty.

And they had always come, willingly.

They licked their lips at the prospect of savagery. They had welcomed the opportunity to be his ripper. To kill seers and gut them for the treasure inside.

Men had been made with evil in them. Men had been made with *him* in them. And the malevolence only had to be beckoned out for it to be easily unleashed on others.

Genocide. War. Murder. Rape. Torture. All the barbarity came from the same place. From the deep, dark pit where malice writhed. The deep, dark pit slotted into every human heart.

It was a test. It was a game. And he was its player.

Make them do evil. Call it out of them.

He had done well. He had stained the world. He had spread his poison. But adversaries came. The seers. He shook with hatred for them and their maker.

Damn the laws of the universe, he thought.

He deserved his prize. He'd played his role since time began. He'd played it well. He'd done his duty and spread his wickedness.

He deserved now to be king, not prince. It was time.

But the fool he had chosen for this task was hesitating.

Hallam Buck, who reeked of evil, was weak. Hallam Buck, whose heart was contaminated by perversion, was frail when faced with his obligations. Hallam Buck was useless.

And where was Spencer? Crawled into the darkness somewhere behind the pillars. *The coward,* thought Jack.

The teenager and his friend had been the first humans to come near Jack for years. In the years after Troy had buried him, he had tried to call others. The ones who built over the well and bricked it up. The ones who built the estate after the slums were torn down.

Although a few men had lingered near his tomb when they heard him speak, none had stayed long enough for his voice to awaken the serpent in their hearts.

Until Spencer.

The boy was decayed. He was wicked. But he had boundaries. He hated killing.

The weedy little cunt, thought Jack.

Hallam raised the knife above the child-seer's head. He'd pulled up her T-shirt to expose her stomach. And he was staring at her skin.

Jack bristled. "Stop looking, you fool," he said. "Kill her first. Cut her throat. It's quicker. Then eviscerate her."

Hallam looked at Jack.

"She's… she's beautiful… "

"Kill her. Do it. Do it, and I'll make you a prince in my world. You can have as many kids as you want, then. I'll have them fucking brought to you on trays. Do it."

Jack would do it himself. He had the will, just not the right.

The laws, he thought*, damn the laws.*

Written into him as they were written into all creation.

If humans knew the truth, they would never enter a church again. They would never walk into a mosque or a synagogue.

A noise alerted him. He turned. Shapes in the distance. He snarled. He narrowed his eyes and saw into the darkness. He exploded with fury. He wheeled back to face Hallam.

"Kill her, you bastard! Kill her now!"

Hallam was looking beyond Jack. His eyes widened.

"Don't stare," shouted Jack. "Kill her."

"It's… it's Faultless," said Hallam. He dropped the knife and backed away.

Jack saw red. His rage became a volcano. He whirled round to face the trespassers.

The man appeared. Jack was going tear his legs off. He readied himself. He saw more clearly. The man had a cold, hard face.

Jack recoiled.

And then he saw the stranger's eyes.

One brown, one blue.

Jack felt something he'd not felt in centuries.

Jack felt fear.

CHAPTER 84.
AN ANGEL.

WHILE Hanbury and Tash circled round to rescue Jasmine, Faultless would take out the head honcho. That was the plan. They'd hatched it in the few seconds it took to find the doorway out of the charnel house into the cavern, where pillars reached up into the darkness and stretched back as far as it was possible to see.

Now, as he darted towards the pale man in the cape, Faultless heard Tash screaming for her daughter, Jasmine screaming for her mother. He heard Hanbury threatening to kill anyone he got a hold of. But then all the noise faded, and Faultless was fixed on his adversary's face.

The eyes were coal-black. The face was moon-white. The hair long and greasy to the man's shoulders. His cape flapped and it shimmered in the darkness. And he had a tuft of hair on his chin, just like –

The man held out his hand, as if trying to stop a runaway train.

Faultless halted. He was aware of struggles going on in the background. Voices echoed. Curses flew. But he was mostly transfixed by the man in front of him, and they stared at each other for what seemed to be an eternity.

The pale man pointed at Faultless with a long, yellow fingernail and said, "You are the darkness… the darkness in the corner of my eye."

"Are you Montague Druitt?" said Faultless.

"I was once."

"Are you Jack the Ripper?"

The stranger smiled. "I was once."

"Who are you now?"

"I like Jack. You can call me Jack."

"Who are you really?"

"I am the lord who gapes. I am the lantern of the tomb. I am the moth eating at the law."

"What the fuck does that mean?"

The man snarled. "It means who I am. You should know."

Faultless shuddered. He should know? The man was staring right at him, directly into his eyes. He furrowed his brow. There was something familiar about the stranger, and that familiarity scared Faultless. It gave him goosebumps. He got the feeling that knowing this man was a bad thing. It was a dangerous thing. And not just for your life but for your soul.

"You're like me," the pale man told him. Behind him, there was struggling as Hanbury laid into Spencer, as Tash fought to free Jasmine. But the stranger paid no attention to what was going on. He seemed fascinated by Faultless.

"Do you know what you are?" the stranger asked him.

The question unsettled Faultless, but he threw one right back. "Do you know who *you* are?"

"You've not faced judgment yet, have you? For a killing."

"Neither have you."

"More similar than you think, then."

"I'm not like you. I don't know what you are."

The stranger grinned. "You don't know what *you* are, either."

"W...what am I?"

"An angel," said the pale man.

"Flattery will get you killed."

"You think you can kill me?"

"If I have to."

"You're not strong enough yet."

"What d'you mean *yet*?"

The stranger looked over his shoulder and then back at Faultless. "You have fucked it all up for me."

"Sorry about that. Couldn't let you kill her, see."

"You can't stop me."

"I *will* fucking stop you."

"I'll have the mother killed if I can't kill the child."

Faultless fumed. He wanted to plough into the man, but something hindered him. Something in the back of his mind holding him on a leash and telling him to wait. The stranger had said Faultless wasn't strong enough *yet* to kill him. Although he didn't understand what he meant, Charlie knew there was truth in the statement.

Now he said, "You touch her, and I'll hunt you down till the end of time, fucker."

The stranger hesitated. Almost as if he believed that literally.

A scream erupted. It was laced with fury. Faultless blinked. Tash was hurtling towards the pale man, coming from the gloom like a laser.

The stranger wheeled to face her. He glanced over his shoulder at Faultless and said, "I'll have her ripped like I had her sister ripped." Faultless lunged forward, his fists bunched. Tash kept coming. Then the stranger said, "Like I had your wet nurse ripped." Faultless charged. Tash clawed. A black shape whipped away to the right, blending into the darkness.

The stranger was gone.

Faultless and Tash ran into each other and fell in a heap.

CHAPTER 85.
ONE AND THE SAME.

FAULTLESS quickly led everyone back into the elevator shaft filled with bones.

He was carrying Jasmine. Her wrists and feet bled where Hanbury had wrenched them out of the cuffs in his desperation to free her. The older man was crying. He panted and held roughly on to Spencer. At first, the youth begged for mercy. Then he shut up, as if resigned to whatever pain Roy Hanbury would inflict on him.

"Are you okay?" Faultless asked Tash.

She was pale. Her eyes were glazed. She swayed and stuttered as she walked. She looked at him, and he saw dread on her face. He'd never seen anything as terrible. It shook him.

"Tash?"

"I'm all right," she said. "Is my baby – "

"She's fine. Fainted, that's all. We've got to get out of here."

They looked up. The lift blocked their way. Panic clutched Faultless. He looked back towards the doorway and the dark cavern beyond.

Was Jack still there?

He thought about their conversation. They'd circled each other like two stags, neither ready to make a move. It was weird. Faultless would have usually laid into a bloke in that situation. But that was no normal man. He was something extraordinary.

So why did he hesitate in killing me? Faultless thought.

The stranger had actually shown fear. Faultless saw it in his eyes. It flashed in the cold, black evil of his gaze.

Staring into the killer's face, Faultless saw something else as well – recognition.

The stranger seemed to know who Faultless was.

You're like me.

The horror of it made Faultless tremble.

You're like me.

What the hell did that mean?

Everything was coming apart. His life was not his life.

He had to find Lew.

The old man's face appeared in his mind. He held his breath and grew cold. Slowly, the face melted away, and in its place came another mask. And its dimensions were exactly the same, only the second face was a younger man's image. Like Lew, he had a tuft of hair on his chin and coal black eyes. He had long hair, dark instead of white.

Jack, he thought. *And Lew?*

His mind began to unravel with the possibility that they were the same person when someone called his name from what sounded like a great distance.

He turned and found himself in the charnel house.

"Come on," Tash told him.

She appeared from the gloom.

"Come on, Charlie, we've found a way out."

She ran into the darkness, and he followed her without asking where she was going, trusting her completely.

She was the only person on earth now he could believe in. But he knew that wouldn't protect her. He knew she was in danger. He could do nothing.

A growing sense of doom spread through him. A seed of something terrible sprouted somewhere deep in his heart. Something terrible that he was born to be, that he would become. Something terrible that would threaten Tash, Jasmine, Roy and everyone on the Barrowmore estate. Something terrible that would blight the whole world.

PART SIX.

DESCENDED TO HELL.

CHAPTER 86.
GRIM WEATHER FOR GRIM TIMES.

WHEN the police finally raided Spencer Drake's squat, they found PC David Rees nailed to the wall. He was dead.

Soon, the whole estate knew about it. Although some residents would probably say it was one less filth on the streets, it did ramp up fear levels. Mysterious deaths did that, especially violent ones. And the violence wreaked on Barrowmore over the past few days had been extreme.

Over the years, there had been shootings, there had been knifings. That was bad enough for most people. But a couple of bullets to the head or a shiv to the guts was really nothing to compare with the mutilations and public displays of cruelty witnessed since Friday's killings in the lock-up.

Rumours of torture and abuse had often buzzed through the estate over the years. Quite a few residents had been involved in crime at some level – drug dealing, money laundering, or loan sharking. And when one of them disappeared, speculation grew about whom they'd pissed off and what had happened to them.

But their punishments, if they were punished, were never made into an event.

Not like these murders.

It was as if the killer wanted his work to be seen. *Well*, thought the man they dubbed the New Ripper, *the killer* had *wanted just that.*

The world needed to know what was at work on Barrowmore. It needed to be aware of what was coming. The murders were a warning. The killer was saying, "This is a taste of the future."

All will hate. All will kill. All will spread my gospel. And my gospel is death.

The New Ripper steadied himself, leaning against the wall. He was lurking near the lock-ups. Something had brought him here. Something had called him. It was the same voice that had been calling him for days, but it was too far away, too distant. He knew what it was. He knew who it was. But he was vague about what the voice wanted.

The New Ripper had answered similar calls fifteen years before. The voice in his head had been strong.

I am the lord who gapes… I am the lantern of the tomb… I am the moth eating at the law…

The voice in his head had said, *Prepare the way… kill one, kill two, kill three, kill four… prepare for the fifth… the fifth we share… our reign shall begin with her blood…*

The man had listened to the voice. He had taken on the mantle. He was an heir to past atrocities. A prince in the kingdom of pain.

But now he wanted his throne. He wanted to be king. He was ready, and the voice beckoned him. It summoned him for one last act, an act that would bring hell to earth.

The meaning of what he did in 1996 was about to become known to him. It had played on his mind for years. It had plagued him mercilessly these past few days. It had got so bad that his work had been affected. But then, he was never that good at his job. He'd winged it throughout his career. He'd got away with – he smiled to himself – murder.

He leaned against the wall, hands buried in his coat pockets. It was cold and wet. The rain had been relentless over the past few days. Maybe it was a sign. Grim weather for grim times. *But let it rain,* he thought. Let it rain blood. Let it rain scraps of meat and shards of bone.

Let the world be saturated in death.

Let me do what I am meant to do.

He was itching to kill again. He was desperate to hear the voice guide him. He was bursting to pin another one down and take things from her body.

He was about to turn and walk away when the door to the lock-up burst open, and a figure carrying a child stumbled out.

CHAPTER 87.
THE ONE SHE WAS
WAITING FOR.

SHE knew someone was coming for her. She felt it. Her mother had warned her, and her grandmother had warned her.

And her dreams had also warned her. They were relentless. Every night, she would wake up screaming, her body drenched in sweat. Every night the same dream. A figure chasing her in the moonlight, gaining on her, despite the fact that he was walking and she was running. It was like a horror film. The menacing villain stalking the heroine. And no matter how quickly she ran, how far she got away from him, he would always be waiting at the next corner.

There was no escape.

And there was no escape for Patricia Faultless, she knew that.

She sat in her flat, drinking. Half-an-hour earlier, she'd stormed out of the pub where she'd had a ruck with Tony. She'd told him of her dreams about being pursued. He'd gone mental, accusing her of having an affair. They'd had a brawl.

Now, her rage dimming, she stared at the TV screen. It showed a game show. Bruce Forsyth was helping people to play their cards right. The couple wore furrowed brows, deciding whether to go higher or lower. But it was easy when you were playing with money. Not so easy when you were playing with your life.

What were the odds on Patricia being born like this? What were the odds on her being given a gift of sight that could end up killing her?

She gulped down the wine and poured out another glass. She was shaking. If only Charlie were here. Her boy. Her miracle. But even he, the menace of Barrowmore, would have to cower before the one she was waiting for.

The one she was waiting for had angels lined up behind him. He was human, but non-human powers controlled him. They guided him. They made him kill for them. They made him rip. He was their hunter and their gatherer. He paved the way. He hoarded the treasures.

Pat put her head in her hands.

Why her? Why had she been born like this? She had never asked for it. They say you have free will, but that was bollocks. No one was free. No one had freedom. Who would ever choose to be born on Barrowmore? Who would ever choose to be born a seer?

"We're descended from very special people," her mother had told her when she was a teenager. "From people who had gifts. We can see things, Patty. We can hear the dead speak. And we can… we can hunt evil."

Pat's mum had made a living out of fortune telling. She'd converted the second bedroom in their flat into a gypsy's den. Candles flickered, and joss-sticks scented the air. Red material was draped on the walls. Thick curtains, permanently drawn, kept out the light. Figurines of unicorns and angels and other mythical creatures peered down from shelves. Red Indian dreamcatcher mobiles dangled from the ceiling. A crystal ball and a packet of tarot cards sat on the small round table at the centre of the room.

It was all pointless. Pat's mum had no need for the paraphernalia. The crystal ball and the tarot were useless. They were what you expected to see if you visited a medium.

But you couldn't tell a future by staring into a sphere of glass, and you couldn't predict happiness by dealing out cards.

It was all fake. Just like the mediums who used them.

But there was nothing fake about Pat's mum. She was real. She could see. She could predict. But it was a curse, not a gift. It was a burden. Because it came at a price.

And the price was death.

You were part of an ancient game. You were pawns. You were puppets.

She wept. The couple on TV chose lower. They should have gone higher. The card came up as the Ace of Spades. Pat laughed through her tears. She stood and went to the front door, checking again that it was locked. Back in the living room, she downed her wine. She felt drowsy. Maybe being drunk would dull the pain.

She wondered if Susan Murray and Nancy Sherwood had dulled the pain. It shook her to think of them, murdered because of who they were.

And then there was poor Rachel. Poor, beautiful Rachel, who Charlie loved. Who Charlie worshipped. Although she was Roy Hanbury's daughter, she was kind and considerate. She was wise. Pat had hoped she would lead Charlie away from the streets. Away from the violence that afflicted his life. But it was too much to wish for.

Charlie was Charlie. The darkness was in him. You could never remove it. That's how he was made. That's how he had been brought to her.

She clutched her chest, recalling that night nearly twenty years previously. She was mourning a lost child. It was a girl, a week old when it died. Losing the baby had been another judgment on Pat that year. Already her dreams of being a model had been wrecked, and then when she became pregnant her boyfriend left her. Someone was punishing her, she was convinced. She was paying for her sins, whatever they were.

But then, a miracle.

Contemplating suicide one night in November 1977, Pat heard a noise outside her front door. It was close to midnight. She guessed it was kids. You wondered sometimes if parents knew where their offspring were. Truth was they never cared much. Not around here.

Pat had gone to the door and opened it. She was ready to shriek at the troublemakers, tell them where to go.

But no one was there. Only a naked baby on her doorstep.

Her Charlie.

Casting a quick glance along the walkway, she spotted no one. She picked up the infant and took it inside.

Her Charlie.

Pat's mother had stared at the baby the following day and said, "If it was left outside the door, mate, he's a gift, ain't he. He's been left there for a reason."

"I want to keep him, Mum."

"Darlin', I think you were meant to. It's in the stars, ain't it. It's fate. It's destiny. He's meant to be yours."

And he was.

Her Charlie.

Now she was torn between wanting him here to protect her and hoping he'd not come home, where he'd probably be killed.

He had been wracked by grief after Rachel's death. He'd sworn vengeance. But no one knew who'd killed her. He said it was the Graveneys. She was a Hanbury, after all.

336

Pat had said, "There's peace between them, Charlie. The Graveneys would never do that to anyone. Not a girl. No way, babe."

Charlie's face had darkened. "You're only saying that 'cause you're shagging that bastard."

Pat slapped him. The first time she'd hit him. "Don't you say that to me, Charlie. Don't you ever."

He looked at her, and his eyes, one brown and one blue, were cold and deadly.

He'd wheeled then and marched out of the house. He was gone for two days. He came back, and they were still cold together. And now, feared Pat, she would die without making up properly with her beautiful boy.

She leapt from her seat, thinking, *I got to find him and I got to tell him the truth,* and pulling on her coat, she went to the door.

She unlocked it and threw it open and stared through the eyeholes of a mask – the mask of a madman.

She tried to scream, but the man in the lunatic's hood clamped a gloved hand over her mouth and forced her back into the flat.

He kicked the door shut.

He spun her around, and he was behind her and he was driving her through into the living room, his breath hot on her neck.

He grabbed her hair and pulled back her head, and the cold blade was on her neck, and she gasped.

The knife cut her, and she cried out.

But then her throat became warm with blood, and she had no breath or voice to scream.

Her body grew cold, and she felt herself drift away, her vision swimming.

Her mouth filled with blood. It ran hot down her chest.

The man loosened his grip on her and her legs gave way and she felt herself fall and fade away and she was dead before she hit the floor.

CHAPTER 88.
THREE DEATHS.

JACK held him against the wall by his throat and said, "Fifteen years ago, I sent a great man out to kill for me. He claimed four seers. He paved the way for my return. There was only a fifth to be killed. Only one more. I gave her to you, Hallam. I gave her to you. I gave you the chance to be a prince in my kingdom. You failed."

Jack tossed him aside. Hallam smashed into the wall. The back of his head cracked against the concrete. Stars burst before his eyes, and he slumped to the ground. He groaned and laid there for what felt like hours.

He sat up slowly. His vision was blurry, and his head ached. Drowsiness overwhelmed him. He threw up. The sour taste of vomit filled his mouth. He cringed and retched again. As his eyes cleared, he saw Jack prowl the darkness, moving from pillar to pillar like a shadow.

They were still in the cavern – wherever that was supposed to be. It was under the tower blocks. But was that possible? Spencer

338

had said how Jack had shown him places and things he never knew existed on Barrowmore. Hallam could tell by looking into Spencer's eyes that some of those things were appalling. Maybe they were things no one should ever see, and once you saw them you were stained.

Hallam certainly felt stained. He felt corrupt. It seemed as if a serpent were slithering inside him, spreading its poison through his veins. And it was all down to Jack. Jack who gave him the chance to live out his desires, who gave him the chance to be a prince.

But Hallam, typically, had thrown it all away. He'd failed to kill Jasmine. He'd failed to be Jack's ripper.

"I… I'm sorry," he said.

Jack wheeled. His black eyes blazed. He swept towards Hallam, who cowered. But Jack was on him, hoisting him to his feet. He screamed in Hallam's face, and his breath was stale. Hallam was nearly sick again.

Then Jack, in his rage, bit Hallam's face. The pain was like fire. He shrieked as Jack's teeth tore into his cheek. Blood ran warmly across his skin. He writhed, begging Jack to let him go.

Jack tore his head away, taking a chunk of Hallam's flesh with him.

Hallam screamed, clutching his face. Blood poured from the wound. It hurt like nothing had ever hurt before.

His flesh filled Jack's mouth – until Jack chewed and swallowed.

"Tasty," he said, smacking his lips. "Shall I eat the rest of you, Hallam?"

"No… please… please… "

"You're crying like a baby. I'm ashamed of you. You've disgraced yourself. I should kill you. I should do what I did with my enemies – I should fucking roast you alive."

"Please… please… "

"One last chance, Hallam."

Relief filled Hallam's heart. "Thank you, thank you."

"Three deaths I want from you."

"Th… three?"

"The first will be the mother. Bring her to me. I want to see her ripped. The second, her child. I just want her dead. The third, the big man. The older one."

"Roy Hanbury?"

"Is that his name?"

"I can't kill Roy Hanbury."

"Why not?"

"Because… he's Roy Hanbury."

"What does his name matter?"

"He's… he's really tough."

"So will you be." He moved towards Hallam. "You will be like a demon. You will be a gelding." He lifted Hallam up against the wall again.

Hallam screamed as Jack's claw-like hand closed around his testicles.

And then Jack said, "You're better off without them, I promise you… I promise you."

Hallam squealed.

CHAPTER 89.
THE MAGICK ARTS.

TASH studied Faultless. He was staring at the portrait of the crucifixion. She went to him and put a hand on his shoulder. He flinched, surprised by her touch.

"You okay?" she said.

"Me? Fine. How's Jasmine?"

"She's sleeping in Dad's room."

They'd come back to her father's house, because her flat had been destroyed. Spencer, meanwhile, had been dragged off to Faultless's rented hovel. Tash's dad stayed with him, keeping an eye. She pitied the teenager but tried not to think about it too much.

Tash had led them out of the cavern. A tunnel snaked away from the elevator shaft where they'd found all those bones. It had been a sewer. The stink could strip the skin from the inside of your nose. Rats scurried. Dirty water ran in a channel under the earth.

She had no idea where she was going, but she had been convinced it was the way out. After all, she'd found her way down there in the first place.

She'd found her daughter and Jack. She'd "seen" them and "known" how to track them down. At the time, she had accepted this knowledge. But now, once more, her gift confused and scared her. Would she always have it? Could it be switched off and on at will?

Faultless said, "I need to find the old man."

"Who is he?"

He shook his head. "He… he looks like… you know… the geezer who took Jasmine – he looks like Jack."

"What's going on?"

"Fuck knows."

"Those bones we found… "

"Don't ask me, Tash, 'cause I've got no idea."

"I'm so scared."

He stroked her hair. They looked at each other. She could see in his eyes that he thought she was beautiful. She could read what he was thinking. It made her quake. It made her want him. But she'd always wanted him. He was Charlie Faultless. He was the man, even when he was a boy. But he was Rachel's. Beautiful Rachel. Thinking about her sister made Tash cry.

"Hey," he said, wiping away a tear.

He touched her face. She kissed his hand. He leaned towards her. Their eyes stayed open. Their eyes said, *Is this the right thing to do?* But their eyes also revealed how badly they wanted each other.

They kissed. His arms around her were strong and safe, and she gasped. Her blood was up. She had heat running through her now. She pressed close, craving him.

When they were done, she must have fallen asleep, because she woke up disorientated.

He was squatting on the floor, his back to her. He wore no shirt. His back bore scars. His muscles rippled. She reached out and touched him and he turned and smiled. She smiled back.

Dressed in his shirt, she sat next to him on the floor. Before them lay more of what they'd found in Jonas Troy's briefcase.

Tash studied a magazine called The Magick Arts. Its pages had yellowed with time, and they felt brittle as she turned them. The pages were full of articles about mediums, psychics, and healers. It featured adverts and illustrations. The journalism was sensationalist. But she found a story about Jonas. She narrowed her eyes and read. The item said Troy was descended from Egyptian shamans, who were the offspring of ancient Hebrew prophets.

"This genuine?" she said.

He shrugged.

"Do you think it's possible at all that the man we saw was Jack the Ripper?"

"He said he was 'once' Jack the Ripper."

"What did he mean by that?"

He shook his head. "He said as well he was 'once' Montague Druitt. So who is he now, or who does he think he is?"

"And who was he before?" said Tash.

CHAPTER 90.
BEWARE THE SNAKE.

IN the pile of papers they found in the briefcase, Faultless discovered a leather-bound Bible. It was a pocket-sized version.

He skimmed through the pages. The writing was tiny. As he flipped through, something caught his eye.

He opened it where a passage had been underlined in ink and notes were scribbled in the margin.

Tash sat next to him on the floor. She kissed his shoulder. It was very matter-of-fact. Like she'd kissed it every day for years.

He smiled. She looked scared.

"What does the Bible say about sleeping with your murdered sister's boyfriend?" she said.

He shook his head. "I think it's okay."

"You sure about that?"

He nodded.

She asked, "What have you found there?"

"It's underlined. Hebrews, chapter four, verses twelve to thirteen. It says, 'For the word of God is quick, and powerful, and sharper than any two-edged sword, piercing even to the dividing asunder of soul and spirit, and of the joints and marrow, and is a discerner of the thoughts and intents of the heart. Neither is there any creature that is not manifest in his sight: but all things are naked and opened unto the eyes of him with whom we have to do'."

Faultless stayed quiet and turned the pages, looking for more marked passages.

"Another one," he said. "Leviticus, chapter seventeen, verse eleven. 'For it is the blood that maketh atonement for the soul.' And then this. Genesis, chapter three, verse one. 'Now the serpent was more subtle than any beast of the field which the LORD God has made.' Someone's written 'Beware the snake' next to the verse."

Faultless felt a chill run through him. He looked behind him, to where Hanbury kept his python. He stood and went over to the vivarium. It was empty. Or it looked empty. He peered in, looking for the reptile under the rocks and branches. He saw nothing.

"Where's it gone?" he asked.

"The snake?"

"Yeah."

"I… why? It can't have nothing to do with Dad's python."

"No, but… I don't know, it just made me think."

Faultless felt a sense of fear flood his heart. The foreboding had grown since he'd come face to face with Jack. It was as if something had been sown in his heart at that moment. Or maybe it was always there, and the meeting had made the seed begin to grow. One thing he knew, he was hesitant to make love with Tash. But he needed to. He wanted her. Not as a substitute for Rachel, but as Tash. It had been difficult because of the feelings he'd experienced in the cavern – the sense that he would stain the world, that he would poison everything. But his desire for her was overwhelming, and for those few minutes, he felt cleansed. The notion that he was tarnished, though, returned quickly once he started reading through the notes.

The phone rang. Tash answered it. She nodded and then put the receiver back in its cradle.

"That was Dad," she said. "He wants you to… to go over and help him have a word with Spencer. Don't be cruel to him, Charlie. And don't let my dad… you know… "

"I'll go over and supervise," said Faultless.

He rose, reluctant to leave her. A knock on the door stopped him. Tash opened it. Don Wilks stood outside, sneering.

CHAPTER 91.
INNER MONSTER.

"I AM not the man I was, Spencer," said Hanbury, "but it would be very easy for me to be him again. He hangs about in my head, son. He keeps asking if he can come out and play again. But I says to him, 'No, you ain't coming out, old Roy, Jesus is in my heart now, and he's my friend.' Did you give them Sharpleys the games console back? Thought not. Maybe if you had, all this wouldn't have happened."

"Don't hurt me, Mr Hanbury."

"I cannot promise that, son."

Spencer had been told to sit quietly on a blanket in Faultless's flat. Hanbury had given him water and some bread. "Jail food, son, so you get used to it." After he'd eaten, he'd fallen asleep. When he woke up, Hanbury rang Tash to tell her.

"Send Charlie over," he'd said. "We can play good villain, bad villain with Spencer. Or maybe just bad villain, bad villain."

As he waited for Faultless, Hanbury thought about his former apprentice.

The boy had been ruthless. Hanbury's lieutenants had marked Faultless out from the time he'd been eleven or twelve. Most lads of that age, you had to discipline. You scared the shit out of them so they learned to stay under the Old Bill's radar. Not Charlie Faultless. He knew how to keep out of trouble while causing as much as possible.

Hanbury started using him to deal drugs and dole out threats when the lad was fourteen. Charlie knew nothing about it at the time – he was dealing for someone on Hanbury's payroll, that was all.

But Faultless really made a name for himself a few months after he was first recruited, when he saved Tash from a pervert.

After that, Faultless entered the fold. He was a Hanbury lieutenant. He was a future Face. And because Hanbury had no sons, he was a possible heir.

But then the Graveney murder happened.

Hanbury shook his head now, the pain of having to exile Faultless sapping his strength.

And then he comes back, thought Hanbury. *And the gates of hell open wide.*

At first it seemed that Charlie Faultless was a changed man. But now bad was coming out of him again – like sweat. He was shedding his respectable skin. His eyes were darkening. He sported that grimace he'd worn as a youth. He was always menacing, but now he reeked of something else. He reeked of malevolence.

All men have a beast in them, Hanbury knew that. But most could control their inner monster. They had different ways of doing it – he'd let Jesus into his heart, while Faultless trained his sights on a different career.

But when the call came, the beast would rear up. The seed of barbarism in a man's heart sprouted again.

"You ever heard of Charlie Faultless, Spencer?" said Hanbury now. "I knew Charlie many years ago, when he was your age. You think you're tough? You don't know Faultless. He was a right cunt. Still is. I can see it in his eyes. And I'm telling you, he ain't got Christ in his heart. He ain't got nothing but darkness in him."

Spencer whimpered.

Hanbury went to get a sack that lay under the desk. He'd brought it with him when they'd smuggled Spencer into the flat. Its contents would be used to scare the teenager into talking.

Hanbury picked up the sack. He reached inside and brought out the python. He draped it over his shoulders. The reptile writhed. Its skin was cool and smooth on Hanbury's nape.

Spencer cried.

Hanbury wondered where Faultless was but thought he'd get the session underway.

"Please don't," begged Spencer.

Someone knocked on the door.

Faultless, thought Hanbury. He went to answer it, the snake still around his shoulders, but as he opened the door he thought, *Why doesn't Charlie have his key?*

The hammer cracked Hanbury in the middle of his forehead.

CHAPTER 92.
21ˢᵀ CENTURY POLICING.

DON Wilks said, "I followed you here, son. Proper, old-fashioned police work. Followed you. What happened to that little girl you were carrying, eh?"

"You could've checked before you hauled me away, Wilks," said Faultless, handcuffed in the back of the police car.

"Yeah, I don't really give that much of a shit. Was her mate got killed, weren't it? What was her name?"

"You're the detective."

"I'm a busy man. Trying to catch crooks and killers. Victims ain't my problem. We got liaison officers and all that politically correct bullshit for them, Faultless."

"Of course. I forgot – you being the face of 21ˢᵗ century policing and all."

Wilks chuckled.

Faultless caught the driver watching him in the rear-view mirror. The copper's eyes were wide with shock. They were saying, *Wilks has got nothing to do with me, mate.*

For a while, no one spoke. Faultless kept his head down, thinking about things. Mostly who he was and where he'd come from. How he could find Lew. Who Jack really was and why he'd told Faultless, "You're like me."

He shivered. His mind went round and round, over the same questions that had haunted him for days.

He'd assumed Wilks was taking him to the closest nick, which was Brick Lane. Thinking that, he never bothered to keep an eye on the roads. But when he lifted his head to stretch his neck, he noticed they were nowhere near Brick Lane.

So he asked, "Where the fuck are we?"

Again, the driver gave him a look and this time his eyes said, *This ain't my doing, mate – I'm following orders.*

Shit, thought Faultless.

"Stop the car, Khan," said Wilks.

"Wilks, what the fuck – "

"Shut it, Faultless."

"Sir," said Khan. "I'm not – "

"And you shut it, too, Khan. Everyone fucking shut it. Everyone do as they're fucking told. Khan, you fucking remember what I got."

In the rear-view mirror, Khan's eyes told Faultless, *I'm fucked.*

Khan pulled the car up on the pavement outside some rusting, metal gates. A sign on the gates said the site was part of a renewal project. It was an old industrial estate. Grey buildings lurked behind the gates. They flanked rutted roads. Pavements were overgrown with grass and weeds. Beer cans rolled about in the wind.

Wilks dragged Faultless out of the car and marched him towards the gate.

"I like fucking with people," said the detective. "Khan, he's a Muslim, see. Fucking loads of them in the Met these days. It's a fucking shambles. Thing is, he's also a homo. Which is classic. Typical fucking Met these days – queers and Pakis."

"So you're fucking blackmailing him, Wilks. Ever the cunt."

351

Wilks opened the gates. They screeched. He shoved Faultless, who stumbled forward. He heard the gates clank shut.

Wilks pushed him, making him walk up the road. It was a ghost-town of a place. Creaking gates. Clanking doors. Dark windows showing gloomy interiors.

They came to the edge of the first warehouse. Wire fencing hemmed in a courtyard just round the corner. Faultless sensed something. He heard laughter. Maybe it was the ghosts. But when he came round the corner, he saw the men.

Four of them. Coppers in uniform with their sleeves rolled up, tapping their batons on their palms in anticipation.

"Two of these fellas, you know," said Wilks.

They were the two filth Faultless had beat up behind the lock-ups.

"The other two are pleased to meet you, Charlie."

The coppers sneered. They bristled. Their hate showed.

Faultless thought, *What have I got to lose?* and he swung his handcuffed wrists in an arc, smashing Wilks in the face. Blood came from the detective's nose. He stumbled away, arms flailing.

The four cops legged it out of the courtyard towards him. Faultless tried to do a runner, but he stumbled.

He heard them behind him, their rage hot on his neck.

And when the first baton strike laid him out, he knew he could do nothing but cover up and take a beating.

CHAPTER 93.
BORN OF JACKALS OR WOMEN.

SPENCER knew he was going to have to die. He was dead the moment he listened to that voice in his head telling him to kill Jay-T. But how could he not listen? It had been so tempting, that voice. It had been demanding. It told him to pick up a brick and smash Jay-T's skull. It had called for blood, and Spencer had given it blood.

And now he was going to pay for everything he'd done. He'd suffer because he'd let Jack down. He'd betrayed him. He'd shown weakness.

There's always a judgment, he told himself now. And maybe that was a good thing. Life seemed pointless. He'd seen too many terrible things to want to live on.

His heart had been corrupted. Not that it was pure in the first place. It had always been bad. But it had never been evil. And now, Spencer knew, it was full of sin. It was a black, pulsing monster in his chest.

He was glad to go with Hanbury when they raided the cavern and rescued Jasmine. He showed unwillingness – just so Jack thought he'd put up a fight. But Jack probably knew the truth. Jack knew most things.

Hanbury had told him to sit quietly in the corner, where Spencer eventually fell asleep. He'd been exhausted. It had been a relief to get away from the bloodshed.

But the respite was brief.

Charlie Faultless was coming, and that was bad news.

Spencer had heard about him. Geezers talked about him in the pub. Dealers muttered his name. Spencer's mum said he was evil. "He was cursed, with his different coloured eyes," she'd warn. "Best thing ever happened to Barrowmore is that he disappeared. Evil, he was, evil." And then she'd lean in and whisper, "They said he wasn't born of a woman, Spencer. They said he was born of a jackal, and you know what that means, darlin'."

Spencer had no idea what it meant. And he had no clue what "not born of a woman" meant, either.

All he knew was Charlie Faultless had returned, and he was on his way over.

Whether he was born of jackals or women, it made no difference to Spencer. The guy was scary.

When Mr Hanbury went to the door with that snake coiling around his neck, Spencer really started to worry.

He tried to think of ways to escape. If Hanbury and Faultless came in now, he might have to make a run for it. He quaked with fear. They'd catch him easily. But he had to try. Just get away from all this. He'd hole up with his cousin in Stepney for a while. Wait until Barrowmore calmed down. Until Jack went away.

He rolled his knees up and wrapped his arms around them, rocking back and forth.

But Jack wouldn't go away. If he killed a fifth, like he said he was going to, then he'd have the whole of London at his mercy.

And that meant Stepney.

Spencer whimpered. Nowhere was safe. Anywhere you looked, you had either Jack or Faultless or Hanbury – men born of jackals or women, maybe. Men born to kill. Not like him. He was born to hide, and that's what he should have done right after he'd stolen the Sharpleys' PS3.

But now it was too late.

And he knew that for certain when he heard scuffling from the hallway and then someone stumbling.

Mr Hanbury staggered back into the living room. The snake writhed around his neck. Blood ran down his face. Spencer gasped in horror.

Mr Hanbury fell to his knees. The snake coiled. Spencer nearly went over to help Mr Hanbury. But then a figure entered the room, and when Spencer saw him, the desire to help went away very quickly.

It was Hallam Buck with a hammer in his hand.

But not the Hallam Buck Spencer had known.

This was a very different looking Hallam Buck.

His face was grey. There was a gaping wound in his cheek. Dark circles rimmed his eyes, which were wide and glittery. His jaw drooped, and something that looked like tar filled his mouth, and it oozed down his chin. Sweat drenched his body, and his clothes were saturated. His groin was bloody. It was a black-red blood. Blood from deep inside. Blood from your heart. His trousers at his crotch had been torn away, and through the blood Spencer saw flaps of skin hang like frayed ribbons.

Hallam Buck had been castrated.

Now the neutered child-killer raised his hammer and went for Mr Hanbury, who managed to kick out a leg and parry Hallam's attack.

Mr Hanbury was on all fours. He was looking at Spencer. His face was a mask of blood.

He said, "Get out of here and find Charlie Faultless."

The snake wound itself around Mr Hanbury's neck. Its black eyes fixed on Spencer, and it seemed to smile. The snake tightened its body.

Now Hallam had regained his balance. He came again with his hammer. The tarry liquid dribbled from his mouth. He smashed the hammer into Mr Hanbury's skull. The old villain's eyes rolled back. He fell on his face.

The snake smiled at Spencer as it strangled Mr Hanbury.

Hallam straddled the dying man. He started to beat him with his hammer.

Spencer cried and shivered. He wet himself. The stink of piss triggered something in him, and he quickly crawled away, keeping tight to the wall. He tried not to look, but from the corner of his eyes he could see.

He could see Hallam like a pendulum hammering Mr Hanbury, the sound of bone cracking and brain mushing making him sick.

He could see the snake's black eyes follow him as he made his escape. The serpent hissed and Spencer was sure the animal was speaking to him and it was saying, *"I am the lord who gapes... I am the lantern of the tomb... I am the moth eating at the law... "*

356

CHAPTER 94.
I AM NOT OWED GOOD FORTUNE.

JUDGMENT, Faultless thought. *This is judgment.*

He hurt all over. He bled from his mouth, his scalp, and his nose. He bled inside too. He was sure of it. He felt death creep up on him.

For years, he thought he'd got away with everything. He thought he'd got away with murder. Tony Graveney's murder.

But justice had been pursuing him. It had been a predator, lurking in the shadows, waiting for him to make a mistake.

And he made one.

He'd come home.

He lay on the bunk in the police cell and put his arm across his eyes. His head ached. He worried he might have a fractured skull. Although his attackers had focused their batons on his body, a few blows cracked him on the nut.

He vaguely recalled them dragging him along the ground and throwing him into a car. He remembered feeling sick. He might have puked. He had a bad taste in his mouth when he came around. He had blood in there, too. Blood and dirt.

When they took him into the police station, he heard Wilks say, "This fella's been beaten up. He's drunk. People are looking for him. We're booking him in for his own safety."

He had looked up at the desk sergeant, and the woman's face had been creased with concern, and she'd said, "He needs a doctor, now."

Wilks had said, "I've got one coming."

Next thing Faultless knew, he was in a cell. Some bloke with bad breath was in his face, shining a light in his eyes.

Wilks's voice nearby was saying, "Give him a cursory glance, Doc. And tell that cow on the custody desk that he's all right."

The bloke with bad breath had said, "Chief Superintendent Wilks, this man is gravely in need of hospital treatment, and – "

"And you, Doc, will be gravely in need of a divorce lawyer and a new reputation when I accidentally give the press the file on you and those under-aged Lithuanian prostitutes."

"I… I thought they were eighteen, all of them."

"The missus would be all right with that, then, will she?"

Then Wilks and the bloke with bad breath had gone and Faultless dreamed of being trapped in a furnace.

He woke up feeling sick. He had no phone, no watch. He had no idea what the time was. How long he'd been here. How damaged he was.

Again he thought, *Judgment. This is what I had coming.*

It was just a shame that Wilks had been his judge. But you had no choice. If you sin, you don't get to choose your punishment – or your punisher.

He'd always known this day would come. He'd never felt he deserved the luck he'd had since leaving England.

Three years before, he'd won one of the US's most prestigious journalism awards. He'd written a piece about two Detroit drug dealers, murdered by a police hit squad. It resulted in four policemen being jailed. But even as he accepted the award and his peers applauded him, a tiny voice in his head was saying, "You shouldn't be here, you fraud – you should be in jail with those killer cops, rotting."

Even on his wedding day to the lavish Cora-Marie Bryant, a former Miss Boston and a New York media lawyer, he was thinking, *This is not what I deserve.*

Two years later, when Cora-Marie left him because he spent all his time on assignments, he felt he did deserve to lose her.

I am not owed happiness, he told himself. *I am not owed good fortune.*

So every time it came his way, he did his best to send it packing.

Soon after Cora-Marie divorced him, Faultless had decided to come back to England. He had to face his demons. He had to face his judgment. But if he were going to be punished, at least he could get some vengeance.

So he would investigate his mother's death, Rachel's death, and write a book about the killings. He would find the killer and name him. And then, if the old Charlie insisted, he would punish the murderer as well.

It would make Faultless feel better about the murder of his girlfriend and the murder of his mother, and it would make him feel better for killing an innocent man.

Well, innocent of those murders. Graveney was hardly Francis of Assisi. He certainly deserved judgment. Just not for murdering Patricia Faultless.

Now he tried to work out the time. It was probably early evening. He wondered how long he'd been holed up in this cell. Wilks would certainly question him over Graveney's murder, and he'd have him charged for beating up those coppers – despite the fact they'd got their revenge.

As he rested, breathing steadily, he started to smell something weird. He sat up quickly. Not a good idea. Dizziness overpowered him, and he was close to fainting. But he mastered his state and steadied himself, his vision clearing, his coordination returning.

He looked round the cell.

The odour was stronger now. It was sharp in his nostrils and made his eyes water.

He blinked, his eyes sore. But then he kept them open. He fixed on something. Something he thought at first was gas.

They're poisoning me, he said to himself.

The gas smelled of bad eggs. It seeped out of the floor, from the crevices in the walls. It poured through the slats in the ceiling.

He tried to hold his breath. His chest tightened. He gasped. The bad odour filled his lungs. He felt sick. He felt queasy. Panic gripped him. He scrambled for the door, thinking, *Bastard filth,* and he clawed at the metal grille, trying to open it.

Then he jerked, as if the floor had actually risen.

He looked down, not believing it. But it was true.

The floor bucked again. Faultless was thrown off his feet. He staggered back towards the bunk. He had to breathe and sucked in the bad air.

It was rotten. It was decayed. He retched.

The floor kicked up again. Something was under it, trying to get out. Something big. It reared again, the concrete splitting now. The floor peeled back. It creaked and groaned.

Faultless rolled up into a ball on his bunk and watched with horror as the ground opened.

A shaft of light shot up through the crack, and it was blinding.

Heat filled the cell. Sweat poured down Faultless's face. Sweat and blood. The earth cleaved. An eruption from below threw up soil and concrete. It rained over Faultless, and he covered his head.

The noise was deafening. The roaring of the earth tearing. The creaking of structures buckling. The sizzling of flames burning.

Faultless kept his head down. He shut his eyes. He gritted his teeth. He waited to die.

But only silence came. Everything grew still and quiet.

He panted, still cowering. The smell remained, but it was now mingling with other odours – smoke, wood, petrol.

He panicked and sat up, and standing at the edge of the abyss at the centre of the cell, smoking a cigar, was Lew.

He smiled at Faultless and said, "I've come for you in your darkest place."

CHAPTER 95.
THE THING ON THE
THRESHOLD.

TASH mopped Jasmine's brow. Her daughter was still running a temperature. It had been a terrible ordeal. But at least Tash felt safe now in her dad's flat. She sat on the edge of the bed, looking at her child.

A chill raced through her veins. Instead of sleeping here in her grandfather's bed, Jasmine could easily be dead.

Tash was still confused about where they had been a few hours ago. The cavern. How had they got there? Had it always existed, beneath Barrowmore? Were there secret places in every city?

And how had they got out? The sewer seemed to go on forever. She thought they would never get out. But finally it led them into the lock-ups. They had to crawl through a manhole cover.

She thought of the journey from the underworld where Jasmine had been taken.

Something inside her had guided Tash out. An instinct. A knowledge. She was psychic. She'd always believed in that kind of thing.

She'd read her stars, and they promised her good luck and fortune, but as yet those pledges hadn't been fulfilled. She watched mediums on TV and gawped as they doled out messages from the other side to weeping audience members. She'd visited fortune tellers and tarot card readers and clairvoyants. She'd paid her money and listened as they told her things that at the time seemed remarkable.

You feel you have so much more to give, Tash.

You enjoy the company of others, but sometimes you like solitude.

You are a creative person, but you're not sure how to best use your creativity.

You are someone who lives for today, but you worry a lot about the future.

You love your family very much, but sometimes they make you sad.

That had been when her dad was in jail. How could the woman have known?

Being psychic would have been great. A gift you could use to help other people. You could be like that Psychic Sally, visiting theatres throughout the UK to help people contact dead relatives, dead friends.

And now she was psychic. Or had always been psychic. But it wasn't exciting. It was terrifying.

All along, her dreams had been real – the nightmares that had plagued her, the visions that made her wake up in a panic.

And this gift, this curse, had been passed on to Jasmine.

Tash brushed the hair out of her daughter's face. It was damp. The child groaned. Her skin was pale and clammy. Her temperature soared.

Don't die, baby, don't die, Tash thought.

Was Jasmine dreaming now of terrible things? Was she seeing something? That monster, maybe? The one who called himself Jack. The one who was going to have her daughter murdered and mutilated.

Rage flared in Tash's breast.

She'd kill him if he came near her child again. She'd kill anyone who threatened Jasmine.

But why would he dismember his victims? She hadn't found the answer in Jonas Troy's scribblings so far. She remembered his notes, trying to think. Only the seers died like this. Only the seers were torn open and things taken from the body. Not only organs, but something else.

She touched her breast.

What do we have inside us?

She felt her heart beat, and it made her think of Charlie. Wilks had taken him. He'd be questioned but ultimately released, Tash was sure of it. Charlie had always been in trouble with the police – and he'd always got out of it.

Her body tingled as she thought of them together. She'd always liked him. But she was only a kid when he dated Rachel. He was bad back then. He was rotten. But that made him more appealing. He still had that darkness about him, but he'd grown up. He was a man, not a boy. She hoped he would stay. She touched Jasmine's brow. She wanted him to stay with them.

The doorbell rang.

She thought, *Charlie*, and rushed through from the bedroom, into the living room.

A dark shape showed through the pebbled glass of the front door. Something coiled in her belly, something urging her not to open the door. But she ignored the warning signs. She opened the door.

It was shaped like a man, but much of the humanity had gone from it, although she did recognize the mutilated face.

It was too late to scream, and it was too late to slam the door. Because in the seconds it took her to gawk at the thing on the threshold, it had forced her back into the house and pummelled her with a hammer.

CHAPTER 96.
THE FIRST EVIL.

AN alarm wailed. Outside the cell, fire blazed. The flames danced and flickered behind the grille in the door. They turned the cell into a furnace.

Faultless lay against the wall, staring.

Lew said, "So are you coming?"

"Where am I supposed to come to?"

"To your fate."

"Who are you?"

"Don't you know?"

"Why would I ask?"

"I am who I am."

"You what?"

"I am who I am," repeated Lew.

"Yeah, that means fuck all."

"Nothing means anything. Are you coming? You have no choice."

"Where am I going, Lew?"

"You're going back where you came from, Charlie."

Faultless looked down into the fissure. The rocks were volcanic. The smell of sulphur wafted upwards. He should have been in a panic. This wasn't normal. But he felt calm. He felt as if he'd expected this to happen.

He asked, "First, tell me about Jack the Ripper."

"Funny name, that."

"I don't know his real name. Who is he?"

Lew smiled. "He is The First Evil."

"I don't understand."

"He was my first dark thought, Charlie. Lust. Greed. Envy. Whatever. All of it. He was the first. The First Evil. And because I thought him, he had to be born."

"Who the fuck are you?"

"I said, I am who I am."

"That doesn't make sense."

"Nothing does. Come with me."

Faultless obeyed. The alarm kept wailing. Outside, the fire burned. But soon, the police would be here. They'd want to know what was going on.

"Why is he killing these women?"

"Charlie, Charlie… they're seers. They hunt him; he hunts them. These are the laws that were written down."

"By who?"

"By me."

"Who the fuck are you?"

Lew smiled and shook his head. "Can't you guess?"

Faultless preferred not to. Instead he said, "Then who the fuck am I?"

"You, my boy," said the old man, "are the Second Evil. Now go down into the fire and wait for me."

CHAPTER 97.
SHINE BRIGHT.

JASMINE staggered out of the bedroom to find Hallam Buck attacking her mum.

She screamed.

Hallam and her mum looked at her. They stared for a second. Hallam looked horrible. His face was pasty and black rings encircled his eyes and his cheek was torn. Something tarry dribbled from his mouth, and he was covered in blood and sweat. Jasmine went cold with fear. He'd already tried to kill her once. He had been going to cut her with a knife. And now he was back to do it again.

Mum said, "Run, Jasmine, run! Go find Charlie!"

For a second she wanted to stay and help her mother. But when Hallam's face darkened and twisted into an expression of hate and he tried to lunge for her, Jasmine yelped and bolted out of the door.

After running into the middle of the road, she stopped and looked back and thought of going to help her mum.

But she was scared. Her legs buckled, and she fell to her knees. She stared towards the door of her grandfather's house and cried.

She yelled, "Mum… Mum," and then looked around, hoping someone would be there to help her.

There was no one.

Night had fallen on Barrowmore. Apart from a few youths, most residents stayed indoors these days. Dread gripped the estate. The murders had seen people curfew themselves and their children. In the dark was no place to be. Not these days.

Jasmine got to her feet and started to go back towards the house. A hand fell on her shoulder. She nearly jumped out of her skin. Turning quickly, she gawped up at the figure who'd come out of the dark. He was soaked. His hair was plastered to his scalp. His eyes were wide with the horror of the things he'd seen.

He said, "Don't go back in there 'cause he'll kill you."

"H… how do you know who's in there?" she asked Spencer Drake.

"Because I've just seen him kill your grandad, and he said he was coming to get you or your mum."

Jasmine said nothing. The information seeped into her brain. She processed it – her grandad was dead – and then slotted it away, because she couldn't cope with it right now. She had other stuff to worry about.

"We got to help her," she said, trying not to think of her grandad.

"It's too late now."

"But my mum's been – "

"It's too late. He's already taken her."

"They never came out."

"They don't need to. I seen all kinds of places on Barrowmore these past few days I never knew existed. Secret places. Places to hide. Places to wait. I wish I hadn't seen, but I have seen, and it's done something to me."

"What about my mum?"

"Come on, Jasmine, we got to hide somewhere – they'll find us."

368

"Who'll find us?"

"Come on," he said and grabbed her arm.

"What are you doing? Don't, I'll scream… "

He stopped and looked at her. "You're in danger, yeah. We all are. I mean, I'm already dead. Or I will be soon. So we got to hide till we can think of something to do."

"I got to find Charlie Faultless."

Spencer gawped. "You know where to find him?"

Jasmine shook her head.

"But ain't you psychic?" he said.

She looked up at him. "How do you know that?"

"Jack… him… he told me."

"You were there when he was going to kill me. Have you come to kidnap me again and take me to him?"

"No, honest. Honest, I ain't. Your grandad dragged me out of there, and he was going to give me a hiding, get me to talk. But I would've talked, anyway. I would've told him anything. I don't want nothing to do with the evil stuff that's been going on here no more. Nothing. I got to do something about what I've done. I… I got to redeem myself, your grandad said. Before I face judgment. So… so I can try to help you."

"Why is Hallam helping him?"

"Hallam's sick. Sick deep inside. And now he's got more poison in him. Black poison that just kills your soul, I think."

She looked around. "It's really quiet."

"Everyone's scared."

"You think my mum's already gone, then?"

He nodded.

She started to walk back towards the house.

"No," said Spencer.

She ignored him and kept going. Fog swirled at the front door, and it wafted out into the street, making it difficult for her to see in the house. She backed up, scared.

369

"It's him," she said. "It's him, Spencer."

"He's not there, now. He's just left his stain on the place, that's all. He corrupts everything. But you can see him. You can find him. That's why he wanted you dead. You and your mum."

"I don't know how to do it."

"Yes you do. Just think hard."

"I can't. I ain't special."

"You are. He says… this Jack… he says you've got powerful souls and you shine. And it's because you shine so brightly you can shed light, he says, on secret things. Things other people can't see. Things like evil. Things… things like him."

"Where's my mum?" she said.

"You got to find her by finding him."

"I can't."

"You got to. And you got to do it quickly."

CHAPTER 98.
SECRETS IN THE CELL.

WHEN Don Wilks got back to the police station, he found everyone gathered outside. Smoke billowed from the building. Fire engines' blue lights lit up the darkening sky. Locals clustered about, probably hoping to see the nick burn to the ground.

Wilks elbowed his way past some women wearing niqabs. They berated him, and he nearly turned back and told them to fuck off back to where they came from, but he was too focused on finding out what had happened.

The desk sergeant stood among a group of coppers, staring at the building as it spewed smoke.

"What the fuck's going on?" said Wilks.

"We had an explosion, we think," she said. "Whole building shook. Then we smelled smoke. The alarms went off, and we got out."

"What about the prisoners down below?"

The woman shook her head.

Wilks stared at the building. Firefighters bustled around the entrance. The door stood open. He thought, *I can leave Faultless down there to die*. But something told him there were secrets down there in the cell. Secrets he needed to know. Revelations he wanted to experience. Memories he had to recall.

At first he walked, striding towards the station's front door. After a few yards, he picked up speed. By the time someone shouted at him to stop and he heard his name being called out, Wilks was running.

He was through the door, the smoke choking him, blinding him. He cried out, flapping his arms to clear some air for himself. His eyes watered. It was pitch black. He stumbled and crashed into the front desk. He veered right, coughing, spluttering.

Something drove him on. A determination born deep inside him. A grit he never knew he had.

There was something down in those cells luring him.

He found the swing-doors and fell through them. Cold air filled his lungs, and he panted. The stairs were clear. No smoke. No fire. He descended, swaying from side to side.

The cries of the prisoners met him as he reached the ground floor. He rammed through the swing-doors. He slid the bars aside and stumbled down the corridor. It was charred. The walls were black. The smell of burning was strong.

From behind the thick, metal doors of the cells, the prisoners begged to be released. They cried and screamed. But Wilks ignored them. He was headed to the farthest cell. The one into which he had thrown a broken Faultless.

He should've had him killed on the industrial estate. But he had wanted to keep him alive, to punish him and make him suffer. The plan was to keep him here overnight and then take him out of his cell again for another beating. Then Wilks would interrogate him and charge him with assaulting police officers and for the murder of Tony Graveney. All he'd have to do then was to hope that the Crown Prosecution Service had the balls to take it to court.

It was a fragile hope. But Wilks had a Plan B. It involved slowly turning Charlie Faultless into a vegetable.

You'll be sucking mush through a straw and shitting through a tube by the time I've finished with you, he thought.

Now he came to Faultless's cell. He threw open the door. He nearly fainted. Faultless had gone. So had the cell's floor. In its place, a huge hole. Heat came up from the hole. Its edges were red hot. Wilks broke out into a sweat. He rocked from side to side, feeling drowsy.

Then he saw an old man, standing at the edge of the abyss.

They looked each other in the eye, and Wilks knew exactly who he was. His gaze seemed to drill into him so he could almost feel it in his body like a wire slicing through him.

The old man said, "You're one of his, aren't you."

And then Wilks knew he was nearly home.

CHAPTER 99.
BLOODSPORT.

"I WISH I could kill you myself," Jack said. "Rip it out of you with my own hands. But I can't. I can't because that's how it was spoken. I have to call out to a ripper. I have to find a really dark heart. I thought I'd found one in Hallam, but he is more sick than evil. He is wrong in so many ways. And Spencer, I knew would never do. Too weak. Convenient for me to be freed from my prison, of course. Easily tempted to kill his friend. But not a ripper. Not the prince of monsters I need. He's betrayed me, the little fucker, and he'll pay for that. He will die very badly."

Tash ached. Her head throbbed. She knew she was bleeding from her scalp. When Hallam attacked her with the hammer, she thought he was killing her. He'd come to get Jasmine, she'd thought, so she had to fight to protect her daughter. That's why she'd told Jasmine to run. But Hallam had come for her, not for Jasmine.

She sat up quickly, gasping for breath. She looked around, not knowing where she was. It was dark and cold.

"You're thinking, *Where am I?* ain't you," Jack said. "Well, you're nowhere. But I'm going to take you somewhere. And on the way, I'm going to show you things – I'm going to show you how everything happened. You and your sort have caused me great torment. But now it will end. Your death will mean my life. The world will fear me. It will see me in all my glory."

Tash was still looking around. Unable to see anything, she focused on her sense of touch. The ground where she lay was rocky. Was she on a mountain or down a mine? It could be anywhere. Not knowing scared her.

Jack went on.

"There's a little piece of me in every human. Evil lurks in them all. It was put in there when you were made. It is sin. Initially, it was dormant. But then it became alive, because one man disobeyed God. And men after that made good use of it. But it will be nothing compared to what I do when I am free of this ordeal. This is a bloodsport. It's been a long war. But with you dead, and my Ripper returning with his treasures, it'll soon be done."

"Would it do any good if I begged you to let me go?"

"Do you think I have compassion? It's not part of my design. Now, we've got to go. We've got to get to the place where you'll be killed and I'll be born. On the way, I'll show you things – that'll be my one and only gift. I'll show you how things became what they are."

He grabbed her hand. She gasped as a surge of energy shot up her arm into her body, slamming into her heart.

Tash jerked. Her chest locked up. She struggled to breathe. Her vision swam. In the dark, she saw a tiny, white dot. It grew, expanding till it became a ball of fire – still small in the vast blackness, but the sole object in this endless space.

And then the ball of fire exploded. Red heat fanned out. It spread across the darkness, filling it with light. Debris sailed off from the centre of the eruption, whirling in the flaming landscape.

Tash found her breath and let out a gasp.

"I'm taking you back to the beginning," Jack told her. "All the way back."

And as Tash watched, worlds formed.

CHAPTER 100.
CREATION STORY.

BIRTH is brutal, Tash knew that. Every birth is the same –
whether it's a mouse or a universe.

It's always an ordeal.

And Tash experienced it – the pain of every birth that had ever
been, from the first to the last.

She learned about this birth and this pain through Jack. The
knowledge flowed from him and into her. He was there, very
nearly at the beginning, so everything she experienced was true;
she knew that.

She felt the heat from the explosion – the explosion that made
everything.

She witnessed what followed – galaxies and solar systems
materializing, stars being born, planets forming.

The sun was made, and she stared right at it without blinding
herself and knew immediately that like everything else that had
been born, it would die.

Hurtling through a sky that went rapidly from dark to light, she
surveyed a world of green beneath her. Forests sprouted from the
soil and spread over the planet. Mountains tore themselves out of

the ground, the groaning world splitting as the great rocks reared up. Water gushed out from the cracks in the earth and washed across the land in great oceans.

As she viewed creation, Tash had a sense that everything she was seeing had a supernatural hand guiding it. It was certainly not a natural event. She became more convinced of this as more life developed.

After the trees and the plants came the animals, the fish, and the birds. She couldn't name some of the creatures she saw. They were strange. Behemoths slicing down jungles with their tails. Leviathans sweeping through the seas. Clouds of insects, miles wide, darkening the skies.

The earth bloomed. It was beautiful. But one part of it was more beautiful than the rest – it was greener, more brightly coloured. It was a garden. And stumbling through it, two people. A man and a woman. They were naked, and their bodies were bloody, as if they had just been born.

Tash gazed at the oasis. She felt jealous that these two humans were allowed to live in such peace and beauty.

Then she spotted something else.

A shadow.

It moved through the undergrowth, taking on the form of a serpent.

Tash felt sick. Its vileness made her skin crawl.

The first evil, she thought and wondered how she could've known such a thing.

And a name came to her. Was it… pillow? Yellow. Something like that?

Pillow… pillow… up-elo…

Tash's chest tightened.

Down in the garden, the serpent beckoned the woman. Tash tried to warn her, but she had no voice. The woman reached for a bright red fruit hanging from a tree.

The images whirled. Tash saw the woman give the fruit to the man, telling him to eat it. And when he did, darkness filled the sky. Suddenly, everything decayed. Weeds sprang from the earth. Thorns wrapped themselves around the trees. Animals that had lived together harmoniously began killing each other.

There was blood, and there was hate.

Tash wept.

She saw two brothers, clad in animal skin. One worked hard, skinning a goat. The other lurked nearby, watching – and the shadow clung to his shoulder.

It whispered in the brother's ear.

Tash heard the words, *Murder him and I will make you king.*

So brother killed brother. He mutilated his sibling's dead body. Soon the killer was coated in blood and gore. He dug his hand into the corpse and lifted something out of it, holding it up triumphantly.

Tash blinked. It was a golden orb. It shimmered. The shadow took the orb and swallowed it and the light dimmed and gloom fell across the land.

The shadow flashed away and raced over the earth, and wherever he went, there was savagery.

Tash cried because of all the suffering she witnessed.

Cities were built. The evil stain passed over them. Men killed. They built armies. They raided other cities. They made slaves of the conquered peoples. They raped women and murdered children.

Empires rose and fell, and blood stained the world.

There was nothing but darkness, nothing but pain.

But then the heavens opened, and what Tash could only describe as angels fell down to the earth. All across the world they mated with human women, and their offspring had light coming from their eyes. Tash felt an affinity with these children of angels and humans. She felt she was one of them. She knew she *was* one of them.

"Who are you?" she heard herself ask. "Who are we?"

We are nephilim, came the answer from somewhere.

The nephilim were all gathered together, and a voice Tash thought she recognized told them, "You are my new creation. You have sight beyond man. You are seers born as adversaries to the *up-elo*. Find him and curse him. But if he kills you in five, the world will be his. It's my bargain with him."

After their arrival, the world, although not perfect, became better. Evil was still on the earth, but it was counterbalanced by more goodness.

Tash saw the seers hunt the shadow. Many times they caught him and imprisoned him with a curse. But he got free each time, because he was able to persuade someone to kill for him. And then he'd hunt the seers, and although he wasn't allowed to kill them, he could employ someone to murder for him. Murder and rip. So many times he'd been close to killing five. So many times the world teetered on the brink of chaos. So many times the seers saved the day.

But how long could this go on for?

The voice she thought she'd recognized came again, saying, "I made a terrible world. What kind of God am I?"

Tash wanted to scream, "Don't abandon us," but she had no voice.

Time swept by. Tash felt sick and dizzy. Suddenly beneath her, a city appeared. Dark and vast. The streets seemed familiar to her, but she was convinced she'd never seen them before.

The closer she got, she realized the place was London. Whitechapel. And the people wore Victorian clothes.

Everything was dirty and smelly, and corruption soiled in the air.

A man she recognized from the illustrations in Jonas Troy's notebooks raced through the narrow streets. At his shoulder was the shadow again.

The man carried a knife that glinted in the moonlight.

The man, Tash knew, was Frederick Abberline.

The Ripper.

As if watching on fast-forward, Tash saw him savage four women. From the bodies of three, he tore out organs, and he salvaged a golden orb, exactly like the one she'd seen the brother hold up. He had killed one woman and was about to disembowel her when a group of men appeared in the alley.

Elizabeth Stride, thought Tash.

The Ripper slipped away before the men saw him. He slipped away before he could rip.

A fifth woman waited in a grubby, little room. She looked scared, waiting for death. She sang a song.

Sweet violets sweeter than the roses covered all over from head to toe...

Tash wanted to comfort the woman and found herself calling out to the her, despite not knowing who she was. But then she did know.

"Mary," she heard herself say, "Mary... "

The shadow came to the woman's door and went in, and it was soon followed there by Abberline.

Terrified, Tash watched him murder Mary and eviscerate her, removing the golden orb from inside her body. He handed it to the dark figure, who swallowed it whole.

The door burst open. Men spilled into the blood-stained room. They were angry. They pinned the Ripper Abberline to the floor. But the shadow fled, despite being stabbed and assaulted.

Some of the men, including Jonas Troy, chased the shadow through the streets.

They called his name... *up-elo... up-elo... up-elo...*

They cornered him and cursed him and threw him down a well.

The world reeled on after that, and Tash followed its evolution – technology, wars, famine, she witnessed it all at high-speed. Finally, life slowed, and she stared in horror at a familiar scene.

Her dad in a flat with Spencer Drake. Outside the flat, a dark figure lurked. Tash cried out, trying to warn her father. But he couldn't hear. And he answered the door when the stranger knocked.

She grabbed her hair and screamed as the ugly, strange looking trespasser pummelled her father with a hammer, before Dad's own snake coiled itself around his throat and strangled him.

Tash shrieked. And then Tash felt she was falling. She gasped for breath and flailed at the air. She started to scream. Gravity dragged her towards the earth, and the ground rushed up to meet her.

She crashed on to a bed, the springs creaking under her weight. She rolled over quickly and took in her surroundings.

"No," she said, "no, please… "

It was the room where Mary Kelly had been murdered in 1888.

CHAPTER 101.
THE GOLDEN ORBS.

DON Wilks, who had been labelled the New Ripper by the press fifteen years before, entered his home in Shoreditch. It was a detached property on a newer estate. All the houses were the same. Three storeys in red brick, with slate roofs. A living room, lounge, and kitchen. Three bedrooms and a bathroom.

And an attic.

And as he thundered upstairs now, that's where he was headed. His secret life was hidden there. His dark past stowed away.

He yanked down the ladder and climbed up, lifting the hatch.

The coldness hit him. And the smell. It was musty and old. He'd not been up in the attic in years. It was the place where he kept the monster. The place where he filed away the voice that called him out all those years ago – the voice of Jack the Ripper, he was sure of it.

I am the lord who gapes… I am the lantern of the tomb… I am the moth eating at the law…

He shivered now, eyes adjusting to the gloom. After waiting until he could see better, he went up.

The chill embraced him. The darkness swallowed him. The voice greeted him.

I have been waiting for you...

Wilks, shaking with fear and excitement, sought out the light switch and flicked it. The attic lit up. The back of his neck tingled, and his bladder felt heavy.

He looked around, gawping as if this were the first time he'd seen the attic. Debris covered the floor. Chunks of wood and bits of masonry. Cardboard boxes were stacked high against the far wall. They contained LPs, books, Christmas decorations, and shoes – boxes of everything his ex-wife had left behind when she went back to her mother's twenty years ago. He should have got rid of them, but they were useful – you could hide things behind them.

He went to them and started to shift them out of the way, and soon the freezer came into view.

Well hidden, he thought. *Out of the way. Out of sight...*

But never out of mind.

I am the lord who gapes... I am the lantern of the tomb... I am the moth eating at the law...

Wilks stiffened. The voice again. But louder now. It made his legs weak. It made him groggy.

Kneeling in front of the freezer, he groaned. He opened it slowly. It hummed as if greeting him. The ice was thick. He clawed it away. He saw the newspaper, buried there. It was like an artefact. Something ancient uncovered.

His pulse quickened. Despite the cold, a sweat broke out on his back. He scrabbled at the ice. Some of it came away, but the freezer, not having been defrosted for fifteen years, was not going to give up its treasure that easily.

Wilks scrabbled around, frantic. He grabbed half a brick and started smashing the ice. Slowly it gave, shattering and sprinkling the floor, where it melted and made Wilks's knees wet.

Finally he was able to tug the newspaper bundles out of the freezer. Also crammed in the ice was a piece of cloth, rolled up. He took it out and looked at it. It was frozen stiff. But holding it brought everything flooding back. It made his stomach churn. He remembered the thrill of the kill.

He stood up, panting. There was one more thing he needed, and he found it in one of the boxes. It was a file folder, which he took back downstairs, along with the frozen cloth and the newspaper bundles.

He defrosted the parcels and the frozen cloth in the microwave. In the living room, he laid the soaking newspaper on a blanket on the floor, and while it dried, he opened the file.

All his notes about Jack the Ripper. The murders had intrigued him from childhood. It was when he first heard the voice in his head.

I am the lord who gapes... I am the lantern of the tomb... I am the moth eating at the law...

Looking through a notebook filled with his childish writing, he remembered telling his aunt that Jack had sent part of a kidney taken from one of his victims to Mr Lusk of the Whitechapel Vigilance Society.

At the time his mum had scolded him.

...little boys shouldn't be thinking about those things...

But he did think about them. They had polluted his brain. And the voices kept calling out to him.

Finally, he became the New Ripper.

He stared at the newspaper parcels. They contained what he'd taken from the bodies of the four women he killed in Whitechapel in 1996. At the time, he had no idea why he'd mutilated them. He was convinced his savagery had meaning, but he wasn't sure what that meaning could be.

In his fury, he'd gutted the bodies, and the voice in his head was saying, *Dig, boy, dig. Find the treasure. Find it for when I return...*

Now he picked up one of the bundles. It was soft and wet, and it dribbled water all over his trousers. He started to unwrap the parcel. The newspaper was soggy and came apart in his hands. But he persevered. And after a little peeling, he saw the golden light shimmer.

He held his breath. Goosepimples raked his body. He stripped away the final layers of newspaper.

He gawped at the treasure.

A golden orb, just a little bigger than an egg. It glowed, a halo of light surrounding it. To the touch, it was soft – like silicone. Like the surgically enhanced breasts of that model he'd groped a few years back.

Stacked from Stepney, he'd called her, though her real name was Stacie.

Her boyfriend farmed cannabis in their flat. Wilks, heading the drugs team at the time, led the raid. The boyfriend got dragged off. The model got emotional. She begged Wilks to let her go.

"If I get done for this, I'll never get modelling work," she'd said.

He'd said, "We can come to an arrangement, darlin'."

And they did – and that's what the golden object in his hand felt like.

He didn't know what the orbs were, but he knew now that he'd kept them for a reason.

Jack was back. Jack was here. Jack had come for his treasures.

And when Wilks delivered them, Jack would make him a king.

He picked up the defrosting piece of cloth. It was his mask. He started to unfold it. It had been fashioned with straps and clips, made to keep a face clamped tightly. It was a mask made for an asylum. For a lunatic. For a madman. For a ripper.

CHAPTER 102.
THE MARCH OF TORMENT.

HE could hardly breathe. Desperately, he sucked in air. But his lungs felt like lead weights in his chest. And there seemed to be a lack of oxygen here. It was blisteringly hot. Molten rock formed the cavern. Lava dripped from them. Fires burned along the passageway ahead of him. Flames crackled, and he could hear shrieks. The smell of burning flesh filled the caves.

Faultless knew where he was.

Am I dead? he thought. *Is this where it ends?*

Lew – or whoever Lew really was – had told him to climb into the abyss, and he'd obeyed. Faultless realized that many of the answers he sought lay down in the deep. He had to go down to find them.

But now he thought everything after the beating by Wilks and his colleagues might have been a nightmare.

The kicking he took must have killed him. Lew saying he was the second evil meant nothing. *It was a dream,* he kept telling himself, *it was a dream.*

And he was actually dead.

And he was in hell.

Everyone has to pay.

He remembered those words.

Was this his payment? The last judgment? The ultimate punishment?

He never believed in heaven or hell. But maybe he should have. Maybe Roy Hanbury had been right. He looked around and felt the heat, felt the agony of the place. Maybe this was hell.

He walked on, clutching his chest. He was hot. His clothes stuck to his skin. Ash rained down. Screams tore through the passageways. He stumbled along. Fire lit his way. The walls were red hot. But as he walked, he noticed that parts of the stone were covered in art – murals depicting suffering.

There were images of torture drawn in blood and soot. Messages had been scratched into the walls. Some of the languages were alien to him. Some were symbols and not words.

Old languages, he thought. *Ancient.*

Some of the messages he understood. He saw one in English. It had been scratched into the stone.

Damned, I am damned. Forgive me, Heavenly Father. Save me from this torment. I beg, I beg, said the message.

It was signed, *George Whittaker, faithful servant of God, July 5th 1703AD.*

There were more messages. Thousands of them in many languages. Some were dated. But dates meant nothing. Time was a human concept. AD was human. But writing went further back than that. And some of this writing stretched to the birth of humanity, Faultless was certain of it. He could sense the antiquity of the languages. He saw a message dated 912AD, but the words – although he recognized some as English – were not understandable to him.

As he stumbled along the passageway, the shrieking became louder. Desperate crying. And wailing. Howls of pain. Pleas for mercy.

This chorus of anguish filled the caves now.

He came to a dog-leg in the passageway. The noise was coming from around the corner.

His heart thundered. His chest was tight. He was sweating. Adrenaline jetted through his veins.

He was going to see something awful around that bend, so he steeled himself before striding ahead.

He stopped dead.

They filed through the caves ahead of him. Thousands of them. Tens of thousands. As far as he could see. They were winding down into the caverns, many columns of them trudging down the many passageways.

They wore suits. They wore nightclothes. They wore uniforms. Some were naked. Some were old and others young. They were men and women and children.

They were all weeping. They were begging and screaming. Faultless heard some of them say, "There's been a mistake, please... I'm a good man."

He heard many begging in the same way. He heard different languages and guessed they were begging too.

But despite their pleading, the figures overseeing this march of torment showed no mercy.

The guards were huge. Some of them must have been nearly eight feet tall. They were dressed in chain mail. Dark stains covered their armour. On their heads, they wore helmets made of skulls. Faultless failed to recognize the animals the skulls had come from.

The guards whipped the people if they slowed down or if they tried to escape.

A man wearing a black suit stumbled out of the line. He was white-haired. He stood over six feet tall and sported a tan. He looked Mediterranean to Faultless. The man's clothes were torn, and he was covered in dirt and ash. Stumbling forward, the man knelt before one of the guards and started pleading in Italian.

Although Faultless couldn't understand what he was saying, he heard the words, "… Gianluca Folcci… Bruccino… " and he was jabbing himself in the chest while he was saying this.

Faultless looked at the man and narrowed his eyes.

He was Gianluca Folcci, Godfather of the Bruccino family.

Panic raced through Faultless. He remembered hearing that Folcci had died yesterday, shot by Italian police.

This was confirmation.

Faultless was in hell.

Folcci begged. The guard glared down at him and then made a gesture. Three other guards rushed forward. They grabbed Folcci. They pinned him to the wall and spread out his arms. Taking metal spikes from their belts, they crucified Folcci to the wall of the cave. He screamed while they hammered the spikes through his wrists and his knees.

While he writhed and shrieked, they stripped him naked, tearing away his clothes.

The guards moved away, leaving Folcci to screech and bleed.

But he's dead, thought Faultless. *How can he bleed? How can he be in pain?*

And then he knew.

Eternal torment. Pain for the rest of time. Suffering without end.

The line of damned souls trudged forward.

Folcci was squealing now.

Faultless imagined his anguish. But then he realized it was going to get worse. From the shadows around Folcci, things slithered. Faultless reared back, cringing. Creatures came out of the gloom. No bigger than squirrels, they had leathery brown skin and tails ridged with spikes. As they clambered all over Folcci, their talons ripped into his body.

His screams intensified.

The demons clawed at him. They bit him. They lashed at him with their vicious tails. They plucked out his eyes. They tore off his ears. One forced its hand into his mouth and yanked, ripping out his tongue.

The Godfather moaned. Blood poured from his mouth. His face was a scarlet mask. His body had been pulped. He slumped. The spikes in his wrists tore at his skin and ligaments.

One of the demons ripped away Folcci's scrotum.

With their bloody trophies, the demons scuttled away into the shadows. But not before one of them stopped and turned and looked Faultless in the eye. The look froze Charlie's bones.

He took a step back, terrified he'd be assaulted in the same way. But the demon scuttled off, lashing its tail as it slipped into the shadows.

Faultless stared at Folcci's mutilated body. The man was still alive.

How can he be alive if he's dead? thought Faultless. *But maybe we don't die. Maybe we just suffer. We leave the earth and either come here or go to heaven, where we continue our lives.*

Faultless crept towards Folcci.

The Italian moaned. His mouth opened and closed. He was a bloody mess – a pile of torn meat.

Faultless stood in front of the Godfather.

"Beautiful, isn't it?" said a voice.

Faultless's bladder almost emptied there and then. He wheeled round.

"You," he said.

"Who did you expect," said Lew, "Satan?"

"I think so."

"Sorry to disappoint."

"Is he dead?" said Faultless.

"Gianluca Folcci left his human life at 11.58pm, Greenwich Mean Time, on February 27, 2011, shot by Italian police. The moment he left that life, he began this one. His eternal life. His suffering has started, Charlie. It will never end. And what a

390

beautiful agony, don't you think?"

"You *are* the Devil."

"Oh, I am everything, Charlie."

"Am I dead?"

"No, you're not dead."

"So is this a nightmare?"

"I suppose it's quite terrifying for you."

"Is it a nightmare or not?"

"No it's not."

"Then why am I here?"

"For the same reason as everyone else – to suffer."

CHAPTER 103.
KINDRED OF CAIN.

"I WAS there at the beginning, and I am here at the last," said Jack. "Hunted and stalked by you. By seers. Born of the angels of heaven and the women of earth. I terrorized the world before they came. I spilled blood and made men do what men love. But then you bastards came and corralled me. You were made to be my adversaries. But our maker gave you souls. The key to my freedom."

Tash had been weakened by her journey. She was sprawled on the bed. She felt wrecked and breathed heavily. Some of the images still tarnished her mind. They were there for good. She still saw them now.

Brother killing brother. The fall of empires. Plagues destroying millions. Floods drowning cities. Nations going to war. Murderers stalking towns. Innocents savaged. Cruelty reigning. From genocide to back-street butchery. From the death of kings to the death of Mary Kelly.

How can we be in the room where she died? thought Tash. *It's impossible.*

But she'd learnt over the past few days that nothing was impossible. She looked around the room. She recognized it because she'd seen the old photos in Jonas Troy's suitcase. The photos that showed Mary's disfigured body on the bed. Was it the same street outside? Had they gone back in time? Had they slipped through a gash in the universe? Was this place like the cavern where Jack had tried to murder Jasmine? Somewhere that existed, but just out of reach. Just beyond the minds of ordinary people. Somewhere you had to look for carefully.

Jack spoke again.

"When Jonas Troy chased me that night, I cursed him. I had been so close to being free. I was sucked down into the gutters, dragged through shit. I was a pariah. A lost soul. One that's got no place in heaven or in hell. But why should I suffer? I was made this way. This is what I am. I am not made to be in pain, I am made to *inflict* it. Luckily, that stupid Spencer came along… "

Tash said nothing.

Jack said, "I shall have your soul. My Ripper is coming home. My 21st century Abberline. He's already paved the way. You know who killed your sister?"

Tash gaped.

"And do you know who killed the Faultless woman? Susan Murray? Nancy Sherwood? He did. My boy. My Ripper. He had so much evil in him. Such darkness in his heart that it was easy to speak to him. Easy to make him hear. We have chemistry, he and I. If I could love, I would love him."

Tash was terrified. "You… you killed my sister, you… "

"Didn't you listen, you tart? Not me. My Ripper. Ripped her up."

Tash shuddered. She felt sick.

Jack said, "I found a kindred of Cain. A descendent with the mark of evil on him. Better than Abberline. Better than all of them."

"Who is he?" The door opened. Hallam Buck entered. Tash stared at him. He looked away and trudged inside. He was pale and bloody, and his crotch was a mass of black fluid and hanging skin.

Tash nearly puked.

But then another figure loomed in the doorway. He stayed in the shadows for a moment so Tash was unable to see his face. But he stood tall and powerful. And then he entered, his face etched with hatred, a satchel slung over his shoulder.

It was Don Wilks, the policeman.

Tash threw up.

CHAPTER 104.
MADE FOR A PURPOSE.

FAULTLESS ripped off his shirt. He gasped for air. He clawed at his body.

This place was a furnace.

He staggered off, trying to find somewhere cool.

Lew laughed. "I said you were here to suffer, Charlie."

Faultless headed for a dark corner, a patch of wall that wasn't molten rock. He never took his eyes off the cool, grey stone till he got to it. Then he turned and pressed his back against it, and it was cold and wet.

"Who am I, Lew?" he said. "What did you mean I'm the second evil?"

"You don't have kids, Charlie."

He said nothing.

Lew went on. "Kids fight, you know. Brother kills brother. It happens all the time. Happens because that's the way I made the world at the beginning. And it's not like I can start over again. I get one crack at a creation."

For a moment Faultless was sure he saw despondency in the old man's eyes. He started to say something, but no words came out. What could he say?

"'Course, that makes no difference to humans," said Lew. "I made them. I put sin in them. I made them weak, easily tempted. But I'm not going to take the blame for that. No way. It's them who are to blame. They kill each other. They lie. They cheat. They rape and ravage the planet I made for them. Bloody ungrateful species."

Faultless stared at the old man. His insides quaked. Was he looking at God? He couldn't believe it. His mind was surely fraying. He wasn't sane anymore. This encounter was taking place in the brain of a lunatic. It had to be. Everything he was experiencing just couldn't be real.

Lew said, "You realize who I am, don't you, Charlie?"

Faultless said nothing. He couldn't speak. And he feared that if he tried, his words would come out in a jumble.

"You think I'm the devil," said Lew.

Faultless stayed quiet and tried to master his body, which was shivering uncontrollably.

Lew continued. "There is no devil. He's just something men made up to excuse their sin. No devil. Only me."

Faultless heard the words, but they made no sense to him. He started to blink rapidly, trying to see if he'd wake up and find himself in bed next to Tash, with all this madness gone from his head.

He didn't. He was still here, no matter how many times he opened and shut his eyes. He was still in hell.

"Once there were many gods," said Lew. "We competed against each other for power. We battled. We created and we destroyed. Finally, I defeated all the others. And I won the right to forge a creation in my own image. I am the alpha and I am the omega. I am who I am. I made the world. Everything in it. You are looking at the face of God, Charlie – and you're alive."

Faultless tried to think of something else. In his head, he played out his life, hoping it would block out the insanity of what Lew was saying. But when images of his childhood sprang into his mind, they immediately reminded him that his life had been fake. He was not a boy from Barrowmore. He was not his mother's son. He was a lie. He was an imposter. He even started to think that he might not exist, and the thirty-four years of his life had just been a few minutes in someone's dream.

"You know who you are, Charlie?" said Lew

He still couldn't speak, unable to put together words that could explain this situation.

"You're my son," said Lew. "Made by me. Born in the very moment after your brother, the one named *up-elo*, the first evil… "

Faultless's heart felt as if it were turning to stone. He grew very cold, even in this furnace. He was going into shock.

Lew went on. "But a moment for me is a million years to man. I made you as a child. A newborn. I brought you down and left you with a seer. The Faultless woman whose child I'd taken a few months before. Her grief made her love you more, see."

Faultless suddenly felt fury rise up in him, bubbling like the lava that ran in rivers through the caves.

Lew said, "I let you loose on that estate and watched you thrive. I watched your mother love you. And then I dropped you into the life of another seer family – ah, the lovely Rachel, the delicious Tash."

Faultless bunched his knuckles. His fingernails dug into his palms, drawing blood. He clenched his jaw so tightly he thought he'd break his teeth.

The old man carried on talking. "Everything happens for a reason. You think life's random? It's not. There are patterns. You see, I knew Patricia Faultless and Rachel were going to die, because eventually they would cross his path. Since you had a role to play, I thought it was better that you play it with fury in your

397

veins. And what better way to make you angry than to have your loved ones killed."

Faultless shook with fury.

Lew continued. "You can be as pissed off as you like, Charlie. Think you can take it out on me? I lift my finger, and you're dust, boy. I happily kill my children, Charlie. Always have. You have a destiny. You're made for a purpose."

"I… I… " Faultless forced the words out and they came in a growl. "I don't… want a fucking… purpose… "

"You have one," said Lew, his lip curled. "You don't have a choice. No one has a choice. Not even I have a choice. Creation is fraying. It's becoming worse every day. I can't do anything about it, or I would. I set it in motion only for *them* to corrupt it. Those good-for-nothing humans I – "

"You made them, you bastard," said Faultless, finally recognizing the situation he was in and acknowledging that he might actually be talking to God.

"I made them good," said Lew. "I gave them every chance."

"You put sin in them – by thinking it. By unleashing it on the world."

"Well… I am not perfect. I was only meant to be a tribal deity, you know. Worshipped by desert people. But when I defeated the other gods, I was allowed to be a creator god. I did my best… "

"This… this is all a nightmare. It's… it's not real… I'm dreaming it… "

"It's no dream, Charlie. You were born for a reason. You were made for something."

Faultless looked around. He cared nothing for his purpose. He now wanted to die. He wanted this to end. He laid his head back against the cold stone and watched the doomed traipse down the tunnels. Thousands of them continued to stream through the caves. Some tried to beg like Folcci. Some tried to flee. But they all suffered like the Italian. They were crucified and mutilated.

Some were flayed. Some had their bellies opened. They didn't die, because they were already dead. But they hurt as if they were alive. Everywhere Faultless stared, there was terrible brutality.

Finally he asked, "What was I made for?"

"You were made to kill your brother."

CHAPTER 105.
SEND HIM BACK TO ME.

LEW said, "That's your judgment, Charlie. That's the price you have to pay."

Faultless was shaking with anger. "The price," he said. "The price for what?"

"For your birth. For the murder you committed."

"And how many have you committed?"

"But I'm God. I create and I destroy."

Faultless sat slumped on the dusty ground. He rested his arms on his knees and his head hung low. He was beaten.

"How did he get to Barrowmore in the first place?" he said. "How did he get to Whitechapel? You, I guess?"

Lew shrugged. "Not me. I don't have as much control as you might think. Now and again I do interfere. An earthquake, perhaps. Famine. The reason I interfere is that death on a massive scale oddly brings people back to me. I made a funny race in humans, I really did." He paused and looked around his domain – his hell. "He wasn't Jack when he came to England. He was someone else. He came with the Crusades in the 12th century. Those were fine days. Men really loved me back then. They murdered lavishly and inventively in my name."

Hate welled up in Faultless.

Lew said, "Some of them came for a cup. You know the story? Holy Grail. The cup I was supposed to have drunk from during the Passover meal when I came to earth in human form."

"And did you?" said Faultless, dislocated from reality now. *I'm asking God questions about The Last Supper*, he was thinking, while a madman's laughter echoed through his mind.

"No. Never. I never came to earth in human form and sacrificed myself. Why would I do that? Why would I put *myself* through torture because men broke *my* rules?" Lew grunted, and his eyes glazed over. "He was called Yeshua, and he was a prophet. One of mine. People have called him Jesus. Made him a god. But he wasn't. He was human. But he was crucified, and he was named the Christ, and his wounds still resonate."

"The wounds of Christ… "

"Those wounds were there from the beginning of time. Like everything I wrote down. Like everything I made. Nothing is random. They have meaning and power."

"And the knights, they never found the cup?"

"'Course not. It doesn't exist. Just another story. But they did come back with original sin. *Him* – my first evil thought. A group of knights raided a Muslim fort in a place called Acre. Hundreds of years before, seers hunted Jack – as you call him – to that fort, and they trapped him there. This group of knights raid the fort. They steal the treasure – in my name, of course."

"Makes it all right, then."

"It does. But coiled up in the gold and jewels was *him*. He had free passage to England. And on the boat over he managed to get into some knight's head who then spilled the blood that can unbind him – just like that little fellow Spencer did."

Faultless said nothing for a while. He listened to the screams of the damned. Then he said, "So I kill him, and he'll be gone?"

"He'll be gone."

"Where? Here?"

"Back into my heart, where I will love him tenderly and torture him endlessly."

"And then there's no evil?"

Lew raised his eyebrows. "Charlie, there will always be evil. It's necessary. It counterbalances goodness. It's vital."

"But with him gone, there… " He trailed off. His eyes widened, and his mouth dropped open. He started to realize something, and the knowledge was like blades inside him. He stared at Lew. "I can't be… you're not… "

"You're his brother, Charlie. You're evil's evil twin, if you like. It's why I thought you into existence. To carry out this task. You are the darkness that comes from my heart. Now you're going to suffer for it."

PART SEVEN.

THE DARKNESS SHALL COVER ME.

CHAPTER 106.
BROTHER KILLS BROTHER.

THE serpent watched from the palm groves.

The elder brother, who was named Havel, had killed a goat. Now he was skinning the animal.

The reek of blood filled the air. From his hiding place, the serpent smelled it, and it was beautiful.

The younger brother, Qayin, lurked nearby, watching Havel at work.

Qayin had a dark look in his eyes. The serpent recognized it. He knew it because it was his look. It was his name. It was *up-elo*. It would become the word "evil".

Havel worked hard at skinning the goat. Havel always worked hard. There was goodness in him. More goodness than *up-elo*. More light than dark. The sin buried deep in his heart was hard to get to. It was easier to find Qayin's sin. Havel loved Yahweh. He praised him and often brought offerings like this goat.

The serpent looked at Qayin again. The evil in the youngest brother shone. It glittered in his eyes. It was etched into his face. The serpent lusted for that look. He wanted to see it in every eye.

The serpent then became a man and slipped from his hiding place.

As he crept towards Qayin, he thought about his existence and cherished it. He had been there from the beginning, when Yahweh had thought of him.

Yahweh, like all gods, was not perfect. He was jealous, angry, wrathful, and cruel. He had made everything and had made it good – or what he considered good.

After creating everything in six days, Yahweh rested on the seventh. His intention was to have a good time with his wife, Asherah, queen of heaven. But that day, Asherah refused to go to bed with him.

She was angry. Her husband had ignored her for six days. He'd been busy making man and a place for man to live. And then he'd even made a mate for man to breed with.

And so on the seventh day, when he went to Asherah and demanded that she give him her body, she said no.

Yahweh raged. Dark thoughts hurtled through his vast, infinite mind. They clashed like stars. They burned. They erupted. The debris from them mingled. And at the centre of the chaos, some of the fragments fused together, and they attracted more pieces from the wreckage. And the splinters of darkness welded into a power.

It welded into The First Evil, the *up-elo*.

It was so strong that it was spewed out of heaven and fell to earth. It crashed into the garden, where Yahweh had put man and his mate.

The First Evil made itself into a serpent and coiled around a tree. It was the one tree in the garden the man and his mate were forbidden to touch. The serpent thought it was stupid to put a forbidden thing in a place that was supposed to be paradise.

It was asking for trouble.

And as he expected, he managed to tempt the mate, the female of the man, to eat from fruit of the tree.

It caused uproar in heaven. Yahweh was outraged. His perfect little creation was flawed. He'd been shown to be a bad designer. Slivers of the evil he'd made when Asherah rejected him had entered the man and his mate. And it was easy, then, for the serpent to call on those slivers. After all, they were pieces of him.

Because they had disobeyed him, Yahweh threw man and his mate out of the garden. The serpent laughed. But he didn't get everything his own way.

He was cursed. He was made a pariah. He would never find a place in heaven. Still, Yahweh loved him because he thought of him as a son. And because of that love, the serpent was allowed to live.

Another mistake by Yahweh.

You should've killed me then, he thought now, watching Qayin.

Over time, the serpent grew stronger. And when Qayin and Havel were growing up, he sensed a rage in the younger brother. He recognized the rage as himself – the piece of him coded into every human.

Now that fury would be unleashed.

Up-elo would show its power for the first time.

It would make brother kill brother.

He went to Qayin and whispered in his ear.

"Yahweh hates you."

Qayin snarled. He never took his eyes off his brother. Havel was hanging the goat up. He had already lit a fire. The smoke billowed. Soon Havel would pray and offer the animal to Yahweh, and then the man would eat the flesh.

"He loves Havel more than he loves you," the serpent whispered.

"And I hate him," said Qayin.

"Havel has something that will make you strong. It is inside him. It shines. Yahweh loves it, and if you take it, you will be as strong as a god. Find it. I will be with you. I will give you the the power to see it and take it. Look at him, Qayin. Look at Havel.

Look at how *good* he is. *Murder him and I will make you king.*"

And Qayin murdered his brother. He cut open Havel's belly. He raked out his brother's intestines and organs. He scooped something else out. He lifted it to his face and gawped. It was a golden orb. Like an egg. It shone brightly. Qayin held it up to heaven and said, "See? See this you gave to my brother? Now I have it."

The serpent moved like lightning – a shadow sweeping across the landscape. He snatched the orb from Qayin's hands and crammed it into his mouth. Gold liquid dribbled down his chin, and he chewed. The orb was soft and broke easily on his teeth. It tasted like honey.

The serpent swallowed the golden orb.

He swallowed Havel's soul.

And already he felt stronger.

He dashed away, leaving a shocked Qayin to Yahweh and his wrath.

CHAPTER 107.
THE GHOST.

"DO you want me to drive?" said Jasmine.

Spencer said, "I can do it."

"Well, you can't. You've had five goes, and you've stalled it every time."

"You're ten – "

"Eleven and a half, and my mum's going to get killed."

Jasmine was trying to be calm. Inside, she was frantic, but her voice remained steady and she wasn't shouting or screaming. She was doing her best to concentrate. But it was difficult for many reasons. First, the car was stolen, and the owner could storm out of his house any second. Second, Spencer didn't have a clue what he was doing, and letting him drive might be dangerous. Third, she might never see her mother again.

Finally, Spencer got going. The car jerked and jumped a lot, but they made it to Commercial Street. It was late at night, but pedestrians and traffic still made the road busy.

"Which way, then?" said Spencer.

She pointed right, and Spencer joined the traffic. He drove nervously. He was sweating, Jasmine could smell it. But she tried her best to ignore him. Her heart was about to explode. She trembled but tried to master her fear.

If she lost her cool, she would lose her mum.

Jasmine knew what being psychic meant. Everyone at school believed in it. Why shouldn't it be true? Why shouldn't she be one? Some girls had mums who were mediums or clairvoyants. One girl had a mum who ran a New Age shop selling crystals and tarot cards and incense. So it was obvious that being psychic was possible. Jasmine had never thought it was possible for her.

But it was.

I'm special, she thought. *I'm gifted.*

A little voice inside kept trying to say she wasn't special. But she had to believe she was. She had to believe she could see things with her mind.

She could see evil.

She gasped for breath. Spencer drove badly. Car horns blared. A cabbie mouthed "wanker" at him. But he kept going, licking his lips and whimpering.

Jasmine closed her eyes and concentrated. In her mind, she trawled the streets. Somewhere in the distance, darkness waited for her. She could sense it. The coldness of it made her shake. The blackness of it made her sweat.

Something that felt like electricity suddenly flooded her veins, and she opened her eyes. On the left stood a pub. It was the Ten Bells. It looked rough.

Jasmine's heart thundered.

"Stop here," she said to Spencer.

"Here?" he said.

They were in the middle of the road.

Before he could do anything, she started to open the door. He shouted at her not to. The car veered to the right. The door flew open. Jasmine rolled out, hitting the asphalt hard. She jarred her shoulder, and it hurt for a second, but she quickly forgot the pain and leapt to her feet.

Spencer ran the car into the side of a bus. Everyone was shouting and screaming. Horns wailed. Tyres skidded. Curses flew. Jasmine kept going, entering Fournier Street, which ran alongside the Ten Bells.

She sensed the havoc she'd left behind. Spencer was caught in the middle of it. She felt sorry for him, but her mother was more important. She never turned back to look.

Although she had no idea where she was going, Jasmine started to head down Fournier Street.

But as she went, ghosts appeared.

She stopped in her tracks, terrified.

Despite the shouts and screams filling Commercial Street as a result of Spencer's accident, her eyes were locked on another unreal scene of chaos.

There was a riot. But it was silent. And those fighting were transparent.

They were ghosts.

They wore old-fashioned clothes. Men with cloth caps battled with big, burly policemen. Women with long dresses and hats clawed at each other. Fists and boots flew.

Jasmine stepped forward, and it was as if she walked right through the figures.

They're not here, she thought. *Only in my mind.*

It scared her. And when she moved into the brawl, she could feel the ghosts pass through her – cold and clammy in her bones and blood.

A man bleeding from beneath his flat cap knelt over a policeman. The copper was big, with red whiskers. His eyes were wide and glittery, and his mouth was open, panting for breath. The bleeding man pressed something into the officer's belly, and Jasmine heard him say, "Keep your hands there."

Then he leapt to his feet, a knife in his hand. He spun round, ready to escape the scene.

But he looked straight at Jasmine and stopped.

She was frozen to the spot. He stared right at her. He was seeing her, she could tell. His eyes flashed. He reached out a hand to her. She reached out to him. It was as if Jasmine knew the man. She felt a connection with him. She felt like she was part of him.

He said, "Go and save her, little seer."

And then he ran past her, looking into her eyes. She turned, her gaze following the ghost, and he headed into Commercial Street, where he faded away. Jasmine faced the brawl again, wondering if the policeman was all right. But he, like the ghost who spoke to her, had gone. They had all gone. Just Fournier Street with its cars and its buildings remained.

The ghost's voice echoed in her head.

Go save her, little seer.

Jasmine turned and ran back into Commercial Street and through the chaos left by Spencer.

CHAPTER 108.
HELL'S THING.

THE guards with skull helmets chained Faultless to a wall. The red-hot stone burned his back. He screamed. He smelled his flesh burn.

"What is this for?" he said.

The guards branded Faultless. They wrote on his body with ink and with his own blood. They painted symbols and words from dead languages all over him. His body steamed. Sweat poured off him. Blood smeared in the perspiration. He screamed.

"These are ancient marks of judgment," said Lew. "You are hell's thing. Everything that comes here knows pain, so you must know it, too. There's none of the humanity given to you by your surrogate mother left. You are an angel again. Does it hurt?"

"Fuck you. This is nothing. I've been fucking blowtorched."

"That was playing."

Faultless's body ached all over. Every inch of him was on fire. He tried to stay upright, but his legs were weak. He panted, desperate for air. "Am I still alive?" he said.

"Do you feel alive?" asked Lew.

"I feel alive."

"There's your answer."

"I don't look alive."

"You look beautiful. I made you; you must be."

"Am I damned?"

"You're damned, Charlie."

"And will I suffer?"

"Always."

Faultless cried out, a long, anguished scream that unleashed all the suffering he'd experienced.

"Why does it have to be like this?" he said.

"The laws of the universe were set when I lit the first spark. I can't change them. What I made is… is greater than what I am."

The old man looked broken for a moment.

"I am flawed, you see. Just like my creation. I'm jealous, wrathful, and impatient. I am prone to cruelty. I hate being ignored. I can be petty. We are what we are. We have to accept our conditions – even we gods and angels."

"I don't accept," said Faultless, his voice quivering with terror at what was happening to him.

"You have no choice. Go fulfil your destiny. Challenge your brother."

"What if I don't?"

"Creation can't cope with much more of him."

Faultless slumped. His mind reeled. He tried to wake up, thinking this was a nightmare. But he wasn't sleeping. Maybe he'd never sleep again.

Lew said, "One more thing," and he shot forward so quickly he was nothing but a flash of light. His hand made a claw, and it had talons lancing from the fingers. He rammed it up into Faultless's solar plexus. Charlie screamed. But the hand drove on, tearing into his body, up under his ribcage. And then closed around his heart. Faultless shuddered. He could feel the cold grip of God on him, every part of his body recognizing and fearing that grip.

The hand tore out of him and brought with it his heart.

Faultless gasped for air. He waited to die. But he didn't. He stared at the organ, clutched in Lew's hand.

The old man said, "You have no need of this anymore. Hearts are for humans. And they are the hiding places of sin. Now you *are* sin."

He ordered the guards to unchain Faultless. For a few moments he was unsteady on his feet. His arms and shoulders ached. He looked down at his torso. It was covered in symbols and words – inked and burned into his flesh. His jeans were rags under the knees, and he could see that his legs had also been written on. He was a book. A book of curses. A book of judgment.

Finally he found his feet.

"What happens now?" he asked, his blood hot. "More torture? Bring it on, you shit."

Lew clapped his hands. "No more now. Now you get ready to fly, my boy."

For a second, Faultless felt nothing. Then a terrible pain ripped through his shoulders. He arched his back. His flesh was tearing. He screamed. "What's happening to me?"

And then bones cracked in his back, and he fell to his knees, in so much agony he thought he would die.

He felt his back burst open. Two things, one each side, erupted just under his shoulders. He knew what they were.

He fell on all fours, exhausted.

"Beautiful," said Lew. "You are beautiful."

And as if it were the most natural thing in the world, Faultless spread his wings.

CHAPTER 110.
THE SOULS OF HIS
ENEMIES.

THE New Ripper, Don Wilks, pulled on his mask, and the thrill rippled through him. He strapped the mouthpiece in place and clipped the restraints over his scalp. The hood tickled his skin. It made him blink, and the coarse material scraped his lips. But it was beautiful. His heart swelled. He was home again.

Through the eyeholes, he looked at Jack the Ripper. Or the one who'd been called by that name.

"You've been waiting for me," said Wilks.

"For you, Donald. For you," Jack said.

"How… how did you know?"

"I know everything. From my caged world I've sought out a disciple – a *true* disciple – all these years. I found you as a child. Your interest in the savagery of what was done all those years ago drew me. It drew me like a siren lures a sailor. It was heavenly."

"Who was Jack? I have to know."

"I was Jack."

"Who did the killings for you? Who was me?"

Jack told him.

"Frederick Abberline," repeated Wilks.

"They sent him to America. They wouldn't hang him or jail him. He knew too much. He was part of the Establishment, see. So they exiled him. Far away from me. I just couldn't reach him there. Couldn't reach him to finish the job. To kill a fifth and free me."

Wilks looked over at Tash Hanbury. She was tied to the old, rusty bed frame. She cried and struggled. *Probably panicking*, he thought. *No idea how she got here.*

But then neither had Wilks. He just followed the voice in his head. Followed it until it became loud. Followed it no matter what stood in his way. Followed it beyond the real world, the rational, followed it and found it somewhere dark and lost.

He scanned the room. It was grim. Everything was decayed, so old and broken. Everything twisted, like his soul. There was a chair and a table and the bed and not much else. But the smell of death hung in the air. And blood stained the walls. Dark, dried blood.

He asked, "Is… is she the fifth?"

Jack nodded. "A woman of Moab and Midian. They are not to be spared, Donald. God orders it. Moses told his soldiers to kill them all. You should do God's work, just like Moses did."

Wilks looked over at Hallam Buck and said, "Who's that? Couldn't he have done it for you?"

"He's my eunuch. My gelded angel. You're my king, Donald. You're my Ripper. My Abberline. First, you have something for me? The satchel?"

Wilks laid the bag on the table and removed from it a large, plastic container. "I didn't know what they were, but I knew they would be important. I thought I'd want to kill more after I started, but… but it didn't seem to be the right time."

416

Jack salivated. He shoved Wilks out of the way and flipped open the container. Four golden orbs shimmered in the gloom of Mary Kelly's slaughterhouse.

Like a hungry animal, Jack scooped the four orbs into his mouth. He chewed. Golden liquid oozed down his face and chest. He swallowed and smacked his lips. Gold filled his mouth. The gold of four souls. The souls of his enemies.

"This is the right time, isn't it," said Wilks.

"Rip her open and take it out of her," Jack said, still salivating. "Rip her so I can be free. So you can be king. Rip her, Donald."

From his pocket, Don Wilks took a butcher's knife. He'd used it to kill his four victims fifteen years before. Now he would use it to kill Tash Hanbury. He crossed to the bed, and she screamed.

CHAPTER 110.
A CHILD OF ANGELS.

JASMINE kept running.

She was headed for that darkness in the corner of her mind. She felt tuned in to the streets, able to see beyond the concrete and the bricks, the wood and the glass, the steel and the asphalt.

She was seeing dark rooms unseen for centuries. Long corridors that lay undiscovered. Tunnels and caves. Nooks and crannies.

She saw life in the underworld – snakes and rats, angels and demons.

It was like being on a ghost train at the fair. Things flashing past your eyes. Skeletons popping up. Screams filling the air. The difference here was that the danger was real.

She kept running, unaware of where she was going. Just following the signals in her mind. Following the darkness.

I am a seer, she thought, and she wondered what that word even meant.

Seer.

Where did that word come from?

Seer.

Why did she think of herself like that?

I am a child of angels.

Her visions now started to comfort her. They suddenly stopped being scary. She was starting to use them, to use the power she had.

She saw bodies buried under the pavements. Corpses in various states of decay, some fresh, others decomposed.

She saw inside people's homes. Husbands beating wives. Wives sleeping with strangers. Kids smoking fags while their mothers boozed. A family praying together for peace. A young girl practicing violin while her dad needled heroin into his veins.

She saw anguish and joy. She saw rage and harmony. She heard it all and it seeped into her and she understood now how to tap into it.

She was learning to see by seeing.

After a while, she stopped running. She stood in an empty street, and for a second, she felt scared again. She was eleven and on her own. It was dark and quiet. There was a barrier across the road to stop traffic. It said No ENTRY on the Tarmac. On one side, an office building towered above her. On the other stood a red-brick building.

Now she was lost. She looked around, confused. Her panic grew. She started to pant, her chest tightening.

A voice in her head shocked her. It was a man's voice. It was the ghost's voice. It said, "Old Dorset Street, little seer. This is where it stood. And there, there stands the entrance into Miller's Court. Where he killed poor Mary. Where your mother waits. Go save her, little seer."

The voice faded. Jasmine stared at a row of green roller doors. They looked like garage doors. She hurried over to one and stared at it desperately. Whimpering, she wondered how she was supposed to find Miller's Court.

Where he killed poor Mary. Where your mother waits.

She lost hope now. She fell to her knees, burying her face in her hands. She cried, calling out to her mother. She just couldn't concentrate anymore. It was too difficult.

How could her mother be behind these doors? How could she be in a place where some woman called Mary had died?

And how was Jasmine supposed to open the doors to find out?

She was about to give up when a shadow moved across the pavement where she cowered. And then she heard flapping, as if a huge bird were beating its wings just above her.

She slowly turned and gawped as the creature descended to the street. Its black-feathered wings fluttered as it landed. Its muscular body was covered in blood and strange pictures and words.

She looked into the creatures eyes. One was brown, the other blue.

CHAPTER 111.
BACK TO THE FIFTH.

WILKS, wearing the lunatic mask of the New Ripper, stood over the woman, the knife in his hand. His breathing hissed. It made him sound like a snake, and he liked that. And he liked it that the man he'd always thought of as Jack the Ripper was standing only a few feet away, watching him. He felt like a pupil being supervised by a teacher. He wanted to do well. He wanted to complete his task and kill the fifth victim.

"You scared of me?" he said in a whisper.

The woman said nothing. She was shaking but trying to fight the fear. Don Wilks had seen that fear before. He'd also seen the effort to ward it off. He'd seen it in Rachel Hanbury fifteen years ago.

"You scared of me like your sister was?" he said.

Tash Hanbury struggled, but she couldn't get loose. She was tied on the bed. Christ, the room smelled bad. The air was stale. A hint of decay laced the atmosphere. But it was an old room. It was a dead place, buried by history. Wilks failed to grasp how he'd got here and how the place could exist – it was Miller's Court, the boarding house where Mary Kelly died on November 10, 1888. Because of his obsession with the Ripper murders, he knew it had been demolished in 1920 by the Corporation of London as part of a rebuilding project. Over the years, more reconstruction was carried out, and places like Miller's Court had faded from memory.

But only faded. They never disappeared completely. They were still here, lodged under London, hidden in its new walls and its modern buildings. Those places and their secrets.

"Do it, you bastard," said Tash Hanbury. "If you're going to do it, do it now."

Just like her sister, he thought. Trying to show she's tough. Like all of them. Like Susan Murray and Nancy Sherwood and Patricia Faultless.

Faultless.

Where was the bastard?

He recalled the old man in the cell. Power had emananted from his frail body. Danger glittered in his black eyes. Never before had Wilks felt such awe. He was convinced the old man had destroyed the police station and had come there specifically to reveal something to him.

You're one of his, aren't you.

Those words felt comforting. He felt he finally belonged.

With that thought, he was able to shrug away any fears he had about Faultless. Wherever he was, it didn't matter anymore.

He kneeled next to Tash Hanbury and pressed the blade to her throat.

"You'll show me you're scared," he said.

She yelled out.

Wilks laughed. "See? See? I was right."

He was still laughing when she spat in his face, and that made him stop. It made him flinch and stand up.

422

She was screaming again, struggling to get free.

"Cow," he said, his blood boiling, "you cow – you show me some respect. You show me awe."

"Fuck you," she said.

"Bitch."

He lifted the knife. He'd stab her in the neck. Make it hurt. Not make it quick, like Jack said.

She screamed. The knife came down.

"*Stop it there*," a voice boomed, shaking the whole room.

Wilks froze. The knife stopped inches from Tash Hanbury's jugular.

"Stop it there," said the voice again, quieter.

Wilks turned. "I was… was going to open her up for you."

Jack stepped out of the shadows. His black eyes were wide, and his tongue flicked over his lips. "We've got trespassers."

"What?"

Jack focused. "A seer and… something else. The seer – it's this one's child again."

The Hanbury woman screamed. She was shouting to her daughter, telling the girl to run. Wilks thought, *Run where?* How had she got here in the first place? It wasn't real. It was on the edges of the world. You had to know where to look to find the cracks that would lead to these lost locations.

He looked at Jack and saw fear in his waxy face.

Jack told him, "Go get them."

Wilks obeyed. He went to the door and opened it, and a long corridor stretched out before him. He took one look again into the room before stepping out into the passageway. Behind him Jack said, "You go too, eunuch."

Wilks walked down the corridor, which was as wide as a road and reached too high for him to see in the dark. The walls were oil-slick and coal-black. Thousands of tiny bones carpeted the ground.

He ran along the passage, brandishing the knife. Someone followed him. He glanced over his shoulder. It was Hallam Buck. Jack's neutered human-pet.

As he turned back to face the way he was headed, he stumbled, flinging his arms over his head to protect himself from the winged creature hurtling down the corridor towards him.

CHAPTER 112.
THE SERVANT OF THE
LORD WHO GAPES.

HALLAM Buck threw himself on the ground when the winged man swept down and attacked the New Ripper. He covered his head as if he were expecting a bomb. His face was buried in the bones on the ground, and they pricked his skin. But pain was nothing to him now. Not after Jack had made him a eunuch and promised him a place at his court. A place of honour.

He peeked through his fingers. He could hear the New Ripper shriek and wings flapping violently.

He was wondering what to do. Stay still or get up and run?

He was no closer to making a decision when he saw her.

Jasmine Hanbury ran down the corridor towards him.

His heart pounded. His excitement grew. Jack had known she was here. He could tell. He'd sensed her. And if Hallam could catch her and bring her to Jack, there would be more praise.

The girl obviously hadn't seen him lying in the bones. It was gloomy, and he could have been just a shape or a shadow to her.

She kept coming. And when she was five yards away, Hallam sprang to his feet.

She skidded to a halt, gawping with horror at the sight of him.

Hallam was uglier than ever. He was deathly pale, with big, dark rings around his eyes. It was a wonder he wasn't dead. But he knew Jack was keeping him alive – keeping him alive to serve in the court of the lord who gapes.

He pounced on Jasmine. She screamed. Above him, the winged man was throwing the New Ripper around as if he were a rag doll.

Jasmine screamed, "Charlie, help me!"

Charlie? thought Hallam and looked up. "Oh God," he said as Charlie Faultless surged through the air on a pair of huge, black wings. Hallam had the girl by the hair and raced down the passageway with her towards the safety of Mary Kelly's lodging house.

As he went he shouted, "I've got her."

The child cried out, screaming for Faultless.

Faultless the winged demon.

Faultless the angel of death.

How had that happened?

The girl called out again.

Hallam bashed her across the face and knocked her out.

As he ran, getting closer to the door with every step, the flapping of wings grew louder, and a dark shape moved above him.

CHAPTER 113.
LOOK HARD.

SPENCER stared at the wall between the roller-doors. He shivered and sweated, aching all over. Drivers had beaten him up after he'd caused the pile-up on Commercial Street. But at least Jasmine got away. He'd watched her go, and when he got the chance to escape the clutches of a bunch of very pissed-off motorists, he ran in the direction he'd seen her go.

And for some reason, he'd reached this private road.

He quickly looked around. Sirens blared in the distance. Cops and ambulances were arriving at the accident he'd caused. They'd probably come looking for him soon, so he'd have to make a decision.

He knew where Jasmine had gone. She'd gone through. She'd found a way. Because she was psychic, she must have known about the places Jack had shown him.

"You have to look hard," Jack had told him, "but if you do, you will always find a way through from your world to these lost places, these hidden locations."

So that's what he did. He looked hard, directly at the brick wall between the two entrances. Something about the spot made him look.

Perhaps it was the damp strip running down the wall or the voices he was sure were coming from behind it. Perhaps he was just going crazy.

But then, as his vision blurred, the dark strip on the wall became clearer, more defined.

He gasped.

"Christ," he said. It was an alleyway. A very narrow alleyway. He climbed up the steps. Now the strip was just damp running down the wall again. He tutted. He stared again, looking hard at the bricks.

Again his eyes blurred, and the dark, vertical band became more definite.

Without blinking, so as not to clear his eyesight, Spencer reached out. He should have touched brick. He didn't. His hand went into the darkness. Into the passageway. He walked forward and then turned sideways. He had to. It was too narrow, otherwise. Holding his breath, he slid into the passageway. The darkness stretched. He shuffled into it. The walls pressed against his back and his chest.

He thought, *What happens if I blink? Will I be crushed?*

Panic flooded his bowels.

CHAPTER 114.
EXECUTION.

FAULTESS, hell's thing, floated down.

Hallam Buck managed to get Jasmine through the door. But Tash was also inside the room, as was the thing born moments before Faultless.

The thing he was sent here to fight.

His brother? How could that be?

He felt gloom and misery overwhelm him. Everything he'd come home to acheive was now lost to him. His goals were altered. His humanity gone. Madness knocked on the door of his mind. His sanity teetered on a precipice.

His psyche quickly fixed on something just in case he went insane – and what he fixed on was his purpose.

The reason he was made.

To fight this creature who threatened hell on earth.

At first, the instinct programmed into him by his maker made him head towards the door behind which Jack lurked.

But then something else took hold. Another desire that had been encrypted into him. But not by God this time. Not by a being Faultless hated.

The desire was vengeance. And it came from love.

He might have been born an angel, but he had been raised a human. Raised by a woman called Patricia Faultless. Charlie loved his mother. He loved her more than anything. He would also love another woman. Given time, he was sure his love for Rachel would have grown stronger than the love he had for his mum.

But destiny drove both women into the knife of the broken man at Faultless's feet.

He wrenched the mask off Don Wilks's head. Sweat sheened the detective's face. Wilks grinned madly, his eyes bulging. He was clearly in agony. Faultless had smashed him from wall to wall, breaking his body. Wilks lay ruined. Bone poked through his flesh. One arm was nearly amputated.

Wilks somehow managed to speak, his voice coming out as a growl. "Fucking cunt," he said. "Where the fuck did you get wings, then, fucker? Ha! You think you're a fucking angel, Faultless, you're a fucking… cunt. And I killed your bitch mother and your bitch girlfriend. Wish I'd shagged them, now. Wish I'd put it in them, the cunts… the… "

"You finished?" said Faultless.

"Fuck you, you – "

Faultless's wing slashed. The speed of the movement made it lethal. It was like steel slicing through Wilks's neck, decapitating him. His head rolled off his shoulders. It crunched into the tiny bones on the ground. Faultless stared into the dead eyes. He felt empty. All the anger, all the pain, was dulled now. Everything he had been was gone. Everything he believed was false.

Executing the man who murdered his mother and girlfriend should've brought satisfaction. It should have brought a release.

Instead, it brought nothing.

He was about to turn around and head for the showdown with Jack when something crashed into him and sent him wheeling through the air.

CHAPTER 115.
SURVIVAL.

TASH came around.

Everything trembled. Dust rained from the ceiling. The floorboards shook. The walls creaked.

She looked around.

"Jasmine," she said, trying to get up, but she was still tied to the bed. "Jasmine, baby."

Her daughter was curled up in the corner. Standing by the door, looking out, was Hallam Buck. He came in and shut the door. He looked scared. It sounded like there was an earthquake.

"Th-they're fighting," said Buck.

"You bastard," said Tash. "Untie me, Hallam. Untie me so I can kill you, you fucking bastard."

He went to the table. He opened a leather briefcase – Montague Druitt's briefcase.

"W-where did you get that?" said Tash.

"It was mine to start with. Faultless stole it."

"It was at my – "

"Yes, and now it's back with its rightful owner."

He fished around inside.

Tash said, "What are you doing?" She looked over at Jasmine. She mouthed, *Get out – run,* but the child stayed where she was.

The trembling got worse.

"What's going on?" said Tash.

"I told you," said Buck. "They're fighting – Faultless and Jack. But he's not Faultless anymore. He's something else."

"Hallam? What do you – "

Buck looked up. Out of the briefcase he brought a scalpel. Tash felt her blood turn to ice.

Buck said, "I'm going to kill one of you, Tash. I got to. I made a mess of things before. I was weak, Jack said. And he ripped my cock and balls off. But if I kill one of you and cut you open, he'll be grateful. He'll let me worship him again. I'm going to be brave and – "

"Don't do this, Hallam," said Tash, panic in her voice. She struggled, trying to get free. "We've got to get out of here. The whole place is coming down. Untie me. Untie me and… and we can be friends."

He laughed. It was a cold laugh. "No point in that anymore, Tash. I got no equipment now. You know what? Charlie Faultless should never have interfered all those years ago."

Tash knitted her brow.

"You don't remember?" he said.

She shook her head.

"You remember being attacked and Faultless saving you?"

"I remember that. It was you?"

"Yeah, me. He stopped me having you, the bastard."

Tash tried to say something, but her throat was too dry.

"I've always liked you," he said, "but, you bitch, you never liked me back."

"I… I… " She didn't know what she was trying to say. What could she say? She could lie. But he'd see through it. He'd know. So she kept her mouth shut and looked at Jasmine and started to think how they would survive this.

Then she thought of something Hallam had said.

"What did you mean Charlie's something else?"

"He ain't human no more."

Dread filled her heart. "What's that mean?"

He said nothing, just sneered.

The fury of whatever was going on outside increased. Floorboards sprang up. The wall cracked. Everything was coming apart, and the noise was deafening.

How was she going to get out with Jasmine?

Hallam was moving towards her with the scalpel now. His eyes shone in the gloom. Debris showered him. He looked like a ghost. He licked his lips, and his tongue stood out pink against his pale, dust-coated face.

Tash arched her back. The ropes cut into her wrists and ankles. She felt the panic rise up. Her chest tightened. Hallam was going to kill her. He was touching her, lifting up her top, and she begged him not to. But his eyes fixed on the skin of her belly, and he rubbed it, his cold, clammy hand making her scream and writhe.

"You like it," he said.

Tash screamed for Jasmine to run. But Jasmine sprang to her feet like a cat, and she was out of the corner in a flash, kicking at Hallam, using what she'd learned at her tae kwan do classes.

It rocked Hallam, and he staggered, slashing with his blade. Tash feared her daughter would be cut. But Jasmine fought like a cornered animal. She had Hallam on the back foot. Her fury had scared him. Tash was still shouting at her to run, but her shrieking eleven year old drove Buck back towards the door with her attacks.

He hacked and sliced at her. And then he kicked and kicked again, anger etching his face now. And Jasmine yelped, stumbling. She bent double. Tash screamed. The scalpel rose. Hallam grabbed Jasmine's hair. He snarled, spit spraying from between his teeth.

"I'll kill you both," he said.

The walls crumbled. The roof started to cave in. The door flew off its hinges.

A man, covered in dirt, flew into the room and barged into Hallam. The three of them – Hallam, Jasmine, and the man – fell in a heap.

"Jasmine, get out," said Tash again.

The man pummelled Hallam. It was Spencer. For a second, Tash panicked because the youth had been with Jack. Her dad had grabbed him when they'd rescued Jasmine. Her dead dad. She screamed with rage. She cursed Hallam and urged Spencer to beat him, to kill him.

Jasmine rose from the pile of bodies and came to her mother, scrabbling at the ropes.

Hallam fought back. He jabbed with his scalpel. He cut Spencer, who shrieked. Blood spurted.

Tash, on her feet now, shoved Jasmine away and kicked Hallam hard in the side. He bent double, gasping for breath. She stamped on his hand, and he dropped the scalpel. She went to pick it up, but Spencer was shouting.

"We got to get out… we got to leg it… everything's coming apart… the whole world's breaking up… "

Blood ran from his arm. He was at the door. Outside, it seemed as if the sky was falling in.

Tash looked for the scalpel again, her eyes skimming the floor, but it was gone. Her chest tightened.

Hallam's got it, she thought.

But he was lying on the floor. A pool of blood formed around his head. It spread, dark fluid leaching across the dirty floorboards.

Tash turned her head slowly. Behind her stood Jasmine. She held the scalpel in her hand. It dripped blood.

"Jesus, we got to go," said Spencer.

Tash snapped into action. She snatched the scalpel from Jasmine and tossed it aside, then grabbed her daughter by the hand and pulled her to the door.

"Go on, get out," she said to Spencer as the ceiling behind her collapsed, burying the dead Hallam under rotten wood and plaster. "Now!" she yelled and shoved Spencer out of the door.

They stopped dead. Tash stared in horror. Everything was disintegrating. Huge walls cracked to reveal the night sky. As their surroundings collapsed, the streets of London came into view – the streets of Whitechapel. Through the crumbling masonry, Tash saw Londoners flee.

They must think it's an earthquake, she thought.

A tremor shook the floor, and she looked down. It was giving way. She clutched Jasmine tightly. The ground was sliding apart as if tectonic plates were separating. And as the earth split and opened around them, Tash saw what was below.

A lake of fire sizzled and bubbled deep down in the crevice revealed by the upheaval.

"We've got to get away now," said Tash.

"Mum, look."

Jasmine was pointing upwards. Tash followed her gaze. For a moment, she saw nothing except the world coming apart. But then in the downpour of debris, two figures whirled.

She couldn't make them out. They wheeled in the air so quickly. They were just a blur to Tash. One had wings. The other seemed to have a huge cape flapping behind him.

"It's Charlie," said Jasmine.

No, thought Tash, *no, never.*

And then Jasmine said, "He's an angel."

And then she remembered Hallam's words.

He ain't human no more.

As she stared up, praying Charlie was still a human who would hold her and kiss her and love her when this was finished, the ground under their feet gave way.

CHAPTER 116.
GOD WEEPS.

THE One Who Made Everything watched as this little corner of his creation came apart.

His children fought, and their battle wreaked havoc and destruction.

It always did. It wasn't the first time he'd sent someone against the *up-elo*, the first evil. But at least today it was a better match.

Thousands of years ago, a blink of an eye to him, he'd sent a man called Noe. Noe had been created good. He'd been fashioned by The One Who Made Everything as a perfect man. But even Noe had sin in his heart. That was the problem now. The blueprint had been set down, and it had this flaw in it – a flaw that came about because the designer got angry after his wife rejected him. But The One Who Made Everything wasn't about to take the blame for that. It was man's fault. He had free will. He could choose. And most times he chose evil. He chose sin.

Man's fault, not mine, he told himself.

But there were high hopes for Noe.

He had a heavy dose of goodness in him. He'd been made especially to face up to the *up-elo*.

But sin was strong. Noe got a taste for drink. He was ratty and rude. And when the *up-elo* came after him, the world paid a heavy price.

Their battle unleashed a flood that drowned the earth. It destroyed virtually everyone and everything.

Noe and his family escaped. The *up-elo* laughed and said to his father, "Don't you have better adversaries for me to play with?"

The story of Noe and the flood threw up fables. They were mostly to do with an ark Noe was supposed to have built to survive the deluge. Another myth. There was no ark. The ark was Noe's heart, where goodness dwelled. It had to survive there or after the flood there wouldn't be any of it left on earth. But sin survived too. Sin always survived. It would always be around, a dark stain in the human heart.

After Noe, The One Who Made Everything decided that *up-elo* was too powerful. The world was decaying even after being purged by the flood.

Back then, he didn't want to kill that First Evil. In a way, it had brought some balance to creation. More darkness made more light. The worse some men behaved, the better others acted. Goodness followed in evil's wake.

But slowly *up-elo* was getting the upper hand. And although The One Who Made Everything couldn't wreck his own creation – that would be an admission of failure – he could at least balance things out.

So what he did was send male angels to breed with human women.

Their offspring he named nephilim. They had the foresight of angels and the craftiness of man.

The One Who Made Everything set out the laws under which they would live. The nephilim and their children were seers who had mind powers enabling them to track down *up-elo*. When they caught him, they should contain him with a curse.

But *up-elo* had a way out.

All he had to do was tap into the sin in men's hearts to secure his release, and then, if he could kill and claim the souls of five seers while he was free, the world would be his. If he was captured and contained before he'd got to five, the seers he'd killed would not count – he'd have to start all over again once he was free.

But there was a catch. There was always a catch.

Up-elo was not allowed to lay a hand on the seers himself. That would have been too easy. He had to recruit a ripper. He had to call to the part of himself that lay in every human heart.

The battle went on for centuries, back and forth. Over time the creator grew weary with his own creation. His attempt to generate balance had failed. He was sad and angry that sin had corrupted the world. He had tried to control it but failed. Finally, there was only one thing to do.

Up-elo had to go. He'd grown arrogant. He was wily and spread a little too much of himself around the world. Even when he had been trapped by the seers, the sin he had distributed during his freedom had tainted the world. War, famine, and plague swept creation. It seemed unstoppable. The earth was dying.

There was only one way he could get rid of *up-elo* without throwing things completely out of balance. He would have to replace it. He would nurture a fragment of the first evil thought and give it life. Send it to earth and give it a destiny. Carve out a path for it so that one day it would come face to face with its brother.

Now was that day.

The One Who Made Everything had to let them fight. He had to be fair to the *up-elo,* to the original sin.

But in truth, he favoured his second son.

He would be a good evil in the world. An equalizer to the goodness that The One Who Made Everything had, at the beginning, tried to instill into everything he'd made. But creation needed balance. It was better that way. It had to continue.

There would always be evil, he decided. Only sometimes it would be a new one. And here it was. Its human name had been Charlie Faultless. Its true name would be unspeakable. It would suffer, and it would bring suffering. It would tempt men to sin, testing them to see if they were worthy of a place in heaven.

It would be the lord who gapes. It would be the lantern of the tomb. It would be the moth eating at the law.

The One Who Made Everything sat back on his throne in heaven and watched the destruction below.

A tear ran from his eye.

CHAPTER 117.
THE FINAL BATTLE.

THEY separated, both of them nursing wounds.

Jack had slammed into Faultless from behind, catching him off guard. He had the upper hand after the sneak attack and managed to injure Charlie. Blood flowed from cuts on his body, and part of his cheek hung off his face.

But Faultless had managed to fight back.

Flapping his wings now as he floated above the earth, he saw that Jack was also badly wounded. His mouth gushed blood. He looked as if he'd been scalped, a section of his hair and the skin beneath ripped away to reveal his skull. His clothes were tattered. As he hovered opposite Faultless, his cape fluttered. Faces contorted in the material. For a moment, Faultless was transfixed.

"They are the souls I've stolen for hell," said Jack. "I keep a little bit of them with me."

"They're mine now," said Faultless.

Jack laughed. "You want them? You want all this?" He gestured to the earth below.

Faultless looked. Whitechapel was in ruins. Commercial Street had been split in two, right down its middle. In the gash, Faultless saw hell burning under the earth. It was a lake of fire. A bubbling mass of molten lava.

"Our war is tearing the place apart," said Jack.

He was right. Faultless saw death and destruction. Buildings collapsed. The ground opened up. People fell into the earth. They were crushed under falling masonry. The carnage spread for miles. It reached the towers of Barrowmore. They trembled as the quake rippled across London. From his vantage point, he saw the ruin of the city.

To the southwest, the Tower of London turned to rubble. The City crumpled.

Looking to the south, Faultless saw the Thames rise in a tidal wave. The waters ploughed through Tower Bridge, smashing through the granite and bending the girders.

Faultless swivelled.

To the east, Barking and Dagenham became a wasteland, and tower blocks collapsed and terraced streets fell like dominoes. Only a few days ago, he'd stared across to those streets from his flat. It seemed so long ago. It seemed that it had not been him staring out of that window.

"Beautiful, ain't it?" said Jack. "All down to us. You and me."

Faultless suddenly thought of Tash. He wondered if she'd escaped. He touched his chest, remembering a warm feeling he'd once had in there when he thought of her. He felt it no longer. He felt nothing after his father had torn out his heart, holding the pulsing muscle up in front of Faultless's face and saying, "You have no need of this any more. Hearts are for humans. And they are the hiding place of sin. But now you *are* sin."

Jack said, "You know I'm stronger than you. You know I was the firstborn. You should give it up. Throw yourself into the fire. It's easy."

Faultless looked into hell. Down there, the tortured screamed. They burned forever in the fire. Their suffering was endless.

"Last chance, Charlie," said Jack. He tore at his clothes. His body bore similar markings to Faultless's torso. Tattoos of ancient writings and lost symbols. The shreds of his shirt floated down to the earth. His still wore his cloak. But it was part of him now. It had fused into his arms and his shoulders. His skin, where cloth and flesh welded together, took on the cloak's colour. It seeped into him, threads penetrating his body and coiling themselves like snakes around his sinews. "I've lived too long to give this up," he said.

Jack brought his hands to his chest and opened himself up like a jacket. His flesh came away like a discarded piece of clothing, and underneath was his true self.

Faultless flinched.

The thing before him was black and leathery. Its dark eyes were set in a ebony, goat-shaped head with curling horns. A black tail lashed the air behind the creature, and its legs were bent backwards at the knee.

A terrible voice came from the thing's throat. "Think you can beat me, Charlie? Look at me. I am the lord who gapes. I am the lantern of the tomb. I am the moth eating at the law."

"No you're not," said Faultless. "I am."

Jack smiled. "Is that what he told you, our father on high? He told you that you were chosen? You were his favourite? Lies, brother. Lies. He's always loved me, because I'm the first-born. I'll hurl you down to hell and send those bitch seers after you – in pieces."

Faultless attacked. He clawed with his hands, and he sliced with his wings. Jack fought back, tearing with his talons, kicking with his hooves, and biting with razor-sharp teeth.

The more they battled, the more the world beneath them broke.

As he whirled with Jack through the sky, Faultless caught glimpses of London. It burned and crumbled and fell into heaps. People were crushed and plunged through the huge clefts that had opened up across the city and sailed down into the fires and into torment.

Faultless and Jack separated for a second time, both weakened.

"Why is he doing this to me?" said Jack.

"Maybe he's had enough of you."

"He *made* me. I am his offspring."

"Fathers can be cruel."

"He loves you more, doesn't he?"

"I don't know if that's a good thing."

"You can't kill me."

"I'll give it a try."

Faultless attacked.

CHAPTER 118.
DEATH OF AN ANGEL.

JACK was more powerful than Faultless expected. Having shed its human skin, the creature seemed to have grown stronger and more confident. And when it gripped Faultless from behind, its talons tearing into Charlie's throat, he thought he'd been lied to by Lew. Just like Jack said.

They wheeled around in the darkening sky. Down below, London crumbled.

He can kill me, thought Faultless, trying to pry the claws away from his throat. *And if he does, what happens then?*

Faultless flexed his wings, flapping them violently in an effort to dislodge Jack.

As they swooped and flailed, Faultless glimpsed the people a mile beneath him, desperately trying to flee the falling city. The earth opened, and hundreds fell into the chasm. Buildings fell and crushed hundreds more. Others drowned as the Thames overflowed.

For a moment, he wondered what he was fighting for.

Is it worth it? Can't I just let him kill me?

444

But then his mind filled with Tash, with his mother, with Rachel, with Jasmine, with Hanbury.

Again he felt nothing for them, but something in the far distance of his mind was calling out to remind him what they had meant to him.

Remember, the voice was calling, *remember your heart…*

A surge of energy raced through Faultless. He grasped Jack's wrists, and with a yell of rage, prized them apart. The skin of his throat came away too, but it didn't affect him.

What was skin when you were an angel?

He yanked his adversary over his head and flung him through the air. Jack sailed through the clouds, sparks flying off his body.

Faultless flapped his wings, guiding himself in Jack's direction.

He speared himself towards the other, rage contorting his face.

As he dived, hawk-like, Faultless saw that his adversary was regaining his balance by using his cape. And then he faced the oncoming Charlie, beckoning him.

"Come on, brother," he growled. "See if you can better me. See if our father lied to you."

Faultless hesitated.

It was enough time for Jack to act. He stretched out his arms, and his cape spread out. The faces that seemed to live in the folds came alive again. Before, they had been masks of pain. But now, suddenly, the expressions had changed.

The faces snared with hatred.

Dozens of them embedded in the cape.

Faultless tried to pull out of his lunge, but it was too late.

They spooled from Jack's cape, hate-fuelled faces attached to the bodies of serpents. They shot towards Faultless, jaws wide to display sharp teeth. Their black eyes glistened, their nostrils flared. And from their throats came shrieks of fury.

Faultless reared up, his wings flapping wildly as he readjusted his flight.

But the first demon struck him, its teeth sinking into his chest. Faultless yelled out and bashed at the fiend's head, but then another smashed into him, latching on to Charlie's arm. More came in, swooping, taking quick bites at him and retreating or sinking their teeth into him and holding on. He howled with rage, striking out at the demons, slicing at them with his wings.

Laughter filled the sky.

A few yards away, Jack hovered. The serpents were still attached to his cape. He pointed at Faultless and said, "After they've finished with you, I'll have them spit you out – what's left, that is."

Faultless fought for his life. He managed to dislodge one of the demons and decapitate it with his wing. The others loosened their grip on him, as if they'd felt the dead serpent's pain. Even Jack faltered.

And then Faultless swooped. His huge wings powered him at a tremendous speed, making him nothing but a blur to anyone who was looking up at that moment.

With the demons still attached to him, he zoomed in a circle around the Jack-thing. Faultless looped around his adversary, winding the serpents around him.

Jack shouted, "No… no… stop… "

But Faultless flew furiously. His wings battered the air. The biting demons tore at his skin. But as they tightened around their master's body, their grip on Faultless slackened.

Soon, Jack was wrapped in his cape and coiled in the serpents. They were knotted together around him and shrieked with panic. They whipped about, trying to escape. Jack screamed at them as he was dragged around. Sparks flew from the coiling mass of flesh formed by him and his demons.

"Let me live, brother," he squealed. "Let me live, and we'll share this world between us… let me live… "

Faultless said, "No," and went in for the kill.

CHAPTER 119.
THE GATES OF HELL.

"BACK, get back," PC Alison Care told the crowd, "Get away from here now." She was standing on the corner of what had once been Fournier Street. Now it was a heap of asphalt, buckled and swollen as if some enormous pressure valve had exploded from below.

Commercial Street had been ripped open. It had been peeled back to reveal a huge, deep cavern that fell away for miles into a fiery pit. Care could smell the sulphur and feel the heat. She knew exactly what was down there. Her father was a pastor in North London, and now she regretted turning her back on God – maybe now was the time she needed him.

Dad had always begged her to return. He'd warned that something like this would happen. Dad had said that before Jesus came back, there would be wars and rumours of war, just like it said in the Bible. There would be famines, plagues, and earthquakes.

Earthquakes just like this one.

"You have to repent," said Dad. "You have to come to Christ, Alison, or you are doomed."

Alison thought that she'd go to heaven by being good.

"No," said Dad. "Ephesians tells us that it is through grace that we are saved, not through our works. The day is coming, Alison. Accept Christ or suffer in hell forever."

Now she wanted to repent. Now she wanted Christ. But maybe it was too late.

Someone screamed. One of many screams. But this particular voice caught Care's attention.

It was a boy, aged about six.

He was standing near the edge of the crevice where the Ten Bells pub had stood, up until a few minutes ago. Now the pub and many of the buildings next to it had gone. They had crumpled and dropped into the earth. The bricks and the mortar, the wood, the glass, the steel, and the people who had been inside them, had fallen into the fire.

The boy screamed again. He was crying. Covered in dust, he shivered, and Care thought he would topple over and fall.

She'd seen hundreds, maybe thousands, die in the past few minutes – at least she could save one.

But then she thought about repentance again.

Faith, not good works, is the way to heaven, she heard her father say.

She looked at the boy. He was shrieking in terror.

Good works were better, she thought. *Heaven can wait.*

She ran to the boy and plucked him up into her arms and turned away from the abyss. But the ground was shaky. It kept rumbling, and it would suddenly rise up like a wave. Just like now. The bulge in the ground lifted Care off her feet, and the boy fell from her arms. She rolled, trying to grab for him, but he slipped down near the edge of the chasm.

Care struggled to her feet.

Cars tipped over, into the gorge that had opened up on Commercial Street. People ran in every direction. Falling buildings crushed some of them. Others fought among themselves to escape, and the weaker ones were pushed into the canyon, where they fell screaming into the fiery depths.

It was carnage.

Her dad had been right.

She started to pray.

But then the child cried again.

He knelt near the precipice.

Care stopped praying and started to crawl towards him.

"Come to me, Daniel, come to Mummy," said a voice.

Care looked. A woman in a white dress stained with blood held out her arms to the child.

The woman stood near the edge of the pit.

She called to the boy again. "Come on, Daniel. Jesus is coming. We have to go and meet him. Jesus is coming."

The boy ran to the woman. She scooped him up in her arms. Care felt terror seep through her. She started to yell, "No, don't," but it was too late – woman and child leapt into the chasm.

Care screamed.

London was being destroyed. Her dreams were shattered. She stayed on all fours, crying. The ground shook beneath her. Commercial Street and the surrounding areas were slowly being flattened. People were dying in the thousands.

And here she was on her hands and knees, doing nothing.

She was getting up when she saw them – a woman with blonde hair, a girl aged about eleven, and a youth in his late teens.

They all stared ahead and strode confidently through the chaos. Around them, Whitechapel collapsed. Death was everywhere. But they just bounded into the road and kept moving.

Care felt she should be close to them. She felt they knew where they were going. She also thought they might know what was happening.

"Wait," she said to them. "Police, wait."

The youth turned. His eyes showed fear. They were glazed over, like he was on drugs.

"Keep moving... we have to get away," the blonde woman told him.

"I order you to stop," said Care uselessly.

The woman told her, "You have to get out of here. Away from the gates."

"What gates?" said Care. "What's... what's happening? You know. Tell me. What gates?"

The woman looked up before staring directly at Care. "When it ends, he'll take everything around here with him. Just get away." The woman then grabbed the young girl at her side by the arm and said, "Come on, Jasmine."

Before Care could stop them, they had gone. She watched them, and the youth looked back and up into the sky, where the woman had previously looked.

Care followed his gaze.

She furrowed her brow, staring hard, trying to focus.

Her mouth dropped open and while she squinted, something kept repeating itself in her head:

The gates... the gates... the gates...

High above Whitechapel, a ball of black fury whizzed and whirled. Watching it, Care could occasionally see feathers or horns or talons or hooves in the spinning mass. The night sky filled with lightning now. It cracked the heavens, and Care was sure that when those cracks appeared, she could see eyes looking through. It made her gasp with fear.

Something terrible was happening.

An old score was being settled.

The end of something approached.

A shape flew out of the spiralling ball of feathers and horns. The rest of the shape followed it, and then Care saw more clearly what had been wheeling about up there.

A man with huge black wings.

A devil, she thought. *Or an angel.*

Others spotted it now, and they all looked up, their attempts to escape forgotten.

Care craned her neck to see the battle.

The winged man grabbed the other shape and pounded it until sparks flew from its body.

The earth gave one last mighty shake, throwing Care and all the other spectators off their feet.

And then the winged man hurled the other figure down, and it plunged, screaming, a tail of fire following it. The shape fell into the chasm. The earth groaned. A tower of fire shot up from the deep to light up the sky like it was day. In the light, Care saw the winged man clearly. He was powerful and beautiful, and his wings held him up easily.

The flaming lance was sucked back into the ground. Darkness and silence fell across London. Care held her breath. Those around her whimpered and prayed.

And then the ground lurched and lifted. Care scrabbled at the asphalt. Her fingers were torn. She cried out for God, repenting of her sins and begging to be saved.

The others who had stayed to watch did the same.

But no one listened.

The groaning earth swallowed them all, sucking them down, along with buildings and cars and streets.

Above her, the gorge sealed, closing Care off from any hope of life. She flailed and fell, thousands falling with her. She looked down, and the lake of fire waited miles below. And as she and the others plunged towards it they all screamed at God for salvation. But God didn't listen.

CHAPTER 120.
RUINS.

EVERYTHING had gone into the chasm. Virtually the whole of Whitechapel. All of Jack the Ripper's haunt.

It had all gone.

All of it apart from one tower.

Monsell House stood alone in a wasteland that stretched from Stepney Green in the east to Bishopsgate in the west.

Even beyond those points, there was destruction.

As far west as Acton, people had died, and buildings had collapsed. In the east, Barking and Dagenham had been flattened. Westminster was a wreck. Big Ben toppled, and the Houses of Parliament had been razed. South of the river, Lambeth, Deptford, Greenwich, and Brixton were rubble.

The earthquake had savaged the city and killed more than eighty thousand.

Emergency crews picked through the obliterated city, searching for survivors, looking for answers.

Foreign aid trickled in. Soldiers kept the starving, desperate population at bay while the assistance was distributed fairly. The government, what was left of it, moved to Birmingham. The prime minister survived because he'd been on a trip to China at the time. But he was one of only a few politicians to be left alive after the disaster.

In what was once Barrowmore, there was now only one human being.

Tash Hanbury sat cross-legged on the roof of Monsell House. She wore a red hooded top under a long man's overcoat. Her gloved hands were tucked into the deep pockets. On her head she wore a Russian hat, the muffs drawn down over her ears. Her jeans were dirty, and her motorcycle boots stained with blood. Over the past few days, she'd had to walk through a lot of human remains.

She'd sent Jasmine with Spencer to safety. There were shelters in Enfield, Bromley, Twickenham, and Wembley.

Then, Tash had returned to Monsell House. Amazingly it stood. She knew it was meant to be. There was no way it could have survived the annihilation unless someone – or something – had a hand in it. The other towers were piles of rubble. The rest of the estate was gone.

Monsell House was here for a reason.

It was here for her.

So she made her way to the roof, climbing up the stairs crammed with dead bodies.

On the roof, she waited.

She drank water and ate stale bread.

And still she waited.

The days were cold, and the nights were even colder.

But she waited.

He would come, she knew it. Whatever he was now, he still, surely, felt something for her. There was still human in him. There was still love.

The wind picked up. Tash looked up. The sky was pitch black. No stars. And then she heard the noise. Like wind beating at a sail. Like wings flapping. She got to her feet, rubbing her hands together. Hope filled her. Maybe if he came, everything would be all right. Maybe he could make it right.

He came from the night, naked. His body was marked with writing and symbols. He had a gouge down the middle of his chest, as if someone had carried out heart surgery on him without stitching up the wound afterwards.

She looked at his body and felt a thrill race through her.

He landed five yards from her and folded his wings into his back.

"Charlie," she said, falling towards him.

"I'm not Charlie anymore." His raised hand halted her. "I am the unspeakable, Tash."

"I love you."

"Don't love me. You'll doom yourself."

"I don't care."

"I… " He trailed off and glanced away.

"What?"

He stayed silent.

"Charlie, what were you going to say?" she asked again.

He looked her in the eye. "Nothing, Tash. My heart's gone. There's no love in me, now."

She started to cry. "What about Rachel? Your mother?"

"She wasn't my mother. And Rachel… " He shook his head.

"So we were nothing to you?"

"You were put in my path. I was put in yours."

"So… so we were meant to be."

"No, Tash. This was meant to be." He gestured at the destruction. They lapsed into silence

After a few moments Tash said, "When I was young, when you were with Rachel… I used to daydream about marrying you, Charlie."

"Forget me."

"I can't. I'm a seer, remember?"

"Don't look for me, Tash. Ever. If you do, you will die. And… and something in me doesn't want that."

She found hope in those words and said, "Charlie, you can love me, you see? Please… "

"Don't look for me," he said, this time with steel in his voice.

"What if I do?"

His face darkened. He said nothing.

She said again, "What if I look for you?"

His face darkened. "Don't you realize what I am? I am pain, Tash. I am suffering. I am sin. I bring only grief. I am the lord who gapes, and out of my mouth comes evil. I am the lantern of the tomb, and I cast my light on death. I am the moth eating at the law, and when it crumbles, there will be chaos. This is what I am. That's my purpose. Go and find love, Tash. You deserve it."

"I don't want it. I want you."

"Go and find it, because if I have my way, there won't be much of it left – it's what I'm born for. We're done. I'll do my best to stay away from you and Jasmine and anyone you love. But I can't promise that I won't corrupt your lives in some way. I just can't promise that."

Tash cried. She said nothing. Charlie – or what had been Charlie – spread his wings and lifted away from the roof. He turned elegantly in the air, and his wings powered him higher. She watched him go.

He said he'd do his best to stay away from her, but she knew he'd be back one day. She knew he would corrupt her life. It was inevitable. Evil came to everyone in the end. When it came to her, she would love it because it had once loved her.

He rose higher and higher and went into the darkness, and slowly the darkness swallowed him. And then he was gone.

THE END.

ACKNOWLEDGMENTS.

There are many who deserve thanks for enabling me to write this novel, and firstly let me cheer Emma Barnes and Anna Torborg at Snowbooks, and proof-reader Robert Clark, who has worked on Prey, Krimson, and Pariah.

Although my agent Mariam Keen of the Whispering Buffalo Literary Agency has not been directly involved with these books, she is what a good agent should be: a shield and a shoulder. I thank her for knowing what's best for me better than I do.

My gratitude also goes to Rudi Gnoyke who read and ruthlessly commented on my drafts. Any failings in the book are down to me because I ignored his suggestions. Thank you as well to Holly Kirwan-Newman who meticulously proof-read my manuscript. Again, any errors are down to me. My gratitude also goes to Greg Lawrence, who read an early draft of the novel and made valuable comments.

Two books I found useful in writing Pariah were Howard Bloom's The Lucifer Principle and The Ultimate Jack The Ripper Sourcebook, edited by Stewart P. Evans and Keith Skinner.

One final and enormous thank you goes to my wife Marnie Summerfield Smith. She puts up with my crises of faith in my abilities, with my moments of doubt in the plot, with my grumpiness over approaching deadlines, and with the late hours as I chase my villain around the labyrinth that is Act Three. She bears it all with strength and resilience. She is mighty and wonderful, and her love sees me through.

Thomas Emson, December 2010

A SNEAK PREVIEW FROM...

PANDEMONIUM ROAD

WHEN THE DEVIL'S ON YOUR TAIL,
YOU'D BETTER DRIVE LIKE HELL

BY
THOMAS EMSON

CHAPTER 1.
EXECUTION.

THE man with wings cut off my father's head. My heart nearly stopped. I wanted to run out of the shed and try to save my dad.

But it was too late.

He was dead.

He'd been executed by the angel of death.

For a while, they had been talking. Dad and the angel. Gesticulating as if they were discussing who had the biggest carrots. But then the angel swiped his wing across the front of my father's throat. If he had been trying to hit my dad, it looked at first like he'd missed.

But he hadn't.

My dad's mouth opened, and his eyes gaped. His head tilted back – and kept tilting back till it fell off his shoulders and landed at his feet.

His body sagged, and he hit the ground.

His blood was on the grass and in the soil, and his head lay in the vegetable patch he'd cultivated for years.

My dad would spend most of his time at the allotment. Since Mum had died, he felt lonely in the house. And because I was never there, he thought it was pointless staying in.

So he'd come tend his vegetables and chat to his mates.

I knew the place quite well, because I hid here sometimes when the police were after me. Hunkering down in Dad's shed, I'd feel strangely close to him. His tools were there – the spade, the rake, the hoe. A wheelbarrow rested against the wall on its handles. A watering can was tucked in the corner. Sacks of fertilizer were piled at the far end. Packets of seeds littered a table, alongside my father's gardening gloves.

It was his place. It was him.

We never said much to each other. I never felt that close to him. He always eyed me suspiciously. But I was a handful.

My parents would argue over me.

Mum would defend me. "They've made a mistake – it wasn't my Jimmy."

Dad would say, "We have to nip it in the bud, Sonya, or when he's older, we'll have a problem on our hands – a six-foot, twelve-stone, big-lad-shaped problem."

I never got to six foot. Five-eight. Ten-and-a-half stone. Not a hefty teenager, but still a big problem.

Whatever Dad used to say to Mum back when I was a kid, it was always he who covered for me when I did get into trouble.

He'd tell the Old Bill I was somewhere else when they said I was behind the wheel of a taken-without-the-owner's-consent BMW doing a ton down the A2.

He covered for me all the time.

When the police came round he'd say, "He's not here," while I'd be cowering in my bedroom.

When the teachers rang to ask why I wasn't at school he'd say, "He's sick today," while I was playing truant with Tyler.

And when the man with wings came looking for me, he did the same.

He protected me.

He told me to stay out of the way and find somewhere to hide.

He'd said, "Son, you stay in this shed and keep yourself out of sight – and whatever you see or hear, do not come out."

So I was stowed away in the shed among his things, the smell of the soil on those tools the same as the smell of my father.

He was the soil, he was the earth.

He was my dad.

And he was dead.

Shock had frozen me to the spot. Only the top of my head and my eyes were visible as I peered out of the dust-covered window.

The winged man stood over my father's corpse, silhouetted against the sun as it dropped behind the horizon.

I started to shake.

Tears burned my eyes. I tried to blink them away, but it only made them flow.

My vision blurred for a moment, and when it cleared again I saw the angel slowly turning his head towards the shed – towards me.

And then he was looking straight at me.

My blood felt icy.

He knew where I was.

He'd seen me.

And he ran straight towards the shed with his big, black wings spread out behind him, flapping against the twilight.

CHAPTER 2.
LAST CHANCE.

CANTERBURY MAGISTRATES COURT,
BROAD STREET – 11.14 AM, JUNE 3, 2011

"YOU'VE had many opportunities, Mr Chance," the magistrates' chairman had said that morning. He was a rat-faced fella and glared at me over his half-moon specs. "I'm not sure you deserve another one."

"I do, your honour," I said.

"Be quiet, Mr Chance," said Rat-Face. I knew him. Not his name, his face. From where I was standing, I'd seen him quite often. My brief touched my arm and smiled, but his eyes were telling me to shut up.

"You are seventeen, Mr Chance," said Rat-Face. "It is time you grew up. Perhaps you should consider your future. Do you have any ambitions?"

I said nothing, playing it dumb – I'd been told to shut up, so I was keeping it shut.

The magistrate sighed. "You may speak."

"Cheers, your honour – "

"I am not 'your honour'. I am 'your worship'."

"Cheers, your worship."

"You should know by now how to address me, Mr Chance – you've been here often enough."

That was true, and I did know. I was just playing the fool.

"Now," said Rat-Face, "your future, young man."

"I'd like to be a racing driver, your worship."

He raised his eyebrows. "Would you? I see. Well, stealing cars and driving them at ridiculous speeds down the A2 and refusing to stop for police are not good preparations for such a career."

"I'd argue it was, your worship."

My brief nudged me.

Rat-Face went crimson. His buddies on the bench bristled. One was a toad-like creature with a comb-over. The other, a woman, looked like a praying mantis. I think the females eat the males. She looked like she could wolf me down. She had steel-grey hair and unblinking eyes. Her mouth was always set in a frown. It had never smiled in all the years I'd seen her at court.

Ratty said, "Perhaps if you showed this court some respect, Chance, you would not be tempted to steal other people's property."

"I doubt that, sir – aw!"

My brief had kicked me in the ankle. It hurt. I had to sit to rub it.

"Are you all right, Mr Chance?" said Ratty.

Before I could say anything my brief stood up.

"Your worships," he said. "James Chance is not a common thug. In fact he is an intelligent young man. Often among the brightest of students at his former schools. But he does have a mouth on him."

"He is gobby, Mr Anwar," said Rat-Face.

A ripple of laughter went through the courtroom. I chuckled too, eager to please. You laugh at people's jokes, they like you a little better. Maybe Rat-Face would warm to me and go easy on me over this taking-without-consent charge.

You've got to hope.

Still smiling, I looked around the court to see if everyone was happy. They were. I felt it was going to be okay.

But then I saw her.

She was sitting at the back, arms folded. She gave me a cold, hard stare. It seemed to go all the way through my chest into my spine.

I found it easier to stare at the three magistrates and their unpleasant mugs than look at her beautiful face.

A sweat broke out on my back.

Her eyes still bored into me, making me feel guilty.

The Old Bill could accuse me all day. The beaks on the bench too. And all the teachers who ever shouted at me over the years. I cared nothing for them. Their indictments meant nothing.

But now, in those eyes, I realize I'd been accused by an angel.

My angel.

And I wasn't sure I could get away with it.

CHAPTER 3.
MY ANGEL.

SHE was sitting on a wall outside the court, waiting for me.

She wasn't happy. Her arms were folded, like they'd been inside, and her foot was going up and down.

I was sweating with nerves.

Dealing with magistrates, police, and lawyers was easy compared to dealing with Samantha Louise Rayer.

Sammie.

My Sammie.

The court gave me probation – again. And a community punishment – again.

It would involve cleaning graffiti off bus shelters and sweeping up litter. A doddle. But punishment was always a piss-take. They never sent you down. No room in jail. And what they call "low-level" criminals, like me, should be sentenced using "other methods".

If they sent me down, I'd probably become a hardened criminal.

I don't read papers or anything, but kids talk. You can get the truth on Facebook. You very quickly get to learn what you can and can't do, and if there's any changes in the law.

Truth is, if you were on the ball, then crime paid.

It was a laugh.

And you were never properly penalized.

Not till you met an angel, that is.

My angel.

I walked towards her, bricking myself.

"Hi, babe," I said.

She never looked at me. Kept her eyes fixed on Broad Street. On the city walls across the street.

I looked at her long, blonde hair and remembered how like silk it was to touch and how lovely it was to smell. A yearning came to my heart, but it was mingled with guilt.

"You let me down," she said without turning.

Sammie was sixteen. She was delicate and deadly. A five-foot-tall whirlwind. Slim like a model and as tough as leather. She was like a doll, and she'd been my girlfriend for two years. I wanted no one else.

Why would I? She was gorgeous.

I never understood my mates. Some of them had girlfriends but cheated on them.

The guys said, "It's just the way – blokes get off with birds and birds expect it."

But not me. I didn't want anyone except Sammie. She made me feel tingly all over. When I was with her, everything was calm. I was never tempted to steal or get pissed. I felt something special for her and wasn't embarrassed to admit it.

I was in love.

She turned round, and her eyes were full of tears. It broke my heart.

She said, "You promised me."

I had promised. More than once. But I'd broken them all.

"Never again, Sammie," I said. "Honest, now. I'll go to college. We'll get a flat together. I love you, babe. I really do."

"I don't think I can be with you any more, Jimmy."

My legs weakened. I had a dizzy spell. A great hole felt like it had opened up in my chest, and my heart dropped into it.

"It wasn't my fault," I said, the stock excuse.

And she knew it.

"Are you serious, Jimmy?"

My mouth opened but no words came out – no crap, no lies, no excuses.

I shut my gob and shook my head before saying, "I'm sorry, Sammie."

She looked away, and she trembled.

"Don't cry," I said. "Please, babe."

"You hurt me, Jimmy."

Her words sliced through me. But I'd heard them before. They always hurt, but I always healed.

And after healing, I'd break her heart again.

She turned to me, her eyes red with tears. It made me flinch to see her pain.

She said, "It's over, Jimmy. I have to finish with you."

I flushed, panic racing through me.

I'd never heard these words before. Not even as a threat. They were devastating. You could've told me I was going inside for ten years, and I would've coped with it better.

"It's over," she said.

She burst into tears and ran off down the road.

I started chasing after her, desperate to salvage our relationship. How would I cope without Sammie? She was everything to me. The glue that held me together.

I was ready to run after her, but a piercing whistle stopped me in my tracks. I wheeled round, saw who had whistled, and sighed.

"You're the last person I need to see," I said.

CHAPTER 4.
WHO NEEDS MATES?

"HERE," said Tyler Jackson, "that's no way to talk to your best mate."

"Best mates don't run off and leave you. Best mates don't disappear and let you take the fall. Best mates back you up."

I walked away from him. I didn't want to be near Tyler or the court. I wanted to be with Sammie and sort out the problem I'd caused.

"And that's what you did," said Tyler. "You backed me up. And I'll never forget that, mate. You're not a grass, and that means something."

He was trotting after me, and I quickened my pace.

I said, "Don't talk crap. You think you're some kind of gangster or something?"

"I know one or two local faces. Does that count?"

"No, it doesn't, Tyler."

"Well, they know me. And you too. We got a reputation, you know."

"Yeah, I know – I'm trying to get rid of it."

"Come on, Jimmy. Here, wait," he said, catching me up. "I got a cracking job for us."

I wheeled and looked him straight in the eyes. "You have got to be joking."

"I never joke. Only with birds."

"And they find you hilarious."

"Sammie likes me."

"You're not reading the signals right, Tyler."

"Come on, it's a great job."

"I said, are you taking the mick? I just got done again, thanks to you. I just got my final warning, Tyler."

"It's always a final warning, mate. You'll be all right. Soft on crime, soft on the causes of crime – you know the law."

"I promised Sammie."

"Didn't do you much good. Last I saw she was legging it down the road. Looked in a bit of a huff to me. She pissed off again? She'll come round. Birds always do."

"Not this time. I'm going round hers. Sort this out. I got to do the right thing, Tyler."

"The right thing is to stick with your mates."

"Just like you did, eh?"

I walked away from him. Tyler had pissed me off. He always pissed me off. We'd been best pals since nursery. He was cheeky and always getting into trouble – always dropping me in it.

I remembered our first encounter. We were four years old.

He stole the nursery teacher's sandwich out of her bag and ate it right in front of the class.

Then he spat out a mouthful of tuna mayo and bread right into my lap.

I gaped at my trousers, covered in crumbs and bits of fish.

"Jimmy Chance," said the high-pitched voice, and I turned to see the teacher standing at the door, scowling at me.

I got the blame, and despite my claims of innocence, there is very little justice in the nursery school system. Circumstantial evidence is enough to condemn you. The burden of proof is not so heavy when you're accusing four year olds of eating your lunch.

So I got told off while Tyler chuckled at the back on the class.

He was a bad influence on me. And sometimes I wondered what kind of mate he was, because he never backed me up. He never stood by me. He was the first to bolt if there was trouble. And he always expected me to take the fall for him.

"That's what mates do," he'd say.

But he'd never do the same for me, despite his pledges of allegiance.

More broken promises, I thought.

But he was a laugh. You were always in stitches with Tyler. You never knew what he would do next. He was unpredictable.

Maybe that was the problem. I needed some stability. I needed Sammie.

As I walked along Broad Street, Tyler shouted after me, "It's a great job. Be fun, Jimmy. Cool car. Mercedes. Come on. You and me, race the cops down the A2. Come on."

Without turning around, I gave him the finger and went to win back my girlfriend.

CHAPTER 5.
SAM'S MUM.

MY head was spinning as I made my way down Military Road.

Court had slipped my mind. My punishment someone else's. Meetings with probation officers could wait.

Those things were nothing. Just a hindrance for a while.

My main concern was Sammie. I just had to get over to hers – and quick. Sort this out. Sort us out. Sort me out.

I was walking home fast. Military Road became the estates off the Sturry Road, where we both lived, just a couple of streets away from each other.

I was sweating, texting as I walked. Texting Sam and asking her to forgive me, please text back, please can we meet.

I was nearly there. My nerves jangled.

Please text back say it's okay, I thought.

My phone beeped. Text. My heart jumped. I checked excitedly. It was from Tyler. I sighed.

He was hassling me: "Meet at mine. Car Stodmarsh."

Stodmarsh, I thought, stuffing the phone back in my pocket.

I got to Sammie's house and stopped outside. Toys littered the lawn, her little brother's stuff strewn across the grass.

I felt a pang, remembering him and me playing football in the front garden, Sammie watching and saying, "You're being beaten by a seven year old," and me laughing, letting him win.

I felt gloomy as I went up to the front door and knocked.

The door opened.

My gloom went, and in its place came a cold, nervy feeling. She glared at me, her blue eyes glinting.

Sam's mum. An older version of Sammie. Delicate and deadly, also tough as leather. Very blonde and very beautiful. I had to admit, Sam's mum gave me the hots. It was good to know that in twenty-five years' time, that's what Sammie would look like.

"She doesn't want to see you, Jimmy," she said.

"Could you just tell her I'm here?"

"She knows you're here. That's why she doesn't want to see you."

"What have I done wrong?"

Sam's mum laughed sarcastically. "Are you joking?"

I was going to say it wasn't my fault, but she might have slammed the door in my face. I said nothing instead, my shoulders sagging.

She let out a sigh. "Jimmy, you know I like you. You're a nice boy, and you got brains. Most important, you're good to my Sammie."

I sensed hope and looked at her with my best "give me another chance" look. Her face had softened.

She went on: "But you've made loads of promises – "

"But I – "

"Jimmy, listen to me. You've made loads of promises, I don't know how many – "

"Four – "

"Four, there we are – four. All of them broken. You can't go on like this. Sammie can't go out with a criminal."

"It's over now, I promise."

473

She pulled a face. "That word again. Promise. Means nothing. Sammie says she doesn't want to see you. It's over. She's very sad about it, Jimmy. But she has made her decision. It's for the best."

"For whose best?"

"For her best."

"I just want her to say it to my face."

"Don't be silly. She's said it to you through me."

"I want her to say it to me, I – "

"It's over, Jimmy," said Sammie's voice from somewhere above me.

I flinched and backed down the path.

She was leaning out of her bedroom window. My heart broke.

Her mum said, "Shut the window and get back inside, Sammie."

I said, "Sammie, listen to me, I – "

Sammie, crying, said, "Jimmy, go away. I can't see you again. I can't. It's… it's breaking my heart. Go away."

She shut the window and was gone.

"Go home, Jimmy," said Sam's mum. "It's over."

She slammed the door in my face.

For a while, I just stood there in Sam's garden with Sam's brother's toys around me. I don't know how long I was there. Seconds or hours. Eventually I trudged away. I looked back once at Sammie's bedroom window. I yearned. I remembered her touch and her smell and the sound of her voice. And losing it all brought tears to my eyes.

CHAPTER 6.
ANOTHER "GOODNIGHT".

WHEN I got home, Dad was sitting in his armchair, watching Coronation Street on ITV2. It was just after lunch, and I could smell beans on toast.

I said, "All right," as I walked in.

Dad said nothing for a minute. He had been at the allotment all morning. He could've come with me to court, but he'd been before and knew how the story ended.

Without looking up at me he said, "You didn't go to jail, then?"

"I did, but I escaped. Me and Charlie Bronson. I'm top of the FBI's most wanted list. Now. Can you hide me in the shed up at the allotment? They'll never think to look up there."

He said nothing, just stared at that bird who used to be in Hear-Say on the telly behind the bar. I stared at her for a bit, too.

Then I said, "Are you going to tell me off?"

"Would it be worth it?"

I sat down on the couch and slung my feet up on the coffee table.

The Corrie ad break came on TV. Cheryl Cole sold shampoo. My dad scratched his chin and sighed. He asked what happened at court.

I told him, and he said, "Same old, same old. D'you get curfew?"

I said yes, and he said, "Same old, same old. Do any good?"

I said yes, and he said, "That'll be the day."

"It's true."

"Seen your Sammie?"

I swallowed, my throat dry.

He looked at me when I didn't answer.

"She's dumped you, hasn't she," said my dad.

I fidgeted with the TV remote control, watching the screen. Red Bus bingo said they sponsored daytime telly on ITV2. Corrie came back for Part Two.

Dad was a bit Mystic Meg-ish in the way that he could suss me out quickly. But maybe it was because I went quiet and my face turned red, and he could probably smell the shame come off me like aftershave.

"Has she dumped you?" he said.

"We had a row."

He shook his head. "Lovely girl. You're an idiot."

"So I'm an idiot for losing Sammie, not for nicking cars, then?"

"Same thing."

I grumbled something.

He said, "Has she dumped you?"

I told him what happened. My dad tutted.

Dad was forty, but he looked sixty. He had grey hair and bags under his eyes. His face was ruddy. That was because he spent so much time outside, the elements affecting his skin. The scotch also helped. He smelled of it now. He'd probably had a tumbler up at the allotment earlier. He never drank in the house. Only in his shed and in the pub.

Forty was old to me, but really it was young. People live anciently these days. But he looked like an old tree, twisted and dry.

It was Mum dying that had made him old.

I was eight at the time, and she'd been ill for a while. I don't remember them ever telling me about her being sick, or that she would die.

She just got sicker and sicker, and he got older and older, till finally she was dead, and he was ancient.

At the time my nan said, "Mum's gone to Jesus, darling."

"Well, Jesus is going to have to give her back," I told her.

"He wants her to be with him, now."

"He's a bastard, then."

"Jimmy, you mustn't say that."

"We've got to rescue her."

"No, darling. She's happy now. She's resting. She's not in pain anymore."

"How do you know, Nan?"

"I… I just know. You've got to have faith, darling."

"Faith?"

"Don't worry, Jimmy. It's going to be okay."

I'm not sure if it was okay. I'm not sure where the line between okay and not okay was. Life just went on.

Dad never talked about it.

Nan tried to but always ended up weeping.

I don't remember crying. I remember dreaming I cried, and the pillow was wet when I woke up. But I'm sure I never actually cried.

After Mum's death, Dad spent more and more time at the allotment and less and less time with me.

When I'd come home from school, Nan was there waiting, and she'd make dinner for me and Dad, trying to talk to us.

Dad grunted. I ate. Nan babbled.

Then we'd watch telly and I'd go to bed. Dad would say, "Goodnight," which was one of the few things he'd say to me all day.

Getting up in the morning, I was nervous and quiet. Dad would be in the kitchen and he'd say, "Morning," and put toast and juice on the table for me and give me my lunch money. When I'd leave for school he'd say, "Be a good boy." And that was it till I got home again to Nan and Dad, and then it was Nan making dinner and telly and another "Goodnight."

Sometimes Dad had to come to school and talk to the headmaster because Tyler had got me into trouble. That was a bit of a change from the old routine, and quite exciting – despite my being in the school's bad books. But Dad never said anything. He never did anything. At the time, when I was eight or nine, I thought he didn't care. But later I realized he cared a lot. He loved me. He just didn't show it.

Like he didn't show it now. He just sat there watching Corrie.

"I'm going out," I said.

He said nothing.